THE
LOST
BOYFRIEND

THE LOST BOYFRIEND

CHRISTINA BENJAMIN

CROWN ATLANTIC
PUBLISHING

Copyright © 2019 by Christina Benjamin
All rights reserved.
Published in the United States by Crown Atlantic Publishing

ISBN 9781081155230

Version 1
Printed in the United States of America
First edition paperback printed, July 2019

To those brave enough to take the road less traveled.

PROLOGUE

H azel

FIELD JOURNAL ENTRY:

It's called the rule of three. We can survive three weeks without food, three days without water, three minutes without air . . . *but how long can we last without our hearts?*

I'm living by a new rule of three. Three seconds to change my life.

That's how long it took for me to make up my mind when James showed up at my door the day after graduation with his heart on his sleeve and a question I already knew the answer to.

But I'm getting ahead of myself . . . let's start at the beginning.

1

Hazel

"HEY KIDDO, how's it going out there?"

Hazel gripped the steering wheel harder. She hated lying to her dad. "It's fine," she said into her cellphone.

"Just fine?"

"It's a college pre-class, Dad, not exactly spring breakers gone wild."

He chuckled. "I know. I'm just proud of ya, kid. Going to college is a big deal. You're a trailblazer, gonna be the first one in our family to get a degree."

Hazel bit down on her shame. She didn't need to be reminded of how selfish she was being. "I don't have a degree yet, Dad." Talking about college degrees was a bit premature considering Hazel still had a few more weeks of her senior year of high school to finish out.

"Just a matter of time," her dad mused. "Did you meet up with Jenny yet?"

Another lie. Hazel swallowed hard. "I'm actually just about to."

"Good. I'm glad you'll have a familiar face out there. Tell her to come visit once in a while, will ya? Vegas isn't that far from Lovelock."

Hazel laughed. Vegas was eight hours from her little hole-in-the-wall town, but it might as well be on another planet.

Not wanting to burst her dad's bubble and tell him no one who lived in Vegas would ever want to visit Lovelock, she changed the subject. "How's Lu, are you giving him attention like you promised?"

"Lugnut is fine, Hazel."

"He hates that name, Dad."

Hazel's grandpa had named the junkyard dog that awful name when he found him, but she affectionately called the adorable Jack Russel, Lu, for short. He looked more like a Lu anyway.

Hazel was only ten when Gramps brought the puppy home and that was it; love at first sight. Her heart hurt just thinking about spending ten days away from him. It was sad, but that damn dog was her best friend—*and who wanted to call their best friend Lugnut?*

"Lu, Lugnut, does it really matter?" her dad grumbled. "He's a dog."

"Yes, he's a very intelligent dog that will pee in your shoes if you piss him off. Pun intended," she replied. "Don't forget to keep him out of Gramps's room. And you have to put Lu's sweater on at night. He hates to be cold."

Hazel heard her dad give a good-humored huff. "Just like someone else I know."

She smiled, the irony not lost on her as she looked at the

snowcapped mountains in the distance. Montana was only a few states away from her home in Lovelock, Nevada, but the landscape couldn't be more different. Towering evergreens and mountains sprouted up from every direction—a big change from Lovelock's flat, brown dust bowl.

Even with the heater cranked in her old Scout, Hazel still felt the chill in her bones. Most of it from the crisp March air, but she knew some of her discomfort was from guilt.

Hazel had never lied to her dad before—*but how could she tell him the truth when she knew how bad it would hurt him?*

She was so busy worrying about her guilty conscience that she almost didn't see the person crossing the street right in front of her.

"Shit!" she hissed, slamming the brakes a split second too late.

"Hazel?"

She shifted the Scout into park. "I gotta go, Dad."

"Everything okay?"

"Yeah, I just ran into someone." *Literally!*

Hazel hung up the phone and jumped out of her car.

James

Seriously! James scowled up at the sky, cursing the universe. *Could there be more signs that I don't belong here?*

He'd been in Montana less than an hour and had almost been killed twice. First landing on that sketchy excuse for a runway and now this.

He glowered at the emblem on the grill of the metallic blue death machine that almost turned him into roadkill.

He'd never seen this make before. *What the hell is an International?*

He'd barely had time to jump out of its way, his long arms reflexively shoving him away from the hood as it screeched to a stop. James shook his head, climbing to his feet slowly to make sure he was still in one piece. Fortunately, he was. *Or maybe unfortunately . . .*

He really didn't want to be here. *Would it be so bad if someone offs me before this fresh hell begins?*

What a nightmare. James looked back at the antique SUV that had nearly crippled him. It looked like a tank. *Is this really what passed as a vehicle in this part of the country?* James shook his head. He was so out of his depth here.

Hillbilly Camp hadn't even started yet and James already wished he was back in his room in Boston surrounded by his computers and camera equipment more than ever.

"I'm so sorry! Are you okay?"

James turned to see the tiniest girl ever running toward him. He couldn't believe she'd been driving that tank. No wonder she hit him, she probably couldn't see over the steering wheel.

"Yeah, I'm . . ." His eyes traveled from her espresso-colored hair to her caramel eyes. She had a smattering of freckles across the bridge of her button nose that reminded him of the cinnamon that dusted the top of a latte. He forgot what he was saying as his eyes traveled down her body, snagging on her feet. "Did I hit my head or are your boots actually hot pink?"

She pulled herself up to her full height, which was comical considering she was five-foot nothing, and crossed her arms, color flushing her cheeks. "Yes, they're pink. Do you have a problem with that?"

"No, it's just . . . they don't really fit the whole vibe you've got going on here," he said gesturing to the torn jeans that hugged her curves like a second skin and the layer of edgy tees, leather jacket and military vest. Not to mention the death machine she'd been driving. Everything about her looked dangerous—except the pink boots.

They screamed bubble gum and Barbie dolls, while the rest of her said . . . well, the opposite.

"And what vibe would that be?" she asked, her tone as harsh as her glare.

James squinted and playfully cocked his head. "Mad Max?"

Apparently, it was the wrong answer because the pint-sized girl scowled at him.

This was why he didn't talk to girls. He was digging himself a grave—and much faster than usual.

Flustered, James changed tactics and extended his hand. "Ignore me, I think I'm still in shock. Ya know, from almost becoming road pizza. I'm Jamie-ur-I mean-James."

Her soft cocoa eyebrows arched. "Which is it? James or Jamie?"

"It's James Forrester, but I prefer Jamie."

"Then introduce yourself as Jamie," she replied.

He smirked. *If only it were that simple.* "Right. And you are?"

"I'm Hazel. Sorry I almost hit you, but you should probably look both ways before you cross the street."

He laughed. This girl had balls. *I like that in a girl, Hazel.* "I think I might've heard that before . . ."

She cracked a smile and it was like a fist clamped around his heart. *Is there such a thing as hit-and-run love?*

"Well, if you're sure you're okay . . ." she said starting to back toward her car.

"Yeah, uh, I'm good. Nice, uh, running into you." He cringed at his own bad joke, but Hazel was smiling at him as he picked up his backpack and started to make his way out of the street, shaking his head as he went.

Fate, you cruel bastard.

It figured the first interesting girl James had met in years would live somewhere that would make it impossible to see her again.

"Wait," Hazel called, scooping something up off the ground and jogging after him.

HAZEL

HAZEL STARED at the hat in her hand. She'd been about to hand it back to Jamie when she recognized the logo stitched onto the front of the brand new ball cap—a silhouette of three mountain peaks, capped in white. *What are the chances?*

"No way!" she exclaimed, pulling a brochure from her back pocket and holding the matching logo up to Jamie's hat. "You're heading to Wander Mountain, too?"

James

JAMES BLINKED at Hazel in shock.

I take it back, Fate. Maybe you've redeemed yourself.

2

H azel

"YOU CAN RELAX," Hazel said, keeping her eyes on the GPS leading her to Wander Mountain's base camp. "I can't run you over when you're *inside* the car."

Jamie smirked. "I'd still be more comfortable if I was behind the wheel."

"Why? Because I'm a girl?"

"No, because you need to sit on a phonebook to drive. Are you sure you're even old enough to have a license?" he teased.

She could tell he was joking because his sky-blue eyes sparkled mischievously, and the corner of his mouth twitched with an itch to smile.

He was appallingly handsome. His striking good-looks almost made Hazel want to ignore him completely, but his comment still bothered her. She'd never been good at keeping her opinions to herself. Her grandpa always told her she had a mule's mouth: too stubborn and loud for her own good.

But in this case, Hazel couldn't help it. Jamie had hit a nerve. She had a chip on her shoulder when it came to being the fairer sex and it didn't help that she was barely five-one.

Hazel scowled at him. "I'm eighteen thank you very much, and I've probably been driving longer than you've been on the planet."

He laughed. "Since I'm also eighteen that seems unlikely."

"Well, I've still been driving longer," she countered.

"How's that?"

"My dad owns a repair shop. I grew up fixing cars."

"Oh, cool. Are you fixing this one up or something?"

Hazel's mouth fell open. "Did you just insult my ride?"

"Uh . . . did I?"

"This is a 1964 International Scout, bub. They don't make cars like this anymore. Bernie is perfect exactly the way she is."

"Bernie?"

"That's her name," Hazel boasted, affectionately patting the dash. "Technically, Bernadette, but Bernie for short."

Jamie blinked at her like she'd just grown another head.

She huffed. "You *do* know cars need names, right?"

"Yeah . . . sure."

She rolled her eyes. "Yeah right, your car doesn't have a name. You probably drive a Prius or something with no character, don't you?"

"Tesla, actually. And its name is Ted."

Hazel burst out laughing. "You did *not* name your car Ted."

"How do you know?"

"First off, you're a guy, your car needs to be named after a woman."

"Says who?"

She shrugged. "That's just the way it is. Unless . . . if you're into guys, then I guess—"

"I'm not into guys!" he blurted out.

"Okay, it's not a big deal if you are though."

"I know, but I'm not and I just feel like I should make that clear. I like girls. Women."

Hazel bit back her grin as she watched Jamie's cheeks flush scarlet. The color crept up from his neck all the way to his ears. He may be cripplingly gorgeous, but apparently even beautiful people suffer from teenage awkwardness.

She decided to take mercy on him—she *had* almost run him over. "Did you really name your car Ted?"

He met her eyes, his mouth slipping into a crooked grin. "Nah. You were right, it doesn't have a name."

She laughed. "I knew it! Okay, gun to your head, name your Tesla."

He frowned and looked out the window, silent for a moment. "Jane."

Hazel raised her eyebrows but nodded. "Solid name. Is she your girlfriend or something?"

Jamie was still looking out the window when he replied. "No. My mother."

"You're naming your car after your mom?"

"Yeah. What's wrong with that?"

Hazel shook her head. "Nothing." *Can you say mommy issues?* Though Hazel didn't have room to talk in that department.

Jamie rolled his eyes. "Oh, whatever, Pink Boots."

That shut Hazel up quickly.

She hated how self-conscious the stupid Pepto-colored footwear made her. She'd gotten more than a few strange looks when she picked up her camp packet at Sinclair's Outpost. But when embarking on a two-week wilderness adventure, one needs a good pair of boots. And it's not like Hazel had the means to buy brand new gear.

She got what she could find at the Lovelock Goodwill, which unfortunately happened to be a tragic pair of hot pink hiking boots. Despite their misfortunate color, they were too good a deal to pass up; five dollars and brand new; still had the tags on them.

Of course they still had the tags on them. Who the hell wears hot pink hiking boots? Especially in Lovelock.

Hazel wished she'd taken the time to at least scuff them up a bit. They practically glowed like some kind of neon billboard that said, *'look at me; cute, flirty, hiker-girl'.*

But that statement couldn't be further from the truth.

Jamie had been right; Hazel was way more Mad Max than her boots gave her credit for. She was a tomboy and proud of it.

Hazel knew her way around an engine block better than a makeup counter and she felt more comfortable with grease under her fingernails than getting a manicure. And flirting? It was more foreign to her than a second language.

She didn't have time for boys or even friends, really. Besides, that's not why she'd come here. She came to Wander Mountain because she wanted to gain as much life experience as she could. So, as intriguing and handsome as Jamie was, Hazel didn't plan on getting wrapped up in him or anyone else for that matter. This trip was about her.

Hazel had expected to meet people with the same mindset at this camp, but all the girls waiting for the camp bus at Sinclair's looked more like they belonged in her pink boots than she did. And when they'd seen Jamie they'd practically swooned. *Honestly, some of the guys swooned too.*

She glanced at him from the corner of her eyes. He wasn't *that* swoon-worthy.

Sure, his blue eyes were nice and he smelled better than a fresh shower, but he was just a boy. A boy with thick brown hair, strong jaw, broad shoulders, narrow waist, long legs . . . Okay, fine, he was a pretty perfect specimen as far as eighteen-year-old guys go . . . but still, she wasn't about to get side-tracked.

Hazel had wanted to come to Wander Mountain since she was thirteen. She probably knew a hell of a lot more than most of the rich kids who were sent here because they couldn't play by the rules. But unlike them, she actually wanted to be here. Wander Mountain was her last chance to have a real adventure, her last chance to live before routine and responsibility swallowed her whole.

That's why she was here. To embrace life, to find herself, to soak up as much of the world as she could in this moment. She let those thoughts center her. She didn't care if her boots were pink. Jamie could make fun of them as much as he wanted. It wouldn't stop her from making the most of every second here.

James

JAMES WATCHED the foreign scenery blur by as Hazel drove. It was nice of her to offer him a ride. Perhaps insulting her boots and car wasn't really the best strategy considering she was a possible ally at this hell camp he'd been shipped to.

When she'd first offered him a ride, he hadn't accepted, despite the instant chemistry he felt toward her. He wasn't in any rush to leave civilization. Besides, being attracted to someone he was going to have to go through wilderness therapy with probably wasn't the best idea. If she was heading to Wander Mountain, then that meant she was probably as messed up as he was—and that wouldn't lead anywhere good.

There was a camp bus making a pick up at Sinclair's Outpost in a few hours. It seemed like a safer option than getting in the car with someone who casually ran down pedestrians. James had thanked her for her offer, but said he was going to take the bus. He did at least offer to walk her to Sinclair's and show her where the camp check in was. But then they'd parted ways.

James had made his way into Junction Café, a tiny eatery attached to Sinclair's. He'd glanced around at the crowded café full of angsty teenagers and instantly had a change of heart—mostly because what always happened to him, happened. Someone recognized him, or rather his family.

James stared out the window of Hazel's car and replayed the awkward interaction in his mind.

"HOLY SHIT, you're Conner Forrester, aren't you?"

"Nope," James replied, pulling his hat down lower.

But the kid kept going, pulling up a photo of Conner on his phone and shoving it in James's face. "You look just like him."

James looked at the picture of his brother in his NFL uniform. Yes, he did look like Conner, and Thomas, and even his father for that matter, but James wasn't them. "Sorry man, don't know what to tell ya."

Another kid chimed in. "Nah, he's the younger one. The one that just broke all those college football records. Thomas, right? I watched your game against USC. You spanked them!"

James felt his cheeks heat with embarrassment. "Wasn't me."

"Dude, we're not gonna ask for autographs," the first kid grumbled.

"Good, 'cause they wouldn't be worth anything considering I'm not either of those guys."

The guys looked at each other, their expressions changing from admiration to arrogance.

"Dick," one of them muttered under his breath.

Looking around the crowded café that boasted, 'the Last Internet for 200 miles', James realized the group of misfit teens staring at him were probably heading to the same camp as him.

Great, just what I need; a whole mountain of people who'll be disappointed I'm nothing like my family.

Pulling his hat down even lower, James tried to avoid the stares of the girls who were now whispering about him. He *did* look like his brothers, but he wasn't nearly as built. They were professional athletes and James was the furthest thing from that.

He glanced at his reflection in the mirrored walls that were trying to make the tiny café appear larger. He *did* look bulkier than usual thanks to the large jacket and the layers he'd piled on ... but still, to think he was an NFL player was a stretch.

James walked up to the counter to order a coffee, or whatever passed for coffee around here. They certainly weren't serving Starbucks.

As he waited his turn, one of the girls who'd been whispering with her friends broke away from her group and slinked up to him. "So, do your brothers have a game around here or something?"

White-hot anger flooded into his stomach. James didn't even have to look at the girl to know what she was hinting at. She was just another jersey-chaser; someone who would pretend to like him to get access to his famous brothers.

It always ended in disappointment when they realized James didn't have anything in common with the athletic gods he was somehow related to. He was used to it, being looked at as a stepping stone, but he hadn't thought he'd have to deal with that out here.

THAT's when he decided to catch back up to Hazel and take that ride after all. It beat waiting at Sinclair's while everyone Googled him.

Things had been going okay when they first started their drive. They'd made small talk and even joked a bit, but their conversation had drifted to a halt thanks to him insulting her car and boots. Now he stared out the window in awkward silence.

James rubbed his temple before pulling his cellphone out. *No service.*

Of course.

It probably wouldn't be any better at the Wander Mountain base camp either.

He'd been hoping to check his emails one last time before going dark for a while. It didn't look like that was going to happen.

James sighed deeply. His father was royally fucking up his life. It wasn't fair. He was eighteen for God's sake. He should be able to make his own choices about his life.

His father's response to that statement flashed in his mind. "Sure thing, son, you can do anything you want, with your money."

But that was the problem—everything James had wasn't really his. His car, his computers, his collection of camera equipment, the massive house he lived in . . . it all belonged to his father.

That's why James was trying to get his business off the ground. If he could finish a few more design projects he'd be able to pursue his dreams and continue his art. He was a photographer, or at least that's what he wanted to be.

He knew he still had a long way to go, but he'd been messing around with photography and illustrator programs since he got his first laptop. He had a pretty deep portfolio of work—good enough to get accepted into SCAD. But telling his father about his acceptance to the renowned art school is what landed James in this situation.

Football or politics—those were James's only choices according to his father.

When James responded that he had no desire to pursue either, his father made arrangements at Wander Mountain. He'd called it a two-week retreat, where James could reconsider his choices.

Apparently, two weeks of wilderness torture was supposed to brainwash him into cowering to his father's wishes. Too bad even two years out here wouldn't manage to make that happen. James wasn't like his father or brothers. And nothing was going to change that.

"Do you always grind your teeth like that?"

James jumped not realizing he'd been doing it. "Sorry," he muttered. "Lost in thought."

He shouldn't be surprised, it was an anxious habit. His stomach was in knots from the resentment he'd been gnawing on. He needed to chill out. He hated when he let his father get the best of him. The man was on the other side of the country and he was still a pain in James's ass. He needed to get a grip.

Exhaling, he decided to focus his attention on Hazel. She

was a pleasant distraction. Completely out of his league but still, he didn't mind enjoying the view.

Her eyes were trained on the road. It was easy to tell she was still annoyed about his earlier comments. She was chewing on the corner of her grapefruit-colored lips.

James tamped down on his sudden urge to reach over and free the fragile skin. He settled for cheating glances at her from under the brim of his ball cap. She was stunning—the kind of girl that didn't even know she was beautiful. Her skin had a warm glow to it, like she spent time outdoors. She didn't wear makeup and her hair looked like she probably hadn't run a brush through it before weaving it into a simple braid.

James itched to take her photo. Not to be creepy or anything. It's just what he did—he couldn't turn off his artist's eye any more than he could stop breathing.

But what use was it? He'd take her photo, then what?

Imagine his life were different?

Imagine he'd see it hanging in a gallery somewhere?

For all his mental posturing, James knew in the end he'd probably cave to his father's wishes. He didn't see any other options.

"So," Hazel finally said, pulling him from his thoughts. "What brings you to Wander Mountain?"

James huffed a laugh. "You mean besides wilderness therapy and outdoor behavioral health?" he asked quoting the brochure resting on the seat between them.

He picked it up and read from it in a mocking tone. "Wander Mountain, where young adults come for adventure therapy. Give your brain a break and experience the outside world. Fresh air, nature, open spaces, everything you need to unclutter your environment and press the reset button without the everyday distractions of technology. Adventure-based experiences will help you find your inner strength.

Build positive relationships while exploring your resilience, resourcefulness and resolve through outdoor challenges that will teach you strategies to make better choices in life."

"What's wrong with that?" she asked.

"Please! It's a bunch of propaganda put together by psychologists and hippie therapists to make our parents feel good about sending us here to brainwash us into being the kids they want, instead of who we actually are."

Hazel's cocoa eyebrows were arched again. "Wow, so I'm guessing your parents are the reason you're here?"

"My father."

"Who does he want you to be?"

"Huh?"

"You said parents send their kids here to make them into who they want them to be."

James exhaled, not entirely sure if he should be going down this road with Hazel. They'd just met, and he was sort of hoping they'd be friends, despite his earlier reservations. But if James admitted the reason he was here, he could certainly count that out.

He'd learned from experience that girls were like wolves. They traveled in packs and could sense weakness, avoiding it at all costs.

Oh well, it's not like I've ever had success hiding who I am before. Might as well find out if you're like everyone else, Hazel. "He wants me to be more like my perfect brothers."

"Who are your brothers?"

"Oh, just football legends."

"Then why didn't your dad send you to football camp?"

Hazel had asked the question deadpan and it made James tear up with amusement.

Okay, so maybe you're not like everyone else, Hazel. "I'll have to ask him that," James replied between his laughter.

When he finally regained his composure, James noticed Hazel was still looking at him expectantly.

"So, you're here to be a better football player?" she questioned.

"No. I don't play football. I can't actually, long story."

Hazel glanced from him to the winding dirt road they were following. "It's a long drive."

James sighed. "I don't really like talking about it."

She gave him a heavy dose of side-eye and was silent for a beat.

Go ahead, say it. I already know you're thinking it, Hazel. It's what everyone thinks.

James knew what Hazel was seeing when she looked at him. Long, lean muscles, a strong athletic build, someone who looked perfectly made for the football field.

James was 6'4, with the same build as his father and brothers. Broad shoulders, narrow hips, long limbs, agile muscles. He even had the same blue eyes, dark hair and wide smile as the rest of the Forrester men—something his father was proud of. But that's where their similarities ended, because James had his mother's heart and that would forever keep him off the football field.

Hazel finally spoke. But she didn't say what James had been expecting. "So you lied to the guys at the café?"

"Not exactly. They thought I was Conner or Thomas. I'm not."

"Does that happen a lot? Getting mistaken for your brothers?"

"Unfortunately."

"Hmm."

James didn't like the judgment he heard in Hazels *hmm.* "What does that mean?"

"I don't know. I'm an only child. I guess I never thought

about what it'd be like to have expectations like that to live up to."

James stared at her with mild curiosity. *Okay, Hazel, you're definitely not like most girls.*

She was still out of his league, but she was becoming more intriguing by the minute.

"You're lucky to be an only child," he replied. "It sucks knowing you'll never live up to the bar the rest of your siblings set."

She smiled. "Are they really that impressive? I mean I know people are crazy about sports and all, but I guess I've never really been into them."

James crossed his arms, suppressing the warmth growing in his chest. *I'm liking you more and more, Hazel.* "They're a pretty big deal. Conner plays pro ball for the Pats and Thomas is on his way there. He's currently playing Division 1 at Stanford, but he'll be drafted this year. My dad played too, now he's in politics, but he makes sure everyone knows his football legacy. It's pretty much all he talks about."

"Impressive."

"Yeah. I guess that's the problem. I'm not *impressive* enough for my dad."

"I don't know. You're pretty good at dodging cars." Hazel smirked. "I'd say that's an impressive trait."

James laughed. "Thanks. I'll add that to my resume."

"What else is on your resume?"

He shrugged. "I don't know. I guess photography and graphic arts."

"An artist, huh?"

"Not if my dad has any say in it. He sent me here because I told him I wanted to go to college for art instead of poli-sci."

Hazel nodded, her calm eyes still on the road.

For some reason her silence made James want to keep

talking. "He thinks I'll come out here and see how tough the world is and realize how weak I am and it'll force me to follow the path he's laid out for me."

Hazel was no longer looking at the road. She was gaping at him, looking completely appalled. "Your dad said that to you?"

"Basically. He told me this would toughen me up, give me a new perspective. I know he expects me to fail. He enjoys setting me up for failure, but I don't care. He can send me to Siberia, it won't change my mind. I don't want a career in sports or politics."

"Are those your only two options?"

"In my family? Yeah."

"What does your mom say?"

James turned his face back to the window. "Nothing. She's dead."

3

H azel

WAY TO GO HAZEL. Bring up the poor guy's dead mother!

She chewed her lip wondering how the hell to follow that. This was when she missed her own mother. She didn't care about the makeup lessons or boy-talk she should've had, what Hazel really missed were the life lessons.

She always thought mothers taught their daughters the secrets to situations like these. How to be compassionate and empathetic, how to apologize, how to comfort people, how to read a room, how to make things less awkward.

Hazel had been raised by her father and grandfather—two gruff military men from the Midwest who didn't pull punches. They solved problems over a can of beer or not at all.

They were the kings of keeping emotions locked up.

She knew they'd both seen some terrible things in their days of service and it was obvious why they didn't want to revisit those ghosts. Hazel couldn't fault them for it. They were great men and they always did right by her. But it was hard at times like these, when she felt unprepared for life outside their rustic little bubble in Lovelock.

It's why she was here—to grow. To make up for the life she should've had if her mother hadn't run away all those years ago.

Hazel glanced at Jamie. Grief clouded his blue eyes and she had a desperate longing to chase it away with the right words. Her grandpa would've said something like, 'what doesn't kill ya makes ya stronger.' But she doubted that comment would bring Jamie any comfort. "I'm sorry about your mom," she finally said.

"Yeah." Jamie gave a heavy sigh. "Don't worry about it."

Desperate to fill the painful silence stretching between them, Hazel did what she did best, chattered nervously. "Well, I'm sorry your dad's a dick, but maybe you can stick it to him by taking some amazing photos while you're here. You can't really ask for a more beautiful landscape."

"I would if he didn't take all my cameras."

"What?" Hazel realized her mouth had fallen open again and snapped it shut. "Why would he do that?"

Jamie picked up the brochure again and flipped to the back, reading from it. "Technology is strictly limited to one personal mobile phone per resident. Use will be monitored by our staff and limited to emergencies only."

"Oh, right." Hazel frowned. "Forgot about that part."

"So, what's the deal with this thing?" Jamie asked, looking at the worn brochure. "It looks like you've had it for like twenty years or something."

"More like five."

He raised his eyebrows.

"I found it when I was thirteen. Someone left it in the back of a car they traded in."

"And snooping around old cars is a hobby?"

"Gramps used to pay me to clean out the cars." She grinned. "I still remember the day I found this," she said pulling the brochure from his hands. "It was shoved under the seat of a yellow 1972 Ford LTD. It seemed like an epic adventure, like something out of *The Hobbit* or something. It felt magical, yet possible at the same time." Hazel blushed realizing she was rambling. "I don't know, it sounds stupid now, but as a thirteen-year-old kid I wanted to go more than anything. I think I really just wanted to leave Lovelock. See some other part of the world." She shrugged. "I held onto it and when I was old enough, I started applying. It just became something I did every year. I didn't think I'd actually get in. But two weeks ago, I got a call, someone dropped out and I was in."

"Wait? So, people have to apply to get in here?" Jamie asked.

"Yeah. There's always a waiting list. I know you don't exactly want to be here, but this is one of the best wilderness therapy camps in the country."

Jamie huffed a laugh.

"What?"

"I'm just wondering how much my dad had to pay to get me in last minute. He thinks money solves everything. I doubt he considered he was taking a spot from someone who might actually benefit from being here."

Hazel frowned, wondering if Jamie realized that was a pretty douchey thing to say. *Did he really think there was nothing he could learn from being here?*

She glanced over at him, catching the amused look on his

face. She shook her head. *Just when I was beginning to like you, Jamie.*

"What?" he asked.

"Nothing."

"It's obviously something. You don't have the best poker face."

"Fine. I guess I think it's kind of a douchebag move to say there isn't anything you can learn from this experience."

His smirk disappeared. "A douchebag move? Do you mean like hitting someone with your car?"

Hazel exhaled slowly. *This is why you should keep your mouth closed, Hazel.* "I apologized for that. And all I'm saying is you're already here. Maybe you should give this a shot. Like you said, you're taking someone else's spot. Don't you think you owe it to them to at least give it your best effort?"

"I don't owe anyone anything," he snapped. "And maybe you should get a little life experience before you go dishing out judgements, Lovelock."

Hazel flinched. *Maybe your dad's not the jerk, Jamie. Maybe you are.*

She wasn't used to men yelling at her. Her father never raised his voice and Gramps was a man of few words. Then again, Hazel had never done anything that really warranted being yelled at. That's why being here without their knowledge was weighing on her. She hated keeping this a secret from them. And if she actually pulled it off, she wouldn't even be able to share any of the amazing things she experienced with them. Not without first admitting she lied—*and why.*

She couldn't do it. She couldn't admit the truth. It would break her dad's heart. He'd given her a good life and it should be enough. She should be grateful.

Hazel hated herself a little more every time the feeling of wanting more snuck in. But she never acknowledged it, shoving it down until it grew like a weed, choking the life from her.

That's why she had to take this opportunity. She had to sew her wild oats, as Gramps would say. She needed to have one selfish adventure, then she could commit her life to giving back to the men who'd given her everything.

Hazel glanced at Jamie. He was staring out the window again. She needed to smooth things over with him. He could easily get her kicked out of the program if he wanted to. Especially if his father was as influential as he said.

She couldn't lose this dream, not when she was so close.

Hazel cleared her throat. "Listen, you're right, okay? I don't know you and don't have any right to tell you what to do. But I actually *do* want to be here, so if you could maybe not mention that I nearly ran you over to any of the counselors, that'd be great."

"I didn't plan on it," Jamie muttered.

"Okay."

"Okay."

Jamie didn't say anything for the rest of the drive and that was fine with Hazel. At least that meant she wouldn't bring up any more dead relatives or say something that set him off again. The only down side of their silence was that it allowed her too much time to think.

She mostly thought about how selfish she was being. It was making her start to second guess her decision to come to Wander Mountain. Her father and grandfather would be hurt if they ever found out, and Hazel had already hurt her best friend, Jenny with her choice.

Hazel had met Jenny Carver in kindergarten, where they

quickly became friends. Jenny was one of those girls who didn't care if you had a brown bag lunch or shopped for your clothes at Goodwill. She was your friend because she genuinely liked you.

As far as Hazel was concerned, there weren't enough Jenny Carvers in the world. And that's why she'd cried for weeks when Jenny and her family moved from Lovelock to Vegas two years ago. They still talked all the time, but it wasn't the same as seeing her in the halls every day.

And up until two weeks ago, Hazel had been looking forward to spring break because it meant ten days with Jenny. That's where Hazel was supposed to be right now; in Arizona with her best friend.

Jenny's parents signed her up for some lame college prep class over spring break because they were worried she'd get into trouble if she went on her boyfriend's ski trip. *Which she definitely would—Jenny always goes for the bad boys.*

Not wanting to spend her spring break alone, Jenny convinced Hazel to come along.

Even though it wasn't a ski trip to Aspen, it was still a hard trip to pass up in Hazel's opinion. The hotel room was already paid for and Jenny promised there would be time to soak up the sun—Hazel's favorite past time.

Hazel hated to be cold, ironic considering she chose camping in the Montana mountains in March over sunbathing in Arizona for her spring break. *But when opportunity knocks, you have to answer.* And sometimes that means sacrifices.

Hazel took her worries out on her lower lip, chewing it while she concentrated on the winding road ahead of her. *What if this is a mistake? What if everyone at camp is like Jamie— spoiled rich kids who don't want anything out of this experience?*

Hazel suddenly worried she'd disappointed Jenny and

given up an opportunity to get ahead on her college classes for nothing.

She heard Gramps's voice in her head. 'Quit hemmin' and hawin'. Make a decision and stick to it.'

It was good advice and Hazel let it fill her with confidence. She was here, her only option now was to make the best of it. Besides, Hazel wasn't even sure she wanted to go to college. At least not the online university she was enrolled in for next fall. She'd only agreed to go to the college prep course because it meant she'd get to spend time with Jenny.

But then Hazel had gotten the call from Wander Mountain.

Jenny was disappointed Hazel was changing her plans, but she was a good friend. She knew how long Hazel had been dreaming about Wander Mountain, so she agreed to cover for Hazel, because that's just what friends do. Of course, she demanded Hazel text every day to tell her all about it—something Hazel was just realizing she probably wouldn't be able to do if the camp was as strict about technology as the brochure said.

Maybe I can write letters.

She'd have to figure something out because her dad certainly wouldn't be okay with zero communication for the next two weeks.

4

James

Yep, this is as bad as I expected.

James found himself sitting around a campfire with twenty or so kids his age, while a therapist with a hippie name he'd already forgotten, forced them to introduce themselves.

They weren't allowed to speak until someone passed them the dirty kickball that had been dubbed the Trust-Ball.

What a crock.

James would've laughed at the ridiculousness of it all if he wasn't so annoyed by how invasive it was.

Not only were they supposed to say their names and where they were from, but why they were here. And if they weren't brutally honest about what indiscretion had landed them in the program, Dr. Hippie whipped out a profile folder and called them out with all the gory details.

None of the issues were that serious. Mostly rich kid problems—caught cheating on a test, stealing from high-end stores for a rush, selling ADHD meds and the likes. At least James's father hadn't sent him to a camp full of hardened criminals.

These kids he could handle. They were just like the over-privileged yuppy assholes he dealt with on a daily basis at his high school, Stanton Prep. Technically, James was one of the over-privileged yuppies too, but he tried to keep his asshole tendencies to a minimum.

Though he'd slipped up with Hazel.

He still felt bad he'd lashed out at her in the car. He wasn't usually such a dick, but there was something about her . . . She got under his skin, slipping past the armor that usually made other people's opinions slip off him like Teflon.

He glanced at her. It was almost her turn with the Trust-Ball. She was sitting cross-legged on a bright patterned camp blanket, her caramel eyes alight with interest as the girl next to her droned on about how she'd hacked into her school's grading system so she could change her ex-boyfriend's test scores to make it look like he was failing. *Cold!*

James made a mental note to stay away from that chick.

Finally, Hacker-girl was done talking and passed the ball to Hazel. James pulled his hat down lower so he could watch Hazel while she spoke.

"Hi, I'm Hazel Walker. I'm eighteen and I'm from Lovelock, Nevada. I'm here because I want to be."

The therapist looked up from his notes. "Ah yes, you must be our Bright Horizons recipient."

Hazel beamed. "Yes, sir, I am."

"Excellent. I remember your essay. Very moving. Everyone, Hazel is our Bright Horizons award winner. Every year, Wander Mountain selects one student with extenuating circumstances who shows great potential for growth and sponsors them with the Bright Horizons scholarship. I think you can all learn a lot from Hazel." He smiled his practiced, therapist-smile at her. "Can you share a little bit about why you wanted to come to Wander Mountain with the group?"

"Um, yeah. I guess mainly to experience life outside of my small town."

The therapist continued thumbing through Hazel's profile. "Is it true that you've never left Lovelock before?"

She nodded.

"You wrote that you feel this is the only opportunity you'll have to see anything but your own backyard. Why is that?"

Hazel swallowed, her cheeks blushing. "Mostly I guess because I don't have the means. My grandpa raised me while my dad was serving our country. The men in my life are incredible. I respect them so much. They gave me a roof over my head, clothes on my back and food on my plate. I'm grateful to them. Now it's my turn to give back to them. So, this is really the last bit of time I have left to do something just for myself."

James watched as Hazel continued to chew her bottom lip, her fingers anxiously pulling at a loose thread in the blanket she sat on. It was plain to see she was uncomfortable with the questions the therapist was asking, but he was too busy skimming through her file to notice.

"Tell us a little about your father and grandfather. They're both veterans, correct?"

"Yes, sir. Both served in the army. My grandpa served in the Vietnam War and my dad did six tours in Afghanistan and Iraq."

"And your father was injured?" the therapist pressed.

"Yes, sir. His unit rolled over an IED. He was the only survivor." Hazel's hands had gone completely still. "That was four years ago. He lost one of his legs and most of his vision in his right eye. He suffered partial hearing loss and severe damage to his heart. He was extremely lucky to survive his injuries. He has a pacemaker now and he uses a wheelchair, but he's still the strongest man I know. Besides my grandpa, who's been living with shrapnel in his chest since Vietnam. He was just diagnosed with lung cancer six months ago . . . That's why I'm here. To learn how to be strong, for them. To find the inner-strength that I'll need to be at my best for them. They made sacrifices to raise me and take care of me. Now I want to do the same."

"Are you their only caregiver?"

She nodded. "Yes, sir."

"What about your mother?"

"She left when I was four. Said she wanted a life, and there wasn't such a thing in Lovelock."

"You wrote something interesting about that. Here it is." Dr. Hippie started reading from Hazel's file. "'My mom called Lovelock a podunk town where dreams go to die. I'm afraid she's right. I'm afraid I'll die here and all my dreams with me'." the therapist looked up. "That sounds like a cry for help, Hazel. Are you contemplating death?"

James felt his face burn with shame when Hazel's eyes flicked up to meet his.

"No," she said. "I'm afraid that I won't ever get the chance to truly live."

Dr. Hippie gave a patronizing smile. "Then we're glad you're here, Hazel. Because together, we'll help each other find our true selves and the strength to grab onto the life we want. Thanks for sharing, Hazel."

HAZEL

. . .

"THANKS FOR SHARING, HAZEL," the circle echoed.

But Hazel kept her eyes on James.

He didn't thank her for sharing. He just continued to stare at her with a haunted expression as storm clouds gathered in his sky-blue eyes.

5

J ames

THIS IS COMPLETE BULLSHIT!

James could feel his heart racing as the stupid Trust-Ball drew closer and closer to him. By the time it was one person away his palms were sweating so profusely that no amount of wiping them on his jeans seemed to help. *How is this form of therapy helpful? Airing out everyone's dirty laundry for the world to see? No thanks.*

It was cruel and borderline destructive.

Hazel, who'd seemed made of steel and sunshine before the Trust-Ball graced her hands, still looked like she'd seen a ghost after sharing why she was here.

Selfishly, James had been listening to each story that followed hers, hoping there would be something worse.

Something to make her feel less alone, something to make what he was about to admit less of a shock. But nothing touched Hazel's problems. Or his own.

I take it back, Fate. You're a cruel bitch to put me in this girl's life.

James could already feel his attachment forming. He and Hazel had so much in common, and she was about to find that out, whether he wanted her to or not.

HAZEL

HAZEL LISTENED RESPECTFULLY while everyone else took their turn sharing. She wished she could say hearing everyone else's woes made her feel better about her own, but it didn't. She knew it shouldn't matter. This was an individual journey. It didn't matter that most of the kids here had perfect lives and were only acting defiant out of boredom. She shouldn't be jealous. *What kind of person does that make me—wishing others misfortune just so I can feel better about myself?*

She'd been raised better than that.

Hazel tried to focus on what the counselor was saying, but she had a hard time listening with Jamie's eyes boring into hers from across the circle. He looked like he was shivering. Hazel could feel his nervous energy from ten feet away. She wondered what he was about to reveal. She didn't know why, but she had a feeling he was the only other one here who could relate to her heartache.

He hadn't even shared with the group yet, but Hazel already knew she'd misjudged him. He might be rich, but that didn't mean he didn't have real problems.

There was something about the way he tried to hide the

pain that flooded into his sky-blue eyes that she recognized. She wanted to tell him not to waste his energy, it was useless. There was no way she wouldn't notice the darkness when it started to push its way in. It was like a storm cloud blotting out the sun.

She knew it was stupid, but she felt an unexplainable desire to be his light in the darkness. Maybe because she knew what if felt like to be lost in the shadows of her own pain. Or maybe it was because she saw pieces of herself in his anger. Perhaps it was jealousy at his willingness to let it out, when she didn't know how. Or maybe she was just so incredibly lonely that she was latching onto the pretty lonely boy whose heart seemed to speak to hers.

James

THE BALL WAS in his hands now. How he'd held onto it with his slick palms he didn't know. Maybe he could've had a future as a footballer if he'd been more fortunate.

"Your turn to share," Dr. Hippie pushed.

James glared at him, wondering what the hell the guy would do if James refused to speak. It's not like he could force him to talk. Maybe they'd have to send him home. His father could send him here, but he couldn't force him to participate.

"No need to be shy, James. This is a safe place. You have the Trust-Ball. You can speak your truths and not be judged."

James fought the urge to roll his eyes. He caught Hazel's eye across the circle. She gave him the most imperceptible nod, and God if that didn't make him want to spill his guts right then and there. *What are you doing to me, Hazel?*

James wished he could tell her that she didn't really want

to know him. That her life would be much better off without him in it. Everyone's would. But he was like a moth to a flame when he stared into her eyes. Had it been just the two of them alone, he would've spilled his soul if that's what she wanted.

"James?" The counselor called. "I'm afraid I have to insist that you share."

"It's Jamie," he snapped.

The fake smile from Dr. Hippie made James grip the ball so hard he was surprised it didn't pop.

"Jamie it is. Now, why don't you tell us a little about yourself? Start with your name, age and where you're from."

James exhaled. It would be easier to get this over with than to fight it. "Jamie Forrester. Eighteen. Boston."

"Told you," a guy whispered.

James whipped his head toward the sound, recognizing the kid who'd mistaken him as his brother at the café.

"Dick," his buddy mouthed making the café guy snicker.

"Jamie," the counselor cut in. "You have a unique family background. Why don't you share that with us?"

He felt his jaw muscles bulge as he gritted his teeth. "They play football. I don't see how that's unique."

"Not only that, but your father is Massachusetts's state senator. You must be very proud."

"Proud's not really a word I'd use to describe my relationship with my father."

"No? How would you describe it?"

"Let's see, he has few loves in his life; football and politics. I'm not involved in either, and I killed the third thing he loved, so you tell me how to describe our relationship."

The only sound was the crackle and hiss of the fire as everyone in the circle stared at him.

James heard his pulse pounding in his ears. His anger was

drowning out the rest of the world. Too bad his temper couldn't actually drown him. He closed his eyes and took a deep breath.

When he opened them, Dr. Hippie was staring at him. "Are you referring to your mother, Jamie?"

So much for privacy. "I'm sorry, but I'm not really comfortable discussing that. It has nothing to do with why I'm here."

"Then why don't you tell us why you think you're here, Jamie?"

"Because my father doesn't agree with my choice of college major."

Dr. Hippie flipped through the folder in his hand. "That's actually not a concern that was mentioned."

James huffed. *Of course it's not.* His father probably wrote something politically correct like, 'my son needs to focus on strategically viable career options.'

Dr. Hippie flipped the folder closed. "Jamie, this program only works if you do. Success doesn't come easily, but if you put the work in, I promise you can achieve a better state of being. You don't have anything to fear by sharing. You can't heal if you don't reveal."

There it is, the perfect therapist catchphrase. 'You can't heal if you don't reveal.'

James almost laughed out loud. "So, you're saying that if I acknowledge killing my mother, I'll magically feel better?" he asked. "Are we going to just bury all my problems in the woods? Because I've gotta say, there might not be enough land here to hold all my guilt."

Dr. Hippie blinked in shock. *Good, I'm finally throwing him off his game.* It was about time the therapist realized James wasn't someone he could fix with catchphrases and Kumbaya.

Dr. Hippie regrouped. "Jamie, our primary focus as

expressed by your father and your school counselors, is to focus on your anger and self-worth. We're happy to set up an appointment for you to discuss deeper issues with one of our more experienced counselors in private."

It was James's turn to blink with a shocked expression on his face.

"Jamie, you may not be ready to admit that you have been dealing with your anger and depression in unhealthy ways, but until you do, you're going to have a difficult road ahead of you. Would you like to take this opportunity to unburden yourself and share with the group? We're all here for you, without judgement."

"Nah, I'm good," James said pushing to his feet and stomping away.

HAZEL

"AT WANDER MOUNTAIN we believe in facing problems head on. The first step to solving your problems is being able to admit them. It's a technique that's true in survival situations and it translates well to real life. No one here is perfect. We don't expect you to be. We're here to give you the tools you need to deal with imperfect situations in positive ways," Dr. Birch said in a soothing voice.

He continued to drone on about tools and techniques, but Hazel wasn't listening. She was too busy watching Jamie's silhouette shrink against the fading backdrop of grays and blues the distant mountain range provided.

She couldn't get his words out of her mind. They'd filled her chest with familiarity when he'd spoken them and now they were lodged there, bouncing around tripping up her heart. She'd been right, he knew the kind of sadness she did. A rush of selfish warmth set her body abuzz. *Is this what understanding feels like?*

You're not alone, Jamie. Maybe Wander Mountain's slogan was true. *You find yourself when you're most lost.*

6

H azel

THE REST of the evening wasn't as eventful as the fireside introductions. After orientation everyone filed into the dining hall,
aptly named Prospects, to grab a quick meal before making
their way to the cabins.

Hazel felt like her head was on a swivel, swinging to-and-
fro every time a door opened. She kept waiting for Jamie to
walk in, but he never did.

Her anxiety over what he was going through killed her
appetite, which was kind of a big deal. You wouldn't know it
from looking at her, but Hazel liked to eat. She was barely a
hundred pounds, but she was all muscle and metabolism.
Gramps always said she ate like a billy goat on a bender, whatever that meant.

A sudden sadness settled over Hazel as she thought about
her grandfather.

She worried about his health, praying it wouldn't take a turn for the worse while she was gone. She already felt guilty enough leaving her dad in charge when he had his own difficulties to deal with. But if Gramps got worse while she was away, Hazel would never forgive herself.

She pulled out her cellphone and fired off a quick text to her dad. They had to surrender their phones soon, so this was her last chance to communicate. As much as Hazel wanted to hear her dad's voice, she was afraid she'd crack and admit where she really was if she spoke to him. Texting was safer.

Hazel sent a quick text to Jenny too, detailing her first day and the fact that correspondence might be few and far between with the strict personal phone use policies.

She asked Jenny to text her dad every other day so he didn't worry. Hazel was famous for forgetting to charge her phone so he wouldn't think anything of it if she was supposedly texting from Jenny's phone.

Still not feeling solid enough to eat, Hazel grabbed an apple and headed out to find her cabin.

Before arriving at Wander Mountain, Hazel had been most nervous about meeting her roommates. But after listening to Jamie's stunning revelations earlier, she hadn't worried about much besides his wellbeing. *What did he mean when he said he killed his mother? What did Dr. Birch mean when he said Jamie was dealing with his anger and depression in unhealthy ways?*

Hazel was starting to get a better picture of the boy she'd spent the afternoon with, and he resembled her with startling accuracy. She never would've thought she could've had anything in common with someone like him. She'd eyeballed the brands of clothing he was wearing when they'd first met and made up her mind about him.

Jamie looked way more relaxed in his Marmot jacket and Patagonia pants than she ever would even if she could afford clothes like that. His father was a Senator and his brothers professional athletes. They probably spent more money on their toilet paper than Hazel spent on her entire wardrobe, but still, she couldn't shake the feeling of kinship she'd felt from the moment she'd met Jamie.

Okay, maybe not the very first moment. But it's hard to feel much of anything with the grill of a Scout between you.

They'd had a rocky start, but Hazel was a firm believer in fate. Maybe he'd been put in her path for a reason. *Are you the adventure I've been craving, Jamie?*

When their eyes connected across the fire tonight, there'd been something so raw and real there that Hazel felt like she was staring into her own soul. It was equal parts terrifying and addicting. She had so many questions, but one thing was certain . . . she needed to know more about James Forrester.

James

IT TURNED out Wander Mountain didn't have a zero-tech-nology policy after all. They just wanted you to buy it from them. *Typical.*

That was fine with James though. His father was footing the bill and thanks to the camp setting up an account for him to charge things like gear, food and personal items to, James found his first glimmer of excitement in the form of a Leica 35mm camera.

He hadn't shot film in ages, but the temptation was too strong to pass up. He didn't even blink at the $1500 price tag and that was before he added a case and film.

James loaded the film, relishing the nostalgic smell of the canister before tucking it away in the camera case. It brought him back to his first photography class, years ago. James had originally thought Mr. Lombard was too old-school to teach him anything worthwhile when he demanded the class put away their digitals and use real film for the entire semester.

Boy had he been wrong.

That class birthed a love like James had never known before. He became addicted to learning every nuance of photography. The ins and outs of manual camera mechanics, the infinite possibilities when it came time to develop the film, how to properly handle negatives and so much more.

Now, as James expertly loaded the film and wound the reel, he was grateful he'd shut his mouth long enough to let himself fall in love with something as beautiful as photography. He already felt more settled with a camera back in his hands. He looped the strap around his neck and headed out into the fading sunlight to capture the world the only way he knew how—through a lens.

HAZEL

HAZEL SWUNG OPEN the door to cabin number nine and was greeted with the shocked faces of three girls passing a bowl.

"Shit!" The girl on the top bunk gasped, swinging down from the bed. "You gave me a stroke, girl. Shut the door."

Hazel quickly shut the door, turning the lock. She turned around to face the room, recognizing the girls from the group sharing session. The one now standing next to her smiling was Kat, the hacker. The other two were Sawyer and Paisley—her roommates, she presumed.

"Hey," Kat said, "I'm gonna take top bunk if that's cool."

"Sure," Hazel replied, dropping her bag next to the only unclaimed bunk.

"It's Hazel, right?" Kat asked.

"Yep."

"I'm sure you remember but I'm Kat," she said grinning. "This is Sawyer and Paisley."

The other girls didn't look up from the bowl they were repacking.

"So, was it true what you said?" Kat asked.

"Which part?"

"That you actually want to be here?"

"Yeah."

Kat studied her for a moment, tilting her head in a feline way that very much resembled her namesake. Then she shrugged. "To each her own," she said and climbed back up to join the other girls on the top bunk.

"Wanna hit?" Sawyer asked holding out the bowl.

It was moments like this that Hazel almost wished she wasn't so inexperienced. Joining her new roommates for a hit would surely be bonding. But smoking for the first time ever while locked in a tiny remote cabin didn't seem like the best idea. "No thanks."

Sawyer looked unimpressed as she returned to her conversation with the other girls. From what Hazel could tell they were rating the sex appeal of the boys in their group.

"No way," Paisley argued. "The tall moody one's the hottest, what's his name again?"

"Jamie Forrester," Kat answered.

"Oh yeah," Sawyer replied. "The one with the famous football family. Hell yeah, I'd get with him."

Kat shook her head. "Athletes don't do it for me."

"He's not an athlete," Hazel said, shocking the girls into silence.

"Do you know him or something?" Paisley asked, her heart-shaped lips pursed like she was sucking on something sour.

"Not really," Hazel replied. "We just drove up from Livingston together."

"Do you think he really killed his mom?" Sawyer asked.

Before Hazel could answer, Kat jumped in. "Nope, already looked it up. She died in a car accident. He was driving, so he probably has survivor's guilt or something."

Survivor's guilt? Hazel swallowed.

She'd often wondered if that's what she had. After all, her mother hadn't been a junkie before she was born. It wasn't until Hazel came along that life became too much for her to handle, making her mother feel suffocated by her worthless existence in Lovelock—her mother's words, not Hazel's.

Sawyer sighed. "Damn, that's way too much baggage for me. He's all yours, Hazel."

"Hey! Not so fast!" Paisley interjected. "I'm the one who said I thought he was hot first!"

"Um, that's not really why I'm here," Hazel said quickly before an argument broke out.

"Smart girl," Kat concurred. "None of us should be trying to get coupled-up."

Paisley pouted. "What else are we supposed to do while we're trapped here?"

Sawyer shoved the bowl in her face. "Get high."

They giggled, but Kat rolled her eyes. "Count me out. I want nothing to do with the Couples' Curse."

Hazel stopped unpacking and raised her eyebrows. "Couples' Curse?"

"Don't listen to her," Sawyer replied. "It's just a bunch of bullshit the camp made up to get us to keep it in our pants."

Kat shook her head, her black pigtails swinging. "It's not.

My sister was at boarding school with the cousin of last year's victim. The one that got preggers up here. When she got home her boyfriend tracked the camp kid down who knocked her up and beat the crap out of him. He's in a coma and the boyfriend's in jail."

Paisley laughed. "That's not exactly curse-worthy. That happens at my school like every other month."

Kat looked completely unfazed by Paisley's brush-off. "I'm just getting started. The year before that, this couple who'd been dating for four years got in a huge fight. Chica swung an ax at him! They still decided to pair up for Crossroads and only one made it back. Year before that, another couple thought they'd conquer Crossroads but before they could get there the boyfriend ended up *'falling'* out of his safety harness. Bam! Brain injury. Turned out his girlfriend was sleeping with a counselor! Coincidence? I think not."

"How the hell do you know all this?" Paisley asked.

Kat gave a mischievous wink. "The dark web is a magical place."

"Well, I'm not looking for a relationship," Sawyer said hopping down from her bunk. "Just a little action," she added, slapping Kat's ass and blowing her a kiss as she sauntered out the door.

"Where's she going?" Hazel asked.

Kat looked at her watch and jumped off the bunk too. "S'more Social!"

7

James

JAMES SAW her walking toward him, the firelight caressing Hazel's features like dawn bathing a new day.

He wanted to photograph her more than ever, but she wasn't alone. Hazel was arm-in-arm with the hacker chick she'd been sitting next to during intros and two other girls he didn't recognize.

Again, he was reminded of wolves.

The girls flanked Hazel—a pack of she-wolves keeping the smallest of them in the middle.

He watched them take a seat at one of the crackling stone firepits carved into the side of the mountain where groups of campers gathered, roasting marshmallows on sticks over the flames. When Hazel sat down, easily melding into the community of Wander Mountain misfits, James turned away.

Forever on the outside, he thought bitterly as he raised his camera to his eye.

It was fine with him. He was used to it.

HAZEL

HAZEL HATED ADMITTING she was disappointed that James wasn't at the S'mores Social. Even for the kids who really didn't want to be at Wander Mountain, it was hard not to enjoy the atmosphere. The air was crisp, but the fire licked away the stinging chill of the evening. And Hazel had never seen such a beautiful set up.

Five firepit coves had been carved into the side of the mountain, large stone staircases leading to each one. The slate decks were each hewn into the earthen walls of Wander Mountain at varying levels.

Hazel sat with the group perched at the highest level. She cozied up on a woven blanket draped over the benches built around the circular firepit. The view was incredible.

When she gazed down, she could see four more glittering firepits glowing like lightning bugs in the distance. The sun had long since disappeared behind the mountain range, but the residual sunlight still reflected across the clouds, painting the peaks the most beautiful shades of dusky blues and pinks.

She could stare at that view forever.

There was nothing like this in Lovelock. Whenever Hazel had a rare moment to stare off into the distance of her vacant backyard all she saw were the dusty browns of the desert and scraggly scrub bushes. Lovelock had mountains in the distance, but the haze of pollution coming from Vegas usually blotted them out.

Suddenly, Hazel was seized by the urge to absorb as much of this view as she could. She popped the S'more she'd been making into her mouth and wrapped the blanket she'd been sitting on around her shoulders, moving away from the fire for a better view.

At this height, she didn't have to walk far. Almost every angle promised views better than any scenic overlook she'd passed on her drive to Montana.

Taking a deep breath, she pulled the clean air into her lungs. It settled her so she did it again. Each breath seemed to sink further into her soul, reminding her why she'd come here and helping her push away her guilt.

This would work. Wander Mountain would make her a better person—stronger and more prepared. Ready to commit her life to caring for the men who had given her everything.

It had to work. She refused to become her mother and be one more person who broke their hearts.

Jamie's words drifted back into Hazel's mind at that moment. *'Are we going to just bury all my problems in the woods? Because I've gotta say, there might not be enough land here to hold all my guilt.'*

Hazel could relate to that sentiment. She'd tried for years and years to bury her problems, but they just kept resurfacing —just like her mother.

She'd come back once when Hazel was seven and again when she was ten. But she'd only ever really wanted money. She didn't crave a connection with her daughter. She didn't want to reconcile with her husband who was busting his ass overseas to keep a roof over their child's head. No, all Lake Walker wanted was her next fix and as soon as she got it, she was gone again.

Gramps had finally asked her not to come back. Hazel remembered the day because it was only six months after her mother's last visit and two days before Hazel's birthday—not that her mother knew or cared.

Hazel had been in her bedroom when she heard arguing on the porch. She'd crept to her window and listened. Lake was begging Gramps to call his son for more money. Hazel knew her father would cave in and give it to her. He always did and Lake always said it wasn't enough. But this time, Gramps refused to call him. Said this was the last time. Told her not to come back again because it was too hard when she left.

Hazel knew it was hardest on her father. He wasn't even there to witness Lake's comings and goings, but somehow, he still felt the loss deepest.

As Hazel got older, she began to recognize the pain in her father's voice whenever he talked about her mother. The same pain was in Gramps's voice too each time he had to explain to his son that his wife had come and gone again.

Hazel didn't know how much money Gramps gave Lake that last time, but it must've been a lot because she didn't come back around.

Gramps never mentioned that last visit, so Hazel didn't either. She didn't want to be the one to remind the men in her life that Lake didn't think they were worth being clean and sober for, so she learned to stop talking about her mother all together. But that didn't stop Hazel from thinking about her.

Sadly, she wondered if a girl would ever outgrow thinking of her mother.

Hazel pulled another lungful of cold mountain air into her chest and held it. She looked around at the vast landscape with hopefulness. Exhaling, she found that she disagreed with Jamie; there was plenty of room to bury her problems in a place like this.

And that's exactly what she planned to do.

· · ·

James

JAMES HAD JUST FINISHED REPLACING a roll of film when he noticed Hazel standing by herself in the distance. Her silhouette was perfectly framed by mountains and trees. Wrapped in a blanket, she looked like she could be from a forgotten time; a young frontier woman, steely and stoic.

He held his camera up and captured the shot.

God she's tiny.

She almost looked like a child from where he stood. It filled him with an overwhelming need to protect her. Especially now that he knew what she'd been through.

Looking at her, with her delicate jaw lifted confidently toward the horizon, he felt like a complete jackass. He'd assumed she was just some hick who thought two weeks in the woods was some kind of vacation. But she had real problems, and compared to her everyday life, this probably *was* a vacation.

No mother. A crippled father and sick grandfather who she needed to care for.

It put James's own selfish problems in perspective.

Yes, he had real issues too. He hadn't even begun to deal with his guilt over his mother's death, or the surges of anger and depression it inspired, but the things that he'd been whining to her about were nothing compared to Hazel's reality.

And though he wasn't comparing his life to hers, he wished he could tell her that he understood. *I get it, more than you know, Hazel.*

Motherless? *Check.*

Cancer? *Been there, done that.*

Pacemakers? *More familiar than I'd like to admit.*

Parental Pressure? *Don't even get me started.*

We're two peas in a pod, Hazel. Maybe one day I'll tell you about it.

But today wasn't that day.

8

H azel

HAZEL SLEPT SURPRISINGLY WELL in her strange new environment. Besides having to brave the frigid weather to pee in the middle of the night, the cabin set up was quite cozy. The only thing missing was indoor plumbing, which is what everyone at breakfast was complaining about.

Apparently, she wasn't the only one who missed the conveniences of home.

"I don't see why they can't put at least one bathroom in each cabin," Paisley whined. "Communal showers are gross and the lighting in there is abysmal. How am I supposed to put on my makeup?"

"The nearest town is two hundred miles away. Who are you trying to impress?" Sawyer grumbled.

"Um, boys. Duh!" Paisley spat.

"Speaking of boys . . ." Kat purred.

Hazel turned her head to follow Kat's stare, her eyes meeting Jamie's.

"Hey, Handsome," Kat called. "Come sit with us."

A flush began to creep up Jamie's neck, but Hazel gave him an encouraging nod. She'd be lying if she said she hadn't been hoping to run into him this morning. It was weird but she was disappointed that she hadn't seen him again last night.

Jamie paused, briefly looking around the crowded dining hall for another option. Apparently not finding one he liked better, he conceded and walked toward their table.

Hazel followed Kat's example and moved over to give him some room.

He took the seat between them.

"So, we didn't see you at the campfire last night," Kat said.

Jamie tentatively pushed his bowl of grits around with his spoon. "Yeah, group events aren't really my thing."

"A loner, huh?" Sawyer winked. "Me too."

Jamie didn't look up. Hazel could feel the tension vibrating from him. If he held his spoon any tighter it was going to snap.

She bumped her shoulder gently against his. "Got something against grits?"

"Is that what this slop is?"

She smiled. "Have you never had grits before?"

He shook his head. "Not a lot of grits in Boston." He tentatively put a spoonful in his mouth and frowned. "I can see why."

"Well that's because you're not supposed to eat them plain." Hazel pointed to her half empty bowl. "You gotta add cheese, bacon, scallions and hot sauce. It's my Gramps' favorite breakfast." Hazel smiled at the familiar memory. "He calls 'em 'desert ice cream with a kick'."

Jamie stared at her for a moment, then surprisingly shoveled a spoonful from her bowl into his mouth. He looked thoroughly impressed as he chewed, nodding his head in appreciation. "He's right. It's much better this way."

Hazel grinned and Jamie took another bite from her bowl.

"Hey, get your own," she said playfully shoving him.

"There's no way I can make mine taste as good as yours. You should just let me have these." He flashed her a grin that made her stomach hurt. *Are you flirting with me, Jamie Forrester?*

Kat's raised eyebrows said she certainly thought so.

Hazel tried to tame her excitement, but the boy was giving her whiplash. One minute he was telling her off, the next he was giving her smoldering looks in group therapy and now he was sharing her breakfast like they'd known each other all their lives. She didn't know what to say.

Luckily, she was saved by the bell—literally.

Dr. Birch stood next to the dinner bell screwed to the wall of the dining hall waiting for everyone to quiet down. "Good morning campers. I hope you're all settling in and have had time to meet your neighbors and enjoy breakfast. Today starts the first step of your journey to self-betterment. If you haven't already, please synchronize your camp-issued watches with the clock on Prospect Tower. Training starts at zero-seven-hundred."

James

JAMES GLANCED down at his watch—not the camp-issued one. There was no way he was parting with his Chopard. His mother had bought it for him and it was worth more than his car. Besides, it kept time just as well as the crappy ones the camp handed out in their welcome packs. It was most likely just a gimmick to charge more equipment.

James pulled the sleeve of his jacket down to cover his contraband watch.

It was almost seven.

He took another bite of Hazel's grits, threw a wink her way and stood up from the table. If he hurried, he'd have time to stop by the camp store and grab a few more rolls of film before hell week started.

Hazel

Hazel stared after Jamie in shock. *Did you just wink at me, Jamie?*

She was about to ask if her roommates had seen it too, but from the looks on their faces there was no need for the question.

Paisley looked like she was sucking lemons again. "You know him, don't you?"

"I *do* not," Hazel hissed.

"You two sure looked cozy to me," Sawyer added.

Hazel felt her cheeks burning. "I assure you, I'm as baffled by that as you are."

"Please," Paisley grumped. "He was sharing your breakfast."

"Yeah, and anyone who knows me, knows I don't like to share my food," Hazel snapped back.

Kat just grinned. "He likes you." She sang the words like she was a third grader.

"Oh, shut up."

"You better be careful," Paisley said bitterly. "Couples' Curse and all."

"Iron out your panties, Paisley," Kat teased. "I'm sure there will be plenty of damaged boys for you to flirt with in group today."

Sawyer rolled her eyes. "Come on, we're gonna be late."

Hazel followed along, still wondering what had prompted Jamie's odd behavior.

He could have split personalities or something. Maybe her roommates were right. He might be more drama than he was worth.

9

H azel

BY DINNER TIME, Hazel was starving. She couldn't remember the last time she'd worked up that kind of an appetite. Morning group had been an intro to all the activities and survival skills they'd be covering over the course of their stay on Wander Mountain. Their group leader, Sage, had broken them up into teams and sent them through a series of drills and agility training that made Hazel's muscles cramp.

After lunch they'd either been assigned to small group therapy sessions or hiking. Hazel had been put in the hiking group, which Sage led at a breakneck pace. He wanted them to be able to think and adapt on the fly.

He said nature didn't take your pace into consideration. They needed to be able to familiarize themselves with their surroundings in any situation.

His point was valid, but Hazel was panting as she tried to

keep up.

Sage practically jogged everywhere as he pointed out plants and herbs and leaves and roots, telling them what did what. Hazel's vision spotted as she tried not to fall behind. She was so winded it felt like she was sucking air through a sponge.

Can lungs catch fire?

It certainly felt like it.

She was too busy trying to catch her breath and watch her footing to absorb anything Sage was saying. They hadn't even left the basecamp trails today and already the altitude was killing her. Hazel could hear her pulse pounding in her head as her body screamed for more oxygen.

Wander Mountain was no joke.

She found herself wondering if it was even possible to acclimate in such a short time as she dragged herself to the dining hall. As soon as she pushed through the door she was hit with warmth and a mouthwatering aroma that pushed all other thoughts away. She read the menu board: Chili Night.

Hazel almost started drooling as she grabbed a tray and rushed to grab a spot in line. This was when her fast metabolism was her enemy. Hazel was used to eating small meals all day long. She always had random snacks with her at school or work. It didn't help that she had the biggest sweet tooth ever and constantly filled her pockets with the random penny candies they sold in the repair shop.

Hazel got her love of sweets from Gramps. The man lived on candy. Over the years he'd turned the tiny waiting room of their repair shop into a general store of sorts, filling it with soda, chips, candy bars and all his favorite sweets from when he was a boy. Hazel was astonished that most of the candy companies from his childhood were still in business. But then again, she understood the addiction to sugar was real.

As she waited in line to fill her tray with chili and corn bread, she spotted brownies going by on another camper's tray. Hazel had to fight the urge to snatch them. When it was finally her turn, she piled her tray with a generous helping of chili, two hunks of corn bread and three brownies.

Yes, three. Don't judge.

Hazel was so hungry she didn't even waste time looking for her roommates. She took the first empty spot she could find and started stuffing her face. Her mouth was crammed full of cornbread when she heard his laughter.

She looked up to see Jamie's sky-blue eyes glittering with amusement. "Worked up an appetite, did ya?"

Hazel eyeballed his empty tray, wondering how of all the tables in the dining hall she'd managed to sit at his. It appeared he'd already finished eating but it was easy to tell from the small stack of biodegradable plates that he hadn't piled nearly as many items on his tray as she had.

"I like food," she said unashamed.

"Clearly."

"Where were you today?" she asked while taking another bite of chili. "I didn't see you out there."

A spark of amusement glinted in his eyes. "Were you looking for me?"

Hazel rolled her eyes and returned to her meal. She was too hungry for flirting.

Seeing she wasn't playing along, Jamie gave a shrug. "Yeah, apparently when you admit to killing your mother in front of a lot of other people you don't get to participate."

Hazel stopped eating.

James

. . .

HAZEL RAISED HER COCOA EYEBROWS. She was hunched over her tray like a starved bear cub. It was quite comical, but the concern in her eyes brought James back to their conversation.

"I had a mandatory therapy session with the Big Kahuna today." He smirked. "Had to make sure I'm not gonna kill anyone else, including myself before they'll let me play with the other boys and girls."

"Oh." Hazel looked down, clearly uncomfortable.

Way to go, Jamie.

He rubbed his forehead wondering how to follow up his tactless sentence. It's not like he wanted to admit he had to meet with the chief counselor this morning to ensure he wasn't a risk to himself or others, but for some reason the truth just tumbled out when Hazel was around.

He glanced up at her. She'd returned to snarfing down her meal. James wished he could just turn the world off for a minute, reach across the table and have a real conversation with her. Their connection was undeniable. She was like a magnet that he couldn't help but be drawn to. *Is it the same for you, Hazel?*

She *had* sat at his table.

As much as James told himself to leave Hazel be, that he'd probably only make her life worse if he inserted himself, he couldn't help it.

He sighed. *I'm sorry I'm so bad at this, Hazel.*

"Why do you tell people that?" she blurted out.

He blinked at her, wondering if maybe he'd actually said his thoughts out loud. "Tell people what?"

She lowered her voice. "That you killed your mother."

The noise in the room dulled as James focused his attention on Hazel. *Do you really want to know, Hazel?*

The intense look in her caramel eyes said she did.

"Because it's true," he said quietly.

"That's not what I heard."

"Really?" James didn't know why he was surprised. He was used to being the source of gossip. "What have you heard?"

"That she died in a car accident," Hazel replied quietly, gazing intently at him from across the table.

He sighed and looped his hands behind his head, leaning back in his chair. "Well, at least the gossip's right for once."

Hazel's frown deepened. "I don't understand. Why did you say you killed her if it was a car accident?"

James rocked forward in his chair, his hands landing on the table as he met Hazel's stare. "Because I was the one driving."

She didn't try to hide her quick intake of breath. *I appreciate the honestly, Hazel.*

"That's not the same thing as killing her," she added softly.

Guilt slammed into him. "Isn't it?"

Hazel's warm eyes softened. "Jamie . . ." she reached her hand for his, her fingertips whisper soft as they met his skin.

Whatever she'd been about to say was drowned out by the squeaking of the chair next to her. A boy had been about to sit down next to her but James gave him the death glare he'd perfected on his brothers. *Sense the room, bro!*

The kid gulped, mumbled an apology and scurried away. But even as James watched him back away, it was obvious the moment between him and Hazel had passed. Her hands were back at her tray as she began eating again.

"Will you be participating tomorrow?" Hazel finally asked.

It seemed like an innocent enough question, but James couldn't help wondering if she was trying to find out if he was stable enough to join the rest of the campers or if he'd be back in therapy.

"Yep. Afraid so."

"Good." She shoveled in another bite. "It's not that bad."

He smirked watching her polish off her bowl of chili like a champ. She was by far the smallest person he'd ever met who could probably out eat both of his brothers.

"What?" she asked when she caught him staring.

"Hazel, I mean this in the most flattering way, but you're eating like they just let you off a chain gang."

She paused spoon halfway to her mouth. She looked embarrassed for half a second and then thought better of it, shrugging as she took another bite of chili, moaning in delicious delight.

James laughed out loud. *You're way too easy to like, Hazel Walker.*

Just when he thought he might actually be confident enough to say one of the stupid thoughts rolling around his head, Hazel's she-wolves arrived.

Hacker-girl slammed her tray down on the table. "Is that man trying to kill us?"

"Who?" Hazel asked.

"Sage! I mean he's gotta be part gazelle. How the hell does he walk so fast? It's not fair. His legs have gotta be twice as long as ours. Speaking of . . . how did you get here so fast? I was on that trail with you."

Hazel shrugged. "The dinner bell rang."

Again, James found himself laughing.

Hacker-girl swiveled her attention toward him. "Ah, Breakfast Boy. If you're going to be a regular dining room fixture, I suppose we should make proper introductions. I'm Kat, this is Paisley and Sawyer," she said introducing the rest of the wolfpack.

"James," he replied.

"I thought it was Jamie," Kat challenged.

He shrugged. "Either's fine."

"You look more like a Jamie to me," Hazel added, making

him smile.

Paisley, the bitchy-looking blonde she-wolf, gave a little humph and turned her attention back to Kat who was still droning on about some guy named Sage and his sadistic teaching methods.

Without anywhere else to be, James sat back, crossed his arms and enjoyed his view of Hazel as her roommates mindlessly chattered about the terrible conditions of camp life. The whole time, Hazel looked as uninterested as he was.

She was much better at pretending she wasn't bored though. She gave the girls a head nod every once in a while and managed an "Um-hm," around bites of food. But James was starting to read her tells. She wasn't engaged.

You're as bored as I am, aren't you, Hazel? You don't care about bitchy high school drama, do you?

Again, he found himself wishing he could shut the world out and get some time with just her. His head was full of questions. It was unbearable to be so close to her, but still feel so far away.

HAZEL

HAZEL HAD TUNED out her roommates once their conversation turned to beauty products and boys. She'd been busy rebuilding transmissions when most girls were learning about bras and makeup in *Seventeen Magazine*. Hazel certainly wasn't the girliest girl, but that had never bothered her. What *did* bother her was that her tomboy ways kept her from joining in when conversations turned feminine . . . another thing she could blame her mother for.

Hazel had been hoping for more out of the girls at Wander

Mountain, but so far, they seemed like wealthier versions of the girls she went to high school with. All Kat, Paisley and Sawyer did was bitch about boys or problems that weren't even problems. Kat couldn't get over her ex cheating on her, Paisley couldn't get over not already having a camp boyfriend and Sawyer . . . well to be fair Sawyer bitched more about weed not being legalized than anything else.

But honestly, why weren't these girls more interested in themselves and finding out who they were, instead of being so worried about who boys thought they were?

Their lovesickness made her sick.

Hazel sighed and tried to remain optimistic as she enjoyed her brownies. It was only day two. There was still lots of time for growth. She caught Jamie's eye again, wondering why on earth he was still at their table. He wasn't eating and there was no way Kat's conversation about Korean beauty products was interesting him.

"I mean seriously," Kat whined. "Do they think Saranghae is cheap? It's like a hundred dollars for half an ounce. It's not meant to be sweated out of my pores into the wilderness."

Hazel almost felt bad for Kat. She was definitely not the outdoorsy type, but Hazel was sure after a few days even Kat would find something to appreciate about Wander Mountain.

Presently, Hazel was deeply appreciative of whoever the dining hall chef was. The brownies she was inhaling were to die for. As she was eating, a dime-sized crumb fell onto her tray. Jamie moved his fork toward it, but Hazel's hand cut it off.

"Whoa!" she cried. "Grits are one thing, bub. But if you even attempt to fork my brownie, I'll take your hand off."

Jamie held his hands up in surrender. "Alright, Smalls. Take it easy."

Kat eyeballed them suspiciously.

"Smalls?" Paisley asked pursing her lips again. "You guys

have nicknames for each other? How cute." Though there was nothing cute about the tone of her voice.

"Smalls isn't my nickname," Hazel grumbled.

Jamie grinned, unaffected by Paisley's pouting. "I guess Shorty works, too."

Paisley stood abruptly, her chair making a loud screech across the floor. "You don't have to rub it in my face," she shouted, snatching her tray and stomping away.

"What's her problem?" Jamie asked.

"She's just jealous that you're in love with Hazel instead of her," Kat said, grinning around her bottle of sparking water.

"We're not in love!" Hazel yelled. "We're not anything, okay?"

Immediately, Hazel felt bad for her outburst. She hadn't meant to be so loud, but she'd managed to draw the attention of nearly every table in the room. The dining hall was uncomfortably silent for a breath before Jamie stood up—his screeching chair breaking the silence.

He stood silently gazing at Hazel for a moment, his jaw muscles working angrily. He didn't say anything at all, and somehow that was worse than if he'd told her off. She'd have deserved it. She could read his thoughts loud and clear. The look in his eyes said it all; 'If you wanna be nothing, nothing it is.'

He gave her a salute and walked out of the dining hall without a word.

James

I GUESS *you're not different after all, Hazel.*
  How disappointing.

10

H azel

HAZEL HAD a knot in her stomach for the rest of the night. She didn't even join the S'mores Social. She wouldn't have enjoyed it. She was too upset with herself to eat—and that was saying something. Hazel never passed up free sugar.

She wished she had her phone. She was ashamed of herself and more homesick than ever. Not being able to check in with her dad and Gramps was only adding to her bad mood. Hazel could really use a dose of Jenny right now. Not only to make sure her best friend hadn't been busted covering for her, but because Jenny was great with boy drama.

Jenny always knew what to do when it came to guys. Hazel knew Jenny would have some expert advice like 'sisters before misters' that would put her camp drama with Jamie into perspective. *Ugh, why did I have to pick the one camp that doesn't allow phones?*

Groaning, Hazel rolled over on her bed. "You're as bad as your roommates, Hazel," she scolded herself. "You didn't come here to waste your time worrying about some guy's feelings."

She stood up, grabbed her shower kit and marched out the door. If she couldn't call home or talk to Jenny she might as well shower and go to bed. At least with a good night's rest she might stand a chance of keeping up with Sage tomorrow.

James

THE SUNSET PAINTED the mountains varying shades of golds and blues. James had already exhausted a roll of film capturing what he could. He loved looking at the world through the steady lens of a camera. Each click of the shutter churned out perfectly picturesque segments of reality. It made it easier to digest that way. He could zoom in, focusing on single aspects rather than the whole.

It was more relaxing that way. Life, as static art.

James wished the world could always feel like that. Still, unchanging—allowing him to cut out the chaos and live in his perfectly framed bubble of reality.

He sighed, knowing it was an unrealistic wish.

With one last look at the pastel sky, he capped his camera and looped the strap over his head as he headed back toward camp. He was just rounding the bathhouse when something barreled into him.

Not something, someone.

His arms flew out grasping her as he tried to muster enough balance for the both of them.

James knew it was Hazel before he even truly saw her. It was the crisp apple scent of her shampoo; ten times more potent now that her shower-wet hair was drenching the front of his hoodie. He had a sudden urge to run his fingers through it.

Is your hair as soft as it looks, Hazel?

He'd never wanted his hands to be tangled in someone's hair so badly.

Instead, he shoved her away. "Christ! You should come with airbags," he grumbled.

She looked up at him, eyes wide and apologetic—or was that pity?

I don't need your pity, Hazel.

He turned to walk away but she called after him.

"Jamie, wait! I'm sorry."

He kept walking.

She ran to catch up. "Please . . . I mean it. I wasn't trying to be a jerk in the dining hall."

He stopped walking and she crashed into him again. James exhaled deeply as he steadied her. It was hard to stay mad at her when she kept falling into his arms. But what kind of person did that make him? *Am I really this starved for affection?*

Hazel had just announced to the entire dining hall that he was worth nothing, but now, with a few bats of her eyelashes, his anger was already warming to lust. His neck flushed as the sensation infected him like a virus. *What is it about you, Hazel?*

It was impossible to stare into those big doe eyes of hers and not see himself in them. He was convinced their souls were made of these same things—equal parts pain and hope.

How else could he explain the unshakeable feeling that she saw him? The *real* him, beyond his last name and the fame that came with it.

He couldn't explain his possessiveness over her, but he had to know her. Especially when she stared at him like she was now—her caramel eyes tipped up, like two open books begging him to devour every page.

Maybe we should stop fighting this, Hazel.

HAZEL

HAZEL BLINKED UP AT JAMIE, blanketed in the warmth of his arms—arms that were still wrapped around her. *Why can't I remember what I was going to say? Or how to take breath?*

All she could do was gaze at the beautiful boy the world kept shoving in her path. She watched his face change, morphing from frustration to friendly as he gave her one of his rare smiles. It was a real one, not the half-crooked 'you-know-you-think-I'm-cute' smile that he probably spent hours practicing in front of the mirror. This smile took Hazel's breath away. It seemed to suck all the light from the fading sky and trap it in her chest, making it impossible to breathe.

Unwrapping his arms, Jamie backed away a step, still grinning like the sun. "If I let you go are you going to run into me again? If so, I might want to warn the camp to up their insurance policy. You're a walking disaster."

She laughed. "Apparently I am. But I think it's only when it comes to you. Sorry about that."

He shrugged and stepped back, adjusting the camera strap around his neck.

"Hey! You found a camera?"

He nodded, holding it proudly. "Found it at the camp store. Turns out Wander Mountain isn't completely against technology as long as they're making a profit." He patted the camera. "Added it to my dad's tab. Figured it's the least he can do for shipping me out to the middle of nowhere."

"They don't happen to have cell phones at the camp store, do they?" Hazel asked, hope creeping into her voice.

Jamie raised an eyebrow. "Need a burner phone for something, Smalls?"

She stuffed her hands in her pockets trying to hide her agitation. *Do you really have to keep going there with the short jokes, Jamie?* "No. I just wish I could check in on my dad and Gramps."

Jamie's teasing tone disappeared. He reached into his back pocket and pulled out a cell phone, unlocking it and offering it to her.

"Oh my God! Where did you get this?"

"It's mine. I kept it."

"We were supposed to turn them in last night."

He shrugged. "Yeah well, in case you haven't noticed, I don't play by the rules."

She wanted to tell him she wasn't impressed by rule breakers or bad boys, but presently she wanted to make a phone call more. "You don't mind if I use it?"

"Knock yourself out."

Hazel took the phone and started to type in her number, but Jamie quickly put an arm around her and ushered her away from the bathhouse.

"Not here," he whisper-hissed. "I may not play by the rules but I'm not trying to advertise that I'm breaking them either."

He led her to a clearing just beyond the trail with an incredible view of the fading sunset. Stacks of smooth rocks had been shaped into a bench for taking in the magnificent views the secluded spot offered. Hazel took a seat and dialed her number while Jamie walked further toward the ledge to give her some privacy. She watched him snapping photos while the phone rang in her ear. He was holding the camera with a tenderness that made her wonder what it would feel like to be touched by him.

"Hello?"

Her father's voice boomed into her ear, chasing away Hazel's embarrassing thoughts.

James

HE WASN'T TRYING to listen, but it was hard not to overhear, even as he focused on the world framed by his camera. It was useless . . . Hazel's voice cut right through him. James had no choice but to try to make sense of her one-sided conversation.

"It's so good to hear your voice, too," Hazel said, her own voice tight with emotion. "I know, but it's not holding a charge." . . . "A friend from class." . . . "Yeah, I'm having so much fun." . . . "Jenny is too." . . . "How are you doing without me? The roof cave in yet?" She laughed. Then she laughed some more. "I know you can. How's Gramps?"

Hazel was quiet. It was a heavy kind of quiet, the unsettling kind that usually followed bad news.

James knew that breed of quiet well. He wanted to turn around, he wanted to look into Hazel's open-book eyes and read every line. He wanted to know everything she was thinking, but he couldn't. Not without being obvious.

Hazel's voice was soft now. "But I thought they said it wouldn't progress that quickly?"

James pulled the camera away from his eyes and glanced in Hazel's direction as he changed a setting. He wished he hadn't looked at her, because now all he wanted to do was run to her side and do anything to take that broken expression off her face.

It was a sin for a face that angelic to look so sad.

Her voice was almost a whisper now. "I know, but—" . . . "Okay." . . . "Okay." . . . "I will." . . . "I love you, too." . . . "I promise." . . . "Will you tell Lou I love him?" . . . "Thanks, Dad." . . . "Goodnight."

HAZEL

SHE TOOK a moment to collect herself before walking over to Jamie to return his phone. Her heart physically hurt when she hung up with her dad. All her anxiety and worries had been realized with that call.

She shouldn't have come here.

Was this all happening because she'd lied? Was it some kind of karmic payback?

No, the world isn't that cruel, Hazel. And honestly you don't matter enough for the universe to scheme against you. This is just plain bad timing.

But even her un-motivational pep talk didn't help ease the hollowness in her chest.

Hazel stood up and tried to rub some of the tension from her brow as she walked toward Jamie. He was still clicking away at the horizon with his funny little camera. It wasn't the sleek digital kind with the massive lenses she was used to seeing.

Even though Lovelock was a whistlestop of a town, they still got their fair share of tourists coming through to take photographs of Main Street, which resembled an old Hollywood Western town. Shutterbugs loved coming by the repair shop to photograph Gramps's collection of old cars.

Hazel had never seen the kind of camera Jamie was using

though. She watched him for a moment. He looked content behind the lens, clicking and adjusting with confidence. He noticed her watching and stopped, snapping Hazel out of her trance.

"Thanks," she said walking forward to hand back his phone.

"Everything okay?" he asked, his sky-blue eyes looking like calm water as he studied her.

No, everything is definitely not okay. But Hazel wasn't ready to talk about it. She nodded then pointed to his camera. "What kind of camera is that?"

His concentration flitted back to the camera. "You know cameras?"

"No, I've just never seen one like that."

"It's a 35 millimeter."

"As in film?"

Jamie nodded, grinning, that real grin again, making Hazel's stomach flip.

"Yep," he replied. "I forgot how much I love shooting real film."

"I didn't even know they still made film."

"It's a lost art," he said fondly. "I mean, don't get me wrong, digital is king, but this was my first love."

"Really? How do you even know if the photos you're taking will come out?"

"Practice, but that's also kinda the beauty of it. The anticipation."

Hazel didn't agree. But what did she know? The only photos she took were with her phone and they were all of her dog. The idea of having to wait to see if she'd actually managed to capture a clear picture of Lu wasn't appealing, but she didn't mind listening to Jamie try to convince her otherwise. She could watch him talk about something he was this passionate about for hours.

Photography lit him up from within. Hazel didn't know Jamie's father at all, but she found herself hating him for even trying to persuade his son from doing something that made him this happy.

Jamie was still musing on about how exciting it was to develop his own negatives. "It's like uncovering something incredibly rare and beautiful."

Hazel nodded, thinking how accurate that description was for him in this moment. He was a completely different boy from the versions of Jamie she'd met before.

This boy, with adventure in his eyes and fire in his smile, he could sweep her heart away in an instant.

"Here," he said motioning her closer. He pulled his phone out and snapped a photo of the last hues of pinks and oranges slipping behind the mountain. "See how it's not nearly as vivid as what your eye can see?"

She nodded.

"Now try this." He passed the camera to her and for a moment she felt lost, not sure where to look without a display screen.

Jamie pointed to the viewfinder and patiently helped her adjust her grip so she could focus the lens. He held his hand over hers as her finger hovered near the shutter. "See how there's nothing between you and the horizon? There's nothing trying to recreate the colors you see. It's just you and your perspective. There's something so peaceful about the natural-ness of it."

Jamie was so close Hazel could feel his warmth seeping into her. And when he spoke, the mist from his breath curled into her damp hair making her shiver. She let him press her finger over the shutter, the click zipping through her like lightning.

"Wanna try it on your own?" he asked.

Hazel nodded and he showed her how to advance the film. She pulled the camera back to her eye and aimed at the glowing mountain range. She knew what she was looking at was beautiful, but she found herself turning the camera back toward Jamie. She wanted to capture the joy on his face in that moment, because it was more beautiful than anything she'd ever seen.

The moment the shutter clicked, Jamie's joy evaporated. His guard went back up as he snatched the camera from her, his tone still light. "I prefer being behind the lens."

He snapped a few of her before she put her hands up, warding him off. "I guess we have that in common," she replied.

Jamie capped the lens and slung the camera around his neck. His eyes looked stormy again when he looked at her. "If you ever need to use my phone, you're welcome to it. Anytime."

Hazel swallowed past the lump in her throat. For a moment she'd managed to suppress the weight of that phone call, but now it came rushing back. "Thanks."

Feeling her eyes sting she turned away, but she didn't make it two steps before Jamie's voice pulled her back. "How bad is the cancer?"

When she turned back to face him, she saw understanding in his eyes and she couldn't hold it in any longer.

11

James

JAMES RUBBED slow circles on Hazel's back as she wiped her tears away with the sleeves of his sweatshirt. He'd pulled it over her head a few minutes ago, though it hadn't stopped her shivering.

The moment he saw the first tear slip down her cheek he'd made his decision to abandon all plans of keeping Hazel at a distance. What kind of monster would he be if he let her suffer alone? He just couldn't do it. Not when he knew how bad that felt.

So here they were, sitting on the stone bench, Hazel crying in James's arms, the night sky alive with stars above them. Hazel kept looking up at them as if praying for strength from the heavens.

He wanted to tell her that was useless. If there was anyone

up there they didn't listen. At least not to him. And from what he'd overheard of her conversation she didn't have anyone's ear up there either.

Hazel was still shaking with sobs. They'd slowed a bit, but James was desperate to ease her suffering. He wanted to lighten the mood. Sarcasm was his go-to coping mechanism for most things. He used it as a weapon to keep people from getting too close, or to keep him from feeling too much. But it worked as a Band-Aid for pretty much all occasions.

"So, I've gotta ask. Who's Lou?"

Hazel sat up, pulling back so she could look at him through watery eyes. "What?"

"You said, 'tell Lou I love him.' Is he your boyfriend or something because it's bad form to talk about your boyfriend on another boy's phone."

She huffed a laugh. "Do you always eavesdrop on other people's conversations?"

He grinned. "Always."

She rolled her eyes, but there wasn't any real annoyance behind it. Strangely, that made him feel worse. He wanted that fiery personality of hers back. He was getting used to it, maybe even starting to understand it.

Hazel was Napoleon in pink boots. She pushed people away with her Little Miss Tough-guy persona so they wouldn't see the vulnerability that lived beneath her skin.

But James had seen it and now he couldn't look away.

"I didn't take you for the jealous type," she teased through a sniffle.

"I wouldn't say jealous, just obsessively mistrustful."

She laughed. *Progress.*

"Well," she replied, "you can rest your suspicions, Lu is definitely not my boyfriend."

He frowned playfully. "Fiancé?"

"Dog," she corrected.

"Huh . . . didn't see that one coming. What kind of a name is Lou for a dog?"

"It's not Lou, like a guy's name, it's L-U, short for Lugnut and before you give me crap about that, I wasn't the one who named him. Gramps did."

At the mere mention of her grandfather, the slight reprieve from her grief vanished.

So much for my distraction techniques. "Are you ready to talk about it?" he asked sensing the time for joking was over.

Hazel sighed and sat back against the bench, her shoulder still pressed against his arm. She stayed quiet for a while, just staring out at the night sky. When she finally spoke, her voice was so quiet, James almost missed it.

"He's stage four," she whispered. "Lung cancer. There's nothing else the doctors can do at this point. We're just trying to make him comfortable."

"He's stopped treatment?"

She nodded. "And now his bronchitis is back."

James took her hand and squeezed. "I'm sorry."

She scuffed the toe of her pink boot into the dirt. "Lung cancer," she muttered, bitterly. "It's not fair. Gramps never even smoked a day in his life."

"Really?" Fear suddenly gripped James. "Does it run in your family?"

Hazel huffed a bitter laugh. "Not unless bad luck is hereditary."

"What do you mean?"

"The cancer's from shrapnel the Vietnam War left in his chest." She shook her head. "He was so proud of it. Told everyone how he got his scars serving his country." She wiped another tear from her cheek. "But I'm not proud. I'm angry! And I know that makes me a terrible person, but I'm angry at how much my country has taken from me. Gramps is dying and my dad . . ." she trailed off. "They're good men. They deserve better."

"It doesn't make you terrible," James said quietly. "It makes you human."

"No, it makes me terrible, because I'm lucky. At least they came back to me. So many other kids don't get that lucky, so I should be grateful. And I am. It's just hard sometimes. It's hard to watch them struggle and not be able to do anything to change it. It's hard to want things for myself when I look at them and see how much they've already sacrificed for me. But I do, I still want things." Her tears were streaming again. "I was so stupid to think I could do this. I knew he was sick. I never should've come."

"Are you going to leave?"

"I don't know. I promised my dad I wouldn't. He said there's nothing I can do, and I know he's right. Gramps is comfortable, but the home health nurse said his bronchitis could turn to pneumonia and at this stage there's not much they can do because he refuses to go to the hospital."

"How long do they give him?"

She shrugged. "A few months, but they've been saying that for years and he keeps proving them wrong." She bit her lip. "It's why I've never left Lovelock. I was always so afraid something would happen to him if I did. But then I got this opportunity and I thought . . . I thought he had more time."

"You should be with him, Hazel. You'll regret it if you're not." James closed his eyes, the last moment with his mother floating to the surface. "Trust me."

She looked at him, her warm eyes full of questions she was too polite to ask. He ran a hand through his hair, gripping the back of his neck as he squeezed the tension out. He never spoke about what he'd been through, but he could tell Hazel needed to hear it.

"My mom had cancer too. She had a better prognosis than your grandfather, but it was a long road. One I traveled with her since I was really the only one around. She got diagnosed right after my brother, Tom, started college. Conner was already playing pro and my dad, well between my brother's games and his Senate campaign he was never around much. So, I'm the one that drove her to and from all her doctor appointments."

James pulled in a slow breath and held it as long as he could, fighting the memories that tried to drag him back to that day—the day he'd lost everything.

"We were coming home from the hospital when a truck broadsided us. I didn't even see it coming. Slammed right into my mom's side of the car."

Hazel's hand slid into James's and he forced himself to look at her. "She made it to the hospital, but her injuries were too severe. I was with her, Hazel. She knew it. In those last few moments, she knew she wasn't alone." He pushed out a breath. "Sometimes I wonder if it would've been easier not to have been there. Not to have held her hand while she let go. Because that was the hardest thing I've ever had to do. But then I think it was easier than the regret I would've carried with me if I hadn't been there."

Tears were streaming down Hazel's cheeks again as she looked up at him, those wide eyes so open. They said so much without ever speaking a word and James soaked up every sentence, knowing he wasn't misinterpreting a thing. He knew, because his heart was stamping out the same words: *I understand . . . you're not alone . . . I see you.*

It's not fair, Hazel. I found you, the one who knows my soul and now I have to let you go.

. . .

HAZEL

HAZEL LET her head fall to her hands. Talking things through with Jamie made her feel even worse. *Who leaves their sick grandpa and handicapped dad to come on a soul-searching adventure? Me, that's who.*

Even just for two weeks; it was selfish and stupid and not worth the risk and she'd known that from the start. James was right, she needed to go home. She needed to be there with Gramps or she would regret it for the rest of her life.

One look at James told Hazel she didn't really have a choice. *Then why does it feel so wrong to leave you, Jamie?*

Hazel squeezed his hand, wishing she could find the words to convey everything she was feeling. But most of all she wished she'd met this version of Jamie from their very first encounter. She wished she'd had two days with *this* boy. She could've learned a lot from him. Maybe she even could've loved him.

They were practically strangers, but after a ten-minute conversation she felt he knew her better than anyone she'd ever met. Proving that point, Jamie handed her his phone without her even having to ask.

"I have to go home, don't I?" she asked.

"Whatever you do, do it with no regrets."

Hazel took the phone and paced a few feet away as she dialed her dad's number again. He picked up on the first ring. "Kiddo? Everything okay?"

"Dad, I know I promised I'd stop worrying and have fun but it's impossible. I can't stop thinking about you and Gramps. I think I need to come home."

"Hazel," he sighed. "We talked about this. You can't live your life for anyone but yourself, kiddo. You're already there. I promise, the best thing you can do for us is make the most of it."

"But Dad—"

There was a muffled shuffling sound and then Gramps's voice boomed over the line. "Hazel Jane Walker, if you cut that trip of yours short even an iota, I'm gonna send that dog you love so much back to the junk yard where I found him."

"Leave Lu out of this, Gramps. And stop getting so worked up. It's not good for your health."

"You let me worry about my health, young lady. You just worry about yourself for a damn change."

"But Gramps—"

"No buts, Hazel Jane. You're my favorite grandchild and you're gonna listen to me."

"I'm you're only grandchild."

"Even more reason for you to make something of yourself. And you can't do that if you're too busy worrying about us to start your own damn life. We had our time, kid. Your dad and me, we saw the world in our day. Hell, we fought for your freedom to wander this blessed country so by God you better do it. You're a good girl, Hazel and I love ya. But if I see your sorry ass on this property sooner than expected I'm gonna kick it to the curb, ya hear me?"

"Yes, sir."

"Good. Now go have some fun. That's an order."

Then the line went dead.

Hazel stared at the phone in disbelief. A laugh bubbled up from her toes and she couldn't help but let it out. She didn't know whether to laugh or cry. *That's Gramps for ya.* Every time she counted him out, he came back swinging.

She turned to face Jamie who had a knowing smile on his face. "So, you're staying?"

"I guess so," she said passing the phone back.

He didn't take it. "Keep it. If you can't go home, you can at least get peace of mind by keeping in touch."

"Thank you."

He smiled that perfect smile and extended his hand. "Well, you heard the man, let's go have some fun, Hazel Jane."

She snorted a laugh. "We've really gotta work on your eavesdropping manners."

12

James

"I CAN'T BELIEVE you've never made S'mores," Hazel said dragging him by the hand toward the closest campfire.

She'd taken his hand after talking to her grandfather and had yet to let go. He wasn't complaining, but he worried he liked the feel of it a little too much. But then again, he liked everything about Hazel a little too much. Even the way her middle name made him think of his mom. *What does it mean that you share a name, Hazel? Is it some sort of sign?*

Normally, James didn't believe in that sort of thing, but normally he didn't feel such an intimate connection to other humans.

The sensation was surprisingly nice, in a terrifying way.

James ambled along beside Hazel, each one of his steps eating up two of hers. He had an urge to just scoop her up and carry her. Not because she seemed helpless—she was still way more Mad Max than damsel in distress—but when one comes across a glittering stone amongst rubble it's a natural urge to snatch it up and claim it.

He watched her as the firelight bounced off her face painting it every shade of bronze and copper. She was like a tiny piece of garnet—sharp and hard around the edges, but full of priceless beauty. *You're gonna break my heart, aren't you, Hazel Jane?*

She was badgering him about the damn S'mores but he didn't mind. He could sit by the fire and listen to her talk forever.

"Eighteen and never had a S'more. It's a sin," she harped.

He arched an eyebrow. "Are they really that good?"

She stopped skewering her marshmallows and gave him a surprisingly serious look. "They're life changing."

TURNS OUT SHE WAS RIGHT. S'mores *were* life changing.

Watching Hazel's face light up as she laughed at his inexperience was pretty damn life changing too. As it turned out, it somehow melted his jaded heart.

He knew the exact moment it happened. It was when she wiped marshmallow off his chin, licking the sticky sweetness off her finger with a grin. James was certain he felt the world shift in that moment.

Something unusual had certainly happened, because he'd never felt the things he was feeling right now. He never expected his pain could bring him joy; his grief, gratitude. But it had. Sharing those things with Hazel had made him feel so much less alone and for the first time James was grateful, because without those things he wouldn't have forged such an instant bond with Hazel. It's why she'd let him in—and he didn't want to let go.

HAZEL

HAZEL HADN'T EXPECTED her night to end on a high note after the way it started. But then again, with Jamie, she was learning to expect the unexpected. She was certain there was more to him than she'd first thought. She liked peeling back the new layers.

Her favorite highlights of the evening had been watching him with his camera and his attempts at making S'mores. The experiences couldn't have been more different. Jamie was all confidence and heart behind the camera, but when it came time to make S'mores he was bumbling and baffled.

He'd failed miserably, but it was quite comical to watch. He swore colorfully when his marshmallows caught on fire, and when an entire S'more adhered to his pants after a graham cracker fell apart, he looked murderous.

She recognized his stubborn streak as he refused her help. It endeared her to him, because she saw a bit of herself in his determination. She didn't like relying on others for help either.

In the end, he'd eventually gotten one right and the moan of pleasure he made when eating it made her stomach clench. Watching Jamie Forrester lick his agile fingers did dangerous things to Hazel's insides. She decided they should probably call it a night.

"Aw, come on. I just figured it out," he complained when she started packing up their supplies. "I could eat like a dozen more of these things."

"Pace yourself, Big Guy."

He smirked at her. "Is that a dig at my stamina, because I promise, I can keep up."

"A lot of self-practice?" she teased.

He barked a laugh. "Oh, Shorty's got game."

She winked. "Let's keep it to one mind-blowing experience a night, Champ."

"I like the sound of that. What's on the menu for tomorrow night, Smalls?"

She rolled her eyes. "Okay you win, your lines are much cheesier than mine, but you've gotta stop with the Smalls."

Jamie stood up, following her from the cozy warmth of the campfire. "What's wrong with Smalls?"

"I don't like it."

"But it's so fitting," he said draping an arm around her shoulder.

Her first instinct was to shrug him off, but he was so warm and he smelled like campfire and graham crackers. She melted into him. *Give a girl a chance, James Forrester.*

"How about, Teacup?"

"What am I, a Chihuahua?"

"Tater tot?"

"Ew!"

"Tiny."

"No."

"Shortcake."

"Nope."

"Bitsie."

"Hell no!"

He scrunched up his face like he was thinking. "How 'bout Fun-size?"

She laughed. "At least that's original."

"And you love sweets. It's fitting."

"Oh, you think you know me now?"

"Girl, you ate three brownies at dinner like you were going head-to-head with Kobayashi."

"Who?"

"Kobayashi." Jamie rolled his eyes at her lack of knowledge. "He's like the Karate Kid of competitive eating."

She snorted. "I should probably be offended by that."

Jamie smiled. "I like a girl who can eat."

Hazel digested the simple sentence, letting it grow wings and fluttered around her stomach nervously. She didn't know if she liked the direction this playful conversation was going. Flirting was one thing, but she felt like every time she took one step forward with Jamie, it always led to two steps back.

She should quit while she was ahead. Especially now that they were standing in front of her cabin, Jamie's warm arm still draped around her shoulders. She didn't want to look up because she knew what she'd see—sparkling sky-blue eyes and irresistible lips curved into that sinful smile.

Jamie tucked a piece of hair behind her ear, his finger trailing the line of her jaw. "You gonna be okay?" he asked, all joking gone from his voice.

She swallowed hard, drowning in the sincerity she found in his eyes. "Yeah. Thank you for tonight."

"Always."

The word was so simple, but it unlocked a door in Hazel's heart that she wasn't ready to open. She craved that word, wanted it to be true more than anything. But it wasn't. It couldn't be.

They may have a lot in common, but they came from two totally different worlds and when this was all over, they'd go back to those worlds. They wouldn't get an 'always'.

It's not like I can bring you back to Lovelock with me, Jamie.

A nervous laugh escaped her lips at the thought of him in her podunk town.

Jamie's smooth fingers tilted her chin up to meet his gaze, his lips moving closer. "Hazel, you shouldn't laugh when I'm thinking about kissing you. It makes your lips irresistible."

Panic sliced through Hazel's heart at Jamie's words. The key to her cabin slipped from her trembling hands, bouncing off the stone path. The noise made her jump out of Jamie's grasp. Her heart felt like a jackhammer in her chest and suddenly the twenty-degree air felt stifling.

She scrambled after her keys, then took a few more steps back.

"You okay?" Jamie asked, taking in her panic-stricken expression.

"You can't kiss me," she whispered.

"I'm pretty sure that's nowhere in the camp handbook. I read it thoroughly. Ya know . . . in case I met a ravenous beauty of fun-sized proportions."

"Jamie, I mean it. We can't."

His easy grin disappeared. "Why not?"

She grabbed his hand and pulled him off the path, her brain scrambling for a way to make him understand. The cold metal of her key dug into her hand, sparking an idea.

Taking the big green plastic keychain the key was attached to, she bent down and drew a large square in the dirt. The moonlight spilled over it, casting shadows that made it look like a hole had opened up in the ground.

Hazel stood up and pulled Jamie into the center of the square she'd drawn.

"Um, is this some kind of kinky Nevada foreplay?"

"I need you to promise me something, Jamie."

He seemed to sense the seriousness in her tone. "Okay . . ."

"Our relationship needs to stay here, inside this box."

"What's so special about this box?" he asked.

"It's full of all the things I need right now. Friendship, understanding, support."

He nodded. "And what's outside the box?"

"Love, heartache, hormones, loneliness."

He frowned, understanding where she was going with this.

"I need you to promise not to cross those lines."

"What if I can't?"

Her chest ached with the loss of him even though he was right in front of her, his warmth still seeping into her through the chill night air. "I'm sorry," she whispered. "This is all I can manage right now. I can respect your feelings if you want something different, but this is all I can give."

His arms wrapped around her and he pulled her to his chest in a hug that was too tight for friends. *Is this a goodbye hug, Jamie?*

She savored it anyway.

James

JAMES HELD HAZEL FOR A WHILE. He wanted to crush the loneliness from her bones. He could practically feel it pouring out of her. He wanted her to know that he saw her and he wasn't afraid. But he didn't know how to express that without crossing her damn lines. So, he held her until his arms ached and she relaxed against his chest.

He swallowed, once, twice . . . trying to find his words. They tasted bitter and he hadn't even said them yet. He knew he would regret them, but he didn't really have a choice.

"Okay," he finally murmured.

She blinked up at him, on the verge of tears. "Okay?"

"Okay, if you want me to promise not to cross these stupid lines, I will."

"Really?"

He nodded and a huge grin broke like dawn across her face.

She hid it quickly. "Okay."

"Okay." *God, I hate that word, Hazel.*

13

Hazel

"So let me get this straight. You met a guy you actually like, and you made him promise not to fall for you?" Jenny asked.

"Yes."

"Haze, you evil genius! That's just gonna make him want you more." Jenny laughed. "I've taught you well."

"It's not a game, Jenny. I really can't get involved with him. With anyone. You know my life. There's no space for another man in it."

"First of all, gross. Your dad and Gramps should never be referred to as the men in your life. And have you forgotten where you live? Lovelock. Desperation is right there in the name, Haze. That town is where love goes to die. You can't be pushing away perfectly good guys who wander into your life."

"That's just it, Jenny. Jamie isn't in my life. He's a temporary distraction."

"You don't know that. It could lead somewhere if you let it."

"No, it really can't."

"Why?"

"First of all, he's from Boston."

"So? What have you got against Boston?"

"Nothing, but it might as well be Bolivia. Boston is practically on the other side of the world when we're talking about Lovelock."

"Nope, not good enough."

"How is that not good enough? I'll never see him again after this!"

"What about college? He could pick a school near Nevada if you're willing to give this a shot."

Hazel rolled her eyes. Jenny; ever the optimist. Suddenly, Hazel wasn't really sure why she'd called her best friend. Jenny wasn't the kind of person to tell you what you wanted to hear. She was a tell it like it is kinda girl. Hazel sighed. *Maybe that's what I need right now.*

All she knew was that if she didn't share the feelings ricocheting around her chest with someone she was going to explode. Plus, she was much too wound up to sleep. And since her roommates were already passed out after surviving an exhausting day with Sage, Hazel had decided to bundle up and sneak outside with Jamie's phone to call Jenny.

Despite Jenny's persistent dating advice, it *was* good to hear a familiar voice.

"What else have you got?" Jenny prodded. "Distance is not enough of a reason to throw in the towel."

"How about the fact that he looks like he spends more on hair product than I do?"

"Ah, a pretty boy, huh?"

Hazel huffed a laugh. "That's an understatement. You

should see him, Jenny. He's devastating. The first time I looked into his eyes I thought I'd fallen out of a plane. They're the color of a perfect blue sky. And he doesn't waste his smiles. He makes you work for them and they're always just a little bit crooked. I don't even know why I like that."

Jenny laughed. "Girl, your 'just friends' plan is a little too late."

"What do you mean?"

"Do you *not* hear the words coming outta your mouth? You're gushing, Haze. You've got it bad for him, sister. I give you two days tops before you're pitching a tent with him, if ya know what I mean?"

Hazel rolled her eyes. "Jenny, I always know what you mean. But I can't let anything happen with Jamie."

"Why not? Have a little fun. I thought that's why you stood me up; adventure in the great outdoors and all that? What's more adventurous than letting some hottie explore your uncharted territory?"

Hazel felt her face flush at the mention of her virginity. Of course Jenny would bring that up. Sometimes she wondered how they remained friends when they lived such different lives. "You wouldn't understand, Jenny."

"Try me."

"Okay . . . I've only known him for a few days but it feels like I've been waiting for him my whole life." Hazel took a breath as she let her own heavy words sink in. "I know it sounds stupid, but the connection I feel with him . . . it goes beyond physical attraction."

"Haze, first of all, I'm not a hooker. I understand the meaning of emotional connection. And more importantly, if you have that with this guy it's even more reason to go for it with him. That kind of thing is rare."

Hazel shook her head. "I just can't. He's been through too

much. It wouldn't be fair to him. Or to me. It's best if we're just friends for now."

Jenny sighed. "If you say so."

"I do."

Knowing Hazel's stubborn streak, Jenny dropped it and switched subjects, catching Hazel up on all the things she was missing in Phoenix. It sounded like Jenny was focused more on keggers than calculus, which at least eased Hazel's guilt about her decision to come to Wander Mountain. She was never much for the party scene and playing wing-woman to Jenny night after night wasn't how she wanted to spend her last spring break.

After Jenny exhausted all her gossip, they said goodnight and Hazel snuck back into her cabin. On her way, she had to walk by the lines she'd drawn in the dirt. Tempting fate, Hazel stepped back inside.

Instantly, she missed the feeling of Jamie's warm arms around her. She was still wearing his hoodie. She sunk her chin down inside it, drinking in his scent. It was already fading . . . *Just like my memories of him will after I leave this place.*

The thought skewered her.

Hazel stared down at the lines in the dirt. No matter how much it hurt now, it would be nothing compared to the pain of letting this become something it could never be. The loss would be too much.

This was the smart move. *Stay friends, don't cross the lines, keep my heart intact.*

Hazel gazed up at the moonlight, repeating her mantra. When the words felt like they had taken root, she marched confidently back to her cabin and climbed into bed.

14

J ames

EVERYTHING about the next three days was perfect, and James owed it all to Hazel. She was the first thing he thought of when he woke and the last when he fell asleep. He couldn't remember the last time his thoughts had been full of something other than guilt and anger and depression.

He realized he was setting himself up for failure thanks to the stupid promise he'd made her, but what other choice did he have? Being around Hazel was addicting. He couldn't give her up. She had this infectious light about her that he couldn't get enough of.

James realized his stupid crush made him a walking cliché.

He'd been so against coming here, but his father was right to send him to Wander Mountain—not for the reasons he thought, of course. The group activities and counseling sessions were a joke, but the way he felt about Hazel wasn't. She made him want to reach inside and pull out all the broken parts of himself and find a way to fix them. She made him want to be better. Not for himself really, but for her.

He realized becoming a co-dependent leech wasn't the healthiest way to deal with his issues, but at least he was dealing with them. Before Hazel, he hadn't even wanted to try. It was remarkable. Just being around her gave him this nourishing energy he hadn't known he was starved for. It's not like she was a ray of sunshine—a shard of gold might be more accurate. But their prickly banter and sarcastic flirting gave him something to look forward to each day. And that was something.

Watching her do the simplest things, like roll her eyes, sucked the negativity out of him and he was beginning to worry he wouldn't be able to function without her. *What will I do when I leave here, Hazel, and you're not around to occupy my mind?*

James was starting to see why she'd drawn those damn lines in the dirt. The trouble was, it was getting harder and harder not to cross them.

Especially while watching Hazel eat the chocolate chips from the mini muffins he'd brought her for breakfast. She had her own of course, but after almost getting forked twice now, he started bringing a buffer plate to their dining table. Something Kat called 'adorbs'.

James was even starting to like Hazel's roommates. It was hard not to like people who disliked Sage as much as he did. They'd all been through four days of hell with that horrible hippie—it bonded them. Well, everyone but Paisley. The girl was still bitter, party of one.

From what he could tell, Paisley's only goal for camp was a

hookup. James wanted to tell her that if she gave her resting bitch face a rest, she might have a better shot. There were a lot of guys at Wander Mountain looking for the same thing. But James had enough of his own troubles without worrying about Paisley.

"So, what does Sergeant Sage have in store for us today?" Hazel asked, between bites of her breakfast.

"I'm so glad you asked, Hazel," Kat replied in her overly peppy morning voice as she placed the day's schedule in front of her. "Today is ropes day!"

Sawyer let her head bang to the table. "I don't even know what that means but I hate it already."

Paisley looked intrigued. "Do you think they're gonna tie us up?"

James nearly choked on his coffee. He smirked at Hazel, eyebrows raised as he jabbed a thumb in Paisley's direction. "This girl!"

Hazel giggled.

Paisley frowned. "What else do you do with ropes?"

"Well, Paisley, thanks for that terrible image, but I think Wander Mountain has a different philosophy in mind," Kat teased.

Paisley scowled. "Like what?"

"I'll tell you." Kat cleared her throat and began reading off the schedule. "Ropes day is a team building event designed to test your leadership, cooperation, determination and reveal your inner strength. Remember there's no healing without revealing."

"Sounds fun," James mocked.

Sawyer made a gagging sound and faked death, something she did at least ten times a day.

James picked up her limp hand from the table and hi-fived

her. "Nice effort. Your deaths are getting more believable every time."

She flipped him off without lifting her head off the table. Hazel giggled again, which only encouraged James.

"Uh oh," he teased, "it looks like somebody needs a time-out. Want me to get you some crayons, Sawyer, so you can draw your feelings?"

Sawyer sat back up and threw her half-eaten muffin at him. Hazel intercepted it and popped it in her mouth. "Damn, the blueberry ones are actually good," Hazel mumbled around her chewing.

James laughed. "Seriously Smalls, does your stomach have an off switch? I'm worried about you." He grabbed her tiny waist and squeezed. "I think we may have to face the very real possibility that you have a tapeworm."

She rolled her eyes and wriggled away from him, but not before snatching his last bite of grits, something he'd perfected thanks to her tutelage.

He mocked offense. "You did not just steal my last bite of grits!"

Hazel gave him a doe-eyed smile, her teeth still full of his breakfast.

"That's it, we're breaking up! I want my class ring back."

Paisley huffed loudly. "Why don't you ever hang out with *your* roommates, James?"

James winked at her. "Because my roommates don't have boobs."

HAZEL

THANKFULLY, the bell rang before Jamie could push more of

Paisley's buttons. Secretly, Hazel didn't mind. Paisley was a bitch. She'd been a pain in Hazel's ass ever since she thought Hazel had stolen Jamie from her. It wasn't true. Hazel had made it perfectly clear to everyone that she and Jamie were just friends. She might wish they were more, but she wasn't pursuing it. And so far, he'd kept his word, not crossing the lines she'd drawn for their friendship.

Sure, they flirted, but Jamie seemed to flirt equally with everyone he spoke to, so Hazel figured their playful interactions were okay. That was just how he communicated. The boy probably couldn't keep his sarcastic tongue in his mouth if his life depended on it. The only time Jamie wasn't cracking jokes was when he had his camera in his hand.

But honestly, Hazel didn't mind either version of Jamie.

Their heart-to-heart had torn down a wall in him that Hazel was envious of. She knew it was their pain that connected them, and she understood why he kept it hidden. She did the same. But it seemed he hid it less and less these days, especially when it was just the two of them.

Admitting what he'd been through with his mother seemed to free him somehow. Hazel wished she could do the same. She was still keeping so many secrets. And her feelings for Jamie were just one more.

15

James

SWEAT CLUNG to every uncomfortable inch of James's over-wrought body. *So much for my streak of perfect days.*

He'd been wrong about ropes day, it wasn't fun. It was torture. And not just because Sage was running them through a ropes course like he thought they were training for the circus, but because James was in Hazel's group today. Not only that, he'd been assigned as her buddy.

That meant he'd spent half the day holding her climbing rope while he was forced to watch her perfect ass wiggling a few feet above him while she scaled the course.

Then, as if that hadn't already given him blue balls, they'd had to complete a tandem zipline together. Hazel's nails dug into his legs the entire time, but James was thankful for it, because it was the only thing distracting him from the fact that the same fantastic ass he'd been fantasizing about all day was harnessed between his legs.

The group activities weren't much better. They were divided up into two teams of ten and clipped into different ropes that were all knotted together in some genius contraption Sage liked to call the Spiderweb of Salvation. It was supposed to teach them to work cohesively as a group, twisting and crawling over each other to untangle the knot. But all it taught James was that his mind and body refused to work together when it came to Hazel. She shimmied her divine little hips against his and he nearly lost it.

And of course, some idiot on their team chose that exact moment to get their rope caught, causing their tangled group to come to a standstill while Hazel was pressed against James hip to hip.

She looked up at him, doe-eyed and flushed.

Down boy! James mentally scolded himself. *Quick, say something witty so she doesn't notice . . .* "Stop trying to seduce me, Hazel. It won't work," he teased.

She laughed and he prayed she couldn't see right through his defenses. Bumping and grinding with forbidden fruit was not his idea of a good time. *Okay, that's not entirely true . . .*

Maybe if it had been just him and Hazel and a bunch of ropes . . . but that wasn't the case. And thinking that way wasn't helping the situation in his pants.

By the time they got to the final group challenge, James was so worked up he couldn't form a thought that didn't involve Hazel and that damn line she'd drawn for their relationship. The problem was, he was dangerously close to crossing it.

Sage's last ridiculous rope challenge for the day was the Tightrope of Trust. The two teams lined up on ropes suspended about two feet off the ground. Each person had to walk across the rope, weaving in and out of their teammates, using them for support. There were guide ropes to hold onto hanging every few feet.

It was simple enough for James, but he was taller than everyone else on his team and could easily reach the guide ropes dangling above his head. He and the five other boys on their team each took up positions equally spaced across the suspended rope so the girls could use them as human poles to hold onto while they crossed.

It was a smart plan since most of the girls couldn't reach the guide ropes and the other team quickly copied it. James cursed as Sawyer stepped on his foot as she clumsily made her way across him, but she eventually reached the other side.

They were down to their last girl—Hazel.

She navigated past the first two guys expertly, but when she came to James she got hung up. It wasn't her fault. She was so damn short and his lanky-ass body was stretching out the rope. She tried to go around the back of him like she had with the other boys, but James was leaning too far out to keep tension on the rope.

"Go around front," he instructed.

She looked worried. "You sure?"

"Yep." Sensing her hesitation, he winked. "Get your mind outta the gutter, Smalls."

She rolled her eyes and went to work crossing in front of him. It wasn't easy and her ridiculous pink boots weren't helping matters. They weren't broken in and the soles looked so inflexible she probably couldn't feel the rope under her feet, which would explain why she kept missing it and groping him.

James was saying silent prayers that she would hurry the hell up, because he was only able to fight the friction for so long. The heavy breathing she was doing certainly wasn't helping. Finally, he couldn't take it anymore. He wrapped one arm around her torso and lifted her off her feet, swinging her past him. Her feet hit the rope exactly as he planned but she hadn't been expecting the move and she couldn't catch her balance.

She swore colorfully and stepped off the rope.

"Walker, try again," Sage ordered.

The last thing James saw was the flash of anger in Hazel's eyes before she stomped back to the platform to start over.

HAZEL

HAZEL'S FALL had cost her team the win and she was livid. Sitting through Sage's post competition monologue didn't help either.

"Now you all need to give yourselves a big pat on the back. You put in some real work today and that effort is not only rewarding in the points you've gained but in the relationships you've built and life skills you just learned how to harness. The points only matter on the mountain, but everything else you'll take with you. Remember that."

When Sage was done handing out scores and reminding them the points would be tallied and posted after lunch, Hazel climbed to her feet and marched toward the dining hall, not waiting for anyone.

Jamie didn't take the hint. He jogged to catch up to her. "Hey, wait up."

She didn't stop.

"Oh, come on, you're not seriously mad we lost, are you?"

Hazel whirled around. "I had it, Jamie. I didn't need your help."

"Aw, are we having our first lover's spat? I've never had one before."

"I'm not kidding! This isn't all a big joke to me."

His smile faltered. "I was just trying to help you."

"That's just it. I didn't ask for your help. I wanted to see if I could do it on my own and you took that away from me."

"Jesus, Hazel, I wasn't trying to take anything away from you. I was trying to get you across the rope."

"You were rushing me."

He threw his hands up. "Yeah, it was a race! Speed is kinda the key factor."

She narrowed her eyes. "That's not why you rushed me though, is it?"

"Uh, yeah, it is. That's how you win, Hazel. You move faster than the other team."

"That's not what I'm talking about and you know it."

James

SHIT! Shit! Shit! James swallowed stalling for time. *You're onto me, aren't you, Hazel?*

"Admit it," she pushed. "Having me that close made you uncomfortable."

"Somebody thinks they're hot shit," he teased.

"Yeah, you! Your thoughts are like damn neon signs, Jamie."

So, you did notice . . . He scrubbed a hand over his face. "Come on, Smalls, you were using my body as a human stripper pole. A guy can only take so much. Cut me some slack."

James watched her anger shift to disappointment, which

was somehow worse. Her voice was low and breathy when she spoke. "You promised you wouldn't cross the line, Jamie."

"And I didn't." He needed to fix this. Desperate to assure her, he reached for her hand but she jerked away.

"No, I told you what I could handle, and this isn't it." She took a quick breath, lowering her voice. "You know what I'm risking being here. I need to get something out of this."

Me, Hazel! You could be getting me! He wanted to scream it, but the rest of their group had caught up to them. The crowd of campers rushed past like water around two unmovable boulders. Strangely, that's how James felt in that moment— like two stubborn stones. Neither of them were going to budge. Hazel was too afraid to let him all the way in and James was too afraid to let her go.

So where does that leave us, Hazel?

"I'm hungry," she muttered. "Let's go to lunch."

16

H azel

LUNCH WAS awkward but Hazel tried not to dwell on it. No one but Jamie seemed to notice her surly attitude anyway. Everyone was too busy talking about Crossroads, the final challenge, that was quickly approaching. It consisted of a five-day hike along an old trapper trail to Gibson Cove. The entire hike was just over a hundred miles. That broke down to twenty miles a day, something even an untrained hiker could handle in good weather and flat terrain. Though they would experience neither.

It sounded like a lot and it was, but Wander Mountain had trained them for it. Sage and the camp leaders had taught the campers all the survival skills they'd need. How to build fire, seek shelter, proper safety and hydration techniques, how to navigate by compass and read a trail map. Now it was time to put that knowledge to the test.

After nearly a week of conditioning, the weather and altitude didn't bother Hazel as much as it first had. It was still colder than she preferred but she'd acclimated to the fifty-degree days and twenty-degree nights. It helped that the Bright Horizons scholarship had provided her with adequate gear—*well, everything but the boots.*

They apparently didn't stock pint-sized shoes in the camp store. *Just my luck.*

But her pinks boots had gotten her this far. There was only one day of group challenges left, the scores of which would determine their hike partners. Everyone was anxious to check the preliminary scores after lunch to see who they'd be potentially paired with.

Everything a camper did on Wander Mountain was scored, from participation in group therapy discussions, to Sage's strange wilderness training challenges. At the end of six days, the individual scores were tallied, and partners were paired up to create evenly matched teams.

Kat was busy explaining her school of thought on the scoring system to their lunch table, scribbling numbers on the back of her schedule. "The ideal spot is to end up somewhere in the middle of the pack. If you scored too high, you'll get saddled with some lame-o who's gonna make you do all the work. If you score too low, you'll get shackled to some jock who'll most likely drag you through the hike at a Sage-pace even if your feet are bleeding."

"And let me guess," Sawyer asked, "you've already figured out the perfect score?"

Kat pushed her glasses up her nose and grinned her wide, wily grin. "Of course. A fifty-one. Exactly what I have."

"Solid plan," Jamie said biting into his grilled cheese. "But we still have one more day of challenges left."

Kat shrugged. "I know. But tomorrow is water day. All I

have to do is not fall out of my canoe and I'll coast into a perfect position in the middle of the pack."

Hazel swallowed her sudden fear along with her spoonful of tomato soup. "Water day?"

"What's wrong? Can't you swim?" Paisley asked.

Hazel glared at her. "I can swim. But who the hell wants to in this weather? The water's gotta be just barely above freezing."

"We'll have wetsuits," Kat remarked. "But speaking of swimming, are you guys gonna do the Polar Plunge tonight?"

"What's that?" Jamie asked.

Paisley's eye turned into saucers. "Are you serious? It's only the highlight of this hell hole."

Jamie turned to Kat. "Translation please?"

Kat perked up. "It's a Wander Mountain tradition. The Friday night before the hike everyone skinny dips in the lake at midnight. Most people do it with their partners; something about bonding and blessings."

Sawyer looked appalled. "It's more than that. It's a sacred Sioux ritual to bathe in the mountain waters under the moon-light before a journey. You have to strip all your material possessions and show mother nature that your heart is pure. Then she will bless your journey."

Paisley snorted. "Okay, Last of the Mohicans. Stoned much?"

"It's called respecting history," Sawyer snapped.

"Anyway," Kat interrupted, turning to face Jamie. "You in?"

Jamie shrugged. "Sure."

Kat's eyes swung to Hazel.

"I don't know," Hazel chewed her lip, "the idea of being naked and freezing doesn't really appeal to me."

The truth was, nothing about being on or in the water appealed to her, unless maybe it was a hot tub. She could swim, but she wasn't the best at it. She much preferred S'mores and campfires over pneumonia inducing Polar Plunges.

"Girl, you better do it," Sawyer warned. "You already have the Couples' Curse against you. You don't need any more bad juju."

"So true," Kat concurred.

Jamie raised his eyebrows. "The Couples' Curse?"

"Don't get them started," Hazel muttered. "And for the last time, we are not a couple! We're just friends."

Kat cocked her head like a smug cat. "And I'm Dumbledore."

James

THE LAST THING James wanted to do was fuel Kat's couple theory after what happened on the ropes today, so he quickly changed the subject. "So, do you know what the challenges are for tomorrow?"

"Of course." Kat pulled another sheet of paper out of her backpack. "Team rowing, canoe relay race, group river traverse and kayak obstacle course."

"Nice." Now those were some wilderness courses James could get behind. He loved the water and growing up in Boston gave him plenty of opportunity to get out on it.

"Nice?" Paisley asked. "You are such a boy. There's nothing nice about having to paddle all day. I'm gonna end up with blisters."

"You might even break a nail," he teased.

She huffed and went back to ignoring him. James was

about to continue pestering her when he caught Hazel staring at him.

"You're actually looking forward to this, aren't you?" she asked.

"Sure. I love the water. Spent most of my summers on the harbor sailing my Hunter 15."

"Are you speaking boat?" Hazel asked. "You lost me, I only speak car."

He laughed. "Yeah, sorry. Hunter is a boat manufacturer. We have a couple sailboats back home. Mine's a Hunter 15. It's small, but it's a great little boat to learn on."

Hazel gazed at him with a mixture of emotion that he couldn't decipher.

"What?"

"Nothing," she replied turning back to her lunch.

"Well, I hope you end up on my team tomorrow," Sawyer said looking at James.

"I don't," Kat replied. "No offense, James, but you'd ruin my score."

HAZEL

HAZEL ROLLED her eyes at Kat while Sawyer pegged their nerdy roommate with a wadded-up napkin.

"What?" Kat grumped. "If there's a way to hack the system I can't help but find it."

Everyone laughed and the conversation drifted back to mundane camp life. But Hazel's mind wandered back to Jamie's confession. It was a new layer to discover.

She hadn't known about his love of water, but she could see the spark in his eyes when he spoke about his boat. It was the same way he looked when he was talking about photography.

It seemed he had two loves in his life.

Jealousy unspooled in her chest.

They talked about everything, including serious stuff like losing parents . . . so, why hadn't he mentioned his boat before today?

That was weird, right?

Maybe not.

Sometimes she forgot they hadn't known each other very long despite how deep their connection felt.

Things moved quickly on Wander Mountain. The program was designed to strip away all pretenses, leaving nothing but raw emotion. It was no wonder so many people ended up hooking up. Everyone was so damn vulnerable with their secrets and shortcomings laid bare. Here, if you fell for someone, you knew exactly what you were getting and there was something attractive about that.

Not that Hazel found Jamie's love of sailing attractive.

Okay, so it wasn't the worst thing in the world to picture him with a tan, wind in his hair as he sailed the open sea. But it was the discovery of another layer that really drew her in. She loved uncovering more about him.

Wander Mountain's annoying 'reveal to heal' motto echoed in her head. The cheesy catchphrase was true. The fact that Jamie felt comfortable enough to share something he loved with not just her, but their entire lunch table showed growth.

Normally, he was all sarcasm and jokes, but she was learning those were just how he hid his true feelings, just like she buried hers by pushing everyone away—especially him.

Jamie hadn't been alone in his feelings on the ropes course, Hazel had felt it too. The way her heart sped up when they were chest to chest, the heat that rioted in her belly every time they were forced to work in close proximity. And when his arms came around her it made her so flustered, she forgot how to function. That's why she'd fumbled so badly on the ropes. She couldn't concentrate with her heart pounding against his.

She shouldn't have been so hard on him. It wasn't his fault she was conflicted. She'd made the stupid rule about not crossing lines. And so far, he hadn't. She wished she could tell him he wasn't alone in his feelings. But that wouldn't be fair and it wouldn't make things easier.

Hazel wasn't going to change her mind. She was here to find herself and she couldn't do that if she got tangled in someone else.

17

Hazel

AFTER LUNCH, Hazel chomped on a lollipop as she gathered outside with everyone to check the scores that had just been posted. Surprisingly, she was one of the top girls in her age group. She looked across and saw Jamie's score was almost as high. That was surprising considering he hadn't really been participating in his counseling sessions, but it appeared his athleticism made up for it. His wilderness scores put him in first place, but his rough scores in counseling pulled him down to third . . . right across from Hazel.

At least that meant there was no chance of them being paired together.

She wasn't the only one to recognize it. "Looks like you're safe from the Couples' Curse," Kat said with a wink before skipping off.

Hazel rolled her eyes as Jamie shouldered up next to her.

"What is all this Couples' Curse stuff?" he asked.

"It's just Kat feeding the camp gossip."

Jamie arched an eyebrow.

"She's got this crazy theory that any couple who tries to do the Crossroads hike together is doomed by some stupid curse because she heard a few unfortunate stories."

"What kind of stories?"

"Mostly embellished ones I'm sure. Fights, pregnancies, jail time, that sorta thing."

Jamie laughed. "Well, I don't know about the pregnancies and jail time, but there's definitely gonna be fighting, and it won't be restricted to couples."

"What do you mean?"

"Smalls, it's a five-day hike with a stranger, crappy food and crappier shelter. That's enough to make anyone a little cranky, especially people unstable enough to believe they found insta-love at group therapy."

"Well, I guess it's a good thing we're not a couple then."

He winked. "Exactly. And we won't get paired up since you're secretly a gladiator. Nice scores, by the way."

"You're not so bad yourself, Stretch."

"Smalls, flattery will get you nowhere with me. I'm all about the sugar," he said, snatching the lollipop out of her mouth.

She laughed, feeling relieved that they were back to their usual witty banter. "Sorry I was a bitch about the ropes today. I think I was just hungry or something."

Jamie slung an arm around her shoulders. "Girl, you gotta get a handle on your hangries. That, sorry-for-what-I-said-when-I-was-hungry, nonsense will only get you so far with me."

She smiled up at him. "Forgiven?"

"That depends, you got any more of these lollipops?"

"Always." She handed him one from her pocket and followed him away from the dining hall where people were still swarming the score sheets.

Maybe she'd overreacted about the ropes. It's not like the loss on the tightrope really affected her score. She was still in a great position. According to the tallied scores she'd probably get paired up with Tanner Jones. She'd had a few group therapy sessions with him, and he seemed harmless enough. He played guitar around the campfire most nights. He had a pretty good voice, too. At least that was something they could talk about on a five-day hike.

Hazel loved music and missed her own guitar desperately. She wished she'd brought it with her when she saw others jamming around the campfires. But she'd purposely left it behind. Music was something she knew, and she was here to experience the unknown.

Relaxing a bit, she followed Jamie to the next item on their schedule; yoga and group counseling in the main lodge. They were in the same group today. Hazel loved when that happened because it allowed her to glimpse further beneath the complex layers that made Jamie Forrester tick.

Jamie grabbed their yoga mats and set them up close to the fireplace. Hazel shrugged out of her jacket and grabbed a handful of candy out of the pocket before she hung it by the door. She kicked off her dirty pink boots and sat down on her mat next to him, popping pieces of sugary goodness into her mouth.

Jamie watched her with curious interest.

"Want one?" she asked.

"What are those?"

Hazel popped a few more of the small red candies into her mouth. "Boston Baked Beans."

"Did you just make that up?"

"No, they're classics."

Jamie scrunched up his face in disgust. "Classic nasty! They look like rotten jelly beans."

She shrugged and ate a few more. "I didn't want to share with you anyway. Besides, you should watch your figure. You've really let yourself go since we got here."

Jamie barked a laugh at her absurd comment. "I'm not just a piece of meat, Smalls. I have feelings underneath all this fat."

She rolled her eyes. Jamie was by far the most fit person on Wander Mountain.

He probably didn't even have an ounce of body fat, something she admired every time they did downward dog in yoga class and his t-shirt rode up revealing his washboard abs.

Hazel shoved the thought away and chomped down on another candy-coated peanut.

Jamie's curiosity got the better of him and he snatched a piece of candy from her and tossed it in his mouth. "Hmm, they're actually good."

"Don't go getting addicted. I'm serious about your weight."

"Smart ass."

"Now, James . . . I think talking about my ass might be crossing the line," she teased.

Jamie gave her one of his sinful smiles. "Trust me, Smalls, if I cross the line, you'll know it."

The comment made goose bumps explode from her scalp to her toes.

For some reason, Hazel couldn't get that taunt out of her head. It haunted her for the entire yoga class. It didn't help that she had a perfect view of the finely carved planes of Jamie's abs and toned arms either. She couldn't stop imagining what it would be like to let him cross the line. To taste those abs, to be held by those arms.

Get your mind out of the gutter, Hazel!

Ugh! She was sweating like a lumberjack and she didn't even want to think about the state of her panties at the moment. Thank God she'd drawn those lines in the proverbial sand, because if just thinking about Jamie felt like starting a forest fire in her pants, the real thing might just burn down her world.

James

YOGA ALWAYS WENT by too quickly for James. He wasn't sure if he actually enjoyed it or if he just dreaded therapy. Either way he wasn't ready when it was time to roll up his mat and walk across the hall to Dr. Hippie's *'sharing circle'*.

Five woven blankets were laid out like magic carpets on the floor. James chose a red and blue one next to Hazel. The blankets where arranged in a large circle, each placed far enough apart that he could've stretched his arms out and still not reached her. Normally, that would bother Jamie. He always felt most comfortable when Hazel was at arm's length, but in this case, distance was probably better.

Being forced to share personal things about his past always made him sweaty and uncomfortable—not his best look.

Today's session was starting out as painful as usual.

Dr. Hippie, whose name James had learned but still refused to use, joined the class, pulling his own blanket into the circle. "First off, I'd like to start this session by acknowledging how far you've come. You've put the work in and that deserves recognition. So, if you would, give yourselves a pat on the back and repeat after me. I have the power to create change. I am focused, persistent and I will never quit. I can achieve greatness."

The class awkwardly followed his lead, quietly murmuring his psychobabble.

"Now, I have to congratulate you on nearly completing the program. Tomorrow will be our last session before you head out on your Crossroads hike."

James rolled his eyes, hating the corny name for the hundred mile hike.

"Some of you may be apprehensive, but I assure you, each of you possess what you need to complete the task ahead. Not just on Wander Mountain, but in life as well. So let's talk about that. The focus of today's session is how to apply the tools you've been given here to your future."

He paused for dramatic effect.

"I want to go around the room and hear what each of you have in your heart regarding your future. What is the secret wish you keep locked away concerning your future? Let it out, give it air to breathe and room to grow. That's the first step to making a wish a reality. Remember, we start to heal when we reveal."

James did his best to listen as people revealed their future goals: to go to med school, to be a mom, to travel. But none of it reached him. They were all simple goals, from people who'd lived simple lives. James wanted so much more than that. And listening to these sheep drone on about their mundane goals only fueled his own arrogant aspirations. So, when it was his turn to share, for once he actually did.

"I want to move to Key West, start a sailing charter and do photography. I don't want to waste any more time doing something meaningless, something I don't wholly enjoy."

"Excellent, James. What inspired this goal?" Dr. Hippie asked.

"I don't know, I guess my love of sailing and photography."

"Where does that love come from?"

"It's something I did with my mother. It's a way I can remember her without all the sadness."

"It's important to hold onto the moments that bring us happiness. Now in this wish for your future, do you see any roadblocks?"

His father's face instantly materialized in his mind. "Yeah."

"And what might those be?"

"There's only one. My father. He's only given me two career paths to pursue and since football isn't an option, it's politics."

"Why do you say football isn't an option?"

James glared at the doctor. For a psychologist the man wasn't very intuitive. "I believe you have a copy of my medical file."

"Of course."

"Then if you know anything about competitive sports, you know they're not an option for me."

The doctor had the good sense to look apologetic, but it didn't stop his incessant questioning. "And how does that make you feel, James? That you weren't afforded the opportunity to play football and continue your family's legacy?"

"It makes me kinda pissed, actually. There are more important things in life than football. Even if I could play, it's not what I want. I want to sail, I want to take photos, I want to share both those things with others and I really want everyone to stop telling me what my future should look like, because I already have my own ideas."

"Good. I can hear the passion you hold for this future wish. Thank you for sharing that with us, James. Passion is an important key in pursuing any future, but as you've said, you know there will be roadblocks along the way of achieving your goals. The goal of our program here at Wander Mountain is to give you the tools to navigate the roadblocks of life in a positive way. Can you give us one example of how what you learned here can help you surpass your roadblocks and achieve your goals?"

James had to fight the sarcastic remarks simmering in his mind. He didn't really see how collecting firewood and tightrope walking were tools any civilized person could ever apply to their life, but he knew how to play this game. Dr. Hippie was looking for the proper response and Jamie had been to enough therapists to know exactly what those were. "Persistence, communication and patience."

The doctor gave him a perceptive look. He knew James was feeding him a line of BS, but he let it go, finally moving on to the next victim.

HAZEL

THE WHOLE TIME Jamie had been speaking, Hazel was picturing it—him tan and grinning, sailing a boat with big white sails through water the color of his tranquil eyes. He'd have a little shop at a marina somewhere for people to look at his photography when they came to book a tour or sailing lessons. There would be photos of sunsets and seagulls and sand and miles of calm blue water that glittered where the sun kissed it.

She wanted that future for him. He deserved it.

It was another secret layer he'd peeled off today and she was strangely jealous that it wasn't one she could keep just for herself. He'd shared it with everyone.

She realized that was the goal of these sessions. To break

the cycle of fear, to be brave enough to admit future hopes and dreams. The trouble was, she had no idea what her own were. How was she supposed to voice that she didn't know what she wanted?

Someone like her didn't prepare for the future, they just tried to survive it.

Hazel's life was one big unending loop of inadequacy. She lived day by day, and she couldn't ever see that changing. Despite what Dr. Birch said, she knew she wasn't meant for greatness. No one from Lovelock was. The best she could hope for was mediocrity, with small slices of happiness here and there.

Wander Mountain was one of those slices.

So was Jamie . . . but she forced that thought away as quickly as it formed. It was too painful to think about letting that kind of happiness go.

Would it make her life even darker when she could no longer stand in his light, or would that light stay with her, illuminating her from within when the monotony of life grew dim? She was hoping for the latter, but there were no guarantees.

The last true loss Hazel had experienced was her mother. But she wondered if that even counted. She wasn't really gone, just missing from her life. And the few times she did come back, her presence only brought more pain.

But Hazel knew true loss lay around the corner. Soon, Gramps would lose his fight with cancer. And after that it would be just her and her dad running a dying repair shop into the ground one boring day after another.

Hazel knew she would lose her dad one day, too. Probably sooner than she should thanks to his injuries. She looked at her hands, feeling them begin to tremble. *What will I do then, with a life half lived?*

What could she even do now?

Hazel couldn't tell her dad she wanted more, not when she knew it would rip his heart out. It's what her mom had said when she left and that had broken his heart. She could never do that to him, not after all he'd given her. Besides she didn't even know where she wanted to go or what she wanted to do, only that she wouldn't find it in Lovelock.

A bone deep sadness settled over her as she realized coming to Wander Mountain had changed nothing. If anything, it made her feel worse about her situation.

What good were all these tools for confidence and success when I have nothing to apply them to?

Hazel had no idea what she wanted to do with her life. She'd been hoping she'd figure it out here, while she was supposedly discovering herself in the wild mountains of Montana. But the truth was, Hazel already knew who she was, she just didn't like that person very much.

Who wants to be the girl destined for nothing?

She wasn't naïve, she'd read enough books to know not everyone gets a happy ending. But it was harder than she thought to surrender that last ounce of hope.

But perhaps now was the time to let go of childish things and grow up.

James

IT WAS Hazel's turn to share and James snapped to attention, listening for the first time since it was his own turn to speak.

Dr. Hippie had just repeated his question, but Hazel just continued to stare like a deer in headlights. James wanted to punch the therapist for causing that look of sadness pulling all the color from her normally warm features.

"There's nothing to fear here, Hazel. Revealing is healing. Putting your wishes out in the world creates opportunity. And sharing with a support group helps hold us all accountable so we can reach our goals faster."

"I'm . . ." she cleared her throat and started again. "I'm not sure I have any future goals."

"You don't have to have it all figured out right now, Hazel. Sometimes this journey is just about understanding yourself better and giving yourself permission to dream."

That statement seemed to upset her even more. She swiped at a tear and James was struck with an urge to pull her into his arms. His jaw muscles ticked as the seconds passed in painful silence.

"Let's try this, Hazel," the unrepentant therapist crooned. "Start by sharing something small. Tell us one thing you enjoy."

She blinked at him, clearing her eyes and blowing out a breath. "I like the sunshine. I hate to be cold. I guess I'd like to live somewhere where it's always warm."

The Florida Keys, maybe? James pushed the greedy thought away.

"Good," Dr. Hippie said. "Let's dig deeper. Tell me one thing you've enjoyed about your experience here at Wander Mountain."

Her eyes flashed quickly to James. They met for a searing moment before she looked away, cheeks flaming. "The people," she said softly.

James felt his heart soar. *Hazel . . . are you giving me hope?*

"Excellent. Making meaningful personal connections is one of life's most rewarding gifts. Do you feel your craving for connection is met in your everyday life?"

She swallowed hard and slowly shook her head.

"Why do you think that is?"

She shrugged. "I don't know. I guess because of where I live."

"Remind us where you call home, Hazel."

James had to fight his laughter. *What a tool! There's only five of us in the room and you can't even bother to remember where we're from? Real smooth, Doc.*

"Lovelock, Nevada," Hazel replied, stealing James's attention back.

"What's the first thing that comes to mind when you think about returning to Lovelock?" Dr. Hippie asked.

"Running." The word slipped from Hazel's mouth like a secret.

James felt his stomach drop. *What aren't you telling me, Hazel?*

"Do you do a lot of running?" the doctor pressed. "Marathons?"

"No," Hazel swallowed thickly. "Not that kind of running. I mean running away."

James balled his hands into fists. Watching her discomfort was making his muscles so tight he thought they would snap. He glared at the doctor. Couldn't this jackass see this wasn't helping her? Hazel's arms were looped around her knees, clutching them tightly to her chest. James was no therapist, but he could plainly see Hazel was retreating into herself.

"Is there anything particular you're running away from?" Dr. Hippie pushed.

A tear slipped down her cheek. "Responsibility."

Dr. Hippie nodded. "Ah, yes. That can be a burden that we all feel the need to outrun from time to time."

James huffed. The therapist had no idea. Hazel wasn't just some brat who was fed up with menial activities like high school drama or a job. She was talking about the responsibility of taking care of her handicapped father and terminal grandfather. That kind of stress was enough to make anyone want to run. Add in medical bills and it was a burden no teenager should have to shoulder.

From what James had gathered over the past few days, Hazel didn't have a lot of money and that meant her family probably wasn't getting the best care. She was way too proud to admit that, but looking at her clothes and the heap of junk she'd driven to the mountain, plus the fact that she was here on scholarship, made it easy enough to put the pieces together.

It killed James, knowing that Hazel was holding all this inside. He wanted to help her. His instinct was to scoop her up and let her bury her head into his chest. He wanted to rub her back while she cried and tell her everything would be okay, that he'd help her figure it out. But he couldn't do any of those things, because no matter how much he wished he could protect Hazel, he couldn't.

He was just as messed up as she was, and his future wasn't his own.

His dream may have sounded nice in theory, but that's all it was—a dream. James talked a big game, but he could never pull it off. If he went against his father he'd be on his own, cut off with no means for survival.

James knew he couldn't live like that. He wasn't strong and resourceful like Hazel. He'd probably crack and go crawling back home after a month of living in some dump trying to survive on hopes and dreams.

One lesson his father had taught him was that money fueled dreams, not the other way around.

James cracked his knuckles to release his frustration as Dr. Hippie's voice filled the room again. "Let's look at this from a different angle, Hazel. Instead of thinking about running from something, think about running toward something. Some goal or wish, something that would fill you with joy. Imagine your ideal future, where you have no limitations. Tell us what you see."

"I think that's the problem, Dr. Birch," she replied. "When I try to picture it, there's nothing. I have no idea what I'm meant to do. And maybe . . . maybe I'm not special. Maybe this is all there is for me."

James had never heard something more infuriating. How could she think there was nothing special about her?

Don't you know, Hazel? You're the reason I'm still breathing.

18

J ames

AFTER AN EXCEPTIONAL LOAD OF BULLSHIT, Dr. Hippie finally ended the session. "We did some really good work today everyone. Keep these hopes close. Continue to speak to them, nurture them. Remember, you are in charge of your destiny. Positive thoughts generate a positive future."

James wasn't listening. He was too busy staring at the back of Hazel's head trying to figure out what the hell to say to her. He needed to make her understand. He wanted to be the guy to save her. He just didn't know how.

"And don't forget to pick up your field journals," Dr. Hippie called. "They'll be part of your final evaluation after the hike."

James followed behind Hazel, grabbing a small waterproof

notebook on his way out the door. When they were finally outside, he didn't hesitate, he couldn't take another moment of her not knowing how he felt—lines be damned.

He grabbed her hand and started leading her away from the crowded camp.

"Hey! Where are we going?" she asked, nervousness lacing her voice.

Good, you should be nervous, Hazel, because I won't allow this to go on a second longer. You're about to get a piece of my mind. He was still too angry to speak so he just kept leading her by the hand, grinding his teeth as they walked.

"Jamie!" She rooted her pink-booted feet to the spot and pulled her hand free. "Where are we going?"

"We need to talk."

"What about dinner?"

James worked the muscles in his jaw and blew out a breath of frustration. He knew he wouldn't get anywhere with her on an empty stomach. The girl was like a badger when it came to food. He ran a hand through his hair, squeezing the back of his neck as he tried to come up with a solution.

"Come on," he finally muttered changing direction back toward camp.

She followed him to the camp store, almost trotting to match his pace. When they got to the door James turned to her. "Wait here."

She blinked but caught the obvious edge in his voice and didn't argue for a change.

He came out a few minutes later carrying a large brown bag. Picking up her hand again he silently led her back away from camp. Still sensing his tension, she followed without question. *Thank God.* He didn't have the capacity or patience to argue with her right now.

Though they'd only just met, sometimes it felt like Hazel

had known him for a lifetime. She was perceptive enough to know he had something important on his mind and that it couldn't be rushed. He knew she could sense the trepidation vibrating through him and he was grateful that she wasn't afraid of it. His temper wasn't anything for her to be fearful of. It was something he was still working through, but it had never brought harm to anyone but himself.

James glanced at Hazel as they approached the stone bench that had become their spot. It displayed a perfect view of the mountain range they would soon be hiking. Hazel chewed her lip anxiously, not meeting his eyes. The worry in her eyes said she knew this discussion was unavoidable, but he wondered if she'd actually hear him out.

They both sat quietly on the bench as James unpacked the picnic meal he'd bought at the camp store—two ham and cheese sandwiches, a bag of gluten free tortilla chips, three Snickers bars and two bottles of kombucha. He opened the kombucha and took a big swig, wishing it were a coke.

It was a pain in the ass that they didn't have any soda on the mountain. It's not like they only served health food. The desserts the Prospect Dining Hall served contained enough sugar to put a man into diabetic shock, so what was the harm in a soda?

James sighed and took a bite of his sandwich. They were missing burger night right now. He glanced at Hazel wondering if she was gonna be pissed. She was staring back at him with a look of bewilderment in her eye that expressly told him she wasn't thinking about burgers.

"Eat," he muttered, stalling for time before he revealed the real reason he'd dragged her out here.

He wanted to get his temper under control before talking to her, but it seemed her temporary cooperation was over.

In true Hazel-style, she did the opposite of what he

wanted. She put her sandwich down and walked over to the rock ledge, sitting on the cold ground as she stared out at the horizon.

James squeezed the back of his neck and counted to ten. *Is it really so hard to do what I ask, Hazel?*

The girl was as stubborn as an ox. He suddenly felt bad for whomever got partnered with her for the hike. Trying to tell Hazel what to do was like trying to stear a rudderless ship.

He shoved the rest of his sandwich in his mouth and pulled out his camera. He snapped a few photos of Hazel. She looked so small—a lonely soul lost in the world.

Was that why this was so hard for him? Because looking at Hazel was like looking in a mirror?

He knew how bad that kind of loneliness could get. He knew what pain and loss and despair could drive a person to do. It's how he'd ended up here.

But is that really a bad thing if it brought me to you, Hazel?

James slung the camera around his neck, grabbed a candy bar and went to join Hazel on the rock.

Hazel

"So, you were just craving a picnic?" she asked with mild annoyance when he joined her on the rock ledge.

He snorted and broke off a piece of the Snickers bar and handed it to her.

She cut her eyes at him. "Bribing me with sugar . . . this must be serious."

"It is."

Hazel popped the piece of candy bar into her mouth,

savoring the way the chocolatey goodness melted over her tongue. She wanted to absorb as much sweetness as possible before this conversation turned sour, and she could tell it would. "Jamie, I don't want to talk about it."

"Too bad."

"What are you gonna do, drag it out of me like Dr. Birch?"

"No, that guy's a dipshit. If he knew anything, he'd know forcing you to talk about what you're going through isn't always the best medicine."

Angry tears pushed at her eyes, but she refused to let them out. "You mean like you're doing?"

"No, because unlike him, I've been there. I know what you're going through."

She cut her eyes at him. "So, you know me now?"

"Yeah, Hazel. I do. I know what it's like to watch someone you love slowly die. I know the kind of damage that can do to a person. Especially when there's not a damn thing you can do about it. I know how bad it hurts to not have any control over your situation in life. I know what kind of dark thoughts it breeds. And I know where those thoughts lead." He took a deep breath and ran a hand through his hair, squeezing his neck again. "They led me here."

Hazel was looking at him now, not with anger or accusation, but really looking at him. Because for the first time since the night he gave her his cell phone, the night she drew those stupid lines in the dirt, Jamie was letting her see him—all the way.

His pain was so strangely familiar, it was impossible for her to look away.

"I've never said this out loud before," he said, his voice strained and quiet. "But I think you need to hear it."

Too entranced to answer, she nodded.

Jamie exhaled slowly. "I tried to kill myself six months ago."

Hazel didn't react. She couldn't. She was frozen in a world that had stopped turning. Because that's what it would feel like—a world without Jamie in it would be a frozen wasteland to her.

The thought speared straight through her heart. How had she ever thought stupid lines in the dirt would protect her? Nothing could. *Not when I feel what I feel for you, Jamie.*

How had she not realized it before now?

Jamie hung his head, a tight smile tugging at one corner of his mouth. "That's why my father sent me here. My official records states it was an accidental overdose, but it wasn't an accident." He huffed a laugh. "Can't even manage to kill myself right."

Hazel slipped her hand into his. "I'm glad."

Jamie leveled her with his stunning sky-blue eyes. "Me too. Or at least I have been ever since I met you."

Hazel started to object, but Jamie cut her off.

"I know, I know, you think you're not ready for anything more than friendship, but I think that's a mistake. I think you're not giving yourself enough credit. You're stronger than you know, Hazel. And we have something here. You can't deny it."

Hazel's heart was pounding because she knew he was right. She'd known it from the moment she first met him. They were alike, kindred spirits, and it brought her immeasurable comfort in knowing she wasn't alone.

It was crazy, to have just met someone, yet feel like they'd lived your same life. But that was the only way to describe it. Jamie knew her, maybe better than she knew herself. His life had been written exactly like hers. He was just a few chapters ahead...

"What if we were meant to meet?" he asked.

She laughed. "Like fate?"

He shrugged. "I don't know what to call it, but I can't pretend I don't feel it. When you said you don't think you're meant to have any kind of future or you don't think there's anything special about you, it felt like you were pulling the words right out of my heart. I've felt that way. I've said those same things, Hazel." Jamie shook his head. "But at the same time, everything you were saying made me want to put my fist through a wall."

Hazel's voice was barely a whisper. "Why?"

"Because, how could I listen to you say that and not tell you how I feel? You're the reason I feel stronger. You're the reason I could even answer that stupid hypothetical future question today." Jamie squeezed her hand. "Hazel, before I met you, I never could've admitted I wanted that future. Hell, I couldn't even see it. I wasn't looking that far ahead. But you make me feel hopeful again." He paused, his sky-blue eyes burning into hers. "Let me do that for you."

Hazel pulled her hand from his and stared down at her lap. She picked at a loose thread on her pants and tried to push his words away. They were too much, they made her feel too much.

Her entire body ached like she had the flu. She wanted to run away, but it was too late. His words were lodged in her chest filling her up from the inside out. There was no way to outrun them. Besides, she didn't have the strength to, not when every fiber of her being longed to curl up against his chest and let him wrap his arms around her.

Everything he said was true . . . she felt it too, everything he felt. She wanted to let him in, let him love her. She could see all of his strength and warmth waiting to heal her if she'd only let him. They were two broken hearts that had somehow found each other when the world wasn't looking.

If they clung to each other hard enough could they remain here, hidden away in this little slice of wilderness where their problems couldn't follow? God, she wished that could be true, but she knew it couldn't and that harsh truth made her feel like she was breaking apart all over again.

Jamie tucked a strand of hair behind her ear and traced her jaw. Hazel closed her eyes and let her forehead touch his. She couldn't look at him. It was too painful to see what she could never have. She needed to be the voice of reason. Going down this road would only result in more heartbreak.

They would never last. *How could we, Jamie?*

When this was over, he would go back to Boston and she would go back to Lovelock and their miserable lives would pick back up again. No, she was right to stop this before it truly started.

Hazel sat up and pulled away from him. "Jamie, you promised."

Anger flashed in his eyes. "Yeah, well, I made a mistake, Hazel. I didn't know you the way I know you now." He shook his head. "Actually, that's a lie. I knew I wanted more right from the start, but I was too afraid to say it. I thought you'd just shut me down. Or I thought if by some miracle you didn't, I would only make things worse for you, because I'm a fucking mess, Hazel. I didn't want to drag you down with me and make things worse for you. But I was looking at it all wrong. Together I think we might just hit bottom."

Hazel gave him a skeptical look. "And that's a good thing?"

She watched him reel in his temper and almost manage a grin. "Yeah, because together, we just might be strong enough to kick our way back up for air."

"We won't work in the real world, Jamie."

"How do you know?"

"I just do."

"So you won't even try? Even after I know you feel what I feel?"

She shook her head. "You have a future, Jamie. A really great one. I won't hold you back from it."

His temper unleashed and he stood up, fuming. "That in there?" he yelled pointing back toward camp. "Everything I said about my future was total bullshit, Hazel! A pipedream! My father will never let it happen."

"And you think he's gonna let you throw your life away on someone like me?" she yelled back climbing to her feet too. "You said yourself, you have two choices, football or politics. Dating a charity case isn't a better option."

Jamie looked like he wanted to scream, but his hand caught at the back of his neck, squeezing hard as he struggled to leash his temper. When he was finally calmer, he put both hands on her shoulders and looked her in the eye. "Hazel, you gotta get that chip off your shoulder. You're not a charity case and until you can see that, life's gonna keep dragging you down."

"Gee, thanks, Dr. Birch, you're so insightful."

James

JAMES WANTED to put his fist through something. The girl made him insane! He didn't know how the hell to get through to her, but he wasn't about to give up.

He wished he could just press his lips to hers and shut her up long enough to show her how he felt. They could be good for each other if she'd stop acting like she had to take on the damn world by herself.

Hazel crossed her arms, gnawing on her gorgeous lower lip so hard it made James's blood boil. He wanted to rescue it. Nothing coming out of his mouth was making a difference to her, but he was pretty sure a kiss might change her mind. Though he doubted he'd get that far. She looked like she wanted to punch something too and he had a sneaking suspicion it was his face.

It was almost comical how similar they were. *Opposites attract, my ass.*

They were clones—two magnets of the same charge, pushing and pulling with electric ferocity. James wouldn't be surprised if he learned Hazel was a Gemini too. He'd ask her but she probably wouldn't tell him. She wasn't giving him any of the answers he wanted today. Maybe he should call her dad and ask him. *Actually . . .*

"Give me my phone," he demanded, holding his hand out.

Hazel's eyes widened. "Are you serious?"

"Yes, it's my phone. I need to use it."

"Why?"

"Do I really need a reason to use my own phone?"

She huffed and stomped over to the bench to pull the cellphone out of her backpack. "You're a dick," she muttered, slapping it into his outstretched hand.

"Yeah, well I'm a dick who cares."

"What's that supposed to mean?"

He ignored her and scrolled through the recent call list until he found the number he was looking for. He pressed call, put the phone on speaker and stared at her while the phone rang.

.   .   .

HAZEL

HAZEL'S HEART started pounding wildly. She didn't like the thoughts that were running through her head.

There's no way he's doing what I think he's doing.

He wouldn't.

He's bluffing.

Then she heard the sound of her dad's voice. "Hello? Hazel?"

Not bluffing!

"Hang up!" she whisper-hissed trying to grab the phone, but Jamie held it out of reach.

"Hello? Hello?" Her father's voice echoed through the woods.

Jamie pushed the mute button. "If you won't let me in, you're gonna let someone in. I'm not gonna let you face your depression alone and end up like me. Talk to your father. Tell him how you really feel."

"I can't!" she snapped.

"Fine, then I will." Jamie unmuted the phone and Hazel grabbed his wrist.

"Please . . . he doesn't know I'm here."

James

SHOCK, followed by regret slammed into James as he stared into Hazel's panic-stricken eyes. A second passed before he remembered he still had her father on the line. He handed her the phone.

"Dad?" she whispered, her voice nearly trembling.

"Hazel? Hey, everything okay, kiddo?"

"Yeah, sorry, bad connection." Hazel switched the phone off speaker and started to walk away from James. She looked back over her shoulder once, her eyes shameful and hurt.

James felt bad for the panic he'd seen momentarily consume her, but not bad enough to let her off the hook that easily. Not until he found out why she was lying . . .

I knew you were hiding something, Hazel.

19

H azel

HAZEL WAS SITTING on the stone bench again, Jamie next to her. It had become their after dinner routine to come out here and watch the sunset. Jamie snapping photos while Hazel watched, soaking up the last of the sun's rays. It was a comforting routine that she'd grown accustom to.

But tonight, nothing felt comforting.

Hazel had just finished talking to her dad, trying to reassure him everything was fine after Jamie dialed him and nearly gave her a heart attack. She'd been so worried he was about to spill her secret that her voice had come out all shrill and squeaky for the first half of the conversation with her dad. Luckily, she'd been able to convince him she was just a bit homesick—which at the moment was true.

Anything was more appealing than admitting her lie.

But Jamie was waiting for an explanation and she knew he

wasn't going to let her get away with anything but the truth. Frankly, it pissed her off. The only thing Hazel hated more than being wrong, was being called out on it.

"You can't just hijack my life, you know?" she muttered.

"I'm not trying to hijack your life."

"Certainly feels like it."

"I called your father because I'm legitimately worried about you. And turns out I should be because you're crazier than I thought if you chose to come to Rambo-camp and lied to your family about it. Where the hell do they think you are?"

She exhaled deeply and let her shoulders slump. It was exhausting keeping secrets from someone like Jamie. He saw right through her, so she might as well come clean. "Phoenix."

"Phoenix?"

"Yes, like the city in Arizona."

"I know were Phoenix is, smartass."

She rolled her eyes.

"What I don't get is why they think you're there. Spill."

When she didn't say anything, Jamie held his cell phone up. He'd re-confiscated it the moment she ended her call. "I could always call your dad back and ask him."

She glared at him. *Why do you have to be as annoying as you are handsome, Jamie Forrester?!*

Maybe if Hazel switched tactics and made Jamie feel like he'd made her see the error of her ways he'd drop the protector act. "Jamie, I really appreciate that you care this much. It's actually kinda sweet, but I don't need you to fix my problems."

He arched an eyebrow. "Are you hitting on me, Smalls?"

She rolled her eyes again. "See, this is why we would never work. You can't take a compliment. I'd end up in jail for smothering you with a pillow because of your ill-timed jokes."

He laughed. "Don't think your feminine wiles are gonna

get you outta this. You're gonna have to try a helluva lot harder than that to change the topic. Now start talking."

"Ugh!" she groaned. "It's not a big deal. My dad thinks I'm in Arizona with my best friend Jenny taking a college prep course over spring break."

Jamie smirked. "Wow, even your fake spring break plans sound terrible."

She scowled at him. "It wasn't a fake plan."

He leaned back against the bench, crossing his long legs at the ankles. "I need to hear this story."

Hazel sighed. "It's not much of a story."

"Don't care."

Knowing he wasn't going to quit nagging her, Hazel decided to just tell him the truth. "I was planning to go to Arizona with Jenny for spring break. Her parents are super strict and thought she'd get knocked up if she went on an unsupervised ski trip with her boyfriend, so they signed her up for this college prep course in Arizona instead. She conned me into going with her since she knows I can't pass up sunshine and time with her. Plus, the hotel was already paid for. All I had to do was pay for the course and drive there."

"But what . . . you decided you'd rather secretly hike the mountains of Montana?"

"I'm getting there," she grumbled. "I made the Arizona plans with Jenny months ago, long before Gramps was doing so poorly. When his health took a turn for the worse, I decided I wanted to stay home. But both Gramps and my dad told me I wasn't allowed to cancel my plans on their account. My dad called Jenny's parents and everything to make sure I wouldn't back out."

Hazel sighed, hating how shallow and irresponsible this was making her sound. "So, I kept my plans, saved some money and was all set to go to Arizona, but then I got a call from Wander Mountain. Their scholarship recipient backed out last minute and I was in. I never thought I would get a spot. I mean I'd been applying every year since I was fifteen. Getting in wasn't even on my radar. But when I did, it just seemed like an opportunity I shouldn't pass up. I called Jenny and she told me to go for it. Said she'd cover for me and everything."

"Then you bought some pink boots, hit a good-looking guy from Boston with your tank and the rest is history?"

"Pretty much." Hazel sighed and took a bite of her candy bar to ease her guilt.

Jamie was silent, which only made her feel worse. She'd expected at least a few sarcastic comments about her selfish and idiotic plan.

"Look," she said, "I know it was a stupid plan, okay? And I know you think this whole program is a joke, but coming here meant something to me." She scuffed the toes of her ridiculous pink boot into the dirt. "It's one of the only future goals I've ever had, so when I had the chance to see it through, I took it. I don't expect you to understand."

Jamie's eyes, which had been fixed on the horizon, swung to hers. "Why wouldn't I understand?"

"We don't live in the same world, Jamie. I know you've been through some awful things, but when this is over you still get to go back to your famous family and a life full of choices. They may not be the choices you want, but at least they're choices."

"You're right, they're not the choices I want. A lot of choices have been taken away from me, but I do my best not to complain about that."

"Don't get all high and mighty on me. You want to run away from your life just as much as I do."

"There's a difference between running away and choosing a path, Hazel."

She glared at him, her temper piqued. "Since we're being so truthful, tell me something. Why did you say football wasn't an option for you in counseling today?"

Jamie hunched over, his elbows resting on his knees while he rolled the empty kombucha bottle back and forth in his hands. "Because it's not."

Hazel could see the fight fizzle out of him. She'd hit a nerve and felt instantly guilty. She was the one at fault here. Just because she wasn't brave enough to tell her family the truth didn't mean she needed to take her frustration out on Jamie. He didn't owe her anything.

She was about to say so, but the serious expression on his face stopped her. He looked like he was working through how to tell her something important.

Hazel hated the prickling fear she felt waiting for his revelation. She wanted to say something snarky, like 'reveal to heal', to lighten the crushing weight it looked like Jamie was shouldering.

Why had she asked him about not playing football?

She knew it was a sore subject.

In therapy, Jamie had eluded to it being a medical reason that kept him from playing, but she had no right to ask him such personal questions. Hadn't that been why she was so upset with him earlier . . . for meddling in her life where he didn't belong?

Hazel was about to apologize when Jamie leaned back against the bench and met her eyes. "I have a medical condition. It's nothing too serious, but it keeps me from playing any sort of contact sports."

She blinked digesting his words. She didn't like them, not

one bit. He looked like an Adonis. *How could this perfect human specimen be sick?*

A million more questions crashed through her mind.

What kind of medical condition?

A life-threatening one?

Can it be cured?

Her eyes raked over his flawless skin, his strong frame, his large hands.

God, you are the worst, Hazel.

All she did was complain about her pathetic life to this gorgeous boy and he was the one with the real problems, and he rarely complained about it. Even now, she'd practically had to drag it out of him.

Jamie watched her expression, a frown stretching across his full lips. "Don't look at me like that, Smalls. I'm not gonna keel over. I just can't play football. It's not the end of the world." He dropped her gaze and shook his head, running a hand through his dark hair. "This is why I don't tell anyone. Poor little rich boy is sick . . . I don't need that in my life."

"That's not what I was thinking," she argued—*although it kinda was.*

"Oh yeah? Enlighten me. What were you thinking?"

"That you probably weren't meant to play football."

His eyebrows rose. "Why's that?"

She slid her hand into his large, soft palm. "Because. You have an artist's hands."

He barked a laugh. "Shit! Now I know you're pitying me. You're never this nice."

"You're right. I'm not. I'm a mess. You're a mess, and Jamie, as much as I like you, and I'm admitting that I do, we'd be a train wreck together if we were anything more than friends."

He blew out a breath and closed his hand around hers, rubbing his thumb slowly across her knuckles. "You're probably right, but it's not gonna stop me from caring about you, Smalls."

Hazel gave him a tight-lipped grin. "Same."

She hated how this felt like a goodbye—the end even though they'd never really began.

Knowing Jamie had some hidden illness made Hazel care about him even more. It was a startling revelation, because she realized she might already care about him too much—more than she'd ever cared about another person in her life.

She'd only known him a short time, but he felt like he might be the best friend she'd ever had. Of course, she couldn't decide if she wanted to kiss him or kill him most of time, so maybe it was more than friendship.

Whatever it was she knew she was smart not to let it go any further. Neither of them were in the right place for more.

Doing her best to reel in her feelings, Hazel smiled at Jamie as he squeezed her hand, wondering why she was drawn to fragile, broken things. An abandoned dog and two disabled vets were her whole world. Maybe she was just destined to love the downtrodden.

But who would love her?

As much as she hated to admit it, she needed someone to care for her heart. Because it was its own fragile, broken thing.

James

JAMES COULDN'T TAKE SITTING THERE a moment longer. It was too sad, staring into those gorgeous caramel eyes.

He saw everything he ever wanted in Hazel's eyes, but he knew he'd never get it. Not now anyway. Maybe someday, when they were both older and stronger. Maybe they'd outgrow the cruel situations life had currently locked them into and they'd get another shot at whatever this was.

At least that's what he told himself because it was too painful to think about the alternative.

In reality though, he felt like this was their chance. The only one they'd get and it was killing him to pass it up.

But what could he do?

He couldn't force the girl to let him love her. He'd been where she was. She needed to love herself first. He still struggled with that himself. It was hard to do when you were a walking disappointment to your father and you carried the guilt of your mother's death around.

A few days ago, James had barely been keeping himself afloat. He couldn't hold Hazel up too, especially not if she wouldn't even grab the damn lifeline he was offering.

He stood up and pulled his tacky camp keychain from his pocket. He stared down at the slogan stamped into the green plastic. *'You can't find yourself without getting lost.'*

What a crock of shit.

He was lost all right, lost in Hazel Walker.

The trouble was, he'd also found himself in her.

He knew he wasn't wrong about them being right for each other. When he was with her, he felt most like himself.

How can that be wrong, Hazel?

James tossed the cheesy plastic keychain in the air a few times, catching it as he weighed his options. He felt like everything was mocking him, the unattainable girl, the perfect sunset his camera couldn't quite capture, the damn keychain with its stupid slogan. James wanted to hurl it off the cliff. Knowing that would serve him no purpose other than getting locked out of his cabin, he did the next best thing he could with it.

· · ·

HAZEL

HAZEL WATCHED Jamie with amusement while he dug his keychain into the ground and drew a wide circle around the stone bench she was sitting on.

"What are you doing?"

"Making our lines a little wider."

"Our lines?"

"You know, the ones you won't let us cross." He grinned up at her. "If I'm not gonna break my promise I'm gonna need a little more room."

"Room for what?"

"Truth, flirting, fights . . . the usual Hazel/Jamie repertoire."

She laughed. "Oh, you mean like tonight's enlightening conversation?"

He winked. "Exactly."

When he was done completing his circle, he sat back on the bench and slung an arm around Hazel's shoulder. His easy tone turned somber. "I meant what I said earlier, Hazel. The way you were talking in group today, it scared me. I don't want you going down that road alone. I've been there. Nothing good comes of it." He picked up her hand. "I may be a mess, but I'm strong enough to help you carry some of your baggage till you find a way to let it go."

She swallowed past the lump in her throat. "Okay."

"You can trust me, Hazel."

"I know."

"Good, 'cause I know you're a badass and all, but letting me know when you need a little support isn't gonna diminish your street cred in my eyes, alright?"

She laughed and bumped him with her shoulder. "Same goes for you."

"Yeah, I guess it goes both ways, huh?" Jamie smirked. "I've got your back, if you've got mine?"

Hazel felt her first genuine smile of the night crack her lips. "Something like that."

Jamie stood up and offered her his hand. "It's a deal."

She got to her feet and clasped his hand. "Deal."

He flashed one of those grins that pulled at her heart like gravity, making her lose her breath and question her resolve.

You're just friends, Hazel. You can't have more. "Where to?" she asked hoping her voice didn't sound as shaky as her heart.

"I say we go to Prospects and get some real food, my picnic sucked."

She laughed. "We finally agree on something."

Jamie slung an arm around Hazel, pulling her into a headlock and mussed her hair until her laughter filled the forest around them. She let him lead her back toward camp, feeling lighter than she'd expected after bearing so much of her soul to another person.

Maybe this whole friendship thing could work . . .

20

James

DINNER WAS A BUST. By the time they got to the dining hall the hot food had been cleaned up. There was nothing left but fruit and packaged snacks, which was why James now found himself sitting around the campfire at another S'mores Social.

He needed to put something in his stomach and he'd grown secretly addicted to the sugary treats that Hazel loved so much. He tried to fight his grin while watching her lick the marshmallows off her fingers.

It was too easy to get addicted to all things Hazel. If he didn't watch it, this girl was gonna steal his heart.

James pulled his focus back to the fire softly roasting his marshmallows. Tonight, they ended up sitting around a campfire that was more karaoke than cooking. The chairs and benches around the fire pit were packed with campers from their age group, including Hazel's roommates. Tanner Jones had his guitar out and was taking requests, belting out poppy country tunes with ease.

Everyone in the vicinity either sang along or swooned over Tanner's voice, including Hazel. After finishing her S'mores she sat elbows on her knees, chin in her hands, grinning as she tapped her feet along with Tanner's songs, quietly mouthing the lyrics to herself.

James glared at Tanner. He didn't see what the appeal was. He looked like Macaulay Culkin trying to impersonate a rock-star—all shoulder-length blond hair and trying-too-hard leather necklaces.

So what? The guy could play guitar and sing a little, it didn't deserve that much adoration.

James rubbed the tension from his jaw as he watched Hazel watching Tanner. *Shit, so this is what jealousy feels like.*

James crossed his ankles and leaned back in his Adirondack chair. He wasn't a fan, of Tanner, or the feelings crowding his chest.

Tanner was the guy Hazel was most likely going to get paired up with for the hike and that didn't bode well for James. Between songs Tanner and Hazel chatted animatedly about music and the bands they liked. It seemed they already had plenty in common, making James wish he'd actually paid attention in music class.

Was it too late to learn how to play guitar?

When Tanner finished crooning another ballad, he took a bow. After the lull in applause he asked for requests.

Hazel who'd been quietly watching, spoke up. "Do you know Tequila?"

"Dan and Shay, right?" Tanner asked, pulling his guitar back to his lap. He strummed out a few notes but then shook his head. "Nah, I love them but haven't mastered that one yet."

"You're nearly there," Hazel said nodding to the guitar. "Just play a little heavier on the G cord."

Tanner's mouth pulled into a sideways grin. "You play?"

Hazel shrugged and seemed to shrink back in herself as she answered. "A little . . . just for myself though."

James perked up. It was the first time he'd heard of this.

"Ah, come on, I'd love to hear it," Tanner encouraged, offering her the guitar.

Hazel shook her head. "No one wants to hear me sing."

"I do," James said.

Hazel met his eyes and he could see her cheeks redden even in the firelight. She gave him the smallest shake of her head and averted her eyes.

"Me too!" Kat called from across the fire. "Play for us, Hazel."

"Play Hazel!" Sawyer chanted getting the whole campfire in on it. "Hazel! Hazel! Hazel!"

"Oh my God, alright!" Hazel groaned taking the guitar. "But I'm warning you, it's not gonna be pretty. I only play for my dog and that's 'cause he can't criticize."

"We'll be gentle," Tanner said giving her a cocky wink that made James want to punch the suggestive smile right off the kid's face.

HAZEL

THE MOMENT the guitar settled in her hands, a familiar calmness washed over Hazel. The coppery scent of the strings, the hollow curve of the wood, the rich tenor of that first strum of cords. It all soothed her, filling her with a comfortable lightness that she'd missed.

She strummed a note and it brought her back home; sitting on the back porch as a child, watching Gramps play, studying every movement of his fingers so she could copy it.

Gramps had given Hazel her first guitar; a gift for her ninth birthday. She hadn't put it down since. Music was how she worked out her problems, how she expressed all the things she didn't know how to say. She could lose herself in a song for hours. Gramps always said the guitar was cheaper than a therapist and as she began to play, she realized he was right.

All the tension and stress of the past few days started to melt away. Even her confusing feelings about Jamie seemed to iron themselves out as the music filled her heart. And for once, she didn't fight it. She let everything she felt pour out in the lyrics of a love song she'd never really understood before this moment.

James

MESMERIZING—THAT was the only way to describe what James was watching.

Hazel came to life with that guitar in her hands.

Her words dripped slow like honey but packed a punch like dynamite. James felt every word she sang as if she'd etched them into his heart. It stole his breath.

How could you ever question what you want to do with your life, Hazel?

This was what she'd been put in the world to do.

It was obvious she felt music with her soul. With her eyes closed and her head bowed over the guitar it was like the song had carried her away and all her problems with it. James wasn't sure what she pictured when she played, but he was certain it was something beautiful.

A curtain of molten bronze, her hair shimmered in the firelight, the slight tug of a smile pulling at her lips between words. James could've watched her like that forever. He was still, so present in the moment that he knew precisely when it happened. When his world shifted again and he tumbled headlong into love with the girl in the damn pink boots.

The song ended and Hazel opened her eyes. She caught him staring and smiled at him, and he wondered if she knew —*that absolutely everything had changed.*

HAZEL

HAZEL WAS breathless and laughing when she finally managed to make her way out of the crowd.

After she'd finished singing, the group around the fire had whooped and hollered for her to play another, but she graciously declined, handing Tanner's guitar back to him. He begged her to sing with him, but Hazel would rather crawl into a hole. She didn't know what had come over her in the first place. She never played for anyone, let alone sang.

Even though the heat in her cheeks told her that her face was three shades of red, she did her best to hold onto the euphoric energy the music had brought her. She didn't like being the center of attention. She was always more comfortable in the shadows, which was where she'd been slinking off to when she felt Jamie's hand slip into hers, forcefully pulling her away from the campfire.

"Everything okay?" she asked, watching his jaw work furiously over something that was clearly bothering him.

He didn't answer, only kept tugging her behind him until they reached the small boathouse at the end of the stone path leading to the lake.

Hazel didn't know what was wrong, but it was definitely something. She could feel the agitation vibrating from him. He dropped her hand and began pacing. It made her skin prickle with nervous energy. She was about to ask him what the hell was wrong when he turned and looked at her, closing the distance between them abruptly.

His warm fingertips tracing her jaw, tilting her face to meet his. The moon painted his complexion sliver and blue, the eerie coloring making the pain etched on his face more pronounced.

"Hazel . . ." he whispered, emotion burning in his voice so intensely it made her swallow all the words she'd ever learned. "Hazel . . ." he said again.

Oh God, please stop saying my name like that, Jamie.

She had to close her eyes because she'd never loved a word more. The way Jamie said her name . . . it was a prayer, a song, an awakening.

She couldn't look at him. Her knees were weak and she knew if she opened her eyes she'd cross every line she'd ever drawn. She squeezed them shut tighter, but she could still feel the heat of his breath on her neck as he whispered her name one last time.

"Hazel . . . I'm sorry." And then his lips were on hers, soft at first and then frantic.

Her lips matched his, like they were running a race for their lives and the finish line was just beyond the other's lips. The passion she felt was so sudden and explosive that she was powerless against it.

She gave herself over to the kiss.

It was dangerous and delicious and everything a kiss should be.

Jamie tasted like burnt sugar and chocolate and she knew those two flavors would forever be tangled with him.

James

HE HADN'T EVEN MEANT to kiss her. He'd been trying to find the words to tell her how he felt—like there wasn't enough room in his chest for all the things she made him want. But when he opened his mouth he couldn't get past her name and the way saying it made his heart react.

His words may have failed him, but his lips hadn't.

Kissing Hazel was like the push and pull of the ocean —unstoppable.

She fit in his arms like she'd been chiseled from the space between them. And for a moment it felt like everything else in the world stopped to give way to the magic that was happening between them. Because that's what having her kiss him back was like—pure magic.

Electric agony tore through James when Hazel finally pulled away. She was wide-eyed, gasping for air. James wanted to lend her his lungs so their lips would never have to part again. He might as well just give them to her. *Take them, Hazel, you already own my heart.*

She blinked up at him, chest heaving. Her hands were still fisted in his sweatshirt, pulling him against her like he was the only thing keeping her on her feet. And after that kiss, maybe he was. He certainly felt unsteady.

The world swayed back into focus as Hazel started to pull

away, but James drew her back in catching her chin as she tried to cover her face.

"Hey," he whispered, but she shook her head.

"Jamie, we can't . . ."

He stared at her. *How can you possible deny it, Hazel?*

She felt the same way he did, he knew it. She'd kissed him back with the same explosive passion now vibrating through every fiber of his being.

"Why?" he asked curling his arms around her slender waist, refusing to let her escape. "What's so bad about this?"

"I can't, okay? I just . . ." She trailed off as her lower lip began to tremble.

Hazel tried to bury her face in her hands but James wasn't having it. He wanted to look into the endless volumes of her eyes and read all the words she wasn't saying.

"Hey, look at me," he begged.

She did, fear shining in her gorgeous eyes.

"What are you so afraid of?"

She finally stopped trying to hide. She blew out a shaky breath and looked up at him with startling honesty. "You. I'm afraid of you, Jamie."

"Me?"

"Don't you get it? If I let myself fall into this . . . into you . . . I may never climb back out."

He tucked a lock of hair behind her ear. "Would that really be so bad?"

"Yes! I'm supposed to be figuring out who I am. Not getting lost in someone else."

"I know you who are, Hazel. Let me show you."

"I can't."

"Give me one good reason why not."

"Because you broke your promise, Jamie."

"Hazel, those lines never should've been drawn and you know it."

"I know it?"

"Yes. You want this just as bad as I do," he moved closer, backing her up against the boat house. "I felt it in that kiss and if you say you didn't, then you're never gonna figure out who you are because you're too busy lying to yourself."

"Get over yourself, Jamie. It was just a kiss." Her words were harsh, but her eyes betrayed her, darting to his lips.

You're lying, Hazel. You want more. He grinned. "Just a kiss, huh? Fine. If it meant nothing, kiss me one more time, right now and prove it."

She swallowed again. "What's that gonna prove?"

He shrugged. "You tell me?"

"I'm not playing this game with you, Jamie."

She tried to push past him but he put his arms up, boxing her in. "Why not? It's just a kiss, right? It shouldn't be a problem if you don't feel anything."

She crossed her arms. "You're not gonna let this go, are you?"

He slowly shook his head. "One kiss, Smalls. And if you can make me believe you don't feel anything, I'll never bring it up again."

HAZEL

"THIS IS RIDICULOUS, JAMIE."

Why was she even considering going along with this?

Duh, because the first kiss was earthshattering!

Ugh! Stop it, Hazel! She couldn't be thinking things like that if she was ever going to make him drop this. And he needed to drop it.

Kissing him would lead to wanting more and that's something she couldn't allow. Jamie would only be in her life for a few more days before they went their separate ways; heading out on a path that would eventually lead them back to their old lives. They'd probably never see each other again. There was no point in pursuing the emotions tightening her chest.

Then again . . . what do I have to lose?

Hazel stared up at Jamie, heat rising everywhere his eyes roamed. He wasn't even touching her and she was already turned on! How the hell would she convince him she didn't feel anything when his lips were on hers?

Her heart was in her throat just thinking about kissing him again. It was pounding so hard he could probably hear it. *How embarrassing.*

Jamie moved one hand away from the boathouse, sliding it down her shoulder until it rested on her chest.

She shivered. "What are you doing?"

He gave her a crooked grin that made her blood simmer. "Your heart's beating awfully fast, Smalls."

"Maybe that's because I'm not used to having guys coerce me into making out with them."

"Are you gonna kiss me or are you gonna—"

She didn't let him finish his sentence. She grabbed the collar of his sweatshirt and jerked him toward her, her lips crashing into his before she lost her nerve.

His shock made the kiss that much more intense. He was still for a moment while her lips met his, controlling the pace, gentle and soft, then all at once he came alive. His lips devouring hers. His tongue parted her lips as he lifted her into his arms pressing her against the boathouse as she hooked her legs around his hips. Her hands were in his hair and his mouth was everywhere.

So this is what it feels like to be swept of your feet?

Jamie was the ground beneath her, the air around her, he was everything all at once. He stole all of her hope then breathed it back into her soul. He wrecked her and she couldn't get enough.

People say they see their lives flash before their eyes right before they die. But for Hazel, it happened when she finally came to life, awakened by Jamie's kiss. She wondered what it meant. Had she not truly lived before that moment . . . before her lips met his?

She saw image after image flash through her mind and all of them were filled with Jamie. The first time he looked up at her from the hood of her car, the time he'd given her his phone, how he pulled his hoodie over her head when she was cold, the way his fingers fit over hers when he showed her how to hold his camera, how he brought her extra desserts at every meal and a thousand other tiny gestures that fit together like a photo album. It was a lifetime of affection in five days.

How had it happened? And how hadn't she known? More importantly, how would she survive this?

But Jamie was right, Hazel couldn't deny the way she felt. His hand was no longer over her heart, he now held it, and all chances of convincing him she was unaffected by his glorious lips were long gone.

And for once, she really didn't care.

21

James

JAMES FORCED his lips away from Hazel's for a breath. The moment the kiss broke, he felt a wide uncontained smile stretch across his face. He tried to stop it, but it was useless, mostly because Hazel matched him with her own gorgeous grin. He pulled her closer and traced quick kisses across her lips. As soon as he stopped his smile returned.

Maybe this was all he could manage now, kissing and smiling. He could live with that. Especially if it meant he could keep Hazel in his arms. She was pressed so close against him that it felt like his heart was beating inside her chest. And maybe it was, because it had never felt this strong. Only Hazel made him whole.

Their kiss, the one that Hazel claimed wouldn't affect her, was still going strong ten minutes after it started. James's lips were chapped, and Hazel's nose felt like an ice cube against his face, but he wasn't complaining. His girl was in his arms and nothing could be better.

She came up for air, biting her kiss-stung lips as he grinned at her. "Don't say it," she groaned burying her face in his neck.

"Say what?"

He could feel her roll her eyes. "You have that smug 'I told you so' grin on your face and I already know what you're gonna say so you can stop gloating."

He laughed, loving the way the sound vibrated through Hazel as she clung to him. "Now, why would I be gloating?"

She lifted her head and looked at him, trying to look fierce. "You were right about the kiss, okay?"

He laughed again and kissed her one more time before setting her on her feet. "You know what this means don't you?"

"What?"

"You're my girl."

She rolled her eyes. "Your girl? That's so ridiculous. Who even says that?"

"We do."

"We're a *we* now?"

"Definitely." He tugged his sweatshirt off and pulled it over her head, drawing her back into his arms.

Jamie loved seeing Hazel in his clothes. Especially when she snuggled down into the hoodie and tried to pretend she wasn't inhaling his scent. "Yep, we're a we and you're definitely my girl."

Hazel frowned, pulling back to meet his eyes. "Can we be serious for two seconds?"

He didn't like the doubt he saw swimming in her eyes but he nodded and let her talk.

"We can't do this, Jamie."

"Hazel, you came here for an adventure, right?"

She nodded.

"So let me be that adventure for the next few days."

"And then what?"

He shrugged. "That's a problem for future us to figure out."

She rolled her eyes. "Real mature."

James smirked. He was trying to be serious, but it was hard with his heart on Cloud 9. "I can promise you adventure, Smalls, but if you want maturity, I'm not your guy." He watched her resolve soften and he pulled her closer. "What do ya say, Hazel Jane? Wanna get lost with me?"

HAZEL

I ALREADY AM. The answer was on the tip of her tongue, but fear made Hazel break out in goose bumps as she tried to make up her mind.

They'd only have one more day together before everyone would get paired up and sent off to hike Crossroads with their partners. Based on her and Jamie's scores there was no chance they'd end up together.

Was one night of adventure with him really worth the potential heartache?

Hazel looked into Jamie's sky-blue eyes and all logic disappeared. The only thought left echoing in her head was a resounding yes. *What have I got to lose?*

Her heart pounded out the answer: *Him.*

She realized she was more afraid of losing him than all the other reasons she'd concocted for staying away. So why was she hesitating? Wasn't one day of bliss better than none? She knew her heart would break when she had to go back to Lovelock anyway. At least this way she'd have a few beautiful memories to take with her.

Jamie held her in his unwavering gaze and Hazel drew strength from it. Finally, she released her inhibitions, stretching onto her toes to press a single kiss to his lips.

"Okay," she whispered against his mouth.

"Okay?"

She nodded and kissed him again. "Okay."

"I think that's my new favorite word, Smalls." Then he swept her off her feet and whooped as he swung her through the cold night air.

It felt like flying—terrifying and exhilarating all at once.

Hazel laughed, surrendering to Jamie's captivating kiss, letting herself get lost in his lips.

James

THE POUNDING of boots on stone was the only thing that made James come up for air. When he pulled himself from Hazel's lips, he saw a stampede of campers rushing toward them, half of them undressing as they ran.

"Midnight Polar Plunge!" someone hollered, while others howled like wolves before rushing by them to splash into the frigid lake just beyond the boat house.

James pulled Hazel out of the way as three guys streaked by. She giggled and buried her laughter in his chest.

"I coulda done without seeing that," he joked.

"I don't know, it wasn't all bad."

"Oh yeah?" James quirked an eyebrow at Hazel, loving the playful grin on her face. "So, we taking the plunge or what?"

"You better," Kat yelled as she came running down the

path with Paisley and Sawyer. She turned, calling back to them as she jogged backward. "Or risk the wrath of the Couples' Curse!"

Hazel's roommates giggled at Kat's ridiculous taunt, but James felt Hazel tense in his arms. "You know they're just messing with you, right?" he murmured.

Hazel nodded, trying to look untroubled, but James wasn't buying it. He wanted to get the carefree-Hazel back before she retreated into the version of herself that was consumed with worry.

When it seemed the crowd of streakers had dissipated, James took a step onto the path and extended his hand. "What do you say, Smalls? Ready to take the plunge with me?"

She hesitated for half a second, then a ghost of a smile grew to consume her whole face as she reached for his hand. "Okay."

His grin matched hers. "Yep, definitely my new favorite word."

Then he yanked her into his arms and took off running toward the lake before Hazel could change her mind, her laughter trailing behind them.

22

H azel

"WHAT AM I DOING?" Hazel whispered to herself.

This was easily the most embarrassing thing she'd ever done. She was standing in a bathroom stall, completely naked except for her stupid pink boots and a skimpy white towel. She'd just finished stacking her clothes neatly on the back of the toilet tank when she heard Jamie calling her.

"Smalls, I'm freezing my nuts off out here."

Hazel groaned. She would've changed her mind about the stupid midnight skinny dipping tradition if Jamie hadn't been waiting for her. But he was already outside in his own towel and boots and it was cruel to leave him hanging.

Plus, she couldn't deny there was a part of her that was curious to see the goods he'd been hiding under all those layers of expensive clothes.

With one final look in the mirror, Hazel took a deep breath and opened the door.

James

JAMES WONDERED if it was normal to be able to pinpoint the exact moment the path of your life changes. For him, there'd been three: when he met Hazel, when he heard her sing and right now, when Hazel Walker breezed out of an old bathhouse in nothing but a towel and those goddamned hot pink boots.

After he picked his jaw up off the ground, he managed a low whistle. "Damn!"

Hazel bit her lip and smiled at him. "If you're gonna make fun of me—"

"There's nothing funny about you, Smalls," he interrupted taking her hand before she could retreat back into the bathroom. He twirled her under his arm, her tiny towel flapping in the frigid night air. "Damn," he said again.

"You already said that," she teased.

"Well, yeah. With the way you look . . . it deserves a second damn." He pressed a hand to his chest. "You're gonna give me a heart attack, girl."

It was funny how a moment ago he'd been questioning what the first signs of hypothermia were and then Hazel walked out of the bathhouse and he suddenly felt like he'd been teleported to the sun.

"Come on," he said starting toward the riotous laughter coming from the lake. "I've never needed an ice-cold bath more than I do right now."

. . .

HAZEL

HAZEL STOOD where the dock met the land. She'd already kicked off her boots. All that was left to shed was her towel.

Jamie stood next to her, a playful grin on his face. He was down to nothing but his towel too. "On three?"

She nodded and he took her hand. The warmth of his fingers made her breath catch. For a split second she questioned herself. These were the kind of memories she wanted to make here. But would it be diminished because she hadn't been strong enough to do it alone?

She looked at Jamie, his warm touch spreading through her, and she knew that she'd never regret this moment. Not a single second of it. Nothing she could share with him would ever warrant remorse. He was the only reason she was standing there, about to take part in an ancient tradition and plunge into a frigid lake.

Jamie was right, he was an adventure. All Hazel had to do was be brave enough to hold on. A tiny seed of fear bubbled up in her. "Don't let go, okay?"

He squeezed her hand and winked. "I got you, Smalls. Promise."

Then they were running, nothing between them and the biting night air.

The moment Hazel hit the water she started to panic. It surrounded her like an icy vice grip, cold and sharp as it stole her breath. Her limbs seized as she struggled to resurface. When she finally did, she couldn't remember how to keep her head above water. She tried to flail her arms, but one was tethered to something—*Jamie!*

The moment she saw him she surged forward, clinging to him with all the strength she had left. The icy water was leaching her energy and she couldn't seem to catch her breath, but Jamie was there. He hadn't let go, just like he promised.

James

"BREATHE," he coaxed. "I got ya."

But Hazel continued to panic, wrapping her limbs around him like a squid, her teeth chattering as she shivered and coughed.

"Hazel, I got ya. I'm not gonna let go," James murmured.

He put both hands on her cheeks, treading water with his powerful legs so he could smooth her wet hair away from her face. "Look at me, Hazel." Her eyes were so wide they could've swallowed him whole. "I'm not gonna let go, okay?"

"O-k-kay," she stammered, drawing in a deep breath that finally calmed her.

James planted a soft kiss on her blue lips. He knew he was enjoying this way too much, but it was hard not to enjoy a frightened Hazel. *Make that a frightened, naked Hazel.*

She was always so damn determined not to need anyone, but apparently the water was her kryptonite. James was sure this moment of fragility would vanish as soon as her feet were on solid ground again so he was lapping it up while he could.

"Ya know," he teased glancing down to where their bare chests were pressed together, "if you wanted to cop a feel you coulda just asked."

Hazel gave a shivery laugh. "I'm too c-cold to even have a c-comeback," she chattered, teeth gnashing together.

"Ready to get out?"

"Yes p-please."

"Okay, you gotta do one thing first."

"What?"

"Howl like a wolf."

"What?"

"It's tradition." James rocked his head back and howled at the moon. It was invigorating.

Hazel eyed him warily.

"Come on. The faster you do it, the faster you can get back to making out with me. That'll warm ya right up."

She rolled her eyes, but a smirk stretched across her shivering lips just before she tilted her head back and howled into the night. James laughed and joined her, letting a howl of joy rip into the night.

When they were breathless from howling and laughing, he pulled Hazel's lips to his and kissed her deeply. She'd finally stopped shivering when he pulled away, but she was clinging to him even tighter.

"Hold on," James whispered slipping Hazel onto his back as he began to swim toward shore; just a little more slowly than necessary.

HAZEL SNUGGLED CLOSER TO JAMIE. She was sitting on his lap under a thick pile of blankets. They were one of the last few campers left around the fire. He knew it was getting late, but he was in no rush for the night to end. It was the best one he'd had . . . ever.

They'd spent the last hour laughing and talking with the other campers who'd been crazy enough to take the Polar Plunge. They'd all huddled around the fire trying to get warm while exchanging stories and experiences, until one-by-one, the promise of cozy beds called them back to their cabins.

Now it was only James and Hazel, and a few other people quietly talking around the fire.

"So, I'm thinking Fiji," Jamie murmured into Hazel's damp hair.

"Fiji?" she asked without even lifting her head from his shoulder.

"Yeah, for our honeymoon."

That got her attention. She looked at him, caramel eyes full of the skeptical sass he loved. He gave it right back to her. "You saw me naked, Smalls. We have to get married now."

Hazel swatted him and rolled her eyes, standing up.

He groaned trying to pull her back down. "Bora Bora? Granada?"

She just shook her head like she thought he was crazy.

"Okay you pick. It just has to be somewhere we can sail."

"Why's that?"

He finally pulled her back into his arms and wrapped the blanket around both of them. "Because," he whispered into her hair, "ever since I saw you naked on that dock, I've been imagining what you'd look like on my boat."

She swatted him. "You said you didn't look!"

He laughed and slid his hand through her hair. "I lied," he whispered, pulling her lips back to his for another endless kiss.

James desperately wished they were alone. He wanted nothing more than to crawl under the blankets with Hazel and not resurface until first light. He couldn't get the image of her bare silhouette in the moonlight out of his mind.

He'd tried to be a gentleman and give her some privacy when he carried her out of the lake, but he couldn't help it. He'd caught a glimpse of her toweling off on the dock and nearly died. He'd never been so jealous of a droplet of water before. He wanted to be the only one exploring Hazel's curves and valleys.

Hazel smirked, her faint blush making her even more beautiful. "You *did* see me out there, right? I'm not really that great in the water."

He laughed. "That's sorta the appeal, Smalls. I think I could get used to rescuing you."

"Anything to cop a feel," she teased.

He winked. "You know it."

"You're terrible."

"The worst. But just for the sake of our future honeymoon plans, you *can* actually swim, right?"

"I do okay in an above-ground pool."

James blanched. "I can't tell if you're joking."

Hazel blushed further and eventually shook her head.

James pulled her closer. "Future tip, Smalls. The next time you let me talk you into something crazy, you might want to disclose important details like not being able to swim."

She glared at him. "I can swim. I'm just not great at it."

He shook his head, admiring her tenacity. "I'm gonna have to get creative with my dates, aren't I?"

"Wait, that was a date?" she teased, grinning up at him.

"Damn straight! You better wrap your head around it, Smalls. I already told you, you're my girl now."

She laughed and let him kiss her. The fact that she didn't argue or have a smartass remark might have been the best thing she said all night.

HAZEL

IT WAS late by the time Jamie finally walked Hazel to her door, but she didn't mind. She doubted she'd be able to sleep anyway, not with the way her heart was racing.

She and Jamie hadn't done anything more than kiss but Hazel felt like she had a fever. Even now, as he caged her against the door to her cabin and whispered awful pickup lines in her ear, she couldn't catch her breath.

How had so much changed so quickly?

Every time he pulled away it felt like he was tearing a little piece of her away with him. They tried three times to say goodnight only to end up back in each other's arms.

Finally, Jamie pinned her with a look that said he'd put all joking aside. "Promise me this isn't a dream," he whispered, pushing her hair back with gentle fingers.

Hazel stared into his gorgeous blue eyes—sky colliding with earth. There was hope and fear in his expression and she wanted to quiet it. "It might be a dream," she whispered. "But I won't forget."

He kissed her one more time. "Okay."

"Okay."

Somehow, Hazel tore herself away from gazing at the night sky in Jamie's eyes and went inside, practically sliding down the door like a cracked egg. Her heart felt like it was in her toes and her throat at the same time. She was exhausted and invigorated. How could one boy make her feel so much?

Hazel startled when she heard Jamie howl into the night just beyond her door. She brought her fingers to her lips, unable to fight her grin.

23

James

HAZEL BLINKED up at James through a pair of sleepy caramel eyes. Her espresso brown hair stuck out from her ponytail at comical angles. She reminded him of a confused owl—it was adorable.

He also loved the fact that she was still wearing his hoodie.

She'd obviously slept in it, a fact that filled him with way too much joy. Her whole disheveled appearance made him want to kiss her and drag her back to bed. Instead, he handed her a coffee. "Twelve gazillion sugars and too much vanilla creamer, just how you like it."

"What are you doing here?" she asked looking at her watch. "It's hours till breakfast."

"I know. I wanna show you something."

"Now?"

"We only have twenty-four hours together before we partner up for Crossroads and I intend to use every last minute to make sure you don't forget about me while you're sharing a tent with Mr. Teen Country Idol."

"Tanner?"

"Yes, Tanner. Now put on your pink boots! We've got places to be, Smalls!"

HAZEL

HAZEL BIT her lip to control the smile that slid into place when she saw the sweet scene Jamie had set up at their stone bench. It looked like he'd dragged the blankets and pillows from his cabin out into the woods to arrange a cozy spot for them to snuggle. *The counselors aren't gonna be happy about that.*

"Just in time," Jamie murmured hurrying to the blankets, towing Hazel along with him.

He hadn't let go of her hand from the moment they left her cabin and she had to admit, it was something she could get used to.

Hazel was never a fan of PDA. She couldn't understand why anyone other than children would want to hold someone's hand. But with Jamie's fingers securely threaded through hers she felt like she could take on the world. And every time his thumb brushed across her knuckles it was like a jolt of caffeine straight to her heart.

She squeezed his hand a bit tighter. She was starting to understand the appeal. It certainly didn't hurt that his fingers were as warm as her mug of coffee.

When they settled onto the blankets, Hazel leaned into Jamie's side to soak up some more of his warmth. "So, any particular reason you dragged me out here at the crack of dawn?"

Jamie grinned and hooked his fingers through her belt loops, tugging her onto his lap. "As a matter of fact there is, Smalls." Then he kissed her.

He tasted like hazelnut coffee and a heart full of hope, and Hazel never wanted to let go of the feeling flooding into her chest. It was terrifying.

"You didn't have to bring me all the way out here for that," she whispered. "You can kiss me anywhere."

A devilish smirk danced across Jamie's face. "Anywhere?"

Heat scorched Hazel from the inside out as she caught his suggestive meaning. "I'm gonna have to call off the wedding if you're gonna try and corrupt me, James Forrester."

His laughter filled the misty morning air. "So, you're admitting I have a chance? I'd call that progress." Jamie's grin brightened as something caught his eyes. "Look, it's starting."

Hazel followed his line of sight and nearly gasped as the first rays of orange light began to burst above the mountains in the distance. He'd brought her to see the sunrise! Hazel's chest felt tight with emotion as she climbed to her feet for a better look.

It was such a thoughtful gesture and when she turned back to face Jamie, not quite sure how to express her gratitude, he was standing there, camera raised to his face. He focused the lens on her and snapped a photo. Letting the camera hang from the strap around his neck, he shook his head with a mystified expression on his face.

"What?" she asked.

"I brought you up here because I wanted to share something beautiful with you, but not even the Montana sunrise can hold a candle to you."

Words failed Hazel as she saw the sunrise reflected in

Jamie's sky-blue eyes. She could see the love he held for her, as vast and brilliant as the horizon behind them. She wanted to be a part of it. She wanted to let his warmth awaken her just like the rays of sunlight slowly bathing the mountains in golden light. So, she did the only thing she could think of in that moment. She stood on her toes, grabbed the front of his shirt and kissed him with everything she had.

James

THEY SPENT the morning watching the sunrise and trading kisses. James felt so relaxed he even let Hazel steal his camera and snap a few photos of him.

"Am I ever gonna get to see these masterpieces I'm taking?" she asked, sitting on his lap and aiming the lens much too close to his lips.

"Give me your address and I'll send you copies."

She arched an eyebrow skeptically. "Was this all a ploy to get my address so you can stalk me when this is over?"

He laughed and it shook her whole body. "Yes, ever since you hit me with your tank I've been plotting my revenge. I'm on phase twenty-seven, sunrise photography lessons."

She smirked. "How many phases are there?"

"Hmm, let's see." He reached for his field journal and pretended to flip through it for a master plan. "Only a few dozen more. But don't worry. I've got you right where I want you." He grabbed her hips and squeezed until she was squealing with laughter.

He'd only just learned how ticklish she was and he planned to totally abuse that knowledge. Mostly because he couldn't get enough of the way Hazel's laughter felt as it rained down around him. It lit his soul with light, his heart with desire.

She was breathless when she finally collapsed into his arms. It was so cold out that he could see the tiny puffs of mist with her every exhalation. He wanted to capture each one and breathe only that air for the rest of his life.

He'd never felt this helpless or free. It was intoxicating.

Hazel's stomach rumbled and Jamie laughed. "I may need to reconsider this arrangement, Smalls. I don't know if I can afford to keep you fed. You're always hungry."

She was pretending to pout when he reached for the small cooler he'd stashed under the stone bench.

Hazel's eyes grew like saucers when he pulled out fresh cinnamon rolls. "You brought me sugar?!"

He laughed. "I know how to take care of my girl."

"I thought coffee and sunrise was good. You're just spoiling me now," she said taking the cinnamon roll Jamie passed her.

It was still warm and Hazel moaned when she bit into the pastry, making every muscle in James's body tighten. He clenched his teeth against the undeniable desire and jealousy clashing in his gut. He wanted to be the one causing her to make those sounds.

She noticed him staring. "What?"

"Is there anything you love more than food?"

She grinned, answering with her mouth full of cinnamon roll. "Nope." She took another bite. "Where did you get these?"

"I have my ways." He winked. "Apparently, I'm charming."

"Do I even wanna know?"

"You're looking at a guy who charmed the pants off the dining hall ladies by telling them about the romantic picnic he was planning for his girlfriend. They gave me a cooler full of these bad boys," James said patting the old Coleman next to him. "Wrapped them in foil with some fancy heat packs to keep them warm, too."

Hazel's eyes widened as she zeroed in on the cooler. "There's more in there?"

"Yep."

"Omigod, I love you."

James picked up his journal again and pretended to write. "Phase twenty-eight: Make her fall in love with me —complete."

Hazel giggled as she tried to see what he was writing. When Jamie realized she might actually see something she shouldn't he snapped the book to his chest.

Hazel crossed her arms. "Are you actually writing about me?"

"No."

"I saw my name."

"So?"

"Oh my God!" her hand flew to her mouth. "Did you write about seeing me naked last night?"

He couldn't help smirking at the embarrassment coloring her cheeks. "Maybe."

"Ew! You're such a perv. Let me read it!"

"I'll make you a deal. Let's write to each other each day we're on our hike and when we get back, we can share them."

Hazel scowled at him. "You wrote about seeing me naked and now you're requesting love letters?"

James pushed the cooler toward her. "Yes, but don't forget I brought you cinnamon rolls."

Hazel rolled her eyes and laughed. "You're impossible."

He pulled her into his arms and kissed her. "You mean impossible to resist."

24

H azel

HAZEL COULDN'T HELP IT. She was on Cloud 9. She didn't even care that Paisley was still scowling at her from her spot by the river.

Paisley wasn't pleasant to be around on a good day and after she'd caught Hazel and Jamie kissing outside the dining hall this morning, Hazel's least favorite roommate was being anything but pleasant.

When Hazel finally managed to let Jamie drag her away from their perfect morning of sunrise snuggling, they took a detour to the camp store. True to his word, he shipped out the rolls of film to be developed. He even let Hazel put her home address on the return shipping label so she'd be the first to see them.

Then they'd stopped by the dining hall to return the cooler.

Paisley, Kat and Sawyer happened to be walking out when Jamie was planting a kiss on Hazel's lips.

"Good morning, lovebirds," Kat greeted, brightly.

"'Bout time," Sawyer mumbled through a yawn.

But Paisley had scowled at them, her silence saying everything.

Kat who was apparently immune to Paisley's death-stare, gave Jamie a hi-five, much to Hazel's chagrin. "Better get all the nookie you can before the Couples' Curse kicks in," she'd teased.

Jamie's response had been to sweep Hazel off her feet and kiss her again.

How could she complain about that?

The only thing she could even remotely find fault with today was the fact that Jamie hadn't been put on her team for their last challenge day. And it was water challenge day. *Yuck.*

Hazel gazed across the river to where Jamie stood, looking much too sexy in his wetsuit as everyone prepared to start the day's hellish events. The next few hours wouldn't be pleasant. It made her grateful Jamie had woken her up early. At least she could hold onto the warmth of those memories while she muddled her way through a day of freezing water sports.

"Alright," Sage yelled. "Gather up, Wanderers. Today is your final wilderness challenge day. The scores you accumulate individually and as a team will determine your final overall ranking and therefore your Crossroads partnerships. As always, I'm here to guide you through these challenges should you need help, but these are team building and partnership exercises. You need to trust yourselves and rely on your teammates for support. The water challenges we've set up for you today are designed to test your strengths in leadership, resolve, problem solving and courage. Today won't be easy for many of you, but it will reveal your strengths and weaknesses so that together we can work through them. Remember, reveal to heal."

Everyone repeated the lame camp catchphrase, but it wasn't up to Sage's standards.

"I can't hear you, Wanderers."

"Reveal to heal!" Hazel shouted along with her fellow campers.

"That's more like it. Alright, let's get this water quest under way."

After Sage and the counselors gave them all a demonstration about how to use their paddles and handle their kayaks, Hazel reluctantly took her place in line. Watching everyone before her haphazardly steer their kayaks down the fast-flowing river did little to boost her confidence. The bright red kayaks looked like little floating kazoos and the closer she got to the front of the line the more her anxiety grew.

The kayaks were unforgiving as the campers tried to navigate them down the river between gates. It seemed like the smallest miscalculation sent them tipping over, which happened a lot since part of the challenge was paddling them through specific gates to collect flags.

The girl who had gone ahead of Hazel had flipped her kayak over and trudged out of the river, teeth chattering. So far, she'd been the only one not able to roll the kayak back up to right herself after tipping.

That was probably the scariest part in Hazel's mind.

She glanced to where Jamie was waiting for his turn on the opposite bank. Sage was running two heats at once so the obstacle course wouldn't take all day. Jamie was a few behind Hazel in line, but his side seemed to be moving faster so they'd probably end up on the river at the same time. That thought gave her comfort.

Jamie smiled when he caught Hazel's eye and gave her a

thumbs up. She tried to give him a confident smile back, but her hands were starting to sweat despite the frigid weather.

The temperature usually climbed to the fifties by noon, but Hazel could tell it wouldn't reach that high today. The clear sky and blustery wind didn't offer any shelter. As Hazel got closer to the water, she felt the spray coming off of it and swore. It felt like freezing rain needling her skin. The majority of her was covered in the camp-provided wetsuit, but her hands and face were exposed to the elements and it wasn't pleasant.

She shuddered, imagining what it would feel like to be submerged in the river. *Incentive to stay upright, Hazel.*

Finally, it was her turn. As Sage helped Hazel into her kayak, she began to panic. She didn't like how trapped she felt once she was in the cockpit, the rubber spray skirt sealed around her.

"You ready?" Sage asked, holding the kayak steady in the raging water.

Hazel could feel the power of the river as the water rushed under and around her tiny bobbing boat. The last thing she was, was ready, but she knew there was no getting out of this.

Hazel looked across the river one more time. Jamie was there, giving her an encouraging smile. She smiled back and took a deep breath, nodding to Sage.

"Alright. We're gonna count you in," Sage barked. "Start paddling as soon as I let go."

She nodded again and held her breath as Sage counted backward.

"3 ... 2 ... 1 ..."

James

. . .

JAMES HAD BEEN WATCHING Hazel paddle to her first gate when someone in line behind him nudged him. "You're up man."

"Oh, um, do you wanna go ahead of me?" James asked. He'd been hoping to watch Hazel's run but the guy behind him didn't look too eager to take his place.

"Nah, I'm good."

James grumbled under his breath, but stepped into the water, grabbing his paddle as he prepared to get in his kayak. He didn't waste any time getting settled in the cockpit. If he couldn't watch Hazel's run, he could at least catch up with her so they could celebrate at the finish line together. Then maybe he'd be able to sneak a kiss in before he had to return to his group for the rest of the afternoon.

He hated that they'd been put on opposite teams their last full day together. After this morning, James was getting far too used to having Hazel at arm's reach. His chest tightened when he thought about having to spend a week hiking the mountains without her. *And longer after that . . .*

He wouldn't let himself think about the distance that would separate them after camp ended. He was convinced something would work out. It had to, because already he couldn't imagine his life without Hazel in it.

HAZEL

HAZEL WAS through her third gate and to her surprise she'd managed to collect all three flags without tipping her kayak. Her time wasn't going to shatter any records, but that wasn't her goal. She just wanted to finish without taking a dunk in the river. Last night's Polar Plunge had been more than enough.

Plus, this time she wouldn't have Jamie to cling to.

Just thinking about him flushed her with warmth. *Focus, Hazel.*

She only had four gates left and thinking about how it had felt clinging to Jamie's naked body had cost her hours of sleep last night. She didn't need those thoughts creeping back into her mind and distracting her from the finish line.

She was almost to the fourth gate, her heart pounding in her chest as she paddled hard to reach the flag. She stopped paddling a bit too late and her momentum carried her straight into the gate. She tried to correct herself with a quick back paddle, but the current had other ideas, whipping her kayak around until she was moving backward down the river.

Hazel panicked trying to right herself. She was twisting and turning in her seat, but the damn spray skirt restricted her movements. She pressed against the foot pads trying to get some leverage and adjust her weight, but she overcorrected and all at once the sky was replaced by freezing cold river water.

She shrieked but the sound was drowned out by a mouth full of water, then nothing at all.

James

JAMES HEARD Hazel's scream and his heart plummeted to his feet like an anchor. His eyes instantly scanned the river for her kayak, and when he found it, all reason left his body.

The red hull was facing the sky as it rushed down the river toward a shallow shoal dividing the river. *Where is she?*

If she didn't pop up before she hit that shoal . . .

He didn't even finish the thought. Instinct and panic overtook his actions, fueling his muscles with adrenaline that had him shredding through the water like the devil himself was chasing him. James was alongside Hazel's kayak in seconds. As soon as he grabbed the stern cleat, he knew something was terribly wrong. The upside-down boat was way too heavy. There was resistance where there shouldn't be.

Fuck! Hazel was still in it!

James didn't hesitate. He tore himself out of his cockpit and hit the water in one breath, not coming up for air until he had Hazel in his grasp. Her legs were still half in her cockpit making it difficult to drag her to the surface. He needed to get her to the bank, but she was still attached to her kayak and pulling it against the current wouldn't be possible.

James forced himself to remain level-headed. He could do this. He had to. He couldn't put Hazel down. She was unconscious and he couldn't tell if she was breathing. Every alarm in his body was blaring at full blast. He had to get her to land.

He cradled her in his arm, putting her back against his chest while he held her head above the rushing water. He braced his legs against the hull of her kayak and used his free hand to steer them like rudder, avoiding shoals and rocks the best he could as the current pulled them down stream.

But it was taking too long, and he could tell from Hazel's utter stillness that she wasn't breathing. With one last surge of energy he kicked against the hull of the kayak trapping her body. It finally budged, letting Hazel slip out to her knees. One more kick freed her completely and James swam the fastest heat of his life as he made a beeline for shore, his heart in his hands.

25

Hazel

WATER FLOWED down the beautiful lines of Jamie's face in glistening rivulets. The sun above his head cast a rainbow-hewn halo around him that made Hazel's heart thump against her ribs in an unsteady way. His lips pressed to hers and she sighed.

How had she ever resisted him for so long? He was exquisitely breathtaking.

Her chest physically burned when he kissed her. *Is this what love feels like?*

"Hazel, please," Jamie whispered.

She wondered what he wanted. Whatever it was she was certain she'd give it to him. She couldn't listen to him say her name like that and not want to give him the world. She tried to focus, to remember what it was they were talking about so she could tell him, *yes, it's yours,* but her head hurt.

Actually, everything hurt.

His lips met hers again and she inhaled a breath—*his breath!*

Suddenly, things began to come back into focus. There was a crowd of faces around her, a hushed chorus of concerned voices joined Jamie's and the sound of raging water rose above all of it. *The river!*

Everything came rushing back at Hazel, including the contents of her stomach. Jamie rolled her to her side and held her while she retched cold water and her breakfast all over the ground. She would've been embarrassed but trying to drag oxygen into her lungs was taking all of her focus.

"Easy," Jamie coaxed rubbing her back. "I've got you. Try to take slow, deep breaths."

After a few seconds she got her breathing under control and he sat her up.

Hazel began to shake uncontrollably in his arms.

"Are you hurt?" he asked.

She didn't think so, more terrified and mortally embarrassed than anything. She shook her head and he pulled her close, pressing kisses to her wet hair while he rubbed soothing circles on her back. She burst into tears and she didn't even know why.

She heard Sage's rough voice breaking through the comfort she'd found in Jamie's arms. "Walker? You alright?"

"She needs to go to medical," Jamie said defensively.

"Can she talk?" Sage asked.

"Yes," Jamie replied.

"Good, then let her." Sage turned his attention back to Hazel, pulling her out of Jamie's arms to do his own assessment. "Did you hit your head, Walker?"

"No."

"Do you feel faint or dizzy?"

"I don't think so."

"Okay." He patted her on the shoulder. "Take a breather and you can go again when we get to the end of the line."

Jamie was in Sage's face in a instant. "Are you out of your mind? She wasn't breathing when I fished her out of the river! She nearly drowned. She's not going again."

"Don't be so dramatic. She's fine. That's what perseverance is all about. When life knocks you down, you gotta get back up again."

Jamie practically growled in Sage's face. "I'm taking her to medical."

"Go ahead. I'm not gonna stop ya. But they're gonna say the same thing I am. She just got scared. Only cure for that is to get back on the horse, so to speak."

"Did they teach you that in boot camp?" Jamie muttered. "'Cause news flash, this isn't the Army."

"No, that's a life lesson, kid. One you might've learned by now if society didn't placate to your every overprivileged wish."

Jamie's jaw twitched so furiously Hazel thought the veins in his neck were going to burst. Somehow, he managed to rein in his temper. "We're going to medical," he muttered through clenched teeth.

"Fine. Like I said, I can't stop ya. But if you both don't get your hides back here for the next challenge, you can expect a DQ for the day."

Jamie turned to face Hazel, blocking Sage from her view. "Hazel, I think you should get checked out by medical. We can come back here after if you want, but I'm not okay with you getting back in the water without a professional evaluation first."

"Okay," she whispered.

"Okay." Jamie took her hand and tension ebbed from his

limbs.

Hazel tried to take a step to follow him away from the river, but her feet felt like lead. She stumbled but before she had the chance to right herself, she was in Jamie's strong arms. She imagined he looked like a fireman carrying a wet kitten, but she didn't even care. All she knew was that he made her feel safe. What else really mattered?

She looped her arms around his neck and buried her face in his shoulder as he carried her away from one of the most terrifying moments of her life. It was ridiculous to be happy right now, but she was.

It was possible that nothing in her life had ever felt as good as Jamie's arms around her in that moment. If she could curl up and live there, she would.

James

JAMES PACED in the waiting room of the tiny medical cabin.

A nurse had taken Hazel back about thirty minutes ago and with each passing second his anxiety grew. He hated not knowing what was going on. Hazel had seemed much calmer by the time they arrived at medical but James couldn't forget the way she'd trembled in his arms as he'd carried her there.

Hazel, who always seemed larger than life despite her miniscule size, had shivered against his chest, curling into him like his arms were the only things holding her together. James thought he'd have enjoyed having Hazel let him comfort her, but it was just the opposite. He felt unwavering fear, because her submission only proved how scared she truly was, and how close he'd come to losing her.

Perhaps he shouldn't have been surprised. He'd always

known the truth . . . that his heart was already in her chest, beating right alongside hers.

He couldn't live without her. And that's why he hadn't hesitated a moment to think about his own safety when he rushed into the water to save her. The second she'd disappeared under water, all the parts of him that mattered disappeared right along with her and he wouldn't be whole again until he had her in his arms.

The sound of the nurse's shoes squeaking in the hall grabbed James's attention.

The stern-faced woman faced him and began to speak. "You can see her now—"

James was already halfway to Hazel's room before the nurse finished her sentence. He felt like he took his first breath in hours when he finally set eyes on Hazel again.

She was sitting on an exam table in an oversized yellow hospital gown that made her look like a child, all knobby knees and sharp elbows. She looked so small and frail, but a shy smile sketched across her face when she saw him, giving James the strength he needed to hold it together and walk into the exam room slowly.

He wanted to run to Hazel and scoop her into his arms, never letting go. But he resisted, terrified that he might cause further damage somehow, because though she was smiling, she looked seconds away from tears.

"Hey," she said when he approached the table.

"Hey yourself." James took her hand. "Are you okay?"

She nodded. "Yep, cleared with a clean bill of health."

He released a breath he hadn't realized he was holding. "Thank God."

Hazel blinked up at him, biting her lip sheepishly. "I'm sorry I freaked you out."

He freed her lip gently with his thumb, letting his hand

linger on her chin. "Yeah, I could do without a scare like that for probably the next hundred years." He placed her hand on his pounding chest. "My heart's fragile enough, Smalls."

Hazel looked like she had a question on the tip of her tongue when the nurse walked back into the room carrying a clipboard and bundle of fabric. "Okay Miss Walker, I found you some scrubs to wear. Sign here and you're released."

James backed away to give the nurse some room. He used the time to put on a brave face for Hazel's sake. She didn't need to see how shaken he was.

When the nurse left them again, he moved back to Hazel's side playfully squeezing her knees. "What do ya say? Wanna blow this popsicle stand?"

"Yes, please."

He gave her a moment of privacy to change and when she met him at the door, he scooped her off her feet again. "Where to, Princess?"

She fought a smile. "I *can* walk, ya know?"

"But why bother when you have such a hot ride?"

She rolled her eyes and he relaxed at the familiar gesture. But then the gold flecks in her caramel eyes dimmed. "I don't think I can do it," she said quietly.

"Do what?"

"Go back to the river."

James clenched down on his swift anger, his jaw muscles flexing. He hated that Sage had even suggested Hazel continue the day's ridiculous water sports after what she'd been through, but James was doing his best to respect whatever decision Hazel made. "It's up to you."

She bit her lip, hesitating before answering him. "I can't do it. I just wanna go back to my cabin."

James exhaled a breath of relief into Hazel's hair and planted a gentle kiss on her head. "Cabin it is."

26

H azel

"JAMIE, don't skip because of me," Hazel argued, her hands wrapped around her torso against the chill as she stood on the stoop outside her cabin with Jamie.

"If you're not going, then neither am I," he said stubbornly.

"Sage will give you a zero for the day. It'll screw up your score."

Jamie crossed his arms over his broad chest. "Does it look like I care? Now get inside before you freeze to death. I wanna take care of my girl."

Hazel smirked, wondering how selfish it made her that she was happy Jamie didn't want to leave her side. Truthfully, the only thing she wanted to do was curl up with him. She'd stopped shaking from her near drowning ordeal, but it would be a long time before she'd forget the panic the icy water had filled her with.

Whoever said drowning was a peaceful way to go had obviously never tried it. There wasn't a shred of peace left in her memory now. The only thing that soothed her was being in Jamie's arms.

Hazel tried to tell herself it was just because he was the one who pulled her out of the water, but she knew it was more than that. He'd saved her in more ways than just rescuing her from the raging rapids. It felt like she'd been fighting against an insurmountable current for most of her life and Jamie was the first thing to give her something sturdy to hold onto. He was the first thing she *wanted* to hold onto.

It was strange that someone who she was convinced was as messed up as she was could anchor her, but he did. Just looking at him gave her strength. Maybe it was because for the first time, she truly felt like she wasn't alone in a world full of people who didn't understand her.

It was true that Jamie Forrester came from a completely different world than she did, but somehow, Hazel couldn't feel closer to him.

James

JAMES FOLLOWED Hazel into her cabin, taking in the familiar set up with fresh eyes. Even though he'd been staying in an identical cabin for the past week there was something exciting about being inside Hazel's for the first time and it wasn't just that he was violating the 'no boys in girls cabin' rule. James simply wanted a further glimpse into Hazel's world.

How could he not want to know more about the girl who'd captured his heart?

Right away, he could tell that the bottom bunk to his right was Hazel's. Her pink boots sat neatly next to the bed and finding his sweatshirt tucked over the rungs by her pillow made him feel way too warm and fuzzy inside. He pulled it from the bed and started to bunch it up, ready to pull it over her head.

"Let me get out of these scrubs first," Hazel said, moving to her dresser and digging through some drawers. She found what she was looking for and turned to face him. "Can you turn around?"

"You know I've already seen you naked, right?" he teased.

"Yes, but that was different."

"How?"

"Because . . . it was dark and you were naked too."

He chuckled. "Are you asking me to take my clothes off, Smalls? 'Cause I totally will."

Her face turned pink. "Just turn around, perv."

He held his hands up in surrender and turned around, smirking when he realized he was facing a mirror that fully displayed her. He was just wondering if he should be honest or enjoy the show when she turned her back to him and took off her top.

All the words he might've said died a slow death as he took in the beautiful curve of her spine in the mirror. Her flawless golden skin created a map that he wanted to explore. Admiring Hazel's reflection was so much more enthralling than the glimpse of her he'd seen that night on the dock.

It made him feel like he was staring at a reflection of his heart. God, how she possessed it. James swallowed hard but the tightness in his chest made it impossible for him to move. All he could do was watch.

Just before Hazel's long dark locks fell into place, his eyes caught on a tiny tattoo inked at the base of her neck. Before he could make out what it was, she shrugged into an oversized black t-shirt that fell to her knees. She stepped out of her borrowed scrub bottoms and turned back to face him, their eyes meeting in the mirror.

Hazel stilled and James slowly turned around closing the distance between them. His fingers were unable to hold back from touching her tattoo. He stroked a hand down her hair and brushed the silky locks aside to reveal the delicate tattoo peeking out from the back of her shirt collar.

"I didn't know you had a tattoo," he said, tracing the tribal starburst pattern that graced her perfect skin. "A sun?"

She nodded.

"Does it have a special meaning?"

She still hadn't said a word, seemingly frozen beneath his touch.

When goose bumps erupted beneath his fingers he backed off, realizing he'd just asked her a rather personal question. "Sorry. You don't have to tell me."

"No, it's okay," she said quietly angling her head so she was looking at him over her shoulder.

He was struck with a sudden urge to photograph her.

She smiled absently as her own fingers caressed the tattoo. "I guess I got it to remind me that no matter how dark it gets, the light will always return in the morning."

Her words shocked him. It was like she'd torn them from his own heart.

He, too, felt like the night brought a poison that could only be burned away with the dawn of a new day.

James blinked at Hazel, wondering how the hell it was possible to feel so completely connected to someone he'd only just met. *But have we just met, Hazel?*

Sometimes it felt like she was the other half of him that he'd always been missing. Maybe people weren't born whole, and this was what finding your other half felt like.

James just stared at her tattoo, not really sure how to convey his feelings.

"I don't think I've ever admitted that to anyone before," Hazel said softly. "Whenever I'm asked about my tattoo, I just say I like the sun."

James took a step closer and slid his hand down Hazel's shoulder, not stopping until his fingers were threaded through hers. He leaned his forehead against her temple, their breath mingling together. "The nights are the hardest for me too," he whispered. "At least they were, until I met you."

He felt her breath catch. "Me?"

"Hazel, I'm afraid you're the only light I'll ever need." He closed his eyes. "And today . . . when I thought I'd lost you . . ." He couldn't finish his thought, but luckily, he didn't have to.

Hazel turned in his arms, her lips brushing against his before he finished speaking.

All it took was the first sweep of her tongue against his and he was lost—a tangle of limbs and lips, hands and hearts. They were so passionately entwined that James didn't know where he ended and she began.

HAZEL

HAZEL'S HEART was fluttering against her ribs like a bird in a cage as Jamie followed her into her bed. This was the furthest she'd ever gone with a boy.

The mattress groaned under his weight, but he felt delicious on top of her. Somehow, their kissing had led them here, pressed together beneath the covers. She shouldn't be surprised. Really the only shocking thing was that they were both still dressed.

Jamie had somehow managed to strip out of his wetsuit while they furiously groped each other, but he was still wearing boxers and a white t-shirt that clung to his muscles in the most delicious way. As appealing as it was, Hazel wanted it gone. She couldn't seem to get close enough to him. And the way he kissed her made her want to climb inside him and know him from the inside out.

She tugged at the hem of his shirt, fighting the urge to whimper as each inch revealed the abs of a god. Jamie helped her, pulling the shirt over his head and tossing it away. This time she couldn't stay quiet. He was too beautiful not to be admired. His pale skin stretched taut across lean muscle, flawless save for a faded two-inch scar below his collarbone.

Had she not been mere inches from him she might not have noticed it at all because her eyes were drawn to the tattoo just above it. The word *Jane* was scrawled in a thin black cursive font that made her chest feel like it was caving in.

Jamie's words from their very first day together came back to her.

Jane . . . it was his mother's name.

Jamie stilled as Hazel's fingers slid over the velvet soft skin of the scar. He closed his eyes and she pressed her lips into his scar, wishing for all the world that she could take away his pain.

James

. . .

WHEN HAZEL KISSED HIS SCAR, James wanted to bury himself beneath her skin and never resurface. It was the single most comforting sensation he'd ever experienced. For a moment, their eyes met and understanding passed between them. They'd both shared a loss that would never truly leave them, but somehow having both experienced it made it hurt a little bit less.

Each touch, each kiss, dulled the bone-deep pain in epic proportion. The sensation was addicting, and James was positive he might never be able to drag himself from her bed.

He shifted Hazel beneath him, her slender legs hooking around his waist. A whimper of pleasure broke from her as he kissed his way down her neck. He had to stop and collect himself as her hips moved against his. Breathing hard in her ear he whispered, "Is this okay?"

She nodded quickly, her breath coming as fast as his. "I've never done this before," she whispered. "H-have you?"

He nodded. "Do you have a condom?"

She bit her lip, her cheeks flushing magenta. "No. And I'm not . . . um . . . taking anything, like preventatively."

"You're not on the pill?"

She shook her head and James let his face crash into the pillow next to her. "You're killin' me, Smalls."

She gave him a look that was part grin, part grimace and buried her face into his neck as if conveying her equal devastation. "Maybe we could still do it . . . I mean if you want to?" she said, anxious hope lacing her breathy voice.

You want this too, don't you, Hazel? James could see the matched desire in her beautiful eyes. And God he wanted her! But he wanted to be safe. No condom, no sex. Besides, knowing she wanted him too . . . it was enough—*for now.*

He grinned at her. "No, when we do it, and we are gonna do it, it's gonna be somewhere deserving of us." He gestured to the tiny bunkbed. "This place can't handle what I want to do to you."

She laughed. "You should really work on your confidence. Has anyone ever told you that?"

"Just you wait," he whispered teasing her with kisses.

"Why don't you put your money where your mouth is?" she taunted back wriggling beneath him.

He raised his eyebrows, loving the flirtatious side she was revealing. "You couldn't handle this," he teased.

She matched his smug grin and pulled her shirt up over her head, tossing it on the floor with his. "Care to test your theory?"

He stared down at her lacey bra and somehow found his words. "Challenge accepted."

HAZEL

HAZEL WAS WRONG, she *could* feel closer to Jamie. And he made certain that she knew it. She fisted the sheets as his lips kissed a trail down her body. When he kissed the hollow between her collarbone . . . *O. M. G!* There were no words.

Did people know how magical that was?

Why weren't more songs written about that spot?

But as his kisses moved lower, Hazel had a sneaking suspicion she was about to find out what truly inspired people to write love songs. The moment his head disappeared beneath the covers, she closed her eyes and let go of everything she thought she knew about the world. Stars exploded behind her eyes as Jamie's kisses shattered her apart.

In the aftermath, as they lay together, a tangle of elastic

limbs and pounding hearts, she knew nothing would ever be the same.

How could it be when she knew, even if she managed to find all the pieces of herself that lay in their wreckage, that she'd never fit back together the same way again? Not when she'd given Jamie all of herself . . . *Well, almost.*

But as he stroked her hair and placed gentle kisses on her cheeks, looking at her the way no other boy had ever looked at her, Hazel realized she didn't care how badly this might end. She'd let this boy break her apart over and over just to see that look on his face a moment longer.

Jamie could have all the pieces of her, because she was already broken when he found her. The difference was, now she knew that he was too, and somehow, the sum of their broken parts made her feel whole.

James

JAMES REALIZED two things at once as he watched Hazel dress. He would be forever grateful to his father for forcing him to come to this god-awful camp, and that he would fight him to the death if need be to make sure she remained a part of his life. James had been wrong to think he knew what happiness was before today. Happiness for him could only ever dwell in Hazel's arms.

He was a fool to think her kissing his tattoo was the most comforting sensation he'd ever experienced. He hadn't even scratched the surface with her yet.

He knew things between them were still building, growing into an inferno of passion that would consume them both if he wasn't careful. It had been nearly impossible to stop what they'd started under the covers, but James had meant what he said. He wanted to wait. Their first time should be somewhere special, worthy of what was developing between them.

And even though it killed him to leave Hazel's cabin, now full of intimate memories and meaningful glances, he did, knowing the best things were worth waiting for.

27

H azel

WHEN HAZEL WALKED into the crowded dining hall, Jamie's hand tightened around hers like he could sense her fear. Earlier, he'd managed to chase away her memories from the river, but as every head swiveled in her direction, she felt like she was drowning again.

After they grabbed their trays of food, Kat spotted them and waved them over. With plates piled full of meatloaf, mashed potatoes and apple pie, Hazel and Jamie joined their usual table.

They weren't even sitting down yet when Kat started babbling. "Hazel, are you okay? I can't believe Sage is being such a jerk, but I knew something like this would happen." She shook her head giving them an *I told you so* look. "The Couples' Curse is the real deal and it looks like everyone's pegged you guys as this year's victims."

"Will you stop?" Jamie snapped. "There's no curse! It's just a bunch of gossip bored camp kids make up."

"Uh, no it's not," Kat argued. "Check the score board."

Jamie balked. "What are you talking about?"

Sawyer piped up. "Do you seriously not know?"

"Does this look like the face of someone in the know?" Jamie replied, crossly.

"Sage DQ'd you both for the day," Kat answered. "It dropped you both to the middle of the pack. You guys are partners for Crossroads."

Hazel blinked back her shock rapidly, hoping she was somehow hallucinating. "What? That's not possible. We can't be partners."

Paisley rolled her eyes, mumbling bitterly to herself. "I would've fallen out of a kayak to be his partner."

Hazel narrowed her eyes at her roommate. "We don't *want* to be partners. It'll ruin us."

"So you're admitting you're an 'us'?" Paisley shot back.

Jamie ignored her, catching Hazel's eye. "Is being my partner really that bad?"

"Couples' Curse," Kat whispered in a ghoulish voice.

Jamie banged his fist on the table making all the girls jump. "Will you shut up? There's no such thing as a curse."

Kat sucked in a breath and Sawyer looked offended. "You know the kind of people who don't believe in curses? The ones who are cursed."

Jamie turned back to Hazel. "This is the kind of shit a bunch of bitter prep school kids invent to make their time here seem more interesting. Tell me you know that, Smalls?"

She swallowed, nodding feebly, wishing she held Jamie's confidence. Normally, she didn't believe in that sort of thing, but she'd already thought things with Jamie were too good to be true. Hazel knew better than to think life was some big fairytale. She'd never expected a happy ending. Guys like Jamie didn't fall for girls like her.

A sinking feeling filled her chest, chasing away all the bliss of earlier. She should've known better. As soon as she'd let herself follow her heart and fall for Jamie, she'd been doomed. Nearly drowning and now their Crossroads partnership were just the early warning signs. Nothing this perfect could last.

James

JAMES DIDN'T LIKE the way Hazel had clammed up.

All through dinner she hadn't said more than two words while her ridiculous roommates filled her head with more curse nonsense. The fact that she hadn't eaten spoke volumes. The Hazel he knew never missed a meal and today, she'd skipped two, missing lunch to romp under the covers with him and now dinner.

James watched in agitated silence as Hazel pushed her food around her plate with her fork like an anxious bulldozer.

This Couples' Curse thing was getting out of control. Enough was enough.

After dinner, James took Hazel's hand and led her up to their stone bench. The sun had already dipped behind the mountains, but the sky was still painted with streaks of amber light.

James sat down and pulled Hazel onto his lap. "Hey," he said, tilting her face to his. "Don't let them ruin this."

She looked at him, her eyes already watering. "They're not wrong."

"Hazel, they're sad, jealous twits. There's no curse."

"I'm not an idiot. I don't think we've been hexed or anything like that. But you can't deny that hiking a hundred miles would test anyone's relationship and ours—"

"Ours is perfect," he interrupted.

Her caramel eyes glowed with heartache. "Jamie, we've known each other for a week. We've been more than friends for barely a day. The last few hours with you . . . they've been some of the best of my life. But that's why we shouldn't even consider doing the hike together."

"Why not?"

"Because, we won't get what we're meant to out of it and we'll risk ruining what just happened between us."

"Or something even more amazing could happen." He took her face in her hands. "Hazel, we only have a week left here. The idea of not spending every second of that time with you guts me. This is a gift."

"Or a curse."

"I know you don't believe that. I was there today," he tucked a lock of her dark hair behind her ear. "I felt what you felt. It was . . ." he shook his head searching for words to sum up his feelings. "You can't tell me it wasn't everything you've been searching for."

She couldn't meet his eyes and he knew it was because he was right. "It's just gonna make it harder when this ends."

"Or it'll make us fight harder to make sure it doesn't end."

Hazel pinned him with a pained glare. "Jamie . . . don't."

"Don't what?"

"Don't fill my head with things that can never happen. We have to be realistic."

"Fine, let's be realistic. I have the opportunity to go on a once in a lifetime hike with someone I can't get enough of. I'm crazy about her and I'm pretty sure she feels the same way too, but her delinquent roommates are filling her head with nonsense."

"It's not nonsense."

James frowned. "Listen, if you legitimately don't want to do this with me because you're uncomfortable to be alone with me or you think I'll hold you back from experiencing everything you came here to find, then fine, I'll be the first to go talk to Dr. Birch and tell him we can't be partners. But if you're scared of some stupid campfire stories or of your feelings for me, I don't accept it, Hazel, because I'm pretty damn certain I'm exactly what you need in your life. You're sure as hell what I need in mine."

She almost smiled and he could tell he was winning her over, which was a damn good thing because he didn't want to tell her that spending a week without her by his side would be detrimental to his health. He could already feel his pacemaker working overtime to keep his heart steady while his anxiety spiked through the heavens.

The idea of Hazel with another partner threw James into a blind rage, not to mention the fact that whoever got stuck with him as a partner would be signing a week-long sentence for emotional torture. James would be a basket case, worrying about Hazel the whole time.

He blew out a steadying breath. It was strange how love and insanity felt so similar.

"Look, I know this wasn't what you had planned when you came here, but this is where we are. I'm pretty sure I'm falling in love with you, Smalls. And if we can survive this, we can survive anything. So what do ya say? You wanna take the plunge with me one more time?"

HAZEL

. . .

DID SHE EVER!

The idea of having a week with Jamie all to herself sounded like paradise to Hazel.

They'd have endless time to get to know each other, not to mention the prospect of sharing a sleeping bag with him made her so warm and toasty they probably wouldn't even need a fire. This wasn't what they'd agreed to. But to be fair, all previous arrangements prior to what happened in her bedroom today seemed null and void.

Maybe we need a new set of lines?

"Jamie, I don't regret anything. Taking your hand the night we jumped into the lake will always be one of the highlights of my life. And what we shared today . . ." she trailed off, blushing at the memories that would live in her mind forever. "But we only agreed to explore this until Crossroads."

"I know that, but here we are. The universe has thrown us together and I'm pretty sure it's for a reason. I'm willing to see it through. The question is, are you?"

Hazel stood on the precipice—her own literal crossroads. She had two choices, Jamie or reality. Reality would ultimately win, the question was how long could she put it off? Spending more time with him would only make it hurt worse in the end.

Jamie seemed to sense her dilemma and gave his final argument. "Listen, the only thing I've learned here that's been worth a damn is that we make our own destiny." He pressed a kiss to her lips. "You're it, Smalls. And if you want this too then you gotta start fighting, right now."

Wow, he was quoting Sage! Hazel knew that took resolve considering how much Jamie hated him. He'd looked like he'd wanted to punch the counselor in the face earlier today. Maybe if Jamie could put his feelings aside to find wisdom in

Sage's words, they actually had a chance at surviving this thing.

Hazel took a deep breath. "I have two conditions."

A wide smile split Jamie's face.

"Stop smiling, you haven't even heard them yet."

"It doesn't matter. I'll agree to anything."

"I'm glad you feel that way because I don't think you're going to like my rules."

"Shoot."

She gestured between them. "We put whatever this is between us on hold until we complete Crossroads."

"And?"

"And we keep it in our pants till after the hike."

"What does that mean?"

"No kissing, hand holding or couple-y things."

"Deal," he replied eagerly.

Hazel cocked an eyebrow. "Did you hear what I said? You can't kiss me or anything. From this moment on we're just partners."

"Loud and clear."

"Then what are you so smug about?"

"I'm not smug."

"You're the epitome of smug." She crossed her arms. "You think I'm gonna cave and crawl into your sleeping bag when I'm cold, don't you?"

He winked. "You got a taste, Smalls. I know you'll be back for more."

She rolled her eyes. "I'm gonna have to pack my own tent. There won't be room for me in yours with that big head."

Jamie walked Hazel back to her cabin, chattering excitedly

about all his ideas for the hike. Now that he'd gotten her to agree to be his partner, he was in full on planning mode. She hated to admit it, but she was actually sort of grateful that her kayak mishap coupled them. Jamie seemed to have a lot of good ideas about how to pack their gear and divide up the hike, most of them she never would've thought of on her own.

Plus, spending the next week with him would be fun. She had to complete Crossroads with someone. It might as well be someone she enjoyed. And it comforted her to know that when she looked back on these memories, he'd always be a part of them.

The thought was bittersweet. Because as much as she wanted Jamie to be a part of her future, she knew that wouldn't be possible. She wished things could be different, but wishing never amounted to anything but wasted time, as Gramps would say.

When they finally reached her cabin, Jamie pulled Hazel in for a kiss, but she quickly held a hand up and his lips met her palm. "Not so fast, bub."

"Oh, come on. Crossroads hasn't even started yet."

"I was serious about my conditions, Jamie. You need to show me you can do this."

"Can't we start tomorrow?"

She was dying on the inside as he gave her his best sinful smile, but her exterior was unflinching.

"Fine," he leaned against her doorframe, his lips a breath away from hers. "But I have one condition of my own."

"What's that?"

"You need to call your father and tell him the truth."

"What do you mean?"

"You're about to go on a pretty serious hike. As your partner, it's my job to keep you safe. I can't do that if your family doesn't even know where you are."

She rolled her eyes, but this time it was Jamie who crossed his arms.

"Sorry, it's non-negotiable, Smalls."

Hazel pushed off her door, swearing under her breath as she fished Jamie's phone out of her pack. "I really don't appreciate you meddling in my personal life."

He only smiled. "You'll thank me later."

She huffed. "Shows how little you know me."

"Good thing we have a hundred-mile hike to change that."

God! Sometimes he was infuriating.

Hazel turned her back on Jamie and dialed her dad's number. She'd thought about putting up more of a fight, but it wouldn't make a difference. Jamie would probably just take his phone back and call her dad if she didn't do it herself. And God only knew what he'd say. At least this way she could control the situation.

She held her breath while the phone rang. What the hell was she even going to say?

'Hey Dad. How's it going? Everything's fine here. Oh, by the way, I'm actually in Montana, not Arizona. But don't worry, I'm about to hike a hundred miles with a complete stranger. Nothing to worry about. Okay then, good talk. See ya in a week.'

Thankfully, the call went to voicemail. She hung up and Jamie scowled at her. "That didn't sound like a confession."

"My dad didn't answer. I'm not explaining this through voicemail."

"Fine, but don't think you're off the hook."

"Fine."

They stood there staring at each other for a moment, Hazel holding the phone in her hand, Jamie holding her heart. She hated how her feelings for him could sneak up on her. One minute they were arguing, the next she was overwhelmed with the need to kiss him.

How the hell is my poor heart going to handle a hundred miles of this?

The blue of Jamie's eyes had taken on the dark tones of the night sky and Hazel felt lost in them as she fell under their spell. She wanted to know everything this beautiful boy held back behind those enchanting eyes. Did the world look different through them? It must. How else could she explain the way he looked at her?

What do you possibly see in me, Jamie Forrester?

Before Hazel could work up the courage to ask, the door opened behind her, interrupting their moment.

"Oh, sorry," Paisley muttered, not looking sorry at all. Then her face lit up when she spotted the phone Hazel still held in her hand. "Ohmigod!" she squealed swiping the phone from Hazel.

"Paisley, that's not mine."

"Well, whoever's it is won't mind if I use it," she sneered already searching her social media.

"Actually, they will," Jamie said, grabbing the phone from her hand. "It's mine and it's only for emergencies."

"But this is a social emergency," Paisley whined, batting her eyelashes at Jamie.

Hazel had to struggle to swallow her laughter. Paisley was an even bigger idiot than Hazel thought if she actually expected her weak ploys of flirtatious eye batting was going to get her anywhere with Jamie. When he laughed in her face, Hazel's chest swelled with pride.

"You've got to be joking," Jamie replied.

Paisley lips puckered into her famous sour lemon scowl. "I never joke about my followers."

Jamie huffed a laugh. "You're one of a kind, Paise."

Paisley beamed. "Thanks."

"It wasn't a compliment," he answered, handing the phone

back to Hazel and turning his back on Paisley. "Try your dad again, Hazel. I'm serious about him knowing the truth." Then he left.

Hazel stood outside her cabin, watching Jamie head off in the direction of his own. She could feel Paisley's eyes shooting daggers into her back. Hazel sighed, knowing the moment she turned around the battle would begin. The last thing she wanted to deal with right now was a barrage of questions from Paisley about why she had Jamie's phone. She knew it could probably be avoided if she'd just let the self-absorbed girl use it, but the child in Hazel didn't want to give Paisley the satisfaction.

She'd been nothing but rude to Hazel since day one. Most days she just ignored Paisley's scowls and bitter comments. Hazel didn't have time to waste stooping to that level of passive aggressive remarks, but she also wasn't going to let the girl walk all over her.

Hazel shoved the phone into her pocket and pushed past Paisley, into the cabin. The rest of her roommates were nowhere to be found. Perhaps they were in the bathhouse or enjoying one last S'mores Social.

Hazel groaned. *Great, at least if they were around, I'd have a Paisley-buffer.*

But no such luck.

Paisley followed Hazel into the single-room cabin, trailing her like a piranha that smelled blood. "You're gonna let me use that phone, right?"

Hazel stopped short and Paisley ran into her back. "Why would I do that, Paisley? Because you're always so sweet to me?"

"Are you kidding me, right now? You're the bitch here. Everyone knows you stole James from me even after I told you I liked him."

"You're delusional. I didn't steal anyone."

"Oh, so you two aren't together?"

"It's complicated." Hazel didn't know why she was even trying to explain their relationship to Paisley. It was pointless, considering she didn't know how to classify it herself.

Paisley narrowed her eyes. "I'm sure it is, what with him being entirely out of your league."

Anger flipped on like a switch. Hazel wanted to punch Paisley in her pretty blonde head. Her words hit home, cutting right to one of Hazel's biggest fears. That she was just an average-looking girl from a podunk town with a dead-end future. She didn't belong with someone like Jamie. She would only hold him back.

The fight drained from Hazel as she sat down on her bed. "That may be true, Paisley, but I'm still not letting you use this phone."

Fury simmered beneath Paisley's flawless makeup, turning her complexion a splotchy mix of pinks. "Well, if I'm not allowed to use it, then neither are you!" With that, she stormed out the door only to return a few minutes later with a counselor in tow.

Hazel felt like a toddler as the guy rooted through her bag and fished out the phone. After being scolded and having the phone confiscated, she was left with only her embarrassment.

Paisley sat cross-legged on her bed looking triumphant. "Betcha wish you'd just let me use the phone, huh?"

"Nope." Hazel rolled over in her bed and shut her eyes.

As embarrassing as the entire ordeal had been, she was clinging to her satisfaction that Paisley didn't get to use the phone.

Actually, Paisley had done Hazel a favor. Now she wouldn't be able to tell her dad the truth and there was nothing Jamie could do about it.

28

J ames

DESPITE HAZEL'S new rules and learning that his phone had been confiscated thanks to Paisley, James had a hard time being anything but excited about the day. Today was their last day at basecamp. Then he'd finally be heading out into the wilderness with Hazel.

How could he not be eager about a hundred miles of uninterrupted time with his dream girl?

After learning about Paisley's antics with the phone, James had decided it was probably best for him and Hazel to eat breakfast at a different table. They sat with his roommates for a change. They weren't as annoying as Hazel's, but they still made it impossible for James to have a real conversation with her.

He didn't like the idea that her father didn't know where

she was. On their way to the lodge for the Crossroads prep meeting, James expressed his concern. "I still think you should call him."

"How? We don't have a phone."

"I don't know. Talk to Dr. Birch. I'm sure he'll let you call him if you explain the situation."

"If I tell him my dad doesn't know I'm here I'll be admitting that I forged his signature on my admissions form. I'll get kicked out of the program."

James rubbed the pressure forming between his eyes. "I don't like it. What if something happens?"

"Nothing's going to happen. We'll be wearing GPS trackers and there's a checkpoint along the trail. Plus, I have the best partner on the mountain, right?"

She grinned at him and his heart melted. "Don't think you're gonna flirt your way out of this, Smalls." But he knew she totally was.

He didn't like the idea of her father not being informed of her whereabouts, but he also wouldn't risk having her sent home if Birch found out she'd forged her forms.

HAZEL

AFTER SITTING through two hours of boring lectures about the rules and regulations of the Crossroads hike, it was finally time to gear up. Thankfully, all of Hazel's gear was included with her scholarship.

She followed Jamie around the basecamp store picking up the items on their check list.

Tent. *Check.*

Compass. *Check.*

Sleeping bags. *Check.*
Flint. *Check.*
First aid kit. *Check.*
Pocket knife. *Check.*
Waterproof map. *Check.*
Rope. *Check.*
Mess kit. *Check.*
Food packs. *Check.*
Hydro packs. *Check.*
GPS band. *Check.*

The sleeping bags, Hydro packs and GPS bands were the only things they each got. Everything else was purposely set up as a single item to force teammates to work together.

Based on his score being slightly higher, James was awarded the navigator role, so he got to be in charge of the compass and map, while Hazel got the food, flint and first aid. There was only enough food for the first three days, but it was up to them to figure out the best way to ration it. When they reached the fourth day checkpoint, they'd be able to pick up their remaining food packs and replace any faulty gear.

Before leaving the camp store, each camper had to put on their GPS band and log it into the system to make sure it was working. They were to be worn on their right wrists at all times, while their camp issued watch was on their left. The compasses were to be kept on their right wrists too, separate from their watches. But Hazel didn't have to worry about that for the time being.

She put her GPS band on and got in line to get it logged in. Once they were all set, she headed out with Jamie to grab lunch, the excitement of what lay ahead taking hold.

At Prospects, Hazel grabbed some pre-packaged sandwiches and headed back out to meet Jamie in their favorite spot so they could get a jump on packing. They still had one last meeting to attend, then it was dinner and bed because Crossroads started at first light.

Of course, Jamie and Hazel wouldn't be heading out until well after.

Scoring a zero on water day had dropped them into the middle of the pack and since start times were based on performance, they wouldn't be one of the first teams leaving camp.

Hazel understood why the teams needed to be spread out, but she wasn't on board with why they all had to be at the starting line at the same time. *Something about morale . . .*

All it meant to her was less time in her warm, comfy bed.

That was probably the only thing she'd miss about basecamp. Well, okay, that and the food. But now that she'd started familiarizing herself with the gear, she found her excitement impossible to shake.

This was why she'd wanted to come to Wander Mountain. The Crossroads hike was a true adventure, designed to make you reach inside yourself, discover your limits and push past them. The notion inspired feelings of freedom she couldn't find in her everyday life. And the fact that she would get to share this experience with Jamie was even more enticing.

"So, what do you think is the best route?" Jamie asked smoothing the map out across his lap.

They were sitting on the stone bench again and even though it was the height of the afternoon, Hazel shivered as the cold stones leeched warmth from her. She checked her fancy new GPS band. It read 41 degrees; well below the norm for this time of year. She hoped that wasn't an omen for the weather to come.

"I'd say the most direct route is the best one," she replied through chattering teeth.

He put an arm around her shoulders. "Au contraire my

fair-weathered friend. Direct doesn't always equal best in the wild."

Hazel rolled her eyes, leaning into Jamie's warmth as she examined the map. "Well, we definitely should avoid any water crossings," she said running her finger across the blue lines of rivers standing between the start and finish.

"Yeah, I don't think that's an option. But you'll be fine as long as there aren't any kayaks."

She playfully elbowed him in the ribs.

"Too soon?"

Truthfully, she was glad he was joking about it. She still remembered the haunted look in his eyes when she'd come to, and how she'd finally made it disappear when she'd taken him to bed.

Hazel swallowed, the heat of that memory rushing through her like a forest fire. She had to put those kinds of feelings aside if they were going to make it through this hike as partners.

She focused on the map again. During today's endless training, many routes had been suggested, but they were also encouraged to blaze their own trail. Crossroads wasn't a race so it's not like they needed to find the route that was the fastest. And honestly finishing early didn't appeal to Hazel. Not when she knew she wanted to cherish every moment she could with Jamie.

"Maybe we should just make it up as we go."

He winked. "It's worked for us so far."

She couldn't help but smile. "Come on, I'm freezing. Let's head back to the lodge so we can get a seat near the fireplace."

Jamie stood up and crushed her against his side, laughing as they walked. "It's cute that you don't think you're gonna end up in my sleeping bag."

She ribbed him again. "I'm not."

He laughed harder. "Day one, Smalls. Day one."

James

JAMES HATED TO ADMIT IT, but most of what Dr. Hippie was blathering on about at the moment wasn't half bad. James didn't know if it was because Hazel was seated comfortably beside him, or if it was possible that their heavy hookup session yesterday had completely reprogrammed his brain. It was probably the latter. He'd been in a ridiculously good mood ever since.

No one stuck at Wander Mountain deserved to be this giddy, but he was.

In just a few hours he'd be heading out on a week-long backpacking trip with a girl who'd stolen his heart. Not only that but she'd also restored his faith in love and his will to live.

James knew it was absurdly cliché, not to mention obsessively codependent to put his happiness in the hands of another, but until Hazel, nothing else had worked. He couldn't argue with fact.

He hadn't had one suicidal thought since he met her. Even his anger seemed to dwell a bit further below the surface these days. It didn't hurt that every time he looked over at Hazel during Dr. Birch's speech, she grinned at him.

See, I'm even calling Dr. Hippie by his real name. I'm a changed man!

James knew Hazel was feeling the same level of excitement as he was. She was eagerly scribbling notes as she listened to Dr. Birch speak. "I want you to take this opportunity to pull out your field journals."

The rustling of movement drew James's attention back to Dr. Birch.

"Crossroads is about more than connecting people through a shared experience, it's also about connecting with your inner-self," he droned. "I want each of you to take a moment and ask yourself this one simple question. It will uncover a profound truth and that's what this is all about. Ask yourselves, *why*? Why are you taking this journey? What do you hope to get out of it? Take a moment to think about your *why*. When it comes to you, I want you to write it down in your journal. There are no right or wrong answers here. The only thing I will tell you is that your answer must come with conviction. It must come from a place of truth and you must be dedicated to the purpose it serves."

The room was full of rustling pages for a moment, then blistering silence. James caught Hazel watching him out of the corner of her eye. He nudged her pink boot with his foot. She gave him a shy smile and returned to her writing. James stared at a blank page in his notebook. *Why?* It was such a simple word with a myriad of difficult answers. He looked back at Hazel and the answer came to him as simple as breathing.

James wrote down his 'why' and closed the journal.

After a few moments, Dr. Birch continued his speech about the motivation behind the Crossroads challenge. "Years from now, when someone asks you about this experience, it won't be the gear you remember, or the physical exertion, or the route you took; it'll be the purpose that sticks with you.

"Keeping your purpose in mind when you confront the challenges that await you not only on the hike, but in life, will center you. This is why your field journal is so important. Keep it close to your chest. Revisit your answer often. Write down how your purpose has helped you overcome obstacles.

Write down how you've fallen short and how you can do better. Know that it's okay to let your purpose evolve.

"This journey isn't about resolving all your issues at once. So let go of those expectations right now. You are a work in progress. This journey will more than likely leave you with more questions about the world and your place in it. That's okay. Make this journey about being present in the moment, observing what's around you. Take in the simplicity and beauty of nature. Scale your problems against the vastness of the wilderness. I guarantee your burdens will weigh less when you reach the finish line.

"If you let it, Crossroads can lead you to what it truly means to live a fulfilled life. So, I encourage each and every one of you to let this journey make your souls larger and your hearts fuller, because I promise you, there is no better adventure or test of personal will and strength than opening yourself up and loving what you find."

There was a riotous round of applause and even Hazel joined in. James let himself get swept up in the excitement. He clapped along with the campers, watching as teammates hi-fived and slapped each other on the back.

"Remember," Dr. Birch said, switching to the final slide of his lecture. The camp's motto flashed up on the screen and the room echoed the statement along with him. "You can't find yourself without getting lost!"

James turned to gaze at Hazel and couldn't contain the smile that split his face.

I'm going to enjoy getting lost in you, Hazel Walker.

29

H azel

HAZEL WAS a bundle of nerves when she woke up on the morning of Crossroads. The sun wasn't even up when her alarm went off, but it was time to get ready.

She tiptoed out of the room and ran through the frosty air to the bathhouse. She wanted one more hot shower before the hike began.

By the time she got back to her cabin all her roommates were up. The tiny cabin was pure chaos—a whirlwind of camp gear and grumbling. Thankfully, Hazel completed all her packing the night before. So, she simply grabbed her pack and slipped out of her cabin, jogging down to Prospects to meet Jamie for one last hearty breakfast.

Hazel scarfed down two helpings of grits. Jamie did the same, eating his, 'Gramps style', as he liked to call it. He'd perfected her recommended mixture of cheese, bacon and scallions. Hazel was certainly going to miss this on the trail. With a grueling twenty miles to cover each day, it didn't leave much time to cook gourmet meals.

Their food pack consisted primarily of trail mix, PB&Js, jerky and protein bars. She'd snuck in a few of her own snacks when she'd been dividing their meals into rations. *Going cold turkey on her daily sugar fix wouldn't do anybody any good.*

She'd also scored half a dozen brownies at dinner last night and even managed to squeeze a box of Boston Baked Beans into the inside pocket of her jacket, along with a handful of Dum-Dums into the cargo pockets of her pants. She'd had to cut the sticks off the lollipops, but the sacrifice would be well worth it when she needed a sugar hit.

Jamie pulled out his field journal and flipped to a new page. Hazel watched him write on the waxy waterproof page. *Day 1: fueling up for the big hike. I'm pretty sure my partner packed enough sugar to send me into diabetic shock. Should I be worried? What if her plan is to fatten me up so she can eat me?*

Hazel shoved him. "Jamie! I'm gonna kill you! This is part of our final evaluation."

He bent his head over his notebook again and wrote. *The death threats have started. Good thing she's so cute.*

"Jamie Forrester!"

"What? We're supposed to write down all our feelings and private thoughts."

"Your thoughts aren't very private," she whispered. "Your smug grin might as well be a billboard that says you've seen my panties."

"I can't help it if I think you're incredibly sexy. And by the way if I look horny, it's your fault. You're the one who let me see your panties, and much more, I might add."

Jamie gave her a devious wink and she gasped. "Excuse me. How is your horniness my fault?"

"You're the one who made the no kissing rule." He bent over the notebook again and wrote. *If I die of blue balls, Hazel Walker is to blame.*

She pinched him hard and stomped out of the dining hall, trying not to smile as his laughter trailed behind her.

James

THIS WAS IT. Game time. The big day. James wondered if this was what his brothers felt like just before kickoff. Crossroads wasn't even a competition, but James felt adrenaline pumping through his veins. He was ecstatic that he'd secured Hazel as his partner for many reasons, but a surprising one was that her presence calmed him.

After a three-hour van ride, he and Hazel were standing at starting line C waiting for their numbers to be called. Every time a new group was called, James felt the nervous energy crowd his chest, but one look at Hazel soothed him.

The group ahead of them had left twenty minutes ago. James and Hazel had ten minutes until it was their turn. Five minutes. Four minutes. Three.

James was steadily watching his watch count down the seconds until their start time. The campers in their age group were the first to head out on the Crossroads journey. The sixteen-year-olds would leave tomorrow, the fifteen-year-olds the following day.

Three starting points were set up, all equal distance to the day four checkpoint. James and Hazel had drawn starting line C. It was the furthest east. It meant they would be traveling southwest to meet up with the checkpoint.

James pushed his sleeve up to glance at the compass. It

was securely fashioned on his right wrist between his GPS band and his prized possession. The Chopard watch was a gift from his mother and he never took it off.

The tiny compass looked like a toy nestled between his beloved watch and GPS band. But as long as it worked, he supposed that's all that mattered.

James checked their heading one more time and then consulted the map. After a moment he folded it and put it back in his pocket, reaching for Hazel's hand. "You ready to get real, Smalls?"

She looked from him to her watch and back. Only thirty seconds remained. Hazel swallowed hard and squeezed his hand. "Ready or not..."

HAZEL

THE HORN BLARED and they were off into the wild Montana mountains.

Hazel and Jamie started the adventure hand-in-hand. She found herself wondering if they would finish that way. *Probably not.* That was no way to be thinking on day one. *Shape up, Hazel.*

"So," Jamie said as they walked side-by-side through the mildly flat forest. "What's our first, life-altering Crossroads conversation going to be about?"

Hazel shrugged. "I'm kinda hungry."

He laughed. "Why do I have a feeling all your journal entries are going to be about food?"

She rolled her eyes. "If you're going to make fun of my healthy appetite, then I won't share my candy with you."

He perked up. "Candy? I didn't see that in the food pack."

"I improvised."

He snorted. "Look at you, my little rule breaker. I must be rubbing off on ya."

"Must be," she replied handing him a lollipop.

He examined it with mild amusement. "Where's the stem?"

She shrugged. "I had to conserve space."

He laughed, unwrapped it and popped it in his mouth, talking around the hard candy. "Okay, now that you've got your sugar fix, time to get real. After all, life doesn't start until you're lost," he said doing his best cheesy Dr. Birch impression.

"That's not even how it goes."

"Whatever, you know what I mean. Tell me something I don't know about you, partner."

"What do you wanna know?"

"College aspirations?"

"Don't have any."

He looked confused. "Then why go to Arizona for a college prep course?"

"I'm enrolled in an online college, but that doesn't count."

"Why not?"

"I don't know. It's not like it matters. I don't need a degree to run the repair shop. I've been working there since I could walk." Hazel's pack suddenly felt heavier after that admission.

It's not that it wasn't true, but to someone like Jamie it probably wasn't very impressive. She'd always been proud of her mechanic knowledge, but after a week at Wander Mountain she was beginning to realize just how unsophisticated she truly was.

She glanced at Jamie. He was watching her patiently. There wasn't an ounce of judgement in his perfect sky-blue eyes. She knew there wouldn't be. Her insecurities were all her own making.

This is why you're here, Hazel. Don't clam up. This is your chance to get a taste of that freedom you've always wanted.

Freedom. It was her 'why' word, her purpose. The answer to Dr. Birch's question. If she opened her field journal right now, she'd see that word: *freedom*.

The answer had come to her easily. The reason Wander Mountain had always appealed to her was because one look at the endless expanse of mountains and open air spoke to her of a pure unadulterated sense of freedom.

"I don't think college is really my thing," she finally admitted.

"No?"

"I don't know. I don't like textbooks or staring at a computer screen all day. I'm more of a hands-on learner."

Jamie quirked an eyebrow and grinned.

She bumped him with her shoulder. "Perv."

"I mean, ya kinda set yourself up for that one."

She rolled her eyes. "If you're gonna make this into a joke I'm not gonna tell you anything real."

He held his hands up in surrender. "Continue."

"I don't even know what I was saying now."

"That school's not your thing 'cause you're a hands-on kinda girl."

She cut her eyes at him. "Right."

"So, what *do* you want to do?"

"That's the thing, I really don't know. I know what I don't want to do, but that doesn't really solve anything."

"Why not?"

"Whining and wishing are just a waste of time."

"Where do you come up with this stuff?"

She smiled. "That's another Gramps original."

Jamie laughed. "I can't wait to meet this guy."

Hazel nearly stumbled. "What? When would you meet him?"

Jamie gave her an affronted look. "I don't know, I just figured he'd want to meet the guy his granddaughter is in love with." He smirked. "How are you going to explain me anyway? Camp companion? Passionate partner? Or should we just wait until the wedding?"

Hazel stopped walking. She hadn't even thought of that. She knew he was being sarcastic, but how *would* she explain Jamie? She'd either return home with a boyfriend or a broken heart. Either way her family would notice.

"You *are* going to tell them about me, right?"

Hazel realized she hadn't planned on it, but she could tell by the tenuous look in Jamie's eyes that wasn't the answer he was hoping for. She started walking again. "I'm not sure. Let's see how this goes."

"I think it's going pretty well," Jamie replied.

"It's day one."

"What, are you afraid the honeymoon period is gonna wear off?"

She arched an eyebrow. "I guess we'll see."

30

H azel

THE WEATHER WAS DETERMINED to end their so-called honey-moon before it even got under way.

Not thirty minutes into their hike the rain began. It was nearly sunset now and the dismal weather had yet to let up.

They'd planned to make camp much earlier, but the weather had slowed their pace. Hazel wanted to stop but Jamie insisted they push on to make it to their predetermined destination.

Hazel hated relinquishing control, but Jamie was the official navigator for the first half of the hike. They would switch once they reached the checkpoint, so she'd just have to trust him until then.

She knew part of his reasoning to keep them moving was because he'd been hoping for a break in the weather to set up their tent. But no such luck. Two hours later the rain was still coming down and Jamie finally relented to make camp.

"I would love a weather app right about now," Jamie muttered as he fished a tent pole through the canvas slots.

Hazel grabbed one end of the pole, helping him erect their tiny tent. "Why?" she asked teeth chattering. "Just look up. It's raining. When it stops, you'll know."

She for one, was happy not to have access to a weather app. All it would do was depress her further to see the plummeting temperature. Besides, she didn't need an app to tell her she was cold, wet and miserable.

When they finally climbed inside the damp tent her mood wasn't much better. The rainfly was at least keeping more water from drenching them, but everything inside the tent was wet already from setting it up in the downpour.

Jamie started unpacking their sleeping bags. At least they were dry. Thankfully, their packs were water resistant.

"I'll work on setting up our bedrolls if you work on dinner," Jamie offered.

"Dinner's ready," Hazel grumbled holding up a bag of depressing sandwiches.

Without the option for a fire to heat one of the freeze-dried camp dinners, they'd have to make do with PB&J's and jerky.

Jamie chuckled softly while unfolding the waterproof mats to lay the sleeping bags on. "I knew it would be food that broke you."

She scowled. "You can't tell me you weren't hoping for a hot meal."

Jamie patted the bedroll and Hazel stripped off her wet jacket and sat down.

"Any meal with you is a hot meal," he teased.

Hazel rolled her eyes. "You're an idiot."

"Sweetums . . . are we having our first fight?"

"Jamie, sense the room. I'm not in the mood for your teasing. You're supposed to treat me like we're partners, remember? And right now, your partner is cold and wet and tired and starving."

His smile faltered and he pushed a lock of wet hair out of her face. "Sorry. I am too. Let's eat and try to get some sleep, okay?"

She nodded, suddenly feeling like she was on the verge of tears. This was ridiculous. They'd only been hiking for one day and already she was cracking?

She wouldn't allow it.

Hazel pushed back her emotions and rooted around in her pack for the rest of their dinner.

Jamie smiled when she handed him his sandwich. He held it up like a drink. "Cheers to surviving our first official day of Crossroads, partner."

The grin on his face made it impossible for Hazel to continue sulking. She bumped her sandwich against his and took a bite, closing her eyes as the deliciously sweet and pungent taste of grape jelly and salty peanut butter assaulted her taste buds. The sandwich might be smooshed but it was the most amazing PB&J she'd ever had. She took another bite and moaned.

Jamie grinned. "I know, right?"

"Is there crack in here or something?" Hazel joked. "This is the best PB&J I've ever tasted."

"Imagine how good real food is gonna taste when we reach civilization again?"

Hazel laughed. "Now you're speaking my language. What's the first thing you're gonna eat?"

"A burger with bacon and blue cheese."

She wrinkled her nose. "Blue cheese smells like feet."

"Your feet maybe."

She fake-gasped. "My feet do *not* smell."

Jamie knocked his muddy boots against hers. "Are those boots of yours bubblegum scented or something?"

She kicked him back. "Jerk."

"Princess."

She rolled her eyes but couldn't help smiling as she ate the rest of her dinner like a savage. When they were finished, she fished out two brownies and passed one to Jamie. His eyes lit up like it was Christmas morning. "These definitely were *not* in the official food rations."

She shrugged. "Guess you're rubbing off on me, rule breaker."

He bit into the brownie and groaned. "I knew I loved you."

Hazel knew he was teasing, but she couldn't contain the butterflies that blossomed in her stomach at his comment. It wasn't the first time he'd jokingly said he loved her, but it was getting harder and harder to ignore.

James

AFTER THEY FINISHED EATING DINNER, James helped Hazel reorganize their packs. They stripped off their damp clothes, changed into the dry long johns they'd planned to wear for the second day of the hike and then draped their jackets over their gear, hoping they'd be dry by morning.

Hazel climbed into bed first. James's bedroll was right next to hers and listening to her teeth chatter all night was definitely not an option. "Ya know, it'd be a lot warmer if we both shared a sleeping bag."

"Partners don't share sleeping bags," she said, stubbornly.

"That's not true. If you and Kat were partners, you'd have no problem snuggling next to her to stay warm."

"That's different."

"Why?"

"You know why."

"Who's the one not treating who like a partner now?"

"Jamie . . ."

He rolled over and looked at her. "I'm being serious. Neither of us are going to get any sleep if we're shivering all night."

She stared at him, uncertainty swimming in her caramel eyes.

"It would only be for warmth," he added softly.

She bit her lip as if contemplating.

"Come on. What kind of partner would I be if I let you freeze to death?"

"Fine, but you have to promise no kissing or . . ." her cheeks turned red, "or any of the other stuff we did last time we shared a bed."

"If I recall correctly, you liked the 'other' stuff we did."

Hazel blushed further. "That's not the point."

He smirked and gave her a salute. "Scout's honor. Just for warmth."

HAZEL

IT TOOK some time to zip their sleeping bags together and get comfortable, but Hazel had to admit, it was much warmer that way. Though her sudden warmth was partly due to her heart racing like a Thoroughbred.

She lay curled into Jamie's chest and no matter how she

tried to calm her frenzied pulse, she couldn't. She knew what had set it off. When she'd first settled next to him, she'd been facing away from Jamie, but with her back pressed to his front she could feel every inch of him against her. She tried to remain still, but each breath she took pressed her harder against him. And when his arm draped over her waist, his fingers accidently brushing her exposed navel, it sent the butterflies she'd been trying to lull to sleep bursting to life again.

It was enough to make her roll over and change positions. At least if she was facing him, there was a small pocket of space between their hips. Plus, Hazel liked listening to the steady rhythm of Jamie's heart. Her head was pillowed on his bicep, her nose only inches from his chest. She ached to trace the scar that lay just beneath his t-shirt again.

She knew it was his mother's name he'd tattooed over the wound, but it was also her middle name and it gave Hazel a strange sense of satisfaction knowing a piece of her would always be with him—etched just above his heart.

Jamie's chin innocently nuzzled her hair and her heart thumped louder. At this rate, she wouldn't freeze, but she also wouldn't get any sleep. So far, Jamie was being a complete gentleman. He hadn't crossed any lines as a partner and he even remained strangely quiet, restraining his normally flirta-tious banter. It made her wonder if being this close was as difficult for him as it was for her.

Being in Jamie's arms and resisting the urge to kiss him felt more strenuous then their entire day of hiking. Hazel needed to give her lips something to do other than fantasize about being pressed to his. *Maybe talking would help.*

"Will you tell me a story?" she asked.

He chuckled softly into her hair, the warm air tickling her senses. "You mean like a bedtime story?"

"Sure."

"Hmmm . . . let me think . . . Okay, I've got one. There once was a princess from Nevada. She wore pink boots and drove a tank."

Hazel pinched him, trying not to laugh.

"Shhh, don't interrupt story time," he teased before continuing. "One day the princess almost ran over a prince. When she got out of her tank to help him, he fell in love with her. They hiked into the mountains and lived happily ever after. The end."

She couldn't help snuggling a bit closer, loving the way his voice sounded vibrating through his chest. She hadn't missed that he'd said he loved her again. She wondered how many times she'd have to hear it before she started to believe it.

She couldn't let herself dwell on it. It was just a fairytale anyway, and she knew better than to give her heart to someone who might carry it away.

"Tell me another one," she whispered.

"I don't know any other bedtime stories."

"Then tell me something real. Something about you."

"What do you want to know?"

A stroke of courage overtook Hazel and her fingers reached up to touch Jamie's chest. "Tell me about this," she said, feeling the subtle raise of his scar through his shirt.

She felt his throat bob against her forehead and wanted more than anything to see the expression in his sky-blue eyes. Just when she was beginning to worry she'd been too bold, he answered. "The scar or the tattoo?"

"Both."

"I got the scar when I was seven."

"What's it from?"

His throat bobbed again. "My pacemaker."

Hazel bolted upright, blinking the shock from her eyes.

She knew all about pacemakers. Her father had come home with one and they were no joke. There were major risks and shortened life expectancies associated with the tiny life-saving devices. And the fact that Jamie had one . . . it took her breath away. Why hadn't he told her?

"It's not a big deal," he said pulling her back to him.

"It's a very big deal," she argued.

"It'd be a bigger deal if I didn't have one," he joked.

"Jamie, you shouldn't joke about this."

He shrugged, smiling at her solemnly. "Joking is my form of coping."

Seeing him lying there looking up at her, his sky-blue eyes clouded with sorrow, she felt her heart break apart. Hazel slid back down next to Jamie, her hand pressed over his heart again, feeling the steady rhythm. "My dad has a pacemaker."

"I know. It's why I didn't tell you about mine."

She frowned. "Did you think I'd treat you differently?"

"No, I thought you'd worry and I don't want to be one more thing for you to worry about."

"Why do you have a pacemaker?" she asked quietly, around the emotion tightening her throat.

"I have Long QT Syndrome. Just like my mother."

"Long QT Syndrome?"

"LTQS2 if you want to be specific. It's a heart defect that basically means my body has trouble regulating my heartbeat. The pacemaker fixes that."

"And your mother had it, too?"

She saw that sad smile return. "Yeah, but I don't mind that I inherited her heart disease. I know it's stupid, but now that she's gone, sharing this with her makes me feel like a part of her is still with me."

"That's not stupid," Hazel murmured, feeling tears prick her eyes.

"Hey, none of that, Princess. I'm perfectly fine. I've been dealing with this since I was born. It doesn't hold me back."

Hazel felt stupid as she swiped at her tears. "It's just that my dad always complains about his. He's tired all the time and he's already had to get it replaced when the battery died."

Jamie placed his hand over hers on his chest. "I'm sorry. I know it's not easy, watching someone you love suffer. But I promise you I'm not suffering. I imagine it's more difficult for your father to get used to his pacemaker because he was used to having a perfectly normal heart. I never had that. The pacemaker actually makes my life better."

She nodded, realizing he was probably right. Her father had to get used to a lot of changes. Losing the use of his leg, partial sight and hearing . . . so much had been taken from him.

A sudden realization popped into Hazel's mind. She looked at Jamie. "That's why you can't play football."

He nodded.

"Doesn't it make you angry? That your choices were taken away from you?"

"Not really. Like I said, I was born with this disease. It's not like one day I woke up and everything I thought I'd have was taken away. I grew up knowing I'd never be a professional athlete." He gave a small shrug. "I'd rather use my head for something other than getting it beat in on a football field anyway."

She smiled at him. "Something like photography?"

"Like photography or sailing or I don't know . . . probably a dozen other things. I don't have it all figured out, but I know every beat of my heart is a gift and it makes me not want to waste time doing things that don't make me happy, ya know?"

I know exactly what you mean, Jamie. "That's a beautiful way to look at life."

He huffed a laugh. "Too bad my father doesn't see it that way."

"Maybe it doesn't matter how he sees it."

Jamie cocked his head and gave her an ironic smile. "I'll believe that when you do."

"My dad would never hold me back from my dreams."

"No, you do that all on your own."

Hazel stiffened at the harsh truth in Jamie's words. She wanted to clam up, roll over and shut down. But part of her was afraid if she stopped talking to him, she'd go back to wanting to kiss him, so she kept the conversation going despite the dangerously personal turn it'd taken. "Maybe I do hold myself back."

"Why are you so afraid to let yourself be happy?"

"Because it's not that easy."

"It's exactly that easy," Jamie replied. "You have to go after the things you want, Hazel."

"I can't."

"Why not?"

"Because the things I want, the things that would bring me happiness, would hurt the only people who've ever loved me."

Jamie's hand cupped her cheek. "Maybe the people who love you are stronger than you think."

She closed her eyes, shuddering against the warmth of his touch and how bad she craved more of it. "You don't understand."

He popped up on his elbow, blue eyes glowing in the lantern light. "Then make me, Hazel. Make me understand why you won't let us be together. Because there's not a lot I believe in, but I believe we're meant to be. I've never felt this way about anyone. And you can't deny that you feel the same."

She was sitting now, her arms wrapped around her knees,

shivering in the absence of Jamie's warmth. "I'm not denying it, okay? But it doesn't matter how I feel."

"How can it not?"

"Because!" she shouted. "If I let myself love you it's just gonna result in more broken hearts. Mine, yours, my dad's, Gramps'."

"What do they have to do with us?"

"I can't leave them, Jamie. It would kill them. That's what my mother did. She walked out and abandoned all of us because she hated living in Lovelock. And I hated her for it, but ya know what I hate more?" Tears stung her eyes as she refused to let them out. "That she was right. There's nothing there. I feel like I'm suffocating every day I'm stuck in that dead-end town, but I can't leave. I can't do that to them. Not after all they've sacrificed to keep a roof over my head. I'm the only one left to take care of them."

Jamie's voice was soft again. "I'd never ask you to leave your family, Hazel."

"And I'd never ask you to give up your dreams for me. Because that's what you'd be doing, Jamie. If you came to Lovelock, you'd resent me."

He took her hand. "No I wouldn't."

"You would," she said, pulling her hand away. "And I'd rather you think I'm a coward than the person who killed your dreams."

"What if you're my dream?"

She shook her head. "Then you need to get a new dream."

Jamie glared at her, anger flashing in his eyes. He squeezed the back of his neck, shaking his head. "You were right. We shouldn't have been partners because this is fucking torture, Hazel! Being this close to you, having you refuse to love me even though I know you do."

"I tried to warn you," she whispered through the stubborn tears that refused to be held back any longer.

He gave a bitter laugh. "Yeah, I guess you did."

"I'm sorry, Jamie. I really wish it could be different. But it can't."

"Don't be sorry," he said severely. "I trusted my heart. My bad, not yours." Then he flopped onto his bedroll and turned away from her.

Hazel did the same, trying desperately not to make a sound as she cried herself to sleep. Jamie was never really hers, but losing the idea of him broke her heart just the same.

Was the price of finding herself, really worth the loss of him?

31

James

I FELL FOR YOU, Hazel, but I guess I never asked if you were ready to catch me.

James realized it probably happened all the time, one partner being more ready for love than the other, but that didn't make it any easier to accept.

The morning had been extremely awkward between them, and by lunch, things weren't much better. It didn't help that the rain still hadn't stopped. The temperature was hovering around thirty degrees, turning the precipitation into stinging freezing rain. James wished it would just turn to snow already. That would at least make it more bearable.

What he wouldn't give to be dry. He'd take being back in the tent with Hazel over this. Even being surrounded by awkwardness and heartbreak had been more comfortable.

James hadn't gotten a wink of sleep, which wasn't helping his mood. Neither was the fact that his fingers were pruning as he ate the last of his protein bar under the sparse shelter of a tree. The silver lining was he was too exhausted to waste his energy complaining. The only thing that would really make him feel better was undoing the conversation he'd had with Hazel last night. But since that wasn't going to happen, he focused on finding their next campsite.

Unfolding the map, James shook the raindrops off the lamination. He hadn't been using it much today because the visibility was shit and taking his gloves off to pull it out of his pack didn't appeal to him. James had been relying mostly on his compass. A quick glance here and there kept them on course. But now, looking at the map, he realized they still had a lot more ground to cover before they could make camp for the day.

They were nowhere near as far as James had expected. Unless they'd somehow gotten off course . . . He glanced around the wooded wilderness. It was impossible to pinpoint their location when they were under the trees. Without the mountains to use as a reference they could be anywhere.

He shook his doubt away. He needed to trust himself. They'd gone over the map a dozen times before they left base camp. He knew the thing like the back of his hand, and they had a compass. It would keep them on course, even in weather like this.

James put the map away and picked up his pack. "Ready?" he asked looking back at Hazel.

They hadn't said more than a few words to each other all day, getting by with only what was necessary.

She nodded and silently slung her pack back onto her back.

James wondered if maybe he should try to coax her into conversation.

Yeah right, his subconscious chided. *Because that went so well last night.*

He sighed, knowing even if he did get her to talk it would lead nowhere. He wiped the frustration from his face.

How the hell had he managed to fall for the one person on the planet more stubborn than he was?

HAZEL

HAZEL HADN'T THOUGHT anything could make the second day of hiking worse than the first. Not after how things ended last night. But she was wrong.

As the freezing rain stung her face, she began to wonder about the validity of the Couples' Curse again, because this kind of weather wasn't the norm for March in Montana.

The entire week at basecamp had been full of blue skies and crisp fifty-degree days—still colder than Hazel preferred but enjoyable with the right gear. *Or snuggled next to a campfire with the boy of your dreams.*

Today's weather, however, was making Hazel's bones shiver.

By the time they stopped to make camp for the night, her fingers were so numb she could barely unzip the tent flap to crawl inside. The rain and wind howled, announcing that there would be no chance of fire again tonight.

Hazel wanted to cry. The only way she'd stayed warm last night was because she'd shared a sleeping bag with Jamie. But the idea of doing that tonight made her sick to her stomach.

She knew that she'd hurt him. Hell, she'd hurt herself. And it was becoming more and more evident that there wasn't enough space for all their hurt inside such a small tent.

Hazel wanted to say something to break the tension, but nothing came to mind as she watched Jamie shake out his wet gear, placing it around the tent to dry. The longer their silence drew out the more agitated she became.

When Jamie laid the map out, she finally spoke. "Noticed you didn't use that much today."

He shrugged. "Don't really need to."

"Memorized the whole thing, did ya, Magellan?" she asked cynically.

He answered with just as much sarcasm. "No, but I know how to use a compass and as long as we keep heading southwest, we'll get where we're going."

"Mind if I take a look?"

He gave her a patronizing glare. "Don't trust me?"

"I didn't say that."

"You didn't have to."

"I'm not trying to fight with you, Jamie."

"Sure feels like it."

She didn't know what to say to that. His defenses were up and every time she opened her mouth it just made things worse.

Jamie finally stopped moving about the tent and sat back on his heels. "Look, we have two more days till the checkpoint. Let's just stick to our roles until then, okay?"

Hazel exhaled deeply, deciding to leave it alone. "Fine," she muttered, turning back to her pack to fetch another unexciting dinner of cold PB&Js and jerky.

She tossed Jamie his half of the rations and sat down to eat her own. She was still bitter about the map. They'd been given it for a reason, but saying so would only add fuel to the fire right now. If Jamie wanted to let his pride be the reason he got lost, so be it, but Hazel wasn't going to get stuck out here. She'd find a way to snag the map tomorrow.

Thankfully, they were both too exhausted to argue more. After dinner they both fell asleep, fully clothed and in their own sleeping bags.

James

THE NEXT MORNING the sound of song birds rustled James from his slumber. Their chirping was a welcome presence. It meant no rain! And it was all he needed to shoot energy back into his exhausted limbs.

He crawled out of the tent and wanted to cry at the hint of blue sky and pale morning light. The temperature had dropped significantly, but at least it wasn't raining.

James slipped back inside the tent to grab his coat and the fire making kit. By the time Hazel emerged from the tent, he had a pot of water boiling.

"Do I smell coffee?" she asked, rubbing the sleep from her puffy eyes.

Jamie held a mug out to her. The smile that split her face made his heart ache—almost enough to forgive her for breaking it.

"Thank you," she said pulling the mug to her nose and inhaling the hot beverage.

"There's powdered creamer and sugar in my mess kit."

She raised her eyebrows. "That wasn't part of the food pack."

"Sometimes it pays not to follow the rules."

She smirked and made her way to his kit.

James felt his heart spark with hope again. He sighed, knowing how useless it was to carve it out each night, when one smile from Hazel would instantly renew it.

32

H azel

THEY MADE good time on their third day of hiking. It was amazing what a cup of hot coffee and blue skies could do for the soul. Hazel was still hungry, tired and cold, but at least she was dry. The only thing still bothering her was Jamie's insistence on remaining the sole navigator.

He didn't consult the map nearly enough for her liking and the fact that he controlled their only compass aggravated her even more. Mostly because now that Hazel could see the sun she had a sneaking suspicion they weren't heading in the right direction.

When they stopped for lunch, she decided to bring it up. "So, how many miles do we have left until we reach the checkpoint tomorrow?"

Jamie stuffed the last bite of his protein bar in his mouth

and shrugged. "Depends how far you want to go before making camp tonight."

"Well, it's not raining so I think we can push it a bit further."

"I agree."

Hazel's stomach rumbled loudly, embarrassing her.

"Why don't you eat another protein bar?" Jamie suggested.

"It's for lunch tomorrow."

"We'll be at the checkpoint by lunch tomorrow. Eat now. It'll give you more fuel for today so we can cover more ground."

He made a good point but looking at their already depleted food rations made Hazel nervous.

Seeing her hesitation, Jamie shrugged. "It's up to you. You're in charge of food."

"Would you be telling me to eat extra rations if I was just some random partner?"

"Who said you get extra?" he asked quirking an eyebrow.

She rolled her eyes and pulled out two more protein bars, passing one to him. Grinning, he took it and started unwrapping it right away.

They ate in silence, but it felt more comfortable than before. Maybe there was hope for them yet. Hazel hated to think that they couldn't figure out a way to navigate their failed relationship into some kind of friendship. Plus, it was kind of impossible to stay mad at Jamie when he grinned at her like that.

Crossroads was designed to test and bond. They'd definitely been tested. Maybe this was when the bonding started.

James

.   .   .

THE TENSION in James's chest loosened throughout the day as he and Hazel moved into a more comfortable rhythm. Knowing the checkpoint would be within their grasp tomorrow put an extra pep in their step. It also made them more liberal with their food supply.

By sunset they'd gone through two more bags of trail mix, the last brownie and quite a few lollipops. The candy was like a fast burning fuel. The more they ate, the better their mood, but the more they craved. Luckily, Hazel seemed to have an endless supply. She pulled a Ziploc bag out of her jacket pocket and offered James the contents.

"You brought Boston Baked Beans?" he asked looking at the reddish, lumpy spheres.

"Duh. They're the best candy ever!"

"That's debatable. They look like jellybeans with botulism."

"Fine, you can't have any."

"I didn't say I didn't want any."

Hazel smirked and held the bag back out. James grabbed a handful and popped a few into his mouth, crunching the sugar-coated peanuts loudly. "They're not bad," he admitted. "I think they're growing on me."

"Not bad?" Hazel scoffed. "I'm not wasting any more of my favorite candy on you."

"I didn't mean it like that. They're good. But what kinda name is Boston Baked Beans? It makes me expect actual beans or something."

"Aren't you from Boston?" she teased.

"Yeah, but I grew up in the house of no sugar."

"Really? You didn't have candy growing up?"

"Are you kidding? My house is made up of professional athletes and heart disease patients. Everything on the menu is either some sort of juice, powder, pill or greens."

Hazel's smile faltered.

"Don't go feeling bad for me, Princess. At least I won't end up with diabetes," he teased popping another bean in his mouth.

She smirked. "I blame Gramps for my sweet tooth. He started my sugar addiction at a young age. And since my parents weren't around to say otherwise, I pretty much grew up on Frosted Flakes and penny candy."

"Penny candy? Does that still exist?"

"Yeah. I mean it costs more than a penny now, but novelty candy is huge. We order it in bulk for the repair shop. Gramps loves stocking the lobby with it. He says he's making up for lost time because he was too poor to buy candy when he was a boy."

James laughed. "I like his method of justification."

"Yep, Gramps has gobs of gumption."

James cocked an eyebrow. "That sounds like another Gramps-ism."

Hazel grinned. "It is. It's funny. Not being around him and my dad has made me realize how alike we are. It's weird, to not appreciate you're like the people you spend your life with until you leave them."

James digested her words, wondering what it meant about him that his time away from his family only made him realize how different they were. His brothers were good people. He had nothing against them, but he'd never really had the opportunity to build that brotherly bond with them. They had nothing in common. James didn't play sports and he was a lot younger than his brothers. He'd spent the majority of his youth with his mother. She was the one whose similarities he shared.

Though he looked like his father and brothers, James knew his personality came from his mother. He'd always wondered if that was because they shared a heart. Not literally of course, but he'd inherited her heart disease and it was something that bonded them.

Despite their varying revelations, James knew what Hazel meant by not realizing her family likeness until she was away.

James had spent a lot of time with his mother, but now that she was gone, he wished he'd spent more—*but then again, no amount of time would ever be long enough between a boy and his mother.*

"What are you thinking about?" Hazel asked.

James pulled himself from his thoughts, astonished by how much ground they'd covered in their recent silence. The mountains they'd been hiking toward loomed closer now. "My mom," he finally answered.

"Jane?"

He nodded.

"Is it strange that her name is my middle name?"

"I think it's nice."

Hazel blushed slightly. "When did you get her name tattooed on your chest?"

"The day she passed away."

"How'd you get a tattoo when you're not eighteen?"

"Sometimes there are benefits to having a famous family. What about you? How'd you get your tattoo before being legal?"

"Jenny did it."

James raised an eyebrow. "She sounds like a rebel. I like her."

"She *is* a rebel."

"Tell me again why her parents thought moving her to Vegas was a good idea?"

Hazel laughed. "I ask myself that question a lot. They said it was because her dad got a better job, but Jenny's theory is that her parents thought she was only rebelling because Love-lock was too small-minded for her big personality."

"So they what, hoped she'd disappear in a big city? Small fish, big pond syndrome?"

Hazel laughed again. "Maybe, although I don't think there's a pond big enough to make Jenny's personality seem small."

Once again, James longed to meet the dynamic characters in Hazel's life. "What's wrong with parents?" he asked. "Don't they realize they're screwing us up making all these major life decisions for us?"

Hazel shrugged. "I don't know. They're just us, a few chapters ahead in their story. They probably have no idea what they're doing. All any of us can do is what seems right at the time."

"Yeah, but don't they remember what it was like to be on the edge of eighteen? To be full of dreams and without the means to chase them?"

"I don't know," she replied sadly. "Maybe it's better to think they don't remember. That all these feelings will just fade away, taking the pain and misery with them."

James stopped walking and faced her. "I don't accept that, Hazel. I don't want to forget the way I feel right now. I don't want to forget my mom. I don't want to forget you. I want to hold onto all of it. The love *and* the pain . . . Otherwise how do we even know we're alive?"

HAZEL

HAZEL STARED into Jamie's wild-blue-yonder eyes and saw a

future she desperately wanted. It stretched out before her. If only she was brave enough to grab it.

"I don't know," she whispered.

"Hazel, I know where you stand and I'm not trying to change your mind, but you have to know that you make me feel alive. And I'd do anything to hold onto that feeling. I'd cross mountains and oceans to make this last if I knew you felt that way too."

She sucked in a breath, trying to stay upright when his words made her want to crumble. *Oh Jamie, if you only knew how much I want that too.*

But she could never have it and no matter how much she learned about herself on Wander Mountain, she knew that fact wouldn't change.

It was one thing to crave freedom, but another thing entirely to capture it.

So, she did the only thing she knew how to do, put her head down and kept moving.

33

James

THE AWKWARDNESS HAD RETURNED by the time they made camp, but still James wasn't sorry about what he'd said. Maybe it was the altitude or the hunger, or maybe the Wander Mountain philosophy was finally seeping in despite his resistance, but he didn't want to live the life he'd been living any more. He knew better than most that life was short and fragile and he didn't want to leave things unsaid.

If Hazel didn't feel the same, fine.

Well, not fine, but he'd learn to deal with it.

The feelings he had for her were real and he was going to keep telling her that even if her answer never changed. At least that way, he wouldn't have to wonder if he could've changed her mind—because living with regrets wasn't really living.

. . .

HAZEL

WHEN JAMIE finally declared they'd hiked enough for the day, Hazel fell into their campsite routine. They set up their tent, collected wood, built a fire and for once, ate their fill. They'd be at the checkpoint tomorrow, no sense rationing now.

Knowing they were almost halfway through their journey filled Hazel with bittersweet emotions. Despite their serious conversations earlier, their evening had been pleasant and quiet, and she wasn't quite ready for it all to be over so soon.

As they sat around the fire, Hazel took in her soundings, trying to soak in as much as she could. She watched the fire spark, embers dancing as they climbed into the night sky while Jamie wrote in his journal. He'd been vigilant about the task, which surprised her.

She hadn't managed to write in hers yet. She knew it was a requirement, but Hazel had never been good at pouring her heart out. What would she even say? That she'd fallen in love with a boy she had no future with?

If it sounded absurd in her head, it would only be more embarrassing on paper. Plus, there was something about writing things down that made them seem more permanent. If she kept her feelings locked up, they were easier to deny.

At least that's what she told herself.

When the fire began to die down, she slipped into the tent to change for bed. Jamie wasn't far behind her. They each slept in their separate sleeping bags again, not even broaching the subject of sharing.

It was all starting to feel routine to Hazel. The soft snoring from Jamie's bedroll, the warmth emanating from his side of the tent, the way his face looked in the faint glow of starlight. Each little nuance brought her comfort.

Hazel shivered, wondering how long it would take before she'd be able to close her eyes and not imagine Jamie beside her. A month, a year—*a lifetime?*

James

MORNING BROUGHT DISTURBING CLARITY.

When James unzipped the tent, he couldn't believe what he saw. While they'd slept the world had been blanketed in white. He had to shield his eyes from the bright snow-covered wilderness that stretched as far as the eye could see. He swore and pulled on his jacket and boots before stepping out into the cold.

The snow engulfed him, his boots buried up to his shins. He couldn't believe how quickly it had accumulated.

This didn't bode well for their pace today. They still needed to cover a lot of ground in order to make it to the checkpoint, but the snow would slow them down. And he was pretty sure besides whatever candy Hazel had hidden, they only had enough rations for breakfast. Yesterday they'd gambled it was better to eat a hearty dinner so they could sleep well, with full stomachs for a change.

At least that part of their plan had worked.

Last night James actually managed to sleep through the night with only a half dozen tantalizing dreams about Hazel—progress compared to the dozen or so that usually kept him awake. But now he worried they'd be hiking into the night without much food to keep them going.

He gazed at the expanse of unending white and did his best to shake off his anxiety.

Oh well, it's only a day. We won't starve.

HAZEL

HAZEL GASPED when she climbed out of the tent.

She'd never seen so much snow in her life! It snowed in Lovelock, but not this much. Mostly it was just a light dusting that melted before it could accumulate into an amount that would cause trouble. But this . . . there was probably a good two feet and that was under the tree cover where they'd camped.

It would be worse when they crossed open ground.

Jamie handed her a mug of hot coffee and the last protein bar. She took it gratefully.

"How did we sleep through this?" she asked gesturing to the whiteout surrounding them.

He shrugged. "I don't know, but we're gonna have to get moving as soon as possible to make it to the checkpoint."

"We'll be lucky if we make it by midnight trekking through this stuff."

"We'll be fine," Jamie said, already heading back to the tent to start packing up.

A stiff wind blew snow from the trees, sending flurries down Hazel's collar. She shivered the foreboding feeling away and followed Jamie back into the warmth of the tent.

Today was going to be a long day.

James

. . .

BY NOON, James's appetite and agitation were growing. They were barely covering any ground in the deep snow and listening to Hazel's chattering teeth was making him anxious.

He'd told her to stop twice and add another layer, but the girl was beyond stubborn. She kept saying she was fine when she clearly wasn't. Her lips were chapped and much too pale, and she had snot frozen to her face thanks to the blistering wind that had kicked up.

James knew he didn't look much better. His eyes were watering from the wind, the tears promptly freezing to his face. He was pretty sure there were icicles on his eyelashes. And why not? Everything else was frozen.

He could barely feel his fingers and the water in their hydro packs had frozen solid. Not to mention that his balls had migrated to his tonsils!

James was beginning to wish they'd never left their tent but thanks to their lack of resolve with their rations, waiting out the storm wasn't really an option. He knew he should pull the map out again, but he wasn't anxious to expose his fingers to the blistering cold.

The rule of three that Sage drilled into their heads popped into James's mind. *Three minutes without air. Three hours of exposure. Three days without water. Three weeks without food.*

He'd never really considered the knowledge useful before, but as James began to lose feeling in his face, he wondered how long they'd be able to last in this kind of weather. *Three hours of exposure.*

They needed to find shelter, and soon.

He pulled up his sleeve to look at his compass again. The sight made him pause.

The needle was pointing back at him, when a moment ago

it had been pointing away. That was odd, considering they hadn't altered their course. He tapped it with his gloved finger and nothing happened. *Could a compass freeze?*

"What's wrong?" Hazel asked, coming up beside him.

"I think the compass is frozen."

"What? That's not possible." She pulled his arm toward her pushing his sleeve up further until she gasped.

HAZEL

HAZEL HAD to clamp her teeth together to control her anger. "How long have you been wearing this watch?" she asked quietly.

"The whole time," he replied. "I never take it off."

Hazel threw her arms up and screamed, scaring the birds in the trees above them into flight.

"What's the problem?"

"The problem is, you've ruined our compass!"

"What?"

"I knew it! I knew this didn't feel right, but would you let me look at the map? Nooo! You had to be the big man in charge."

"What are you talking about?"

"I'm talking about the fact that you set a compass next to a magnet and expected you could trust it!"

Jamie blinked his frozen eyelashes at her and Hazel wanted to scream again.

"Jamie, the compass is compromised. We could be hiking in the wrong direction!"

"I don't understand."

"Watch batteries are coercive. They disrupt the magnetic field of the compass needle."

"How the hell am I supposed to know that?"

"Anyone who's ever changed a car battery knows that! And they told us at base camp! That's why you were told to wear the compass next to the GPS band, away from the watch."

"Well, I'm sorry, I guess I didn't get the memo."

"Maybe if you weren't so busy trying to get into my pants you would have!"

"Are you serious?"

Jamie looked offended but Hazel didn't care. "I'm dead serious. You screwed us. God, Jamie! Why can't you just follow the rules?"

"Alright! I get it. I'm sorry. I didn't know it was such a big deal."

"Well you should've! The counselors weren't trying to make you give up your fancy jewelry for no reason, Jamie. They were trying to prevent this exact situation!"

"Okay, Hazel! I said I get it! I screwed up. I wasn't trying to be some flashy douchebag. This watch is from my mother! I never take it off."

Hazel was too mad to let Jamie's comment dull her fury. "I want to see the map," she ordered, dropping her pack into the snow so she could dig out her binoculars.

She needed to find some sort of landmark so they could figure out where the hell they were and get back on track. Her fingers shook when she pulled her gloves off to de-fog the binocular lenses. A quick scan of their bleak white surroundings made her heart race.

Everything looked the same.

They could be anywhere!

Hazel marched out of the tree line they'd been traveling

through to get a better view. Pulling the cold binoculars to her face she was met with more of the same, until . . .

"I see something!" she shouted.

Jamie was by her side in an instant as she focused the high-powered lenses on the spot where she'd seen an unnatural shape. There, in the distance, sat a small cabin. It looked old and decrepit, but it was shelter and even better than that, a landmark.

Hazel assessed the distance. It was probably a little over four miles away. With conditions so poor it would take them most of the day to reach it. She had a decision to make. Waste time and energy hiking there for shelter or try to get her bearings and plot a course back to the Crossroads trail and the checkpoint they desperately needed to reach?

She slapped the binoculars against Jamie's chest without a word and hiked back under the trees to get a break from the wind while she consulted the map. She did her best to calculate a fifty-mile radius from their starting point and worked backward from there. Based on the mountains in the distance, she had a sinking feeling they'd somehow veered off course in a northerly direction.

As she dragged her finger along the northern ranges on the map, she prayed she wouldn't see anything to confirm her fears, but sure enough, she located a tiny drawing of a cabin. The words, *Trapper Outpost*, identified it and Hazel's heart sank.

She knew that cabin. It was Old Man Murphy's.

The counselors at Wander Mountain credited Old Man Murphy, the iconic fur trapper from the eighteen-hundreds, as the pioneer who paved the way for most of the surrounding settlements. He was also the camp's benefactor, eventually gifting the land deed Wander Mountain's camp was built on to the state. The camp's owner had snatched the property up for next to nothing in the late eighties. But all that knowledge was useless to Hazel. It did nothing but help her realize how lost they truly were.

Jamie rejoined Hazel, finally looking as somber as she felt after he dropped the binoculars from his eyes. "Please tell me that's not Old Man Murphy's cabin?"

"I wish I could."

A deafening silence settled between them.

The trouble with being so close to Old Man Murphy's cabin was that it meant they'd hiked nearly fifty miles off course in the wrong direction.

Hazel wanted to collapse as the realization of their situation sunk in. They were lost in a snowstorm with no food or water and it would be days before anyone from the camp would come looking for them.

"What do we do?" Jamie asked.

Never one to give up, Hazel scrutinized the map. "We get back on course."

"Now? Are you crazy?" He moved closer, peering over her shoulder at the map. "It's a four-day hike to get back to where we started, probably longer in these conditions. Plus, we're out of food."

"Oh, now you can read a map?" she sneered.

Jamie glared at her. "We need to find shelter. The camp will send someone to our GPS location when we don't show up at the finish line. Or maybe sooner if they notice how far off course we are."

"You *would* want to throw in the towel, wouldn't you?"

"What the hell's that supposed to mean?"

"It means I didn't come out here for a vacation."

"And I did?"

She shrugged. "If the shoe fits."

Hazel stomped away from him and re-evaluated the map.

She knew she was being a jerk, but she couldn't help it. She was beyond frustrated that once again she'd allowed someone else to dictate the course of her life. She should've fought for control earlier, but that was her problem, wasn't it? She always let others choose her path for her.

But no more. It was time she took the reins.

Hazel had come to Wander Mountain to find herself and soak up as much freedom as she could. What better way than to tackle the wilderness on her own?

It was doable. Humans were capable of astonishing feats when they were determined to succeed, and Hazel had never felt more determined than she did in that moment.

Her keen eyes covered the terrain on the map and a route began forming in her mind. One that would skip the checkpoint and take her straight to the finish line. If she left right now, she could do it and only be maybe a day or two off the pace.

It wouldn't be ideal in these conditions or without real food, but it was still possible. She was convinced the weather wouldn't last. Snowstorms were rare this time of year. The cold front would break and the snow would melt, giving her water. As far as food, she still had some candy left. The hike would take a week max. She wouldn't starve in a week.

She finally folded the map and turned back to face Jamie. "I'm not giving up. I'm gonna hike to the finish."

James

JAMES ACTUALLY LAUGHED, but as he watched Hazel slip the map in her pack he realized she was serious.

"Hazel..." he started, but she cut him off.

"I'll need the tent if you're not coming with me."

"You can't be serious."

"Why not? Because I'm a girl?"

"No, because this is a reckless stupid idea. We're not prepared for this kind of weather. We have no idea if anyone else is even still hiking in these conditions. They may have held everyone at the checkpoint until the storm passes."

She shrugged. "Maybe, maybe not."

"Listen, I'm sorry. I know how bad you wanted this experience and I screwed it up for you, but I'm not gonna let you do something stupid just because you're pissed."

"You're damn right I'm pissed, Jamie! I knew it wasn't a good idea to partner with you, but you wouldn't take no for an answer. And I knew we weren't going the right way days ago, but you wouldn't let me see the map. I'm done letting you be in charge of my life! I'm hiking out of here. If you want to come with me, fine. If not, stay at the cabin and I'll tell them where to find you. But you're no longer in charge of anything that affects my future."

James was livid. Hazel was being ridiculous. Standing there with her arms crossed, kissable lips pressed in a determined scowl, he wanted to hoist her over his shoulder and carry her to the cabin where he knew she'd be safe. Maybe if he could just get her there, he could talk some sense into her. Splitting up was the worst thing they could do, but he'd have better luck explaining that to a rock than Hazel at the moment.

Swallowing his pride, James prepared to beg. "Fine, Hazel, be pissed at me. Hike out of here, I don't care, but do it tomorrow. We only have a few hours of light left and right now isn't the time to make rash decisions like this. We're both cold, wet, tired and hungry."

"And you think we won't be tomorrow?" she challenged.

"I *think* we should spend the night at the cabin and reevaluate our situation in the morning. We're not thinking straight right now."

"Actually, I'm *finally* thinking straight," she said dropping her pack to the snow again and starting to rummage through it.

"What are you doing?"

"Dividing everything up so we can go our separate ways like we should've from the start."

She tried handing him some candy and part of the first aid kit, but he refused to take it. "Stop it!" he yelled shoving her offerings back at her. "I'm not letting you go by yourself."

"I don't need you to come with me!"

"Well too fucking bad!"

Hazel tossed the candy and first aid supplies into the snow next to James's pack and unhooked the tent, strapping it to her own pack before hoisting it onto her back.

James watched with amusement. "I'm just gonna follow you."

She met him with seething anger. "Don't! Just stop making this harder than it is."

"What are you talking about?"

"This . . . us . . ." she said gesturing between them. "We don't work. We never have. We've been fooling ourselves thinking this would ever have a different ending. I mean look at us. We're lost in the middle of nowhere. That never would've happened if we had any other partner." The anger in her voice simmered to sadness. "We're too wrapped up in each other for our own good."

"Hazel . . ."

"No. We never should've met. I'm the one who wasn't supposed to be here, so let me be the one to fix this. It's time we sever things before we do more damage. And if I'm the only one strong enough to do it, then you have to let me."

James didn't know what to say. Every word coming out of Hazel's mouth was the truth, but that didn't stop him from hating it. He couldn't let her walk away from him.

Not like this.

"Maybe you're right, but we started this together and I'm not willing to end it any other way. Hike to the cabin with me tonight and tomorrow we'll hike out together."

She looked at him, weighing his offer.

He wanted to say more but he knew pushing Hazel wasn't a good idea. Another word from him was just as likely to tip the scales in the wrong direction.

This had to be her choice.

HAZEL

HAZEL CONSIDERED HER OPTIONS.

She knew if she spent the night at the cabin it would put her another day behind, but she also knew she wouldn't be able to get rid of Jamie right now and at this point, that's all she wanted.

It was time she cut him out of her heart and started healing. She couldn't do that if he was with her every step of the way. But she knew if she tried to blaze her own path now, he'd follow her no matter what she said.

The best she could hope for was to sneak out before he got up tomorrow.

"Fine," she muttered.

"Fine."

34

James

IF JAMES THOUGHT GETTING to the cabin was grueling, getting inside was just as tough. The place was buttoned up like Fort Knox, which made no sense because the dilapidated old structure didn't even look worth saving.

Vines and roots were trying to reclaim it, climbing up the log siding like a ladder. The windows were spattered with centuries of dirt and grime so thick he couldn't see through them. But somehow, the door was sturdy. It took all the strength James had left to kick his way in.

Unfortunately, he hadn't helped their situation by splintering the doorframe. The damn thing wouldn't shut properly now and the only way they could keep the door closed was by shoving a piece of old furniture against it.

But at least they had shelter.

That was about all the cabin offered. It had long since been abandoned. The only things that remained unharmed by disuse were two rickety chairs and an old table, currently propping the door closed.

An old wooden counter ran the length of the back wall. It had probably been used to sell furs at one time. Currently, it reminded James of something he'd find in some trendy Boston pub, making him slightly homesick.

The only other items inside the cabin were a few dusty taxidermy creatures that were so rotted they barely resembled their animal forms. James had been hoping to find something they could eat, but from the thick layer of dust coating everything, it was evident no one had lived here in a very long time.

"At least there's a fireplace," he said assessing the room.

Hazel was already busy building a fire. They'd been lucky to find a stack of old timber behind the house when they were looking for a way inside. The wood had been covered by an old moth-eaten tarp and was so brittle James had no doubt it would spark up immediately.

He worked on setting up their bedrolls while Hazel tended to the fire. James knew the instant the fire caught. He began to cough as the cabin quickly started to fill with smoke.

"Did you open the flue?" he asked.

Hazel glared at him. "Of course. I'm not an idiot."

James rolled the tension from his shoulders and did his best to let the comment slide, walking over to the fireplace to inspect the situation. He cranked the lever for the flue, closing and opening it again. The smoke continued to billow into the stuffy cabin. The smell wasn't great either. "Something must be obstructing the chimney."

"Ya think?" Hazel added, her voice dripping with sarcasm.

James sighed, hating that it was his fault things were so awful between them. "I'll climb up to the roof in the morning to see if I can fix it," he replied. "For now, we'll just have to leave the door cracked."

Hazel silently helped him move the table so they could crack the door open. After a few minutes, the smoke began to dissipate. Sleeping with the door ajar wasn't ideal, but at least they wouldn't die of smoke inhalation.

Without another option, James finished setting up their bedrolls and settled in for what was sure to be another long, miserable night.

HAZEL

"I THINK something died in that chimney," Hazel muttered from her bedroll.

She was closest to the fire, but the warmth almost wasn't worth the musty smell of decay wafting toward her on the tendrils of smoke.

"I'll check it out in the morning," Jamie murmured, sounding like he was already half asleep.

Hazel turned away from the fire and snuggled deeper into her sleeping bag. She closed her eyes. It didn't matter if he fixed the chimney. She was leaving at first light.

As USUAL, things didn't really go according to Hazel's plan.

She woke far from first light. The only reason she woke at all was because of the awful noise coming from the chimney. The fire was out and it was so cold in the cabin she could see her breath. She shivered, pulling her sleeping bag tighter around her, trying to cling to the warmth.

The noise started up again and Hazel worried whatever had died in the chimney was coming back to life! She turned to rouse Jamie, but he wasn't there.

She sat up quickly, her senses on high alert.

Not finding Jamie beside her was even more alarming than the noise coming from the chimney. But then she saw a note resting on his bedroll. *I'm on the roof. Hopefully I don't fall on top of you.*

Hazel hated the blossom of emotion that bloomed in her chest at his words.

God! Even his handwriting makes my heart ache. "Now or never, Hazel," she muttered to herself.

She knew if she didn't leave now there was a chance she never would and not just because she'd run out of food and energy—because of Jamie. Despite the fact that she knew she and Jamie would never work, the idea of leaving him again was difficult to swallow. She listened to his footsteps on the roof. She had to leave now while he wasn't able to stop her.

Hazel sprang into action packing up her bedding and rifling through their packs. She divided everything so she wouldn't be leaving him high and dry. She even left him half her remaining Boston Baked Beans. The only thing she took for herself was the tent and the map. If he planned to wait at the cabin to be rescued, he wouldn't need it.

Dressed and ready to go, Hazel stood at the door, her nerves tingling.

Would he see her as soon as she darted down the stairs of the little front porch?

Would he try to stop her?

What if he didn't?

She might never see him again and she hadn't even left a note.

She hated herself for leaving this way, but what could she even say? *I wish my life was different?*

Wishing was wasteful.

She gave herself a quick pep talk. "You can do this, Hazel. It's just like ripping off a Band-Aid."

She took a deep breath and quietly opened the door.

James

JAMES MOVED SLOWLY, carefully choosing each step on the unstable roof. Getting up had been a challenge. There wasn't a ladder, or any trees close enough to help him. The only assistance he got came from the lumber he'd found in the backyard.

He managed to stack the remaining pieces at an angle against the cabin and use it as a ramp to climb up. It took a few tries, but after a running start he made it.

As a precaution he'd tied a rope around his waist and then around the chimney. Although if he fell, he doubted the chimney would hold him. If anything, it would probably make matters worse and fall directly on top of him. But James was doing his best not to think about that.

He wasn't a fan of heights, but he didn't want to suffer another miserable night. Sleeping with the door open had made the wood they burned useless. It had barely taken the chill off the air and they didn't have enough lumber to keep wasting like that. That is, *if* he could convince Hazel to abandon her crazy plan and stay at the cabin.

James figured he'd have a better chance of persuading her not to hike out if he could fix the chimney. So here he was . . .

Upon first inspection, it was easy to see why they'd had

trouble with the chimney. Someone had fastened a tarp around the opening, probably a winterizing technique, but it was the reason they'd been unable to clear the smoke. Luckily, their fire last night had eventually burnt through most of the tarp. But there was enough of it left that smoke had still been slowly puffing into the cabin when James woke this morning.

Wanting to eliminate the problem, he stripped away the remaining pieces of charred tarp and peered down into the stone flue. He could see another blockage. It looked like some sort of animal had tried building a nest in the chimney. There wasn't much left thanks to their fire.

James found himself hoping Hazel hadn't been right. He didn't like thinking some poor creature had been trapped inside the chimney when they started the fire.

Shaking the thought from his head, he grabbed the branch he'd dragged up to the roof with him, hoping to dislodge whatever remained. After a few tries he cleared the lingering blockage. He was surprised Hazel hadn't popped her head out. The charred debris raining down into the fireplace had probably startled her from her sleep.

Satisfied that he'd managed to solve at least one problem, James began unfastening the rope from around the chimney. He gathered it up in his arms and started to move toward the side of the roof where he'd built the ramp when he noticed a familiar pop of pink in the distance.

The color was bright against the blinding white snow and James would know it anywhere—Hazel's pink boots.

His heart plummeted.

Pack strapped to her back, Hazel was taking determined steps across the clearing, moving further and further away from the cabin.

.   .   .

HAZEL

THE FURTHER AWAY HAZEL GOT FROM the cabin the worse she felt about leaving Jamie without any explanation. She couldn't shake the feeling that she was no better than her mother, sneaking off for her own selfish reasons without any thought for how her absence might affect others.

Her heart protested each step she took. *You're a hypocrite, Hazel!*

She knew how awful it felt to be abandoned, yet here she was, doing it anyway.

Hazel tried to justify it to herself, but no matter how sound her reasoning for hiking out on her own, she knew it was cowardly and wrong. And the thing that made each step more painful than the next was that she knew Jamie would never do the same to her. Not even if the roles had been reversed and she'd been the one to get them lost.

She felt tears sting her eyes as her heart silently protested. Every part of her longed to turn back. In her anger yesterday, finishing the hike had seemed like the most important thing in the world. But now, it felt foolish and selfish and she didn't know why the hell she'd ever wanted to do this to begin with.

Even if she somehow made it to the finish line, what would it prove?

Her life wouldn't change.

"Be strong, Hazel!" she muttered to herself.

But she *was* strong. She already knew that. She never would've survived the hand she'd been dealt if she wasn't.

Her father and grandfather had raised her to be resilient and responsible. They'd also raised her not to leave others behind.

Hazel's steps faltered. *What am I doing?*

She didn't have anything to prove. Not to herself or to the world.

She'd come here to find herself, when maybe all along that wasn't what she'd been searching for. Maybe she'd always been searching for the strength to make the choices she wanted, not the ones that were expected of her.

The memory of Jamie's sky-blue eyes flashed in her mind, the feeling of his lips pressed against hers and suddenly, what she wanted materialized in her mind, clear as day.

It was him.

It had always been him. She'd been trying desperately to deny it because that had seemed the easier choice. But she knew better than most that the easy path was not always the right one.

She knew if she chose Jamie, their path wouldn't be easy, but she didn't care. She wanted to fight for him, fight for *them*. There would be no truer test of her strength than fighting for love.

That's what she wanted to put her energy into, not making it to some stupid finish line that someone else created for her. Hazel knew who she was, and it wasn't someone who put herself before others. *That was her mother.* And that was the one person Hazel never wanted to be.

As the thought solidified within her, Hazel heard Jamie calling her name and turned to face him with so much hope in her heart she could hardly contain it.

But then she heard something else and it stole the breath from her lungs . . . and all her hope along with it.

35

James

IT WASN'T a moment after James called her name that he
heard it . . . the heart wrenching sound of the ice splintering
beneath Hazel's pink boots.

She turned, her body stiff with fear. She was too far away
for James to make out her expression, but he was grateful he
couldn't see it. It already felt like someone had jammed an
icicle into his heart. Seeing the fear in Hazel's warm caramel
eyes would've gutted him.

The moment he'd realized the large, flat expense she was
hiking across was an iced-over lake hidden beneath the snow,
he began to panic.

James screamed her name again. "Hazel! Don't move. I'm
coming."

But what the hell was he going to do? She was a hundred

yards away and adding his weight to the splintering ice field would only make things worse.

He quickly began gathering the rope in his hands. *If I can somehow get close enough to throw it to her . . .* But then he heard the ice crack again, ringing out like thunder in the frozen silence and his heart filled with dread.

HAZEL

HAZEL SCREAMED as she felt the ice begin to shift under her feet. The sudden storm had frozen the lake and hidden it beneath the solid layer of snow, but it wasn't solid enough and the longer she stood in one place, the more she felt the ice begin to shift.

This wasn't happening.

Not now.

Not when she finally figured out what she wanted.

Hazel took her pack off and slowly lowered it to the snow-covered ice, taking a step away from the extra weight. The ice groaned and hissed like an angry beast being rousted from its slumber.

"Please," Hazel whispered over and over again. "Please, please, please."

She was begging God and mother nature and anyone who would listen, not to let her die like this.

This can't be how it ends.

She looked up at Jamie on the roof of the cabin. *Is this the last time I'll see you?*

Her heart split at the same time as the ice. Hazel screamed, her eyes locked on his beautiful face as the ice gave way and the dark, icy water swallowed her whole.

36

James

THERE WASN'T a reasonable thought in James's head as he propelled himself toward Hazel.

His feet began moving before he remembered telling them to, pounding over the shingles he'd so carefully traversed moments before. Somehow, he made it all the way to the edge of the front porch roofline without it caving in. But that was the least of James's worries. All he cared about was getting to Hazel.

So much so that he hadn't thought his plan through before leaping into the air.

He hit the frozen ground so hard the impact knocked the wind out of him. The snow did nothing to cushion his fall and his chest seized with pain as he tried to catch his breath and get his feet under him again.

It took him longer than it should have, but nothing was broken. At least he didn't think so, but he couldn't be sure. The sheer amount of adrenaline coursing through him made James feel like he could outrun a train.

Even as he struggled to his feet, James never let his eyes stray from the darkening hollow in the ice where Hazel had disappeared. The surface rippled but she didn't resurface and that's what drove him forward.

He frantically ran onto the ice, only stopping long enough to tie his rope to the closest tree in case he fell through too.

By the time he reached the spot where she disappeared, James had come unglued, screaming Hazel's name and clearing the snow as he desperately tried to see through the splintering ice. It groaned and popped under his weight, but he constantly kept himself moving, trying not to stay in one place too long so he might have a chance at finding her before it was too late. It was the only thought left in his frenzied mind —*Find! Her!*

Three minutes without air...

How much time had passed already?

James pushed the panic away and kept moving. "Hazel!" he roared, over and over, sending birds to the sky. "Hazel!"

But there was no answer, only the frantic beat of his heart echoed in his ears. But James wasn't about to give up. From the brief time he'd known Hazel he'd gleaned that far too many people underestimated her and he refused to be one of them. He wouldn't give up on her, even if it cost him his own life— it's not like he'd want one without her anyway.

James had known the moment he first set eyes on Hazel that she was going to change his life, he'd just imagined things ending differently.

This can't be the end, Hazel.

"Come on!" he begged. "Please, please, please. Don't leave me! Not like this!"

Then, a flash of pink beneath the ice caught his eyes.

James felt his heart leap!

He'd never been so happy in all his life to see those ridiculous pink hiking boots. He cleared the snow further and dropped to his knees, his eyes locking on Hazel's frantic ones, her tiny hands pounded the underside of the ice.

James balled his hand into a fist and punched the ice with all his strength. Over and over, until he felt nothing but pure rage and love coursing through him, driving him on when all reason should've stopped him. The ice became a slurry of blood and water as he continued to pound his fist into it. After the first few fractures James couldn't feel his hand anymore and that was probably a good thing considering he was pretty sure he could see bone through the mutilated flesh of his knuckles. But he didn't care. He had one goal and he wasn't stopping until he achieved it.

Get. Hazel. Back.

When his fist finally broke through the ice and James grabbed hold of Hazel's soaking wet body, pure joy exploded in his chest, making the world sway around the edges. He wrenched her out of the water, her wild gasp for air music to his ears. But there was no time for relief. He quickly dragged Hazel away from the fracturing ice by the hood of her jacket before scooping her into his arms and sprinting back to dry land.

She was gasping, shivering and coughing, all while trying to speak but James couldn't make out what she was saying. He was concentrating on staying upright as his vision began to spot, his own lungs feeling as though they'd been the ones trapped beneath the ice, starved for air.

When he finally made it back into the cabin, he collapsed with Hazel in his arms.

"I-I'm s-s-sorry," she chattered.

James didn't care what she was, as long as she was alive. But he couldn't get the words out to tell her so. He couldn't manage to get anything out. His chest heaved, his heart racing as his vision swam again. He felt lightheaded. What the hell was wrong with him? Was this an adrenaline crash? Or maybe hypothermia setting in?

He couldn't think straight!

Focus, James!

Wander Mountain had trained him for this, but for the life of him, James didn't know what to do next as a million thoughts tangled in his mind. He needed to wedge the door shut. He needed to start a fire. They needed to get their wet clothes off.

But in what order?

One look at Hazel's blue-tinged skin and shivering lips and his mind cleared. He sprang back into action, helping Hazel to her feet as he teetered on his own.

"Take your clothes off," he ordered, already working to help her out of her jacket.

Her fingers were shaking too badly to get the job done herself and when James let go of her to steady himself, she collapsed back to the floor like a wet noodle.

"Hey, stay with me, Hazel. Keep talking. You have to stay awake."

"I-I'm s-s-sorry," she stammered out again.

His first instinct was to tell her everything was going to be okay . . . but was it? The reality was that their situation had just become even more dire. With the plummeting temperatures, they were now facing hypothermia. But there was so much worry filling Hazel's big, caramel eyes that James was flooded with the overwhelming need to comfort her.

"It's okay," he said softly. "Just help me get you out of these wet clothes."

She silently did her best, her body shaking so badly she could barely function.

James took over for her even though he was shaking just as severely.

"Bet you didn't think this would be how we'd end up naked again," he teased trying to lighten the situation.

Hazel tried to smile through her chattering teeth as her fingers wrestled with the buttons of her pants. James batted her hand away, ignoring the screaming pain in his own. In no time, he had Hazel stripped and wrapped in his sleeping bag. As much as he wanted to crawl under there with her, he knew there was more to be done. They needed fire.

With the last of his adrenaline, James ran outside to drag in more wood. Once he had a fire roaring, he secured the door, stripped off the last of his own damp clothes and slid under the sleeping bag, pulling Hazel to his chest.

Her teeth were still chattering loudly and her whole body shook with icy tremors.

"I was c-coming b-back," she sputtered.

"It's okay," he whispered, tightening his arms around her as exhaustion finally claimed him. "It's going to be okay."

37

James

SLEEP WASN'T ALWAYS KIND. That was something James knew well.

After his mother had passed, his dreams had been haunted by her ghost. Now, a new ghost joined his nightmares —Hazel, trapped under the ice, screaming up at him for help.

James awoke with a start, his fists still clenched like they had been in his nightmare where this time, he'd been unable to break through the ice. Thankfully, it was just a dream. Hazel's shivering body pressed against his, reassuring James that it hadn't been real.

"It was just a dream," he reminded himself, though every time he closed his eyes, he swore he could still hear the echo of Hazel's scream.

He would never forget that sound for as long as he lived.

When Hazel fell through the ice, every future hope James ever had started to pop like balloons on a dart board. Perhaps that's why he'd fought so hard to get back to her—he knew if he lost her, he'd lose himself too.

Even though she was in his arms now, he couldn't stop his heart from breaking. *You were leaving me, Hazel.* He tried to push away the feeling of abandonment that rushed in, but it was impossible. After losing someone you loved, it got harder to reason with your heart.

Even though it hurt to think Hazel had been leaving him, it didn't hurt worse than if James hadn't found her buried beneath the ice. Strangely, he felt that's where her heart was— still buried beneath a field of ice so no one could ever get close enough to hurt her.

You let me in once, Hazel.

As James pulled her closer, pressing a kiss to her forehead, he couldn't stop hoping she'd do it again. He let that hope fill his chest as he closed his eyes again.

JAMES JERKED AWAKE. *What is that noise? And why is it so cold?*

As the world came back into focus he remembered where he was.

So it hadn't all been a nightmare?

The fire was out and his own teeth were chattering so loud he wondered if that was the sound that had woken him. He looked at Hazel. She was still much too pale for his liking. He brushed her matted hair away from her face—at least it had dried. He kissed her forehead and took her pulse. It seemed steady enough and her temperature was a bit better than yesterday.

Wait . . . is today a new day?

He looked at the dull light filtering in from the dirty window, the cold coals of the fire . . . How much time had passed? It was hard to keep track when he couldn't fight the pull of exhaustion that constantly lulled him to sleep.

He needed a plan.

Dragging himself from the warmth of the sleeping bag, James shrugged on some dry clothes he found in his pack. He grabbed a spare long-sleeved shirt for Hazel too and dressed her in it for an extra layer of warmth. Then he shrugged on his jacket and went in search of more wood. By the time he finished stacking a few days worth inside the cabin he was dead on his feet, swaying as spots swam in his vision again.

What the hell was wrong with him? He couldn't catch his breath and his heart was pounding against his ribs much too quickly. He fought the waves of dizziness long enough to pack an old bucket he'd found full of snow and set in near the hearth. Then he built another fire.

This time, before collapsing next to Hazel, James set his watch alarm to wake him up every two hours so the fire wouldn't go out.

THE NEXT TIME James fully woke he knew something was wrong, both with him and Hazel. A full day had passed in a haze of two-hour sleep intervals.

Every time the alarm went off, James had stoked the fire and added a few logs before letting sleep drag him back into the depths of its hellish embrace. But somehow, reality seemed worse than his reoccurring nightmare of Hazel trapped beneath the ice. Because in reality she was so hot she could've melted an iceberg.

James pressed his lips to her forehead, confirming what he

already knew. Hazel was ravished by fever. The shirt he'd dressed her in clung to her pale body, damp with sweat.

He needed to do something. There was Tylenol in the first aid kit and maybe the bucket of snow had melted to water by now. That would help Hazel.

Gathering his strength, James tried to stand up. The moment he was on his feet, the world began to sway. He collapsed, crashing to the floor as his vision eddied into blackness.

WHEN JAMES WOKE UP AGAIN, he was shivering. The fire was out and he was laying on the hard cabin floor a few feet away from Hazel. *What the hell?*

He crawled back over to her, noticing the beads of sweat gathered on her brow and cheeks. She even had a tiny pool of perspiration amassed in the perfect dip that made up the Cupid's bow of her lips. *The fever.*

His memory cleared and he remembered he'd been trying to get her Tylenol.

He had to try again.

It took a tremendous amount of effort, but this time, James managed to complete the task, staying on his knees until he'd been able to crawl to the first aid kit. The water in the bucket had melted enough for him to refill his hydro-pack, giving Hazel water to take the pill with. She hadn't even opened her eyes, but he'd been able to coax her to swallow the pill and drink.

It wasn't much, but it was progress.

Once again James stoked the fire, then dragged his pack back over to the bedroll so he'd have their supplies nearby. Finally, he crawled back under the sleeping bag with Hazel.

She was like a tiny inferno, but her warmth felt like heaven against his chilled skin.

James rummaged through his pack until he found what was left of their rations. He laid them out on the piece of tin foil he'd saved from his last PB&J. The smell of peanut butter clung to the empty foil making James's mouth water. He would kill for a PB&J. Now, all they had left were Hazel's candies: two lollipops and eleven sugar coated peanuts.

He unwrapped a lollipop and sucked it for a moment, savoring the sweet tang of sugar. It made his jaw ache with hunger. After not nearly long enough, he shared the lollipop with Hazel, encouraging her to suck even though she was barely conscious enough to do so.

James's hand throbbed in pain as he held the valve of his hydro-pack open so Hazel could take another sip of water, while he propped her up with his good hand. He knew a few Tylenol might help take the edge off his injury, but they only had three left and he didn't want to waste them with the fever still clinging to Hazel's flushed skin.

Besides, he was pretty sure he had at least fractured a few bones in his hand. Tylenol would only be a temporary relief. What he really needed was a doctor. And not just for his hand. His racing heartbeat told James that he was facing a much more serious threat.

He was beginning to worry he may have dislodged his pacemaker when he jumped off the roof. It was the only explanation he could think of for his wild pulse and dizzy spells. James took a sip of water and tried to keep it together. He didn't have any other choice. It was all just a waiting game now.

38

H azel

WHEN HAZEL OPENED HER EYES, it took her a moment to get her bearings. She was warm and comfortable with a pillow under her head. It was dark where she was, but she could make out a tube by her mouth and she heard a faint beeping.

Was she in the hospital? Had she been rescued?

She blinked the room into focus and all hopes of rescue were dashed. Hazel was still lying on the floor in the old cabin. She was comfortable because she was on a bedroll, and she was warm because she was wrapped in Jamie's embrace, both of them beneath his sleeping bag. She'd mistaken his bicep for a pillow and the tube near her mouth was from his hydropack.

But what about the beeping?

When she sat up to investigate, Jamie rousted. He looked

terrible, his skin pale and his eyes bloodshot. But the moment that he saw her awake a huge smile curved his chapped lips.

"Thank God," he whispered sitting up to pull her into a hug that felt entirely too good.

After a moment he pulled back to inspect her, brushing the back of his fingers across her forehead and cheeks. "You had a fever," he explained.

"I did?"

He nodded. "How do you feel now?"

His hand was still on her forehead, fussing over her like she imagined a mother would. "Okay . . ." she said slowly, but her hesitation wasn't for herself.

As Jamie moved closer so did the beeping. It sounded like a dying watch battery. She knew that sound.

Shit! Terror gripped Hazel as her mind jumped to the worst possible conclusion.

It can't be. Yet she knew it was.

She'd heard that sound before. It was the same noise her father's pacemaker made when it malfunctioned, or the battery began to run out.

"Jamie?" Hazel whispered, praying he'd tell her she was wrong, but when their eyes met, she knew it was true. "Your pacemaker?"

When he didn't immediately answer, a lump the size of Nevada formed in her throat. Hazel gently placed a hand over Jamie's struggling heart, barely feeling the tears slipping down her cheeks. "How?"

"It doesn't matter."

"How?" she asked again.

He ran a hand through his disheveled hair. "I don't know. Probably when I jumped off the roof."

"You jumped off the roof?"

His sky-blue eyes darkened. "You fell through the ice, Hazel."

She sucked in a breath. This was her fault. She never should've come to Wander Mountain. Then she never would've met Jamie and put his life in danger.

She could feel the thready pulse of his heart beneath her palm and it split her own heart in two. "I'm sorry," she whispered.

"It's okay," he said softly, bringing his hand up to cover hers.

She gasped when she saw the state of it. "What the hell happened to your hand?"

His swollen purple fist barely looked like a hand at all.

When she gingerly touched it, Jamie flinched. "You were trapped." The words seemed to transport him back to an unpleasant memory that left him shuddering. "I had to get you out," he murmured, his eyes gravely serious.

She found herself wanting to apologize again, but a million 'I'm sorrys' wouldn't make up for what her selfishness had cost him. The only thing to do now was find a way to start repairing the damage she'd done.

Hazel carefully inspected Jamie's hand, her stomach recoiling when she saw bone pushing through the skin.

"Can you move your fingers?" she asked, her voice full of concern.

He tried, his face a mask of pain as he managed a small twitch of movement.

"You need a splint," she said quietly.

"Yeah. Among other things," he replied with a smirk.

She knew he was trying to lighten the mood, but she didn't like the joke. Not when all of this was her fault and what Jamie really needed was a hospital.

She could treat his hand but what good would that do if his heart gave out?

With worry stuck in her throat, Hazel worked silently for the next hour, cleaning and setting Jamie's hand. She was doing her best to be as gentle as possible, but she could tell he was in pain, even if he was doing his best to hide it for her benefit—a trait that only made her feel worse.

Once she disinfected his cuts, she shredded the sleeve from one of his shirts to use as a bandage. She carefully wrapped his hand, threading the material around each finger and over his knuckles where the gashes were so deep she could see bone. She wanted to give him some cushioning for when she applied the splint. Since she didn't have a real one, she did her best to fashion one from what they had.

She cut the six aluminum stays out of the back of Jamie's pack. The pack wouldn't hold its shape without the twelve inch supports, but they were the perfect length for a splint and lightweight enough not to make moving his arm more difficult. The hardest part was getting Jamie to flatten his fingers out. He could barely move them so Hazel had to slowly stretch each one out herself.

"Exhale through the pain," she instructed as she quickly secured the makeshift splints with the tape from the first aid kit and left-over shirt scraps.

"Why are you so good at this?" Jamie asked through gritted teeth.

Hazel huffed a nervous laugh. "I'm glad you think I know what I'm doing."

"You've got me fooled. Maybe you should be a nurse."

"Yeah?" she asked stretching out his last finger.

He hissed in pain. "You'd be a hot nurse."

This time her laugh was genuine. "Okay, I think the pain has warped your brain."

He grinned and shook his head. "You might be right, but I'm already picturing you in a naughty nurse costume."

She rolled her eyes, but it was hard not to smile back at him. If the playful conversation was distracting him from the pain, she wouldn't take that away from him.

Hazel continued to work while Jamie mused about his nurse fantasy. When she was finally finished, she sat back on her heels and evaluated her work. "Well, it's not pretty but it should hold and it's the best chance you'll have to use your fingers."

Their eyes met and the unspoken words hung in the air between them. *If we survive this...*

Jamie broke the silence first. "Thank you."

Hazel turned away from him, the pain in her chest too much to bear. The last thing she deserved was his thanks. "You need to eat something," she said, sorting through the pack and coming up empty.

"The last of the rations are over there," he said pointing to a thin strip of foil by the hearth.

Hazel's heart sank when she saw one lollipop and a few Boston Baked Beans.

Three weeks without food...

The rule of threes raced through her head.

Humans can survive three minutes without air, three hours of exposure, three days without water, three weeks without food.

She'd already tested the air and exposure theories and didn't have any desire to experience the rest.

Thanks to the snow, they had water, but food was going to be their biggest challenge. Three weeks was a long time though. Surely someone would find them by then.

Hazel grabbed two of the sugar-coated nuts and crawled back over to Jamie. She handed him one, then she grabbed a Tylenol from the first aid kit.

He pushed it away when she tried to give it to him. "We should save it."

"You're in pain," she said gently. "Just take it."

"Pain is tolerable," he argued. "These are the only drugs we have left. We should save them."

For what? She wanted to ask, but she didn't have the heart.

She didn't want to argue with Jamie. So instead she threw another log on the fire and settled next to him on the bedroll, counting each of his irregular heartbeats until she fell asleep.

39

H azel

HAZEL STARED up at the ceiling trying not to count Jamie's every breath. His chest rose and fell steadily for now, but how long before that changed?

Worry had woken her at dawn. Not that she'd really been sleeping. She and Jamie had switched on and off with fire duty throughout the night even though Hazel said she didn't need his help. She wanted him to conserve his energy, but of course he didn't listen. Their matched stubbornness might have been comical if their situation wasn't so dire.

Jamie's racing heart filled Hazel with unease. In the silent stretches throughout the night where sleep had escaped her, she racked her brain for pacemaker protocol.

It all led to one simple, hard fact—*Jamie needed to get to a hospital, and fast.*

Hazel worried they were wasting the precious time he had

left hoping for rescue that might never come. She took stock of their meager rations again, wondering at what point they might have to consider trying to hike out on their own. They could probably afford three days in the cabin before starvation set in. But if they waited until their supplies ran out completely, they might be too weak to attempt leaving.

Hazel glanced at Jamie again and mopped the beads of sweat clinging to his brow. His fever started last night, probably brought on from the trauma of setting his broken fingers. Around midnight, she'd crushed up a Tylenol and mixed it in a cup of water. Jamie was so out of it, he didn't notice the bitter taste. It seemed to help for a while, but now the fever was back.

She didn't know if it was from pain, infection, his racing heart or countless other unknown factors. All she knew was she didn't like it. Shivering while sweating was never a good sign.

Unable to watch him suffer, Hazel slipped from under their shared sleeping bag and went back to the first aid kit to prepare another Tylenol tonic. She grabbed two pieces of candy for Jamie too, not wanting to give him more drugs on an empty stomach.

This time, Jamie stirred fully awake when Hazel tried to get him to drink.

"Morning," he said groggily.

His bedhead and sleepy smile were enough to make her heartrate match his, but she forced herself to focus. "Here, you need to drink this."

He obediently took a sip and cringed. "This water doesn't taste right."

"It's the best we've got. Drink." He obeyed and Hazel handed him the two candy-coated peanuts.

He raised his dark eyebrows at her. "Two?"

"I had two," she lied. "We've got to keep our strength up."

Jamie surveyed her face skeptically before he finally popped the two candies in his mouth. He finished off his water and laid back down, holding his arm out for her to join him. "Come keep me warm."

There were a million reasons why she shouldn't curl back up in their makeshift bed—she should tend the fire, melt more snow for water, protect herself from the heartbreak she knew was coming—but nothing was enough to keep her from him. Not when it was her fault he was in this mess.

Besides, when he looked at her like that—all crooked smiles and hopeful eyes—she was powerless against the pull in her chest. They might not have much time left and she was determined not to waste it.

When Hazel carefully settled next to Jamie, his whole body seemed to relax. He wrapped his good arm around her and inhaled her hair. She imagined it smelled horrible, but still, she felt him smile against her.

"Will you tell me a story?" he asked.

She laughed, remembering how she'd asked him the same thing on their very first night of this disastrous adventure. "Is being lost in the woods not exciting enough for you?"

"Every moment with you is exciting."

At that, Hazel's heart sped up, matching the rhythm of Jamie's, because he was right. Ever since she met him, her life had been one nonstop adventure after another.

She closed her eyes, letting herself feel how much she craved him and the way he made her feel alive.

James

.   .   .

WITH HAZEL NESTLED against his side, all felt right with the world again.

James ran his fingers over her silky hair, memorizing the feel of it. He felt her eyelids flutter close against his neck.

"Story," he murmured into her hair, wanting to hear her voice.

"I don't know any good ones," she whispered.

"How did I fall in love with such an unimaginative girl?" he teased.

Hazel sucked in a breath and tried to cover it with a yawn.

James loved the way her pulse raced whenever he said that perfect four-letter word. *Love.* He wondered if it would lose its potency on her if he said it over and over. He knew he'd never grow tired of saying it. He loved her, and there was nothing like the true threat of death to cement that notion.

James had known he'd fall for Hazel the moment she literally crashed into his life. He exhaled, smiling quietly to himself over the irony of love, life and loss. *It never happens the way you expect.*

For a while he lay still, enjoying the quiet sound of Hazel's breathing, but as he began to feel sleep pull him under, he spoke, not quite ready to give up this time with her. There was so much more he wanted to tell her, but how to begin . . .

"Okay," he said softly. "I've got a story."

Hazel snuggled closer and James felt like his chest might burst.

"There once was a prince who fell in love with a princess that he met in the frozen forest. Her heart was trapped in ice and he made it his goal to thaw it. So, he stole her from the frozen forest and brought her to a land of sunshine to live with him on his ship. At last, her heart melted and she fell in love with him too, and they lived happily ever after."

.   .   .

HAZEL

TEARS BURNED Hazel's eyes as she tried to discreetly wipe them away. She didn't deserve him; this boy full of so much love and hope and dreams. She wished so badly she did, because the longing for his fairytale to be true threatened to drown her with loneliness.

"Hey," Jamie murmured, noticing her tears. "What's wrong?"

"I think we need to leave."

He started shaking his head immediately. "They'll come for us. When we don't turn up at the finish line, they'll track us. We need to stay here."

Hazel bit her lip and closed her eyes, voicing her fears. "We can't die here, Jamie."

He pulled her against him and kissed her head. "You won't."

She didn't miss his choice of words. '*You* won't.'

But what about him?

Fear made her brave. Hazel sat up, looking down at Jamie with heartbreak in her throat. "I was coming back. When you called me from the roof . . . I'd already made up my mind to come back."

He swallowed thickly, but stayed silent.

"I just wanted you to know that. I wasn't going to leave you, Jamie. I promise."

"Okay," he replied softly.

"Okay."

Hazel was about to lay back down but her heart wouldn't let her. For once, she needed to get it all out. She might not get another chance.

"No, it's not okay. I'm an idiot. I care about you, Jamie. I want all the same things you do. But I just . . . I don't know. I'm scared to let myself want you."

Jamie took her hand and squeezed, her own pained expression mirrored on his face.

"I don't want to lose you," she whispered. "Because I think . . . I think I'm in love with you."

His face twisted into the most beautiful smile she'd ever seen. It hurt her heart to look at him, so she let him pull her close and pepper her with kisses.

"I knew you loved me," he teased, and she couldn't help rolling her eyes.

When she looked at him, he was grinning. "You knew, huh?"

"Uh huh," he replied, smiling like a fool.

She didn't even try to fight her own grin. "Was it my kind words or sweet temperment that gave it away?"

Jamie laughed. "All of the above." But then his expression softened. "Even if you never figured out how to tell me . . . I knew . . . but thank you for saying it anyway."

Hazel felt breathless as she stared into his sky-blue eyes, set aglow by the firelight. Now that she'd said the words, she felt emotions welling inside her like a tidal wave. She'd always kept them locked up; hidden away in a box within a box inside her frozen heart. But now that her feelings were loose, she couldn't recapture them. She didn't want to. The sensation was liberating.

"I love you," she whispered, "so you better not die on me, okay?"

"Okay," he said softly, before his lips met hers.

And this time, it felt like things actually might be okay.

So, for once Hazel stopped worrying and let herself get lost in Jamie's kiss.

40

H azel

TIME PASSED UNPREDICTABLY in the cabin. One day, then two, then five. For the most part, Hazel didn't mind. She kept herself occupied caring for Jamie and that was a job measured by heartbeats, not hours or days.

When she was snuggled against Jamie's side, it was hard to care what day it was. Their love kept them warm and with his lips pressed to hers, she barely noticed her hunger. Besides, what was hunger when they had dreams to sustain them?

"When we get out of here," Jamie murmured against her temple, "we're going to sail my boat straight to Key West."

"Does your boat have a fireplace?" she asked gazing past him to the glowing coals of their fire.

"No."

Hazel slowly propped her head up on her elbow and smiled down at Jamie. "Then I'm not leaving."

He grinned at her. "Okay. When we get out of here, we'll sail to Key West and buy a house with a fireplace. How does that sound?"

"Do houses in Key West have fireplaces?"

He tucked a lock of hair behind her ear. "Ours will."

Hazel's heart galloped in her chest. It happened every time they played this game of daydreams and Jamie said things like *ours* and *we*. She knew with each day that passed it became more and more unlikely they would survive. And each day words like *ours* and *we* became more important. Their food was long gone. Words were the last hope fueling them now.

Crossroads was over, yet no one had come for them.

The snow outside was melting and with it, their chances of survival dwindled. Soon there wouldn't be enough to melt for water and the prospect of braving the lake that had nearly killed her didn't excite Hazel. There might be other options, but she didn't like leaving Jamie for more than a few minutes at a time. His heartbeat was too unsteady, the beeping of his pacemaker an ever-present reminder of the ticking time he had left.

It made her anxious. But so did most things these days. Especially the fact that her father and grandfather were probably out of their mind with worry.

By her calculations, Hazel should've returned home two days ago.

Was Jenny still covering for her?

Had Wander Mountain called to report her missing?

She knew it was stupid, but she prayed they hadn't. She didn't want her dad to have to come all the way to Montana to join the search party—if there even was one. But that was the kind of thing her dad would do. He was ex-military. 'No man left behind' was practically his motto.

But what about Gramps? Who would care for him if her

dad came to Montana? And what could her dad even do out here? The terrain wasn't exactly wheelchair friendly.

"You're worrying again," Jamie said, stroking her hair.

She sighed. "I just can't stop thinking about my dad."

"They're going to find us, Hazel."

"How do you know?"

"Our GPS—"

"What if the GPS trackers don't work this far out?" She sat up, feeling her pulse throb inside her head. The lack of food was making her lightheaded. When she focused on Jamie, she did her best to disguise the fear in her voice. "What if they gave up looking for us?"

Jamie took her hand. "Hazel, my father may be a dick, but he's a powerful politician. He'll make sure we're found. The publicity alone guarantees it."

She frowned. This wasn't the first time they'd had this conversation either, but it still didn't make her feel any better. "Do you think your father's in Montana?"

He shrugged. "If it means good publicity, yeah."

"I worry that my dad will come here too," she said quietly.

Jamie pulled her back toward him, stroking her hair when she was nestled against his side again. "Do you think he could make a trip like that?"

She nodded. "He's the strongest person I know. Not much stops him."

"Not even his injuries?"

Hazel blinked away the pain. She hated talking about her father's injuries. He was so much more than their sum, but to most people, that's all they saw. "He's only in his chair because it helps him get around faster. He has a prosthetic, but he hates it. Says the only thing it's good for is . . ." Her voice trailed off as she realized what she'd been about to say, making tears well in her eyes.

"What?" Jamie asked.

She didn't want to say it out loud. Somehow, Hazel felt like whispering her father's promise inside the rundown cabin would make it impossible for it to come true. But not saying it almost hurt worse, because now more than ever, she wished for it to come true.

"My dad promised to keep his prosthetic long enough to walk me down the aisle on my wedding day. He practices once a month so he doesn't get rusty." She hiccupped. "Guess it doesn't matter now."

Jamie took her face in his hands. "Hey, we're not giving up. Your dad is a badass hero and mine's a ruthless asshole. I'd say that's the makings of an epic rescue team if I've ever heard one."

She laughed, despite feeling miserable. "Is your father really that bad?"

"He manipulates people for a living, so you tell me."

"But don't politicians help people, too?"

"Some do, but that's not why my father went into politics. He doesn't care about helping people, he just craves the attention he lost when his football career ended. That's why I've never really cared about not being able to play. I don't care about fame or fortune. Not after I've seen what it does to people. Fame fades. And when the spotlight is gone what are you left with? Nothing." Jamie shook his head, his eyes locking on hers. "I know what I want Hazel, and I'm gonna fight for it until my last breath."

More tears leaked from her face. She hated when he said things like that, mostly because she counted every breath he took when she lay awake each night staring at the stars through the holes in the ceiling. But talking about Jamie's fragile heart only made them both feel worse, so instead Hazel asked him something she'd been thinking about these past few days.

"Do you believe in soulmates?"

He smirked. "I don't know. Do you?"

"If you asked me that a few weeks ago I would've said no."

His sky-blue eyes bore into hers. "And now?"

"I think I do."

Jamie chuckled. "Starvation has made you romantic."

"No, it's made me stop being afraid of having something to lose."

He frowned. "I think it's made me more afraid."

"Of what?"

"Of losing this," he said, putting his hand to her chest. "I don't know if I believe in soulmates, Hazel. But I believe in us. And I believe fate brought us together."

"What's the difference between soulmates and fate?"

"I think soulmates is just a phrase that poets made up and greeting card companies stole. But fate is something bigger. It's like a magnetic pull that leads us to the places and people we belong with."

"Kind of like a compass?"

Jamie's smile was so full of sorrow that it broke Hazel's heart for the hundredth time since they'd met. "Just like a compass," he said, pulling her close and kissing her forehead. "I worry that without you, I'd have to live my life with a broken compass, wandering and lost for eternity, and I . . . I don't want that for you."

She caught the first tear she'd seen him shed during this entire ordeal. "Jamie . . ."

"Promise me," he begged. "Promise me if I don't make it, you won't stay lost."

"Jamie—"

"Hazel, I need you to promise me."

She bit down hard to keep from crying or screaming or both. "No," she said through her fury. "I'm not going to make that promise, because you're going to make it." She stubbornly set her jaw. "We both make it or neither of us do."

And with that, she gathered her remaining strength and climbed out of bed.

Hazel wasn't about to lay down and die. Not when she finally knew what to live for.

41

H azel

BY THE TIME the sun decided to grace the sky, Hazel had a plan.

She'd worked through the night by firelight, comparing what she remembered of the Wander Mountain map to the old dusty relics that had been left behind in the cabin. Their map had been lost along with the rest of the contents of her pack when the iced-over lake melted, claiming the last of her supplies.

Thankfully, she'd found a few useful old maps while digging through the cabin for more items to feed the fire.

That was days ago, though. They'd burned through everything she'd found since then, including the remaining wood from the lumber pile outback and the old chairs. Now they were down to the decaying taxidermy, which gave off a toxic odor when burned, making Hazel wonder if the temporary warmth was worth it.

When Hazel had first discovered the maps, Jamie had told her to burn them, but something made her hesitate. She'd tucked them away as if she knew she'd need them. And she had.

During her many restless nights, the old maps helped Hazel pass the time. She familiarized herself with the hand-drawn charts, wondering what it must've been like all those years ago when they were made. She found herself fantasizing about being one of the pioneer families who'd escaped to these mountains to start a new life.

Sometimes she liked to pretend that's what she and Jamie were, two people in love, forging a future in the only place they could have one.

It beat the stark reality—that they were lost and might very well die here, trapped in a prison of their own making.

Her making.

Hazel was the reason they were trapped here and that's precisely why she was so determined to find a way home.

Things hadn't seemed so desperate when Hazel had first let herself daydream over the maps. Jamie had still been adamant that they would be rescued. But now with their rations gone and water scarce, even Jamie was starting to give up.

Hazel knew she'd waited too long. Walking out on foot wasn't a realistic option for Jamie now. Even she was weak from lack of nutrition and she had a healthy heart.

She often fell prey to dizzy spells if she got up too quickly in the middle of the night to keep the fire alive, and it was hard to ignore the relentless growl of her empty stomach or the way her clothes hung off of her now.

But she wasn't about to give up. A plan had come together in her mind last night when she'd been scouring the maps.

One of the older charts she'd found showed where all the rural homestead sites were located. The closest one, the Furlow House, was only about thirty-five miles from them. That was a good day's hike if she pushed it. The nearest town was still nearly two-hundred miles from the Furlow House, but Hazel was banking on there being some form of aid at the old homestead.

Best case, the house would be occupied. Even if it wasn't, she could at least hope for a working phone and maybe some canned goods. Worst case, it would be in as bad shape as the cabin and they would've used the last of their energy for nothing.

But at least we'd have tried.

She couldn't just sit there and slowly die.

Hazel knew her plan wasn't foolproof, but she was out of options. If they wanted to live, they were going to have to take a calculated risk and they were going to have to do it today.

She looked at Jamie, still asleep in front of the fire. The temperature inside the cabin was so cold that Hazel shivered continually. But still, there was a layer of sheen covering Jamie's brow. He was getting worse.

Their window of opportunity was closing. If they didn't leave today, this would be where he died and that wasn't an option. Not while Hazel still had breath in her body.

Jamie had rescued her, twice now. It was her turn to save him.

Hazel knew she would make better time if she left for the Furlow House on her own, but she couldn't do that to Jamie. She'd tried to leave him once to disastrous repercussions. She'd meant what she said to him; they survived this together or not at all.

Last night, after she'd formulated her plan to hike to the Furlow House, she'd spent a good part of the evening constructing a sled out of the remaining pieces of Jamie's pack and the tarp from the wood pile. This way she could drag their sleeping bag, bedroll and diminished supplies. But more importantly, if Jamie needed it, Hazel would have a way to transport him.

Now all she had to do was convince him that her plan would work.

James

EVERY TIME JAMES awoke to the heavenly sight of Hazel's gorgeous caramel eyes staring down at him, he was convinced he was dead. Especially when she woke him with a bright smile and eager words.

If this is heaven, maybe I'm okay with dying. But the thought evaporated the moment Hazel's warm fingers touched his cheek.

He'd never get enough of the sensation that rushed through him when she brushed his skin or kissed his lips. No, dying wasn't what he wanted. Not if it meant losing Hazel and everything she made him feel.

She was speaking again.

It took James a moment to decipher what she was saying. It was getting more difficult to focus these days. He didn't know if it was strictly from the lack of food or something more. The persistent beeping of his pacemaker made him think it was the latter, but he was well practiced in avoiding things he couldn't control.

"Let me show you," Hazel was saying, helping James into a sitting position.

She propped a makeshift support behind him. James hated how natural it was becoming for her to care for him. She already took care of enough people in her life. Hazel needed someone to take care of her for a change and James wanted to be that person, not the other way around.

He blinked and the brittle drawing she'd set in his lap came into focus. It was a map.

Hazel was speaking again, and James wrestled to hear her over the pounding in his head.

". . . it's only a day's hike. If we leave today—"

"Leave?"

"Jamie . . ." she met his eyes, worry laced with determination dancing in hers. "We're out of time. If we don't leave today . . ."

He didn't make her finish the sentence. He knew what a few more days without food and water would do to them. He could already see the changes in Hazel's gaunt cheekbones.

He swallowed thickly, knowing full well he probably wouldn't survive a day of hiking with his heart pounding like a spastic snare drum, but he couldn't say that to her. He didn't want to add more weight to the already heavy burden she was carrying.

He knew she blamed herself for their situation, but in his heart, James knew he was at fault. He hadn't followed the rules. Not one of them—hers or Wander Mountains.

If he'd had a handle on his grief, he would've taken off his mother's watch like instructed and their compass wouldn't have led them astray. If he'd listened to Hazel and not crossed the lines she'd drawn, they wouldn't have ended up partnered together. She wouldn't have fallen through the ice and his heart wouldn't be dying. *Or would it?*

From the moment he met Hazel, she'd captured his heart the way no one else ever had. So how could he have denied himself? Staying away from her would've hurt his heart just as badly as his fall from the roof had.

Hazel watched him with bated breath.

James sighed. It was hard to blame his heart for loving her, no matter what the outcome. And though he knew the love of his useless heart wasn't worth much, it was all he had left to give. James would've carved his selfish heart out to erase the worry from Hazel's face.

He took her hand. "You want to leave today?"

She nodded.

"Okay," he said confidently.

"Okay?" she asked, sounding surprised. "So, you think this will work?"

"I think you're stubborn enough to make it work."

"*We're* stubborn enough," she corrected.

James looked into Hazel's unwavering eyes and felt his heart strengthen. He would keep fighting. He had to—for as many beats as his heart had left.

42

H azel

THE COLD AIR bit life back into Hazel's stiff limbs as they took their first steps away from the cabin. The ground had begun to thaw, leaving a spongy slush that was unpleasant to walk through. Mud and ice squelched underfoot, making each step laborious. If they made it to the Furlow House by nightfall it would be a miracle.

Hazel glanced up at Jamie from under her lashes. She was surprised he'd so readily agreed to leave. Normally, he dismissed her suggestions to move from the cabin. *Did that mean he'd truly given up on being rescued too?*

Hazel hated the way that thought dashed her hopes. She hadn't realized just how much she'd come to rely on Jamie's hopefulness to fuel her own. They were equally matched in that way—balancing each other's deficiencies. He'd cared for her when she needed him; at Wander Mountain and both times she'd battled the water and nearly lost. Now it was her turn to care for him.

She tightened her hold around his waist. His arm was anchored over her shoulders. Holding up his towering frame wouldn't have been easy if she'd been at full strength. But after days without adequate food or water, her energy was depleted, making the task of supporting Jamie's towering frame nearly impossible.

After a few more grueling steps, fear began to whisper in Hazel's ear. *Turn back. You'll never make it together. He's weighing you down.*

She closed her eyes against the terrible thoughts running through her mind and prayed for strength. That's when her father's voice came to her, steady and true. *'No man left behind, Walker. Choose a course and follow through. One step at a time.'*

Emotion swelled inside Hazel, filling her with strength and resolve. She wanted to cry with joy as she let her father's words bolster her, but she couldn't afford to waste the energy. Instead, she steeled her spine and kept moving, one foot in front of the other, not planning to stop until her body physically gave out.

James

"I JUST NEED A MINUTE," James said struggling to pull breath into his burning lungs.

The world had gone out of focus again, blurring around the edges. He'd made it further than he'd expected on this journey. They'd gone nearly thirty miles.

He knew he was slowing Hazel down, but every time he even began to suggest she go ahead without him she cut him off. He had a feeling she was afraid he'd give up without her there to remind him what he was fighting for. And maybe she was right.

He'd had to stop to rest more than a few times. And each time James grew more worried that he wouldn't find the strength to get back up. Yet somehow, the pleading look in Hazel's eyes pulled fortitude from a reserve he didn't know he had. Although this time, he worried maybe he'd finally depleted it.

James was so dizzy he felt sick. Had there been anything in his stomach, he would've thrown up. Thankfully, all he could do was dry heave until he collapsed into a fit of sputtering coughs.

Hazel jumped to his aid, forcing him to lay on the makeshift sled she'd been dragging. "We need to get your heart rate down," she ordered after checking his pulse.

"Tell me about it," he tried to joke, but the words came out strangled, making him sound anything but funny.

"I think you've been upright too much today. It'll put less stress on your heart if you lie down."

"True, but hiking isn't usually done lying down," he argued, attempting to sit.

She pushed him back. "James, you need to lie down."

He knew Hazel was serious when she called him James, but he still couldn't help trying to lighten the mood. Sarcasm had been his friend and weapon most of his life. Even now, at death's door, it came to him naturally, soothing his fears.

"If you really want to lie down, I can think of a few things we could do," he said with a wink.

Hazel rolled her eyes.

"What? You can't blame a guy for trying on his deathbed. It would be rather embarrassing to have, 'died a virgin,' on my tombstone."

Her eyes widened. "A virgin? But you said—"

"I know what I said," he interrupted. He remembered every moment of their time together. Especially the time they'd ended up in Hazel's cabin and nearly had sex.

She looked at him, questions burning in her eyes. "You lied?"

"I wanted you to think I knew what I was doing."

Hazel blushed. "It certainly seemed like you did."

He smirked, reaching a hand up to caress her pink cheek as the memories of that perfect moment washed over him. "That was the single best moment of my life."

"Mine too," she whispered.

"I'm sorry I lied. I want you to know everything else we shared was true."

"Why did you lie?" she asked.

He huffed a gentle laugh. "Would telling you I was slightly terrified have been sexier?"

She surprised him by nodding. "Sometimes it's nice to know you're not the only one who's afraid."

"Then in that case, Hazel Walker, you terrify me. My heart has been in my throat since the moment we met. At first, I was scared you wouldn't see me and when you did, I was scared you wouldn't like what you saw. But for some crazy reason you do. And now I'm even more afraid that you'll wake up and change your mind. I'm scared I'll wake up and all of this will have been a dream, because I'm not someone who's used to getting what he wants."

Tears welled in her bright eyes as they caught the last of the sun's warm rays. "How do you always manage to put my exact worries into words?" she whispered.

"Because we're meant to be."

James pulled Hazel to him until their lips met in a blaze of passion. When they were forced to break for air, he stared into her eyes, seeing his very soul reflected in them. This couldn't be the end. He couldn't have found what he wanted most in life, only to experience it for such a brief time.

It wasn't fair.

He brushed Hazel's hair back from her flushed cheeks. "The one thing I'm most afraid of is a life without you."

"Me too."

"Maybe I conceded too easily to this hike."

"What do you mean?" she asked, concern glowing in her eyes.

He grinned. "I should've begged you to have sex with me first. Now I've lost all my leverage."

Hazel laughed. "I wouldn't have agreed."

James felt his pride wither. "Way to kick a man while he's down."

"You didn't let me finish," she teased. Hazel placed a gentle kiss on the corner of James's mouth. "If you had asked me to sleep with you before we left the cabin I wouldn't have agreed because, when we do it," she placed another kiss on the opposite corner, "and we are gonna do it, it's gonna be somewhere deserving of us."

James laughed the moment he realized Hazel was quoting what he'd said to her just before their mind-blowing romp in the sheets. He gestured to the frigid wilderness surrounding them. "You're right, this place couldn't handle what I want to do to you, Hazel Walker."

It was Hazel's turn to laugh. "Then we'd better keep moving so you can make good on your promises."

43

H azel

WITH ONLY A FEW miles left to go, Jamie's resolve finally collapsed. He'd laid down on the sled to rest but this time he'd been unable to get back up. Hazel had been waiting for it for miles now. And although it terrified her to see him so weak, she tried to think of it as a blessing when he finally gave in to exhaustion and fell asleep. At least now he couldn't argue with her when she strapped him to the makeshift sled and began to drag him the last few miles.

She'd suggested it hours ago, but his pride kept getting in the way. Pulling him wasn't easy. But keeping him upright and watching him struggle for each step hadn't been easy either. At least now she could lean into the last bit of the journey with everything she had left.

They'd come a long way, both physically and metaphorically. And although Hazel had never been more exhausted, she somehow felt stronger with each step that drew them closer to the Furlow House.

When it came into view, renewed energy surged through her. But as the sky darkened and the house grew nearer, Hazel's hope quickly evaporated when she realized she saw no signs of life. No light in the windows, no smoke curling from the chimney, no dogs barking in the yard, no livestock inside the acres of fencing.

The Furlow House was abandoned, just like her hope.

THOUGH HAZEL WANTED nothing more than to collapse and curl up next to Jamie, something inside her wouldn't allow her to surrender. She kept going, dragging him over the barely frozen mix of slush until they were at the doorstep to the two-story white farmhouse.

It wasn't in ill-repair like the cabin. From the looks of it, the house had been built around the same time, but unlike the cabin, the Furlow House had been kept up and modernized throughout the years. The glass in the windows looked new and clean and there was a spicket next to the front porch that gave Hazel hope of finding running water inside.

She'd tried the spicket first, but when nothing happened, she realized the water might be turned off in order to winterize the property. She needed to find a way inside.

Turning back to Jamie, she knelt down and whispered to him. "I'll be right back. I just need to find a way inside. I'm not leaving you, okay?"

He mumbled an incoherent response and she kissed his forehead, tucking the sleeping bag higher around his neck. She hated to leave him even for a moment, worried that if he woke and she wasn't there he'd panic. She knew *she* would.

But then again, she'd always been crippled by her fear of abandonment.

Shaking her worry from her head she tried to focus as she carefully made her way around the property. Exhaustion was taking its toll on her. She needed to find a way inside before she collapsed. Each step felt heavy, her motor-skills impaired as she tried unsuccessfully to pry open any of the doors or windows.

Hazel's heart was pounding from exertion, making it harder and harder to think. She needed to get inside the house. The temperature was dropping rapidly now that the sun had set. They wouldn't survive the night without shelter, and she was much too fatigued to manage a fire.

Her eyes darted to the barn in the distance. It was only a few yards away, but the distance seemed daunting after a day of hiking. But still she forced her feet to keep moving.

Hazel unbolted the creaky barn doors and wrenched one of them open, falling to her knees at the sight that awaited her. She cried out when her eyes caught the familiar glint of metal, rubber and glass. A large nineties model pickup truck stared back at her, sparking the hope that she'd thought she'd lost.

Adrenaline drove Hazel to her feet as she raced to the truck.

Gas! That's all I need.

She sent up silent prayers. If the truck had gas, Hazel could make it run. She'd been working on trucks like this since she was a child. She could rebuild an engine and repair a transmission before she learned how to wear a bra. Hotwiring this truck would be a piece of cake. The only thing that would get in her way now would be an empty gas tank.

Hazel climbed inside and went to work. After a few minor setbacks, mainly figuring out the battery needed to be reconnected, she stripped the starter bundle and tapped the wires together. When the truck roared to life Hazel shrieked with joy. And when the gas gauge climbed to almost a full tank she wanted to dance.

She climbed out of the truck, flung the barn doors open and drove out into the night, feeling more alive than she'd ever been.

44

H azel

HAZEL COULDN'T STOP GLANCING at Jamie. She knew she needed to keep her eyes on the road, but the way he was breathing and the high-pitched beeps of his pacemaker made it impossible for her to focus.

The measured beeps had changed frequency and pattern about an hour ago. Jamie hadn't noticed, but Hazel didn't take comfort in that. He'd been asleep for the entire drive, only stirring for a moment when she'd loaded him into the truck.

He was seat belted into the passenger side and she couldn't help wishing she'd put him in the middle so she could reach him easier. As it was, all she could do now was hold his hand and drive like hell.

When she'd first started the drive, she'd wondered if leaving at night was the best idea. It was easier to navigate in daylight. Plus, a night of rest would've definitely done Hazel a world of good. She was constantly rubbing her eyes and slapping her cheeks to stay awake. She'd even rolled the window down on her side, using the blast of icy air to keep her awake.

But now, as she looked at Jamie in the pale moonlight filtering in through the trees, she knew the decision to leave right away was the only one she could've made. The urgent beeping of his pacemaker only served to backup that theory.

Hazel glanced at the map laid out in the seat between them. She did it more out of habit than necessity. She had the route to Livingston memorized. Studying that map had been her salvation in the many sleepless nights in the cabin. Now, she prayed it would deliver salvation of the physical kind.

Gripping the wheel with both hands, Hazel sped through the moonlight night, racing Jamie's heart to the finish line.

James

UNNATURAL WARMTH and the flickering of light woke James. There was a foreign softness beneath him that creaked and swayed. The world blurred by in a dizzying display of watery light. He tried to focus but his head was swimming. He reached a hand out, feeling for Hazel, but met something cold and smooth. *Glass?*

Hazel's voice sounded from nearby. "I'm here," she said softly, her hand finding his. "I'm right here, Jamie. Hold on, okay?"

He turned his head to look at her. She was sitting a few feet away, bouncing and swaying along with him. The predawn light glowed behind her, making her look even more angelic than usual. "I love you, Hazel."

"I love you too, Jamie. But you have to hold on. We're almost there, okay?"

"Okay," he whispered, letting himself fall back into the arms of sleep.

HAZEL

HAZEL WHIPPED the truck into the first parking lot she found. It was a tiny gas station and convenient store on the outskirts of town. Her heart leapt with relief when she saw the neon word, OPEN, glowing in the window.

Not even bothering to close her door, she rushed to Jamie's side and helped him out of the truck. He was barely conscious as she dragged his lanky body into the store.

The clerk looked up when the door chimed, his face suddenly alert. "What the—"

"Call 911," Hazel blurted out. "Now!"

HAZEL DIDN'T KNOW what took longer, the grueling two-hundred mile drive from the Furlow House or the ten minutes it took the ambulance to arrive.

Jamie wasn't doing well. He sat on the floor of the convenient store with Hazel, their backs resting against the cooler case. Each breath he took was labored and shallow. The clerk had given them water bottles and food, but Hazel was too worried to eat.

She spent the agonizing minutes waiting for the ambulance feeding Jamie tiny sips of water. She took it as a good sign when he refused to drink more unless she did.

"Stubborn to the very end," she teased.

He gave her a weak smile and reached for a candy bar in the pile of supplies the clerk had given them. Hazel's heart ached when he selected a Snickers bar, her memories flooding with the last one they'd shared.

She helped him unwrap it, breaking off a piece and handing it to him, just like he'd done on the day he made her the worst picnic ever.

How she longed to be back there—healthy and whole.

She'd been so foolish to think she knew pain. She hadn't a clue! *This* was true pain. Watching someone you love near death, suffering while hope was within reach. But there was nothing else Hazel could do now but pray that she'd done enough.

Tears sprang into her eyes when Jamie took the candy bar from her and broke off a piece for her.

Hazel shook her head. "Only if you eat a piece first."

He let her place a piece of the candy bar in his mouth, his eyes sliding shut as he tried to chew it with the little strength he had left. She offered him more water and he took it. Even swallowing seemed to pain him.

She let Jamie catch his breath and when he laid his head in her lap she held in a sob, stroking his sweat-damp hair. "Please hold on just a little longer, okay?"

"Okay," he whispered, closing his eyes.

Hazel grabbed his hand and squeezed. "Jamie! Keep your eyes open. Don't you give up. Do you hear me? We made it. The ambulance will be here any minute."

She swore she could almost hear the sirens mixed with the beeping of his pacemaker.

Suddenly, silence cut the air around them, the reassuring sound of his pacemaker abruptly stopping. Hazel and Jamie looked at each other—saying nothing and everything in that frozen moment.

Jamie's fingers tightened around Hazel's. "Promise you won't leave me," he begged.

"I promise," she said with all the strength she had left. "I promise, Jamie."

"Okay," he whispered, giving one last shuddering sigh before closing his eyes.

This time Hazel was sure when she heard the sirens. Because it was the only sound loud enough to break through the deafening absence of Jamie's heartbeat.

45

H azel

THE NEXT FEW hours were the longest of Hazel's life. Time seemed to stand still once she let go of Jamie's hand. She'd kept her promise to stay by his side for as long as she could. Even in the ambulance she'd refused to leave him, but when they arrived at the hospital, he was whisked away, through doors where she couldn't follow.

She didn't know how long she knelt on the cold tile floor of the hospital hallway staring at the gray double doors that were keeping her from fulfilling her promise. She stared at them with hatred until someone finally put her on her own gurney and started to wheel her in the opposite direction.

At first, shock had dimmed her reaction, but when she started to move away from Jamie, she felt like her heart might explode. She scrambled off the gurney, screeching like a crazed animal when the nurses tried to calm her. "No! I'm not leaving him! I promised. I can't leave. I have to stay here and wait for him."

The commotion drew onlookers and more hospital staff. Hazel should've been embarrassed but she didn't have the strength to care. All of her worry was for Jamie. She couldn't stop replaying the silence of his heartbeat in her head. The paramedics had restarted his heart twice in the ambulance, but it was the silence between the beats that continued to send ripples of fear through her.

"Miss, you have to come with us. We need to treat you."

"No! I'm not leaving him. I promised, Jamie . . ." her voice cracked on his name and she began to sob.

"You're with James Forrester?" a man in blue scrubs asked.

Hazel turned to face him. He'd just come through the dreaded gray double doors carrying a chart. "Yes!"

He strode forward, extending his hand. "I'm Dr. Halyard. Are you family?"

"No," she sobbed. "He doesn't have any family here."

"I see. Are you able to get in touch with them?"

She shook her head. "I don't know them. His father lives in Boston. He's a senator, I think."

The doctor nodded to a nurse behind Hazel. "Please see what you can do to get in touch." He looked back at Hazel. "Is there anything you can tell me about James's medical history?"

"He has a pacemaker. It started beeping about a week ago when he fell off a roof."

Dr. Halyard's eyebrows rose, then he scribbled some notes on the clipboard. When he looked up his dark eyes were serious. "Do you know why he has a pacemaker?"

"He has Long QT Syndrome."

He scribbled again. "Do you know if he takes any medications?"

"No, I'm sorry. I don't." She scratched her head, wanting to be of more help. "We've been together for that last two weeks and I've never seen him take anything but Tylenol if that helps."

The doctor smiled warmly. "It does. Thank you, Miss . . ."

"Hazel Walker."

"Miss Walker. I'll do my best to keep you updated." Dr. Halyard turned to head back toward the double doors.

"Wait," Hazel shouted. "Please, I just need to see him. I promised I wouldn't leave his side."

Dr. Halyard took Hazel by the hand and led her to a chair, sitting down beside her. "James is being prepped for surgery. As soon as he's finished, I'll come find you and let you know how it goes."

Hazel began to wring her hands. The idea of sitting here waiting in this sterile room made her skin crawl. "Is there anything I can do to help him?"

Dr. Halyard stood up. "Yes. You can let my staff take a look at you, Miss Walker. If James survives this, he's going to need you at your best."

It was all Hazel needed to hear.

～

AFTER SPEAKING WITH DR. HALYARD, Hazel was the model patient. She honestly couldn't care less about herself. She only cared about Jamie. But she needed to do something to keep her mind occupied and letting the nurses poke and prod her helped.

After filling out a mountain of paperwork, Hazel was admitted to the hospital for severe dehydration and malnutrition. She was shocked to learn she'd lost fifteen pounds since coming to Wander Mountain. She was even more shocked when she found out they'd been missing for a total of sixteen days.

Time was a funny thing. It could seem long and short at once. Like now, as Hazel lay in her hospital bed, counting the seconds that ticked by waiting to hear how Jamie's surgery had gone. She'd only been alone in her room for a few minutes, but already it felt longer than the entirety of the stretch they'd been lost in the wilderness.

Maybe it wasn't time that changed. Maybe it was reality.

Realizing you're alone turns minutes into an eternity.

The only reprieve Hazel found was when the nurses finally got ahold of her father. Hearing his voice on the phone instantly brought tears of joy to her eyes.

"Hazel?"

"Dad," she sobbed. "I'm so sorry."

"Are you all right, baby?"

"Yes."

He blew out a sigh of relief. "Thank God. That's all that matters. I'll be there as soon as I can."

"Dad, you don't have to come all the way—"

"Hazel. I'm already in Montana."

"You are?"

"Of course. You're my daughter. Not even hellfire coulda kept me from finding you. I've been in Montana from the moment I found out you were missing."

His words wrapped around her, the echo of the warm embrace his arms would soon bring. But then fear slammed into her chest. "Dad, what about Gramps? Who's taking care of him?"

"Your Gramps is as tough as they come, kiddo. Though I have to admit, he's pretty pissed I wouldn't let him come out here to help with the search and rescue efforts."

"Search and rescue?"

Her father chuckled gruffly. "Apparently it's a pretty big deal when some senator's kid gets lost. Though my Ranger buddies did a helluva lot more than his pricey investigating team."

Hazel's cheeks heated. *What a disaster.* "I'm really sorry for all the trouble, Dad."

"The important thing is you're both okay."

The words that had been floating around her head since she arrived at the hospital stuck in Hazel's throat, but she forced them out. "I don't know if he's going to be okay, Dad."

Her father was silent for a beat. "Kiddo, you did the best you could, right?"

"Yeah," she whispered. *But did I?*

Could she have driven faster?

Could she have made Jamie leave the cabin earlier?

A million different scenarios filled her mind before her father spoke again.

"Hazel, try to get some rest. I'll be there when you wake up, okay?"

"Okay."

"I love you, Dad."

"I love you too, kiddo."

Hazel tried to rest but it was impossible when her every thought was consumed with worry for Jamie. Even her hospital bed made her think of him. It was too soft and it crinkled when she moved. It made her long for the musty bedroll and sleeping bag they'd shared. The thought was ridiculous, but she couldn't shake it.

She missed the rundown cabin. She'd grown used to the strange openness of things there. Everything in the hospital was confining. From the bedrails to the thick walls and heavy doors. The only place she felt at peace was in the small chair by the window, where she could stare out at the mountain range in the distance.

That's where she was sitting when Dr. Halyard came into her room. Hazel abruptly stood when she saw him, fear the only thing powering her fatigued muscles. She wanted to ask how Jamie was, but she was terrified of the answer. Once she heard it there would be no turning back.

It was impossible to tell the outcome from the doctor's emotionless face.

Hazel moved forward, gripping the rails of her bed for support. "Is he . . ." she whispered.

"The surgery went as well as we could have hoped. James is being moved to the cardiac recovery unit as we speak."

Relief hit Hazel so hard she staggered, causing the doctor to rush forward and catch her. He started to help her into her bed, but she resisted. "I want to see him."

Dr. Halyard shook his head. "Sit down, Miss Walker. We need to talk."

She didn't like the sound of that. Instead of the bed, she moved back to the chair. Dr. Halyard leaned against the wall, crossing his legs at his ankles. He looked absurdly young to be a doctor, but the weariness in his eyes made him seem older.

"It's not suitable for James to have visitors yet. He hasn't woken yet and until he does, we won't know the extent of his injuries."

"Injuries?"

Dr. Halyard gave her a look of pity that made Hazel want to be sick. "Miss Walker, there's no doubt in my mind that getting James to the hospital when you did saved his life. I wish I could tell you more, but since you're not immediate family, I'm not at liberty to discuss James's medical condition further. I'm afraid you won't be able to visit him without permission from his parents either."

"Parents? It's just his father and they're not close. You don't understand, I just want to see Jamie. I told him I wouldn't leave him."

"Miss Walker—"

"If he wakes up and no one is there . . . I don't want him to think he's alone."

A deep sadness washed over the doctor's face. "I wish the circumstances were different. I can't discuss James's condition with you. All I can tell you is that sometimes, patients in his situation don't wake up."

A hollow pit opened up in the world as Hazel struggled to remember how to breathe.

"What?"

"Chronic heart conditions are very serious. Sometimes patients who've undergone this kind of prolonged heart stress don't recover. And even the ones who do, aren't the same as they were before. I'm not trying to scare you, Hazel. But you should be prepared."

She swallowed hard, choking on each bitter word the doctor said.

'Don't wake up?'

'Not the same?'

But hadn't the doctor just said Jamie was recovering? That she had saved him?

Hazel didn't understand, and before she had a chance to wrap her mind around it all, the doctor was walking toward the door. He paused, turning to face her once more. "Also, I feel I should mention leaving your room is not advisable."

She blanched. "What? Why?"

"I'm not sure if you're aware, but you and James have created quite the media frenzy around here. I'm afraid it will only get worse when the Senator gets here." Hazel blinked, trying to follow the doctor's words. "Have you gotten in touch with your family yet?"

Hazel nodded. "My father is on his way here."

"Good. Then I'd advise you stay in your room until you have an adult present."

"Did I do something wrong?"

"No, but in my experience, the media tends to do more harm than good. You've been through a harrowing ordeal and should be given adequate time to heal."

She didn't know what to say. No amount of time would be enough to heal her if Jamie didn't pull through. She felt numb.

"Try to get some rest," Dr. Halyard said, then he was gone.

Hazel really wished people would stop saying that.

BY DINNER TIME, the idea of rest had become a joke that every nurse who entered her room told.

'Try to rest, Hazel.'

'You'll feel better once you get some rest, dear.'

'Rest will do wonders for your recovery, Miss Walker.'

Telling her to rest was as effective as reasoning with a toddler. The more the nurses tried to force it upon her the more restless she became. It didn't help that every time a nurse breezed into Hazel's room she jumped, hope spiking in her chest as she asked for news on Jamie. But each time she was filled with disappointment.

The nurses either didn't know how he was or had nothing new to tell her.

By dinner she'd worked herself into such a ball of nerves she threw up the little food she'd managed to eat.

"You poor dear," the nurse said, helping Hazel clean

herself up. "You're going to have to take it slow. Your stomach isn't used to having much in it."

But Hazel knew that wasn't the problem. She needed to see Jamie, and until she did, she wouldn't be able to keep anything down. But she knew she'd have to bide her time. The nurses weren't going to go against hospital policy for her.

Hazel would just have to find a way to Jamie herself.

When the nurse tried to hand her another blue hospital gown to replace her vomit-stained one, Hazel made her first move. "Actually, do you have any extra scrubs I could wear? I've been so cold in these gowns and all my clothes are ruined."

The nurse gave her a warm smile. "Why don't you take a warm shower and let me see what I can find for you?"

When Hazel got out of the shower there was a pile of pale pink scrubs on her bed.

Step one!

Now she could at least leave her room without looking like an escaped patient. Plus, she hadn't been lying about being cold and clothingless. The hospital gown she'd been given was much too thin for her liking and the idea of sneaking into Jamie's room with nothing on underneath it wasn't very appealing.

The memory of the last time she'd been wearing a hospital gown in his presence seared her heart. It was the day he'd rescued her from the kayak and carried her all the way to the clinic. He'd seemed invincible then.

Hazel shivered, unable to wrap her mind around the idea that he wasn't still that same boy. The one who'd fished her out of a river and fiercely stolen her heart.

No. I won't give up on you, Jamie.

She refused to accept it. They'd gone through too much to come this close only to fail. He had to be okay.

When the nurse came back into Hazel's room, she closed her eyes and pretended to be asleep. She would play the part of the obedient patient if it would get her to Jamie. And right now, that meant pretending to get the so-called 'rest' they'd prescribed.

But as Hazel lay in bed with her eyes closed tight, she let her mind seek out a plan.

Soon, she thought. *I'll be there soon, Jamie. Just hold on.*

Hazel thought the words over and over in her head, willing them to somehow reach him so he would know he wasn't alone.

46

H azel

THE SOFT YELLOW hospital socks with the non-slip treads made Hazel's footsteps soundless as she moved down the hall. It turned out rest was exactly what she needed.

She'd woke at three in the morning, clear headed and full of energy. Both traits she needed to pull this off.

It had been easy to disconnect her IV and slip out of her room unnoticed, but walking through the halls with the confidence of someone who both belonged and knew where they were going was more difficult.

Though she was wearing a pair of pink scrubs, the absence of shoes and a badge was a dead giveaway. She needed to be swift.

By the time Hazel made it to the elevators she was breathing hard. Maybe she hadn't gotten as much rest as she thought. She knew she'd slept because she'd dreamt she was back in the cabin, wrapped in Jamie's warm arms staring up at the stars through the tiny gaps in the old roof.

It was funny how much she missed the place that had nearly killed them. But with Jamie by her side, she'd never really been scared for herself. She feared for his health and for the worry their families were going through, but she'd always felt safe with him. She missed that feeling now as she scanned the signs on each floor, trying to find her way back to him.

When the elevator doors opened to the fourth floor, she read the words 'Cardiac Recovery Unit' on the directory and knew she was in the right place.

The lobby area was deserted, and Hazel didn't come across a single nurse as her socked feet silently shuffled over the shiny white tile. She'd made the right choice to wait until the night shift was on to come exploring. It lowered her chances of getting caught. But now that she was on the cardiac floor, she didn't know how she'd actually find Jamie.

The idea of poking her head into each room wasn't appealing. She didn't want to intrude on anyone's privacy, much less get mistaken for an actual nurse. That would be the surest way to get caught and she'd come too far to be sent away now.

Steeling her reserve, Hazel walked past the nurses' station that sat nestled between the rows of rooms. Two bleary-eyed nurses sat there, too focused on their monitors to pay her much attention. Hazel released a breath when she'd made it past them with a subtle nod of acknowledgement. Her heart was pounding now because she knew exactly where to go.

Behind the nurses' tired heads had been a beacon of hope —a dry erase board with four names on it. One of them read: Forrester, J. And next to it, was a room number.

Hazel's heart felt like she was wearing it outside her chest when she pushed her way into Jamie's dark hospital room. *This is it, no going back now.*

She was about to see the boy she loved and find out if there was any of him left.

Please, she silently prayed. *Please let him be okay.*

She couldn't imagine Jamie not being Jamie. In the short time she'd known him he'd changed her life. She'd grown attached to his crooked smile, sarcastic humor, quiet truths, fierce dreams and most of all his persistent affection.

Seeing him and finding out he wasn't really him anymore would be worse than losing him all together. It would be like losing him over and over again each time she looked at him. Hazel knew what that was like. Each time her mother left, Hazel lost another piece of herself. She didn't want that for Jamie's family, and neither would he.

Hazel paused just outside the striped curtain that separated her from the boy lying in the bed just beyond it. She took a deep breath, trying to prepare herself. She closed her eyes and forced herself to remember him the way he'd been .. . just in case.

Then, she pulled the curtain back.

Despite Dr. Halyard's warning, she wasn't prepared. There were tubes and wires everywhere. A ventilator kept Jamie's chest rising and falling while the leads covering his newly sutured chest measured each of his steady heartbeats on the monitor near his bed.

Jamie looked so small beneath the sheer amount of equipment keeping him alive, but Hazel felt even smaller. She wasn't equipped to handle this. She'd been wrong to come here, but somehow, her feet kept her moving toward his bed.

This can't be his future. Being strapped to this bed, these machines.

It's not what he'd want.

Jamie had dreamt of sailing and art, not a life of sterile rooms and measured breaths.

When Hazel reached his side, she slipped her fingers into his hand, shocked by his warmth.

"I'm here," she whispered. "Just like I promised." She stifled a sob. "I'm going to stay as long as I can, but I'm not supposed to be here." She smiled past the lump in her throat. "You've turned me into a rule breaker, you know. So, if you could wake up sometime soon that would be great."

The only answer was the whir and hiss of the ventilator.

Hazel pulled a chair closer to his bed and took up his hand again. She kissed it, once, twice, then she let the tears come. "I'm sorry," she whispered. "I'm so sorry, Jamie. You don't deserve this."

Hazel couldn't stop thinking that it should've been her in the hospital bed. Her future cut short. All of this was her fault. She'd twisted fate when she'd dared to reach for something that wasn't meant for her. If she'd just stayed home none of this would've happened.

She wished she'd never found that Wander Mountain brochure. The Couples' Curse might not be real, but Hazel was beginning to think she was cursed all the same.

Everyone who loved her suffered. Her grandfather, her father and now Jamie. The only one who escaped was her mother, because her mother had never loved Hazel, and she'd been smart enough to leave.

Maybe her mother had it right. Maybe that was the best thing Hazel could do for anyone—leave before she made things worse.

"I'm sorry, Jamie," she whispered again. "I'm sorry I loved you."

She stood up and let go of his hand.

James

. . .

HER VOICE FELT SO NEAR. Her touch so real. James was convinced he wasn't only dreaming of Hazel this time. If only he could open his eyes, he was certain he'd see her gorgeous caramel ones staring back at him. But he couldn't.

Each command he tried to force on his body felt like swimming upstream. But he was desperate to get to her. The sadness in her voice haunted him. He wanted to call her name, say something to soothe her, but each time he tried to find his voice he felt like he was drowning. His chest ached with an unnatural tightness and his body's unwillingness to respond was maddening.

Hazel's words broke through to him again. *'I'm sorry, Jamie. I'm sorry I loved you.'*

His hand suddenly felt cold.

Was she leaving?

But she said she would stay.

His soul screamed out to her as he struggled against the current dragging him down with everything he had left.

HAZEL

JAMIE TWITCHED, his fingers curling into a fist. Alarms sounded and lights flashed on his monitor. Light flooded the room as two nurses rushed in. Hazel scrambled back against the wall to give them room, her own eyes wide with fear.

Was this it? Was she going to be forced to watch him die?

It was too much. Hazel collapsed into a ball, wrapping her arms around her legs and burying her head in her knees. She could do nothing but sob while the nurses worked swiftly.

Their rubber-soled shoes squeaked around her, ignoring her presence while they spoke efficiently to each other. Suddenly, the storm of lights and alarms stopped, just as abruptly as it started.

Hazel was afraid to lift her head, but then she thought she heard her name. She couldn't be sure because of all the coughing and wheezing coming from the bed. *His coughing!*

Hazel's eyes snapped open and when she saw Jamie staring back at her she passed out.

47

J ames

JAMES COULDN'T STOP SMILING as he watched Hazel sleep. It hadn't been easy to convince his doctor to move her hospital bed into his room, but after threatening to call his father, the doctor caved. *Sometimes having a famous family came in handy.*

The nurses assured James that Hazel was fine. They said she'd merely passed out, understandable after everything they'd been through.

Once the nurses got Hazel settled in the bed they'd rolled in next to his, they'd given her a mild sedative to help her sleep and although James could watch her sleep forever, he was anxious for her to wake. He knew life would get chaotic once his father arrived and James wanted to set some things straight before that happened.

Getting out of bed on his own wasn't really an option for

James yet, so he resorted to throwing tiny ice chips at Hazel to rouse her. He stopped when her eyelids began to flutter open. She looked so angelic as the predawn light shaded her features with hues of blue and gray.

"Hello, gorgeous," he said, unable to keep the grin from his face when she blinked at him in utter shock.

"Jamie?"

"The one and only."

"You . . . you're you," she stammered.

"Who else would I be?"

Hazel was out of bed in an instant, rushing toward him with tears in her stunning eyes. She stopped short of throwing herself over his bedrails when she saw the hideous staples marring his chest. James cursed the new scar that was keeping Hazel from his arms. But she didn't pay the wound a second glance. Hazel's shaking hands were too busy running over his face like she thought he might be a ghost.

"You woke up?" she whispered.

He caught her hand with his good one and pulled it to his lips, brushing a kiss across her knuckles. "You asked me to."

"You heard me?"

"Every word," he replied, concern finally creeping past his elation. "You said you loved me, Hazel. Past tense."

Shame clouded her face, but James caught her chin and forced her to look at him. "Talk to me."

"This is my fault, Jamie. Everyone I care about ends up getting hurt and I . . . I care about you too much to keep hurting you."

"Then don't, Hazel."

"That's what I'm trying to do," she said, pain straining her features.

"Hazel, the only thing that could ever hurt me is not

having you in my life. This wasn't your fault. This was genetics and my shitty heart."

"If I hadn't been an idiot and fallen through the ice your heart would be fine."

"And if I hadn't gotten us lost you wouldn't have fallen through the ice. We could place blame all day, Hazel, but the fact is we survived a situation that not many do. That proves we belong together."

She swallowed hard, still looking uncertain as she averted her eyes.

James had fought too hard to lose her now. "Hazel, you saved my life."

"Barely," she murmured.

He took her hand. "Hey, I'll take barely any day. Barely is what separates living from dying. Sometimes barely is all we get. So barely is enough for me. As long as I have you in my life, it's more than enough," he said pulling her close enough to press his lips to hers.

When she pulled back, they were both breathless.

James wiped the shining tears from her cheeks. "Hazel, I love you. And the only time I want to hear about our love in the past tense is when it's lined up next to our present and future. Okay?"

"Okay," she whispered.

He searched her eyes for any hint of doubt. When he found none, he felt the tension leave his body. He scooted over in his bed and patted the mattress. "Now get over here and keep me warm."

HAZEL

. . .

H AZEL HAD NEVER BEEN SO happy to oblige. She carefully climbed into Jamie's hospital bed and curled up on her side next to him. He pulled her arm across his stomach and sighed into her hair.

She laid her head on his shoulder. "Am I hurting you?"

Jamie grinned. "I've never felt better."

Hazel closed her eyes, finally feeling whole for the first time since they'd been found.

"Tell me a story," Jamie whispered.

Hazel smiled and kissed his bare shoulder. "We're not lost anymore. We don't need stories."

"We were never lost, Hazel," he murmured. "How could we ever be lost when we're together?"

Her heart ached as it swelled with love. This couldn't be real. She didn't get happy endings. But here she was, staring at the only boy she'd ever loved, both of them together, against all odds. Hope rimmed her eyes with joyful tears as she spoke the words her heart longed to say. "I love you, Jamie."

He tightened his good arm around her and kissed her head. "I love you, too."

In the warmth and safety of Jamie's arms, Hazel felt sleep calling her. Unwilling to let it claim her just yet, she spoke. "Maybe I have a story for you after all."

"Tell me," he murmured.

"There once was a girl and a boy left to wander the woods alone. Both were desperate to be found until one day they realized they were in love and as long as they were together, they could never really be lost at all."

He grinned and pressed a kiss to her forehead. "Your stories are my favorite."

She shook her head. "You know yours are better."

She felt him smile against her hair. "You're right. Which one is your favorite?"

She smirked. "The dream you told me about, the one where we live in Key West in the house with a fireplace in every room so we'd never get cold."

Jamie gently brushed her hair back and gazed into her eyes. "Hazel, that doesn't have to be a dream anymore."

She looked up at him, drowsy with sleep. "No?"

Jamie shook his head and kissed her slowly. "We could make it our reality. If you want."

Hazel smiled and kissed him back, not quite sure how to live in a world where dreams became realities, but with Jamie by her side, she knew no matter what the adventure, they'd survive it.

She let a smile light up her soul as she replied. "I want that more than anything."

EPILOGUE

H azel

IT'S CALLED the rule of three. We can survive three weeks without food, three days without water, three minutes without air . . . *but how long can we last without our hearts?*

Hazel stared at the last entry in her held journal.

A smile filled her chest as she realized she was living by a new rule of three. *Three seconds to change her life.*

That's how long it took for her to make up her mind when James showed up at her door the day after graduation with his heart on his sleeve and a question she already knew the answer to.

A lot had happened since she left the Montana hospital sixteen weeks ago to a flurry of news crews and cameras. The press may have died down over the story of the lost lovers, but the love between Hazel and James had only grown.

Hazel hated the miles that separated them while they finished their last few months of high school in Nevada and Boston, but she soon realized distance was nothing in the face of their love. Especially with both of them focused on making their dreams a reality.

Some challenges were easier to overcome than others. The hardest for Hazel had been Gramps's passing. Strangely, it had been the thing that made Hazel realize following her heart was the right choice. That and the heartfelt conversation she had with her father the night of Gramps's funeral.

As Hazel finished packing the last of her things into her suitcase, her father's words came back to her.

"Life is short, Hazel," he'd said. "You've got to live it to the fullest."

She remembered how much her heart hurt in that moment—for her grandfather, who'd lost his battle with cancer, for her father, who'd lost his father and friend, for herself, who'd lost her grandfather and mentor. It made her choice to move to Key West to be with Jamie even harder.

Hazel had already struggled with the notion of not staying in Nevada to take care of her father after all he'd done for her. But they'd discussed it at length when she'd returned from Montana. Once Hazel had come clean with her father about her feelings for Jamie and her worry for her family and their struggling business, her father had set her straight.

He'd taken her face in his rough hands and said, "Kiddo, I'm so proud of you. All I've ever wanted outta this life is for you to be happy. To know that you've found someone you love . . . well, it makes all I've worked for worth it."

Hazel remembered what she said to him, because she would never forget his response. She'd said, "Dad, are you sure it's okay for me to leave? You and Gramps literally fought to keep a roof over my head and clothes on my back. I don't mind staying and pulling my weight. It's the least I can do."

Her father's face had gone red with anger. "Hazel, don't you get it? I risked my life so you could have one."

Now, just the memory of that conversation made tears well in her eyes.

"The least you can do should never be enough for you," he'd added and those words resonated with her. Because he was right. He, like so many other soldiers, had fought so those they love could have a life filled with dreams and happiness. Settling for a life that was anything less was an insult to that kind of sacrifice.

She'd never thought of it that way before. But viewing her life through her father's eyes and thinking in the terms of what he'd sacrificed for her joy, gave Hazel a whole new passion to pursue her life to the fullest.

She still worried about her dad. That would never change. She loved him and he was the only family she had left. But she respected him too much to settle. Sticking around to fill their home with worry wouldn't do either of them any good.

Whenever she started to feel anxious about leaving him alone, she thought about how strong he'd been when he'd scooped her into his arms in that Montana hospital. He'd been her rock as she recovered. Caring for her had forced him out of his comfortable routine. He'd even started using his prosthetic more, giving up the chair a little more each day.

"Hey kiddo," he called as he knocked on her bedroom door and pushed his way into the room. "You almost ready?"

She turned to face him, needing a moment to collect herself before answering. It stole her breath every time she saw him standing tall and proud like he was now.

He angled his head, studying her. "What's wrong? You haven't changed your mind, have you?"

"No."

"Good, because I wasn't looking forward to unloading the truck," he teased. "I got all of Lu's stuff in the back. Just need your suitcase."

Hazel hesitated. "Dad . . . are you sure this is okay?"

He gave her a stern look. "Hazel Jane, if I have to seatbelt you onto that damn plane myself I will. We've talked about this. I'm fine. And I refuse to be the person to steal the kind of joy I see in your eyes when you talk about that boy of yours. So, you're going to Florida. That's an order."

"But—"

"Do you love him, Hazel?"

"Yes," she said softly.

"Then no buts. I wish someone had been there to tell me to go after your mother. Maybe things would've turned out differently. But I'm not making that mistake with you. I see how happy you are, Hazel, and it makes me so damn proud. Promise me, you won't let anything hold you back from what you want in life."

"I promise," she whispered, fighting tears.

"Good. That's all I can ask." He took a deep breath and exhaled as he looked around her empty room. "Maybe I'll sell this place and retire. Who knows, without you hovering all the time I might even be forced to go out and find my own happiness."

She huffed and rolled her eyes, trying to be offended, but it was hard with tears of joy blurring her vision.

Her father strode across the room and pulled her into his arms, holding her tight. "Nothing makes my life feel more fulfilled than seeing you happy, Hazel."

"I love you, Dad."

"I love you too, kiddo." He kissed her head. "Now finish packing or you're gonna miss your flight."

She finished zipping her suitcase and looked in the mirror. He was right, she *did* look happy. She'd gained back most of the weight she'd lost in Montana, she'd cut her long dark hair to just above her shoulders and she'd gotten another tattoo. She and Jamie had gotten them together, the day he flew out to meet her father and Gramps after graduation. The day he'd proposed this crazy plan—the one she said yes to in three seconds flat.

Hazel ran her fingers over the freshly inked words and smiled feeling her soul light up. She couldn't wait to start this new adventure with Jamie. In just a few short hours she'd be on a flight to Florida. Knowing Jamie was there waiting for her filled her with more joy than she could contain. *It was a feeling she planned to chase.*

James

JAMES SLATHERED sunblock over his new tattoo. Every time he looked at it his heart felt too big for his chest. It was the perfect symbol of his and Hazel's love and the future they were planning. The tattoo had actually been her idea and it was the perfect way to solidify this crazy plan of his.

Sometimes James had to pinch himself to believe it was actually happening. He knew it would seem more real once Hazel finally arrived. He looked at his watch—the one his mother had given him, the one that had nearly cost him everything, yet somehow gave him more than he'd ever imagined.

He doubted he'd ever be able to look at the timepiece without bittersweet feelings. The watch would always remind him of his mother and of just how lost he'd been after she passed. But the watch was also a symbol of his love for Hazel. *It was the reason they'd gotten lost; the reason they were found.*

James hoped someday soon he'd be able to think of his mother and remember the love rather than the loss. After all, this new adventure of his was made possible by her.

After James returned home from Montana, things were much different for him. His relationship with his father wasn't miraculously fixed, but they were both working to better understand each other.

Nearly losing James had made his father open up about his own struggles dealing with the loss of his wife. His father admitted he projected his pain onto James and thought he was doing the right thing by forcing him to follow in his footsteps. Mostly because it was all he knew, and he was afraid to let James fail and let both his son and his wife down in the process.

But when James turned eighteen the day after graduation, his father handed him a letter from his mother. She'd written *'chase your dreams'* on it. Inside was an inheritance check with enough zeros to make his jaw drop.

He'd told his father his plan and bought a plane ticket to Nevada the same day.

That was weeks ago now and everything was falling into place. James was already in Key West. He'd found a slip for his new sail boat and just yesterday he'd signed a lease on a two bedroom cottage within walking distance to the marina. He couldn't wait to show Hazel the fireplace. He also couldn't wait to give her the field journal he'd wrapped painstakingly with pink wrapping paper. He knew she hated the color, but after those hot pink boots of hers, it would always be her color in his eyes.

James had envisioned her reading his words a thousand

times. It was their love story, told through the account of the days they spent getting lost, then finding their way into each other's hearts. It was his most precious possession and he couldn't wait to share it with her. Just like he planned to share everything with Hazel—his hopes, his dreams, his life.

The winds changed and James checked his weather app. He looked at the wind meter on the mast and grinned. Polishing the last of the cleats he stood up and patted the wheel affectionately. "What do ya say, shall we stretch our legs a bit before my girl gets here?"

As if in answer the boat bobbed up and down in the crystal-clear salt water.

James grinned and started to unfurl the sail.

HAZEL

"OKAY, Lu. Are you ready for this?" Hazel asked her dog as she seat belted his carrier into the seat between her and her father.

He laughed. "Does this guy of yours know how much you talk to your dog?"

Hazel snorted. "Jamie talks to him, too."

"Two peas in a pod, kiddo."

She smiled. "Three," she said, "Right, Lu?"

Hazel was grateful Jamie and Lu had instantly formed a bond. Her dog was her first love and he wasn't known for his affectionate personality, but when she'd seen Jamie talking to the scruffy terrier at her graduation party, her heart had melted. And when Jamie suggested Lu come along on their adventure, she knew she'd made the right call.

"Well," she said, buckling her own seatbelt, "here goes nothing."

She was backing out of the driveway when the mail truck came tearing down the road, beeping and kicking up dust.

Mr. Watts got out, his face cherry red as he jogged up to the window. "Glad I caught ya before ya left us, Hazel. Found a package for you wedged behind the bins. Looks like it's been there a while. Sorry about that," he said apologetically. "Better late than never though."

"Thanks," she said, reaching out the window to take the parcel. Her heart leapt when she saw the familiar packaging of the film company.

"I didn't know you were into photography," Mr. Watts added.

"Neither did I." Hazel grinned, her fingers caressing the envelop. Scribbled below her address was a note from Jamie that she hadn't seen him write the day they filled out the developing forms. She traced his words and felt each one imprint into her heart. *Everyone deserves a happy ending, Hazel. If you're not happy that means this isn't the end.*

Tears sprang into her eyes.

"Everything okay, kiddo?" her father asked.

"More than okay," she whispered.

Hazel waved to Mr. Watts and put the truck back in drive with the package still in her lap. She knew what was inside and she knew she would need privacy to revisit the photos she and Jamie had taken on Wander Mountain.

That trip had changed her for the better, but sometimes it was still hard to look back at all they'd endured to reach their happy ending. But thankfully, they had, and that was really all that mattered.

. . .

James

JAMES LET the autopilot steer the boat while he snapped a few photos of the serene turquoise waters he was quickly growing accustom to. Life in the Keys was easy to fall in love with. He almost couldn't imagine it being better, but he knew in a few short hours it would be, because Hazel would be there.

He lowered his lens and inhaled deeply, letting the salt air soothe him. It had been good for his recovery. He felt a little stronger every day. He was fully healed from his surgery, but more than the scars remained. He knew how lucky he'd been to survive their ordeal on Wander Mountain.

James owed his life to Hazel. If she hadn't made the decision to drag him out of that cabin when she did, he would've died there. But beyond that, it was her most recent decision that really seemed to save him. She'd said yes—to him, to his crazy plan, to a life together.

Sometimes he still couldn't believe it. They were really doing it, following their dreams of moving to Key West and opening a charter business. With any luck, a small photography shop would follow. But for now, James was beyond satisfied to be doing what he loved and sharing it with the girl of his dreams. She'd changed his whole life.

James hoped his charter business would offer others the opportunity to see the world differently, too. He wanted to show people how to escape the world long enough to reconnect with themselves and what brings them joy.

That's what Hazel and Wander Mountain had done for him.

This was his way to give back. *His mother would be proud.*

James absently brought his hand to his chest and rubbed his scar. It had become a habit, not because the wound pained him, but because of what it reminded him of—Hazel, and the second chance at life she'd given him.

He'd always thought of the heart as nothing but a muscle—in his case, one that didn't even work right. But ever since meeting Hazel, James knew it was so much more.

He'd survived Wander Mountain, but it wouldn't have had the same meaning without Hazel. Everything they had gone through taught James that he was stronger than he knew. But the thing that made them strongest was being together. And knowing that they were going to be facing the future and chasing down their dreams together filled him with a zest for life that he couldn't explain.

Hazel had given him more than a second chance at life. She'd given him a new heart. This one was more than just a muscle. This one was so full of love and life that it sometimes made him feel reckless and foolish. *But then again, maybe that's what a heart should be.*

James tugged on the jib and let the wind fill the sails. His chest swelled with excitement as he turned the boat toward home; because that's what Hazel was—home.

HAZEL

HAZEL SAT on the dock with Lu, her feet dangling over the edge of the empty slip as she peered down into the clear water. Lu's tail twitched excitedly as he watched the fish flit in and out of the shadows below. "What do ya think, boy? You like it here?"

As if in answer, Lu barked, his ears pricked forward in attention.

Hazel laughed. "Me too," she murmured, scratching his head. "Now all we need is, Jamie."

She'd managed to catch an earlier connection and arrived at the airport an hour ahead of schedule. She'd taken a cab to the house hoping to surprise Jamie, but he wasn't there. The ideal weather told her he was most likely at the marina. So, she and Lu had taken the opportunity to stretch their legs and soak up the tropical sights as they made the short walk to the docks.

But Hazel saw the fault in her plan when she arrived at Jamie's empty slip.

He must've taken the boat out for a sail.

She couldn't blame him. The weather was perfect. She leaned back on her elbows and let the sun warm her skin. She couldn't get enough of it. Especially after looking at the blustery photos from Wander Mountain on the plane.

Hazel had finally opened the package once she was in the air. Seeing the photographs of her and Jamie together gave her goose bumps. She was glad she'd waited until she was hurtling through the air to look at the photos, because seeing herself through his eyes . . . she couldn't get to him fast enough. She'd never looked happier, and that was only the beginning.

Their relationship had grown so much since they'd returned from Wander Mountain. It was strange how the distance had only strengthened her affection for him. But in his absence, it became clear that she'd never really had a choice other than loving him. Hazel's heart had chosen Jamie's the moment their paths first crossed. And she knew she would make that same choice over and over again.

The idea of it excited her so much that she didn't even mind waiting on him. She knew they had a whole wide-open future together. There was no need to rush. This was the start of their life together and she planned to enjoy every minute of it.

Hazel pulled her knees up to her chest and hugged them, holding onto her excitement as she gazed out across the tranquil turquoise water. She couldn't believe this was her world now.

In the distance, the shape of a sailboat caught her attention. There were dozens of them dotting the alluring water, but this one in particular spoke to her. As it drew closer, she suddenly knew why. The massive logo adorning the crisp white sail was one that Hazel was familiar with—her tribal sun. It was the very same design she'd tattooed to her back in remembrance of her mother and her quest to quiet the pain of her loss.

Hazel climbed to her feet and tented her hand over her eyes as the boat drew closer. Her heart was pounding so hard she could hear it over the cries of the seagulls. The boat turned and the sunlight sparked across the gold letters adorning the stern. Hazel gasped when she saw the name he'd chosen for the boat. *Hazel Jane.*

It made her heart feel like a water balloon near bursting.

She swallowed past the lump in her throat and waved when she saw Jamie at the helm. The fact that he'd thought to put so much of her on his boat filled her with overwhelming emotion. And when she read the words stenciled beneath the sun, she felt a wave of heat course through her body like a summer storm.

She did her best to collect herself, grateful for the time it took him to slowly maneuver the massive sailboat into the marina, but it was all for naught, because as he drew closer, the power of those words truly hit her. It had become their quote; her favorite by Tolkien. The one they'd gotten tattooed after graduation to remind them of all they've been through and all that was yet to come. *Not all who wander are lost.*

The fact that Jamie had added the quote along with her sun tattoo made her dizzy with love. This boy owned her heart and she planned to spend the rest of her days proving it to him over and over.

She may have been the one who saved him on that mountain, but James Forrester rescued her heart when it was lost.

EXTENDED EPILOGUE

J ames

JAMES FINALLY SAW Hazel standing on the dock. The sunlight painted her hair a burnished chestnut and a bright smile lit her face. His heart physically skipped a beat, not an easy feat considering the tiny device in his chest controlled each one.

He steered his sleek Hunter 50cc into the marina. The brand-new sailboat cut through the water like a dream and James couldn't wait to get his dream girl aboard.

"Hello gorgeous," he shouted.

Hazel jumped onto the boat and into his arms as soon as he docked.

"What are you doing here already?" he asked.

"My flight got in early."

"Well, then, are you ready to have an adventure?"

She laughed and the sound filled his chest. "Now?"

"What better time than now?"

"Okay," she replied excitedly.

James grinned, still loving that simple word so much.

He only hoped he could get Hazel to say it one more time.

HAZEL

HAZEL COULDN'T GET over the feel of the wind in her hair as they cut through the crystal blue water on the sleek sailboat. Jamie stood behind her at the helm, laughing and pointing out tiny islands that glittered like jewels on the topaz horizon. She couldn't help thinking that this was some kind of dream that she would wake from any minute. Life couldn't be this good. *Could it?*

But as she leaned back into Jamie's warm chest, his arms around her as he held the ship's wheel, she let herself settle into the feeling of pure joy that radiated through her. This was her life now, and it really was everything she'd never let herself dream of.

Even Lu seemed to sense the easy joy of this life from where he lounged on the cozy white cushions. The wind ruffled his wiry fur as he sniffed the salty air. The old junkyard dog looked like he was meant to live on the luxurious boat. Hazel smiled, hoping she'd adapt as well, though it wasn't hard with views like this—*turquoise waters and the man of her dreams.*

"This is incredible," she said.

"And it only gets better from here," Jamie replied.

"What do you mean?"

"I have a surprise for you."

"You mean more than naming your boat after me and putting my tattoo on the sail?"

He kissed the space where her neck met her shoulder, then whispered into her ear. "This is only the beginning of the surprises I have planned for you, Hazel Jane."

Despite the balmy Florida air, his words made her shiver in the best way possible.

James

ONCE HE'D ANCHORED the boat, James took Hazel by the hand, excitement sizzling his every nerve. He felt like a kid at Christmas as he led her on a tour of the elegant white sailboat. Two helm stations, two baths, three bedrooms, a full kitchen and a roomy living/dining room, all in clean lines of gleaming teak wood and white leather.

"What do you think?" he asked as she looked around the living room in wonder.

Hazel looked awed. "I think I'm glad I said yes to this crazy plan of yours."

"This crazy plan of *ours*," he corrected. "But I'm glad you feel that way."

"Oh yeah?" she teased snuggling playfully into his chest and gazing up into his eyes. "Why's that?"

"Because I have one more question to ask you, and I'm hoping you'll say yes."

She quirked a curious eyebrow, but James didn't give any hints. Not when he was so close to the moment he'd been waiting his whole life for.

"Come on," he said, taking Hazel by the hand once more.

. . .

Hazel

Hazel gasped when Jamie led her into the ship's final bedroom; the master suite. The white linens of the bed were covered in bright pink rose petals in the shape of a heart and there was a pair of new pink hiking boots in the middle. She wanted to laugh, but when he clicked a remote and a dozen LED candles flickered to life, her breath froze in her throat.

This was it. They'd finally found a place truly deserving of their love and there was nothing in their way now, nothing stopping them from taking that last step as a couple. Of course she'd say yes. She'd wanted to say yes to him a dozen times already, but timing and circumstance were never on their side.

But now . . . now the world was theirs and Hazel couldn't wait to claim Jamie as her own.

She turned, prepared to leap into his arms, but Jamie wasn't standing where she thought he'd be. He was kneeling.

Another gasp escaped her lips. Hazel had never had to exert so much energy to remain standing when she saw what he was holding in his hand.

James

"Hazel Jane, I have one more crazy, big question to ask you," James said, his voice tight with emotion as he held his mother's diamond ring in his trembling hand. "Ever since you and your ridiculous pink boots crashed into my life, I knew it would never be the same, and I don't want it to." He swallowed, fearing he wasn't making sense. He wished he wasn't so damn nervous; it was making it hard to get the words out even though he'd rehearsed them a hundred times.

"What I'm trying to say," he continued, "is that I can't imagine my life without you in it. So," he took a deep breath, "Hazel Jane, will you say yes to a lifetime of adventure with me? Will you marry—"

"Yes!" she screamed launching herself into his arms at last. "Yes! Yes! Yes!"

James laughed and scooped her up, swinging her around until they landed on the bed in an avalanche of laughter, tears and kisses, barely pausing long enough to slip the ring on her finger.

He didn't even care that he hadn't finished his proposal. The only thing that mattered was that one little word. And as Hazel said it over and over again, it outshined all the other words he knew. *Yes* . . . How he loved making her say that word. And if the rest of the night went according to plan, he'd be hearing it a lot more.

HAZEL

SUDDENLY, Hazel was beyond grateful they'd waited until this moment to have sex. Nothing could be more perfect or memorable than having her first time be here, in this moment, when they'd just gotten engaged.

Holy shit! I'm engaged!

Jamie laughed. "Um, yes, you are."

She blushed. "Did I say that out loud?"

"Yep. And you also said yes to my proposal, so no takebacks."

She smiled and climbed into his lap to press another long kiss to his lopsided smile. "I'd never take it back."

He sighed into her kiss. "Good."

When they came up for air, Jamie threaded his fingers through hers. Her hand looked so small in his, even smaller now that there was a gargantuan diamond ring adorning it. "Do you like it?" he asked.

"Jamie, I love it, but this ring must've cost you a fortune."

He shook his head, his finger lightly tracing the smooth platinum band. "Actually, it's my mother's, so that makes it priceless, just like you."

Hazel didn't know her heart had the capacity to grow larger than its current state of all-consuming love, but at Jamie's tender words, it did. "You want me to have your mother's ring?"

He looked at her, his sky-blue eyes momentarily uncertain. "Is that okay?"

"Okay? Jamie, I'm incredibly honored."

The smile that lit his face was like watching sunlight burst through the clouds. He swept her into his arms and laid her back against the bed in a flurry of passion. Hazel clung to him, eager to show him just how much his incredible gesture meant to her.

They were all fumbling fingers and desperate desires. Their shirts fell away first, but when Hazel got to Jamie's belt, he stopped her. "Not here."

"What?" she mumbled, momentarily stunned.

Had she heard him wrong? Her mind was hazy with passion. That was the only explanation, because there was no way Jamie was telling her no. Not now, when they'd waited so long to take this final step. What better place was there than here? What better time than now?

She reached for his belt again and this time he sat up, a sly crooked grin carving his handsome face. "Hazel, this isn't the place."

"What do you mean? This is the perfect place."

Jamie glanced around the room and shook his head. "Nope, it's not quite worthy of our love."

Hazel's mouth fell open as she scanned her surroundings, trying desperately to see what was lacking. The room was large in ship standards, but small in reality. The white sheets were already disheveled, a tangle of rose petals and pink boots. But Hazel didn't care. Now was not a time to be picky. She'd waited a lifetime to be with this boy and she didn't want to wait a moment longer. "Jamie," she murmured, "I thought we were done waiting."

"Just a few minutes more."

Hazel pouted and he planted a slow, teasing kiss on her puckered lips.

"I know I'm irresistible, Smalls, but I promise you, this will be worth the wait."

James

JAMES WAS DOING his best to stay strong, but the want in Hazel's eyes nearly crippled him. He wanted to be with her too. It physically hurt him to pull away when she'd started to undo his belt, but they'd come too far to give in now. He would settle for nothing but perfection for this. After all, it was their first time. Not just together, but ever. It was a rare moment and one he knew they'd remember forever.

It was a gift he wanted to give her, one they could look back at and measure their love against forever. All he had to do was get her to go along with it. Not wanting to waste another precious moment, James scrambled off the bed and pulled a backpack from his closet and put it on.

Hazel blinked at him. "Are we going somewhere?"

He grinned. "I told you we were going on an adventure."

"But where? And how long? I didn't bring anything with me. I don't even have a toothbrush or a bathing suit."

James's grin only grew. "Smalls, give me some credit." He pulled another backpack out of the closet. This one was pink, the same shade as her new boots. "Everything you need is in there."

Hazel unzipped the bag and pulled out the only two items inside; a white bikini and toothbrush. She laughed. "Okay, mind reader. What about Lu? I didn't bring his food."

James patted the heavy pack slung over his shoulder. "Got him covered too. Any more objections?"

He could see Hazel's excitement growing as she shook her head with mock irritation. "Nope, I'll just shut up and follow you."

He burst into laughter.

"What?"

"Nothing, I'm just hoping I can get that in writing. It'd be perfect for our wedding vows."

She playfully shoved him, but he pulled her back, pinning her against the door for one more thorough kiss. She was breathless when he released her, staring up at him with those gorgeous caramel eyes of hers wide open, her longing deep enough to drown him whole.

James pulled away, restraining his desire. "Put on the bathing suit," he said softly, as he tucked a lock of dark hair behind her ear. "Then meet me on the deck."

HAZEL

. . .

TWO CAN PLAY at this game, Jamie Forrester. Hazel took a deep breath for courage and climbed the stairs to the deck, her pink boots thumping heavily.

"I'm ready," she called.

Jamie turned around and nearly fell over. He stumbled, dropped the set of keys he'd been holding and stuttered so profusely that Hazel almost felt bad for him. But if he was going to give her a skimpy little white bikini, it was only fair that he suffer the consequences. Of course, he probably hadn't planned for her to wear it with nothing but her hot pink boots. *But hey, a girl's gotta do, what a girl's gotta do.*

"What?" she asked coyly, twirling a strand of her thick dark hair around her finger.

"Uh n-nothing, you, um . . . you look . . ." he swallowed hard, "nice?"

It was too easy. She snorted a laugh. "I think I'm gonna like being married to you, Jamie Forrester."

"I think I'm gonna like it too," he said, quickly pulling her into his arms.

"So where are we going?"

Jamie struggled to tear his eyes away from her. Finally, he managed to look past her and point to a tiny island on the horizon. "Over there."

Now it was Hazel's turn to swallow thickly. It was no secret that water wasn't her friend. She prayed Jamie wasn't going to suggest they swim there, but once he recovered the keys he'd dropped, he pointed to the dingy at the back of the ship. "Don't worry, Smalls, I've got you."

She sighed in relief, loving how well Jamie knew her. "Yep, I'm definitely gonna like being married to you."

. . .

James

IT WAS a constant struggle to keep his eyes on anything but Hazel in that skimpy white bikini and hot pink boots, but somehow James managed to get them safely ferried to the tidal island he'd found last week. Lu ran ahead, chasing shorebirds up the white sand as they trailed closely behind.

Hazel's hand was securely fastened in James's. He wondered if she could feel his nervous energy. He'd been planning this moment since they first met, and when he found this little deserted island, he knew it was the perfect spot. He just hoped Hazel thought so too.

He'd have his answer soon enough. James let his eyes rush ahead to where the beach curved inward to a sheltered alcove. It's where they were headed.

HAZEL

HAZEL'S EYES couldn't take it all in fast enough. The glittering clear water, the white pristine sand, the lush green plants and palms. It was paradise.

"Who lives here?" she asked.

"No one."

"Really? Why not?"

Jamie shrugged. "There's hundreds of little sandbar islands like this. They come and go depending on the tides and weather. This one is larger than most and it's special."

"Why?"

"You'll see."

In a few more steps, the beach curved sharply in toward

the island. They followed the path of the sand until it disappeared, swallowed up by the plants and rocks jutting out from the center of the key. There in the shade of the old palm trees was one of the most beautiful sights Hazel had ever seen.

She stopped in her tracks, the stunning scene stealing her breath.

A tiny house sat nestled on the highpoint where the beach met the trees. It grew out of the limestone like it had been hewn directly from it. It was a simple square structure with worn white walls, a rusted tin roof and large open-air windows adorned with peeling Bermuda shutters. Through them, Hazel could see white lights and candles flickering inside.

"How?" she whispered.

Jamie held up that remote again, winking at her.

"Jamie, it's . . ." she didn't have the words to tell him how perfect this place was, but with Jamie, she didn't need words. He already knew.

"Finally, a place worthy of our love," he said softly.

She turned to him, tears in her eyes. "Make love to me, James Forrester."

And he did.

James

HAZEL DIDN'T HAVE to ask him twice. James swept her off her feet and into the little cottage he'd spent the last week preparing. They lay tangled together in the modest white bed, the only piece of furniture in the entire space, surrounded by white lights and flickering candles. When James looked into

Hazel's eyes, he saw his whole world, his heart, his life, his future—*his everything.*

He was so glad they'd waited for this perfect moment together. Because it would live in them forever, just like their love.

HAZEL

THEY MADE love well into the night, matching the rhythmic push and pull of the ocean. Afterward, they lay together, woven limbs and the beating of a single heart. Hazel rolled onto her back and smiled as she gazed up at the ceiling, a tiny gasp escaping her kiss-stung lips.

"Just when I think you're out of surprises," she whispered.

Jamie rolled onto his back too and pulled her closer, gazing up at the same beautiful view. "When I was in the hospital, you said you wished we could go back to the cabin," he said softly.

"I remember," she whispered, tears stinging her eyes. "There was something comforting about being in a world with only you and the stars."

He kissed her hand and pressed it to his heart. "We'll always have those memories, and I'll remind you of them whenever I can."

"This is perfect," she said, never taking her eyes off the stars that winked to life between the gaps in the salt-worn tin roof.

It was like having a direct line to the heavens. That thought sparked a memory that took root deep in Hazel's heart. She couldn't believe she'd ever thought that no one up there was listening to her. *How could they not when she had more than she'd ever dreamt of?*

She knew Gramps was up there, smiling down at her, and Jamie's mom, too. It was a comforting feeling to be surrounded by so much love. And as Jamie wrapped his arms around her once more, Hazel let go of the last bit of fear she'd held in her heart. Because her love for him was so encompassing, it left no room for fears or doubts—only love.

James

THE NEXT WEEK flew by in a flurry of passion on their little paradise island. James and Hazel spent their days exploring the island with Lu, snapping photos, hunting crabs, chasing birds, snorkeling and lounging in the sun.

Hazel was finding her sea legs. The water didn't frighten her as much as it used to. With his help she mastered snorkeling. James had never seen someone more natural, or more sexy with a spear gun. They ate like kings! Fresh fish and lobster every day.

But the nights . . . the nights were James's favorite. They were spent in each other's arms, making love under the stars or next to a campfire or sometimes in their tropical cottage.

He could've stayed there forever. It seemed the feeling was mutual, because when Hazel saw him packing up the candles and white lights from their make-shift home, she frowned. "Are we leaving?"

He nodded. "The honeymoon is over, as they say."

"So soon?" she teased. "I thought it would be at least a month before you got sick of me. If you'd packed me a razor I'd even be shaving my legs!"

James set down his pack and pulled Hazel into his arms. "Hairy legs are nothing, my love. Are you forgetting I've seen you at your worst?"

She snuggled into his chest. "It's weird isn't it, how the cabin was both the worst and the best of us?"

James closed his eyes, wrapping his arms around her tightly as he inhaled the scent of her apple shampoo. It instantly brought him back to Wander Mountain. He kissed the top of Hazel's head. "I guess that's what happens when we get lost, we find our strengths and weaknesses."

She tilted her head back to look up at him, those big caramel eyes full of love. "We were never lost, Jamie," she reminded him. "How could we ever be lost when we're together?"

He let his emotions crest as he kissed her until they were both back in bed, breathless and tangled in each other.

"Can't we stay a little longer?" Hazel begged, her head resting against his bare chest.

James stroked her silky hair and smiled at her, excited to give her one more surprise. "We could, but I think we'd get a bad review."

The tiny crease between her eyebrows deepened. "What do you mean?"

He held his wrist up and looked at his watch. "We pick our first charter guests up in less than an hour."

"You're joking."

"Nope."

It took a moment for Hazel to read his expression and when she could sense he wasn't teasing she sat bolt upright. "Jamie! I haven't taken a proper shower in a week! And my hair! Omigod!" she was on her feet now, slipping back into her bikini. "And Lu! I've got to give him a bath. He looks like a sandy gremlin!" she huffed as she scurried around the cottage collecting her things. "Jamie! I can't believe you did this. We're not prepared to have guests! I don't even know how to sail yet."

"It's okay, they won't mind."

"They won't mind? Aren't they coming on a *sailing* trip?"

"I think they're mainly coming because I told them it was a free vacation."

Hazel paused. "You gave away a free trip? Jamie! Do you know what kind of creepy weirdos that attracts?"

"Smalls, you'll like them I promise."

"Jamie—"

She was about to launch into another argument when Jamie's phone started to ring. The sound was so foreign that Hazel jumped.

James used the silent reprieve to hold up a finger and take the call, grinning when he saw the number flashing on the caller ID. "Shhh . . . That's them calling right now."

The look of horror on Hazel's face was so comical James wished he'd had his camera to snap a photo. "Hello?" . . . "Yeah." . . . "You're here?" . . . "Great. We're on our way."

James hung up the phone and Hazel gaped at him. But all he did was wink, slip on his shorts and sling his backpack over his shoulder. "Oh, by the way, you're right. A free vacation only attracts weirdo's like your best friend and her boyfriend."

"What? Jenny and Gavin are our first charter guests?"

"Seems so since their flight just landed."

"Omigod! Jamie Forrester! This is the best surprise ever!" She frowned. "Wait, did you just call my best friend a weirdo?"

He smirked. "If the pink boots fit."

She threw a flip flop at him and he caught it with ease. James watched that determined smirk he loved spread across Hazel's face a moment before she launched herself at him. He caught her just as easily as he had the flip flop, letting her topple him onto the mattress just for fun.

"Call them back," she whispered seductively pinning him to the bed, her luscious hips locked over his.

James throat suddenly went dry with longing. "Why's that?"

Hazel smirked devilishly. "Because I have a sudden desire to get lost with my fiancé."

ALSO BY CHRISTINA BENJAMIN

YOUNG ADULT CONTEMPORARY ROMANCE

(All Boyfriend Books are Stand-Alone Novels and can be read in Any Order)

The Practice Boyfriend (Book 1)

The Almost Boyfriend (Book 2)

The Goodbye Boyfriend (Book 3)

The Holiday Boyfriend (Book 4)

The Stand-In Boyfriend (Book 5)

The Maybe Boyfriend (Book 6)

The Accidental Boyfriend (Book 7)

The Summer Boyfriend (Book 8)

The Wedding Boyfriend (Book 9)

The Winter Boyfriend (Book 10)

The Lost Boyfriend (Book 11)

THE BILLIONAIRE BOYFRIEND SERIES

(All Billionaire Boyfriend Books are clean romance and are stand-alone novels)

Sebastian: A Clean Billionaire Romance (Book 1)

Cooper: A Clean Billionaire Romance (Book 2)

Donovan: A Clean Billionaire Romance (Book 3)

Eric: A Clean Billionaire Romance (Book 4)

Jacob: A Clean Billionaire Romance (Book 5)

Do you or your kids like to read Middle Grade Fantasy books like Harry Potter or Percy Jackson?

If so check out Christina's Pen Name - C.J. Benjamin and her completed series: Geneva Sommers

Geneva Sommers and the Quest for Truth (Book 1)

Geneva Sommers and the Secret Legend (Book 2)

Geneva Sommers and the Myth of Lies (Book 3)

Geneva Sommers and the Magic Destiny (Book 4)

Geneva Sommers and the First Fairytales (Book 5)

ABOUT THE AUTHOR

Author, Christina Benjamin, lives in Florida with her husband, and character inspiring pets, where she spends her free time working on her books, eating chocolate and drinking wine.

Christina is best known for her bestselling Young Adult romance novels, The Boyfriend Series, which proves that book boyfriends are like chocolate... you can never have enough. Check out the Boyfriend Series for fast, fun, YA romance reads. These destination novels let you fall in love in a new city with new characters, every time.

And don't miss her new Billionaire Boyfriend series for clean romance reads.

Join her secret Facebook group to beta read, chat about books over a glass of wine and a dessert. Click here to join her Facebook Group.

Interested in joining Christina's Newsletter for updates and book releases? Click Here to Join Christina's Newsletter.

Follow Christina's Amazon Page to get updates when new books are released. Click Here to Follow on Amazon.

For more information visit:
www.crownatlanticpublishing.com

To my readers,

I want to personally thank you for taking the time to seek out this great little indie book. Writing is truly my passion. I believe each of us can find a small part of ourselves in every book we read, and carry it with us, shaping our world, our adventures and our dreams.

Following my dream to write frees my soul but knowing others find joy in my writing is indescribable. So thank you for your support and I hope you enjoyed your brief escape into the magic of these pages.

If you enjoyed this story, don't worry, there's plenty more currently rattling around in my rambunctious imagination. Let me and others know your thoughts by sharing a review of this book. Reviews help shape my next writing projects. So if you want more books like this one be sure to shout it from the rooftops (or social media.) ;-)

- Christina Benjamin

PLEASE LEAVE A REVIEW HERE

ACKNOWLEDGMENTS

I'd like to thank everyone who made this book possible.

To my amazing editors, Molly and Megan, two incredibly generous women who take time out of their busy lives to help make these books shine. There are not enough words in the world to thank you for all you do, but I will continue to bribe you with wine and cookies. I'm so blessed to call you friends.

To Vince, my sweet puppy, for literally sitting by my side during every word, edit and rewrite. You inspire every pet I add into my worlds of words, especially Lugnut, in this story. My books wouldn't be the same without you. You are the stinky heartbeat at my feet and I wouldn't trade you for the world.

To all the weird and wonderful places I hid away to write this book. My car, my bed, Sky Valley, Las Vegas, St. Augustine, my dreams.

To the brave men and women who are bold enough to take a chance on love, knowing it might not work out. The world could use more of you. Bravery and belief can do powerful things.

To everyone who has ever been crazy enough to follow their heart.

To my parents for teaching me that love conquers all.

And to all the people in the world who still believes in it.

And to my amazing, incredible readers. Thank you for taking the time to read my books, and thank you again for reading this one to the very end. Writing is the best way I can share little bits of my soul with you. Books have always helped me forge bonds with others and find a deeper understanding of myself. My goal in sharing these stories is to heal, inspire and entertain. I hope you found some or all of the above in my words.

But most of all, this book is for my incredibly patient and loving husband, Philip. You are my everything. Your unwavering love and encouragement is a gift beyond my dreams. You are joy incarnate and you force me to pour my best self onto each and every page of our lives. Each word I write is molded by my love for you and how it has shaped my life. You taught me not all who wander are lost and I'll always take the road less traveled as long as you're by my side.

Made in the USA
Monee, IL
30 July 2020